Jamaica Road

LISA SMITH

dialogue books

DIALOGUE BOOKS

First published in Great Britain in 2025 by Dialogue Books
An imprint of John Murray Press

1

A CIP catalogue record for this book
is available from the British Library.

Hardback ISBN 978-0-349-70357-2
Trade paperback ISBN 978-0-349-70358-9

Typeset in Berling by M Rules
Printed and bound in Great Britain by
Clays Ltd, Elcograf S.p.A

John Murray policy is to use papers that are natural, renewable and
recyclable products and made from wood grown in sustainable forests.
The logging and manufacturing processes are expected to conform to the
environmental regulations of the country of origin.

Carmelite House   The authorised representative
50 Victoria Embankment   in the EEA is
London EC4Y 0DZ   Hachette Ireland
                                       8 Castlecourt Centre
                                    Dublin 15, D15 XTP3, Ireland
                                       (email: info@hbgi.ie)

www.dialoguebooks.co.uk

John Murray Press, part of Hodder & Stoughton Limited
An Hachette UK company

For Jonathan, with love

1981

1

The smell of chlorine stung my nostrils as I entered the Grove Street Baths. It was the third week of January, a grey Friday morning and our first swimming lesson since the start of term. The boys had strolled to the pool with their hands in their pockets, sparring insults and dirty jokes. The girls partnered together, linked arms so they could lean in and whisper to each other. I'd been paired with Amy Walker. Although she was friendlier toward me than the other girls in class, we were not friends. Since starting at John Evelyn Comprehensive last September, I hadn't yet managed to find the group where I belonged. Amy and I had walked the half-mile in silence, with our hands at our sides.

'Walk, don't run,' said Mr Jones, the head of year who doubled as our P.E. teacher.

As usual, the girls filed into the changing cubicles that lined the left-hand side of the pool, while the boys headed right. The Victorian built baths had seen better days and there were always a couple of cubicles awaiting repair for broken locks, or doors that had come off their hinges. I looked back and noticed Mark Barrett was among the boys being redirected to the empty stalls on our side.

Ted Butcher's voice echoed across the pool. 'You'll come back to school smelling nice from all that talc and Impulse spray you can get off the girls!'

Mark flipped his mate the middle finger, with an ironic smile.

He had come from Samuel Pepys Primary, the same school as me, where he'd always been popular. I'd heard that Michelle Sullivan had let him touch her minge behind the big kitchen bins, although it was 'only through her knickers'. Mark's popularity had migrated with him to secondary school. He wasn't the best looking boy in class but he was good at football and knew how to make girls laugh. Even me. Last Tuesday while I sat on a bench, close to where the boys in our year played footy, a long ball had been kicked from the other end of the concrete pitch. It sailed over the heads of most of the players but Mark ran to get beneath it, his grey-blue eyes marking the direction of travel. Although he managed to head the ball back into play, he tripped and fell, landing at my feet. I immediately asked if he was all right, instinct making me reach out to him. He'd winked at me before taking my hand and heaving himself up.

'I think I'll live,' he said, smiling. The creases around his mouth softened his face. I'd looked away, grateful my cheeks concealed embarrassment. Afterwards, I thought how his lips were surprisingly full for a white boy.

I closed the cubicle door and turned so I was standing back-to-back with Amy. It was an unspoken rule that nobody ever exposed their top and bottom halves at the same time. You took your knickers off first then pulled your costume on before removing your skirt; that way nobody would get a glimpse of your vag. Since I'd started wearing bras, I'd been stealing the odd look at other girls' chests. If they were my age I'd be interested to see if they had started developing yet, and how far behind or ahead of me they were. With older girls, like my seventeen-year-old cousins Marcia and Margery, I'd examine how their clothes fit – and wonder if their breasts looked like mine. A couple of weeks ago, while I was helping Marcia change her brothers' bed sheets, we found pictures of topless girls that Kiplyn had tucked beneath his mattress.

'That dutty so-and-so can't keep his hands off his cocky these days,' said Marcia holding up pages torn from the newspaper. 'Look how this nasty gyal steal Black women's style, then turn around and call it the Bo Derek – look, cha!' The grainy black-and-white print showed a cheery young woman whose fair hair was braided into cornrows with the plaits draped either side of her naked boobs. Later, when I was getting ready for bed, I stood bare-chested in front of the wardrobe mirror and posed like the girl in the picture: standing at an angle, arching my back, assessing the contours of my new, small breasts.

In my ordinary clothes these changes went unnoticed. But now, in the changing room, as I drew the swimsuit up, the polyester fabric revealed just how much I'd grown in the past month. Amy's glance landed on the bumps pressing against my costume, then skittered away. I followed her out, folding my arms across my chest and walking as quickly as I dared along the concrete edge towards the shallow end.

I looked across to where the advanced group were already swimming in the deep water, salvaging fake bricks from the bottom of the pool and learning life-saving skills, such as how to turn the pyjamas they'd brought to the lesson into floating aids. In order to 'move up' you had to be able to swim fifty metres without stopping. So far I'd tried twice and failed to meet the distance. I pretended not to hear when some of the white kids would say, 'Blacks can't swim because their feet are too flat', or 'their bones are too dense – they don't find it easy to float'. I knew that wasn't true and was determined to prove it.

Mark popped up from the water brandishing his fake brick and accidentally splashed Michelle Sullivan. This made her squeal with delight, so he splashed her again with playful purpose.

'Chop-chop Daphne, look lively girl!' Mr Jones's voice bounced off the pale-green wall tiles.

I realised the other basic learners were already shivering in the pool. I slid into the icy water and spent the next forty minutes swimming as many widths as possible in order to warm up.

At the end of the lesson, I was among those Mr Jones se-lected to try out for the advanced group. There were three other candidates and me. While most classmates went back to their cubicles, there were always a few that hung around the poolside gawping. The first two swimmers gave up after one and a half lengths. Adrian Parker went next and passed the test; afterwards his mates gave three cheers. Then it was my turn. I descended the metal ladder, paused to compose myself then launched into breaststroke, remembering to keep a slow, steady pace. I was conscious of eyes watching me glide through the water. Were they expecting me to fail again? Or maybe worse, were they judging my bum, my hips, my frog-like legs? I reached the shallow end, turned and began the swim back. I'd never got beyond the pool's halfway point on my return leg before. The black mosaic tiles on the poolside read 'DEPTH 5'8"'. I felt a jolt of fear, doubting whether I had strength left. I forced myself to keep looking forward, holding my head higher to stop water from splashing my face, panicking as my legs sunk. I neared the end of the pool, arms outstretched. I missed the bar by inches and my face dipped into the water but I came up spluttering and grabbed the rail. I'd done it. Mr Jones commended me for not giving up. There was a smattering of applause from the remaining spectators as I hauled myself up the ladder. I was exhilarated, but I could feel my swimming costume sagging around my backside and my chest. I hurried to my cubicle, keen to get out of sight.

'Amy, I did it. I've done my fifty. I'm moving up,' I said, opening the door a crack and slipping inside.

But Amy was nowhere to be seen. Instead, I found Michelle standing in front of me, a lemon-yellow beach towel wrapped around her like a toga.

'Where's Amy?'

'Button it,' she hissed, gesturing for me to get behind her.

The whitewashed panels separating each cubicle fell shy of the floor by almost a foot. Usually, girls would use this gap to pass each other hairbrushes, mirrors and talc. Michelle crouched down on the cold wet tiles, bowing until her chest was on her thighs. She tilted her head this way and that until she found the best vantage point to spy into the changing room next door.

'Nice arse!' she whispered.

'What the fuc—' Mark only just managed to stifle his surprise. 'What d'you want, Michelle?'

'I'll show you mine, if I can see yours first.'

I heard a snigger; Michelle giggled too. I wrapped my towel around myself like a cape. I shivered. Intrigued.

'Stand back a bit then,' she ordered. 'I can't see nothing from there . . . that's better!'

Michelle rose to her feet and looked at me. 'You better not say nothing.'

I shook my head. She turned her back to me and began adjusting her towel, while I peered over her shoulder at the gap between the floor and the dividing wall. Michelle tittered as Mark's face appeared below the woodwork. I clutched my towel tighter. A rush of blood pulsed through my fingers making them tingle. Then Michelle held her towel open. In my head I counted nine seconds before she covered herself.

'Is that it?' said Mark.

'For now!' she whispered, turning away from him.

She pushed me aside and reached for her underwear. There was a glow in her cheek. I looked down at the gap. Mark was no longer there. Michelle assumed the obligatory back-to-back changing position and had already wriggled into her bra and applied deodorant before I had even begun to undress. I writhed around under my towel, peeling off the damp costume, letting it slop in a heap around my feet. Using my toes to push the damp cossie aside, I glanced down at the floor. There he was, his eyes glistening in the semi-gloom. Michelle still had her back turned, but Mark wasn't looking at her. This time he was watching me. The tingling I'd felt in my fingers returned. Slowly I opened my towel. The cool air pimpled my skin but it was a nice feeling. I felt a prickling sensation around my crotch. That was a nice feeling too. Was this how

Michelle had felt? Or those women who posed in the pictures my cousin kept under his bed? But then, hadn't Marcia called them *nasty gyals?* I hastily covered myself. Heated by shame. Mark disappeared. Still damp, I pulled on my underwear and hurried into the rest of my clothes, keeping an eye on the gap beneath the partition, wondering what I had done.

We returned to school for our next lesson, which was English. A boy was standing beside Miss Peacock, watching as we filed into the classroom. The intensity of thirty pairs of eyes staring back forced him to shift his gaze to the carpet.

'Settle down.' Miss paused, waiting for absolute hush. 'Now, I'd like you all to welcome our new pupil This is Cornelius Small, although I believe you prefer Connie?'

The boy nodded.

'Connie Small, Connie Tall more like,' muttered Mark. 'Look at the bleedin' size of him!'

He was certainly the tallest twelve-year-old I'd ever seen. His pullover was slightly too short in the arms and his trousers had a crease where the hemline had been let down, yet still only just grazed his ankles.

There was a murmur of giggles and Mark revelled in the response to his quip. Miss Peacock ignored him, raising her voice slightly.

'Connie has recently arrived in England. He's come all the way from Jamaica.'

Michelle leaned into Mark. 'Given half a chance your Phil and his mates would send him right back where he came from in ... what was it again?' she asked, her voice a couple of notches above a whisper.

'A leaky banana boat!' said Mark.

He caught me looking at him and covered his mouth. I looked at the pencil I was holding and began twisting it between my thumb and index finger. I could still feel Mark's eyes on me. I was determined not to give him a reaction. Never let the effect their words had show, or else you became fair game. I'd learnt that as a skinny six-year-old pressed up against a wall, while ten-year-old Phil Barrett and five of his followers taunted me with their own version of the Hokey Cokey:

'You stick your right fist in, your right fist out, your right leg in, and you kick the nigger out . . . ' I had seen Mark skulking behind his big brother's gang. He wasn't singing but he had just stood there with his eyes down, digging between the cracks of the paving stones with the toe of his boot. I'd hidden my face in my hands, but I could still smell their eggy breath and feel the spray of spittle as the big boys moved in closer.

Eventually, one of the mums that helped out with playtime duty came to my rescue. 'You ought to be ashamed of yourselves,' she said. 'Ganging up on a little girl like that when she can't help being Black.' While Phil had merely smirked at the telling off, Mark had at least looked chastened. After that, Mark never singled me out. He'd come out with the odd gibe about West Indians, Pakistanis or the Irish; but then he also teased kids who were fat, or ginger, or wore glasses. And unlike Phil, who would rough up his targets, Mark stuck to verbal put-downs, the wittier the better – anything to make people laugh.

'Daphne, isn't Jamaica where your family are from?' asked Miss Peacock.

Now I felt all eyes fix on me. Over the past few months I'd found a position in my form group's pecking order where I could be invisible most of the time. I'd continued to drop the letter 'h', to say "indoors" rather than "at home", and always referred to lunch as dinner, and dinner as tea.

'Yes, Miss. But I was born here—'

'So since you're both Jamaican, you can help our new classmate settle in.'

She gave Connie a pat on the back and he walked across to where I was sitting, his lanky frame propelled by swaying shoulders. Up close, his clothes looked even more drab. I had some pretty tired hand-me-downs in my wardrobe but I'd never worn anything quite that bad to school. My grandma, Miss Gladys, was a terrific seamstress and when it was her turn to withdraw savings from the pardner, she had invested in a sewing machine so she could do piecework as well as her private commissions. I had homemade skirts that I'd co-ordinate with the clothes that had been passed down to me. While I still put up with the occasional dig at my sensible T-bar shoes, at least I wasn't the only girl who wore them. The only acceptable footwear if you were a boy living around our way were either Dr. Martens or trainers, preferably Adidas or Gola. Connie was wearing plain black plimsolls. I knew that come break time he'd get called 'a joey' or 'a fleabag' and such. I tried to think up cutting replies he could use against the bullies, but I'd never been any good at answering back. Then I decided it would be best not to get involved.

Connie eased himself into the chair beside me, his long legs poking out beyond the desk. He looked at me, his mouth twitching into a nervous smile. I turned away, stony-faced, and stared at the blackboard.

*

'*It is. A truth. Universally. Acknowledged. That a. Single man. In. Possession. Of good. Fortune . . .*'

Craig Evans limped through our class reading book. I was sharing my copy with Connie and had placed the book squarely at the centre of the desk; enough space for both of us to see the pages without any physical contact. Connie sat forward, the palm of his right hand supporting his chin. The longer it took for Craig to stumble through the sentences, the closer Connie leaned in. It was as though he couldn't bear the suspense of whether Craig would be able to read the next word, let alone make it to the end of the line. As he moved nearer, I caught a whiff of bergamot from his Afro. DAX Pomade.

'Thank you, Craig.' Miss Peacock looked up and surveyed the class. 'Now, who shall we have next?'

I loved reading. Over the years I'd imagined myself at an English boarding school like Malory Towers or Miss Cackle's Academy For Witches and my fictional companions didn't call me a monkey or tell me to go back to my own country. Reading had made primary school bearable and so far it had been helping me at secondary school too. I'd while away break times with my nose in a book, trying – and for the most part succeeding – to not look lonely. I'd recently started reading the newspapers and would often go to the public library where they had the posher papers, as well as the tabloids we got at home. Reading the papers made me feel grown up. I was finding out about politicians, other places in the world and movie stars. I was also learning new words like 'recession', 'redundancy' and 'synthesizer'. When Mr Jones tested us at the end of last term, he had praised me on having the reading ability of a fifteen-year-old. Still, I never volunteered to read aloud in class. Nobody did. Connie's hand shot up.

'Oh, a volunteer,' said Miss Peacock. 'Please continue, Connie.'

'Mr Bennet was so odd a mix-ture of quick parts, sar-cas-tic humour, re-serve and caprice . . .'

Connie pronounced every word with precision, a foreigner speaking the Queen's English. Yet rather than sounding clipped and robotic, the syllables lengthened and were smoothed by the lilt of his accent. I'd only ever heard grown-ups speak with a Jamaican accent, never someone my own age. Connie's voice wasn't much deeper than the other boys in class, but without the spiky, south-east London timbre, it sounded mellow. A muffled chortle filled the classroom, but Connie wasn't put off. He read with real eloquence. Miss Peacock allowed him to complete a whole page. After Miss thanked him Connie turned to me, beaming. I was tempted to just stare him out and put him off thinking of me as a potential friend, yet my lips slipped into a smile. But only for a moment. We continued reading until the bell rang for break time. I rose quickly, grabbed my coat and ran out before Connie had a chance to attach himself to me.

The bench where I normally spent break time was under a plane tree close to the football pitches. I unfolded the local paper Mum had brought home last night and rested it on my lap. On the front page was another picture of the burnt-out house with soot-streaked brickwork and blackened windows. Before last Sunday, this three-storey Victorian terrace would have looked similar to the one I lived in. Now it had been reduced to a shell.

HOUSE PARTY INFERNO:
DEATH TOLL RISES TO 11
MORE TEENAGERS SERIOUSLY
ILL IN HOSPITAL

The news report didn't tell me anything new. Nobody knew how the fire had started. One witness said that a cream-coloured Austin Princess was parked suspiciously close to the house, another claimed to have seen something hurled through the ground floor window. I turned to page two.

POISON IN THEIR PENS
GRIEVING RELATIVES GET HATE LETTERS

Relatives of the Black teenagers who died in the blaze at a birthday party in New Cross have had hate mail sent to their homes. One letter, posted from Catford, states, 'What a great day it was when I heard about the niggers going up in flames. I hope the bastard that mugged me was there.' A police spokesman said, 'these letters are sickening to read but the Black community ought not to jump to conclusions about a racial element to the crime. We are keeping an open mind.'

Mum had scoffed last night after reading the article aloud and Miss Gladys kissed her teeth. I looked up from the paper. There was a smattering of brown faces dotted around the concourse, mostly students that came in by bus, from the edge of the neighbouring borough. There were three other brown girls in my year, two Nigerians and a girl called

Tara who referred to herself as 'half-caste, *not* Black'. None of them were in my form group. I felt too self-conscious to introduce myself but I'd nod if we passed in the corridor and they would sometimes nod back. I couldn't see any of these girls about now. As usual, the boys were playing footy and Mr Jones was rolling a cigarette. A few girls lounged on the grassy mound, plaiting each other's hair. For the past week, the fire had been all we'd talked about at home, yet at school I hadn't heard anybody even mention it.

My eyes snagged Mark on the football pitch, his shaggy brown hair flopping around his face. His warm breath appeared as puffs of white in the cold air as he zipped up and down the pitch, demanding that the ball be passed back to him. I wondered when he would drop some wisecrack to everyone about seeing me naked in the changing room. That I'd allowed him to see me naked. What on earth had made me do such a thing? I shrunk into my coat, doing up the top button and raising the collar. I told myself to just keep my head down, to stay out of his sight. Hopefully, nothing would be said today and after the weekend it would be forgotten about.

Connie emerged from the school building wearing a khaki-coloured parka. He spotted me and proceeded to walk over; head high, shoulders back. I fumbled with the pages of the newspaper, my gloves unable to get a good grip. Connie nodded a greeting but rather than sitting beside me, he remained standing, watching the football. I was relieved but I still couldn't concentrate on the article I was reading.

After a couple of minutes, the ball hit the goalpost and rolled off the pitch. Connie took his hands out of his pockets and trapped the ball with his left foot, then elegantly flicked and caught it. Mark came running up.

'Oi! Sambo, hands off!'

A crease appeared in Connie's forehead. His open, expectant smile faded.

'My name is Connie.'

Mark scoffed. 'Yeah, and in't that a girl's name? Think I'd prefer Sambo.'

Connie allowed the ball to slip from his hands and it thudded onto the concrete.

'My name is not Sambo. It's Connie,' he said, his voice low but firm.

'Whatever. Can't you take a joke?'

Then Mark was back on the pitch without a second glance. Connie watched him weaving between the other boys, effing-and-blinding his way towards the goal. I watched him too, with a sick feeling binding my stomach. Mark may not have directed the racial slur at me, but hadn't I been sitting right there? He had given me a scrap of attention, and it had made me believe that maybe he didn't really mean the cruel things he said. How could I have lulled myself into such stupidity? I felt as exposed as I did in the changing room, but heated by a different sort of shame.

'Just ignore him from now on,' I heard myself say. 'He's an idiot.'

Connie put his hands back in his coat pockets and continued to gaze at the pitch. Mark had scored a goal and was running about the playground with his arms aloft, his teammates chasing after him, cheering and tugging at his jumper.

'You'll get used to it here.' I lied.

2

At home time, the usual mass of navy-blue-clad bodies spilled from the school gates on Jamaica Road. Although the Comprehensive brought together fifteen hundred pupils from across the north side of the borough, over half of the students lived on the Marsh Town Estate. The vast housing complex's silver-grey maisonettes sprawled northwards from the school grounds, eventually nestling at the banks of the Thames. At its centre were two tower blocks: Milligan House and Hibbert Court, each twenty-four floors of concrete, steel and glass. Like most street names and places around our way, Marsh Town remembered the days when Britain had its empire and the local docks were thriving. At school we learnt that Mr Milligan and Mr Hibbert were two nineteenth-century businessmen whose fortunes came from their 'interests' in the West Indies.

Mum had put her name on the waiting list for a flat on the estate five years ago, but we were still waiting. I lived half a mile away in a house on a street the council had earmarked for demolition in the 1960s but had never got around to pulling down. 59 Lime Grove had draughty sash windows and an ice-cold bathroom squashed between the kitchen and the outside loo. The house belonged to my Auntie Sybil and her husband Earl.

They and their four children slept in the three bedrooms on the first floor, while Mum and me had the attic room. Miss Gladys slept on the ground floor, in what was once the dining room.

It was Friday and my cousins had gone to hang out with friends after school; I stood alone at the Pelican crossing. The cold was seeping through the knit of my scarf. I wound it around my neck once more, doubling the thickness, then I pushed the button again.

'You walk home by yuself?' Connie said, arriving at my side.

'Yeah.' I replied without looking at him. I willed the green man to appear.

'Mi have an orange mi save from lunch, you want some?'

'No. Thank you.'

All day I'd been trying to be helpful without giving him, or anyone else, the impression that just because we were both Black, we were the same. I'd only spoken to him when it was absolutely necessary during lessons and had expected that after his run-in with Mark Barrett he would follow my example of how to behave. But Connie had made no attempt to keep his head down. He'd volunteered to hand out history textbooks, collected our science test sheets and put his hand up to answer every maths question the teacher set us.

When the traffic lights finally changed I walked across the street and into the park, just managing to keep abreast of Connie's leisurely strides. There were thick privet hedges around the park's entrance, so you couldn't be easily seen from the road. I decided that I could afford to be a bit friendlier now we were further from school. Perhaps I could make him understand the rules. I was deciding how to begin when Connie spoke up.

'So you an English gyal.'

'Yeah. Well, sort of. I was born here. My family come from Jamaica, my mum arrived in 1962 before independence.'

'You ever been to Jamaica?'

'No, but my grandma's told me loads about it. She came over in the '70s, when I was just a baby. When did you get here?' I asked.

'Weeks ago and mi still nuh warm up yet!'

Connie chuckled, a deep, husky sound, his shoulders rising and falling in time with his laughter. There was a dimple in his right cheek I hadn't noticed before. I smiled, then quickly covered my mouth and gave a fake cough.

'Althea have t'ings to sort out before mi could start ah' school.'

'Who's Althea?'

'Mi muddah.'

'How come you call her Althea?'

Connie shrugged. 'I call her that from when mi was small. She say when mi call her Mamma it mek her feel old. Mi likkle breddah call her Mammy though, him two so she nuh mind that much. Althea's a top-notch hairdresser; she plan to open up her own salon and call it *Noir*, which mean black in French. At the moment she work for a dragon name Mrs Samuels, but she determined to have her own place in the next t'ree years, by the time she reach thirty.'

'What? Your mum's only twenty-seven!'

'Nearly, her birthday's not till July. My birthday is November 28th. When yuh born?'

'May.'

'Yuh Gemini or Cancer?'

'I dunno. Gemini I think.'

'Good. An air sign. Althea say Fire and Air get on well.'

My mum said only *eediats* believed in horoscopes, but I didn't say that to Connie. He carried on talking about his mother and her plans, his face all smiles while I calculated that Althea must have been fifteen when she had Connie. Auntie Sybil was always on at the twins, Marcia and Margery, about the misery and shame of being a teenage mum. Yet Connie's mum hadn't been held back, she'd travelled halfway across the world. I silently mouthed her name, letting my tongue savour the softness of the syllables 'Al-the-a'.

My mum's name was Alma, which I once read meant 'nourishing, kind soul'. When I suggested that her name went well with her job, she kissed her teeth. 'Mi name could be Florence Nightingale but some of dem ward sisters would still treat mi like dem skivvy – not a qualified nurse.' Mum was forever telling me how people would be more impressed by my brains than my face, my hair or my name. But from what I saw at school my intelligence didn't count for much, and as far as I could tell, being popular went hand-in-hand with being pretty, which meant having silky hair and white skin. Black beauty also seemed to be measured by hair and the lightness of your complexion. The Black women in the Miss World pageants on TV were never dark and they never had Afros. Like Mum, I had good hair, but we both had mid-brown skin. Mum would be thirty-six in October, an old woman compared to Al-the-a.

Connie continued strolling along beside me, right up until we arrived at my gate.

'Wow, this is a proper ol' time house!' he said, tilting his head back. 'Is here you live?'

'Yeah. Whereabouts do you live?'

'Hibbert Court.'

'But that's back on the estate. You've gone in completely the opposite direction.'

Connie shrugged.

'Will you be all right going back on your own? I mean, it's getting dark.' Connie was silent. 'D'you actually know the way back?'

Connie looked down at his plimsolls. 'Well . . . mi not altogether certain.'

Miss Gladys was standing at the kitchen stove, using the bright blue flame to singe bristles off chicken wings. Whenever I saw grandmothers on telly they were wrinkly, bespectacled white women in pastel-coloured cardigans and flat, fluffy slippers. Miss Gladys wore bell-bottom pants that hugged her broad backside, and she was partial to high heels, faux fur coats and wigs. Her red-brown face was plump and unlined, that is, until she laughed.

She looked up when I entered the room and raised an eyebrow. 'Hey babylove. Ah who dis yuh bring come 'ere?'

'This is Cornelius . . . Connie. He's a new boy in my class.'

'Please to meet yuh, Connie.'

'Howdeedo mam,' he mumbled.

'Bwoy! Yuh put mi in the mind of Rita Daniel's grandson, Willis. Is last summer him come up from yard. Is which part ah Jamaica yuh from?'

'Mi live with mi grandparents ah St Elizabeth.'

'Mi should ah guess. It's all that good yam and green banana that mek yuh so big and strong. Daphne, slice a likkle bun and cheese for yuh and yuh friend nuh.'

'He can't stay. I never meant to bring him here. He's sort of lost his way home.'

Connie looked down at the rug, shifting from one foot to the other.

'Where yuh live?' asked Miss Gladys.

'Up ah Hibbert Court mam. Mi muddah usually work late on Friday and her ... fiancé ... who we live with ah work nights at the car plant and mi nuh fi disturb him, so she gi' me dis.'

Connie partially unzipped his parka and pulled out a latchkey attached to some string. Miss Gladys switched off the gas hob.

'Well it nuh too far from here. Yuh can have a slice of bun and cheese before we go.'

It was dusk by the time we entered the estate, but Connie and Miss Gladys were walking at Caribbean pace, chatting like old friends.

'So yuh muddah work ah Mrs Samuels's salon, that's up near Market Street, me hear she often ah look for staff. Yuh father deh 'a'ere too?'

'No mam, him run off to America before mi born. Althea say him did plan fi send fi us, but it never work out.'

Connie spoke with such lightness that at first I thought I'd misheard him. I didn't have a dad either, but had never told a soul. I hadn't thought it was unusual until I started school. When I told Mum I'd heard the other kids say that you needed a mummy *and* a daddy to be born, I remember a frown appearing across her forehead. It was the first time I realised how deep the furrows were – how the lines left faint traces when she eventually relaxed her face. 'You did have a daddy once,' she said, 'and all you need to know is that he walk away, leave us and we better off without him. Now, me send you to school to listen to the teacher – not the pickney, dem nuh know everything and dem nuh need to know you business neither.' So, I played along, drawing pictures and writing stories that featured my mummy and a daddy.

As I grew older, I'd noticed Mum did her fair share of playing along too. She kept a thin gold band in her purse and would slip it on whenever she went with me to doctors' appointments or parents' evenings. Later, when I moved up from the infant school to the juniors, I overheard Michelle Sullivan and Joanne Cole talking about how kids without dads were called bastards and that their mums were slags who couldn't keep a bloke. I felt so ashamed. I'd vowed to never let on to the kids at school and I hoped that Connie wouldn't go blabbing about his lack of a dad, assuming that it was normal.

'Yuh muddah lucky she find work so quickly,' said Miss Gladys. 'T'ings nuh good right now. Plenty people ah lose dem job.'

'Mi muddah nuh just come ah England,' said Connie. 'She deh here t'ree year almost. But last summer Gramma get sick. Although she tell him not to, Papa write to say him cyaah cope. So Althea send for mi, even though she nuh land.'

Miss Gladys's pace seemed to slow down even more. When she spoke her voice was low. 'What? She nuh land yet?'

Connie paused, biting his bottom lip. 'Mi nuh really suppose to mention that part.'

Miss Gladys nodded, she smiled at the boy. 'It's all right. Mi understand.'

I didn't. I wanted to know why Connie suddenly looked so uncomfortable. But Miss Gladys didn't ask any more questions.

The lift smelt of wee and pine disinfectant and groaned as it staggered up to the eighteenth floor. The doors cranked open, revealing a long passageway lit with bulbs that had a pale blue tint. We followed Connie along the corridor until he came to number 1815. He slid his latchkey into the lock but before he could turn it, the door swung open revealing a tall woman whose cornrow braids were heavy with beads. Her dark brown skin reminded me of the lignum-vitae woodcarvings on my grandma's dressing table. This must be Al-the-a. A small child dressed in blue pyjamas, rested on her hip.

'There yuh are sweetness! Mi lef' work early and expect to find yuh here already.'

'I went to the park. Then mi wasn't sure how fi get back here. Sorry.'

'Mi was about to go look for yuh—'

'Who's that?' Althea was interrupted by a man's voice coming from inside the flat. 'Is that the bwoy? Where him deh till now?'

Connie swallowed and looked down at the floor.

Althea leant back to reply. 'Yes darlin'. Connie reach.' Her voice faltered and there was an awkward stiffness that wasn't there before. 'Him safe and sound. He's here with a nice woman and a gyal from him school . . .'

She trailed off as a tall man in a donkey jacket appeared, his broad frame filling the doorway. He had a long, handsome face with high cheekbones and when his dark eyes flitted across to me, I felt I should keep very still. Then suddenly his look softened. Creases fanned out from the corners of his eyes and although his smile revealed slightly crooked teeth, I thought he was very good-looking. He turned to Connie.

'Glad yuh come back safe. But man must learn to act responsible and with more consideration.'

'Actually, my granddaughter invited this nice young man to our home after school. That is why he got lost. I would have telephoned but he didn't want to disturb you so I thought we'd better bring him back immediately, which is a pity as we would have love for him to stay and have dinner with us.'

I was taken aback by this new story from Miss Gladys, as well as by the way she was speaking. She only ever used her Proper English voice when she spoke to white people; it was her way of showing that she was not to be trifled with. I looked up at her but Miss Gladys's gaze was glued on the man in the doorway.

'Well that *is* very kind of you mam.' His tone had adjusted too, and now I detected the trace of a South London accent. 'I'm working nights and I like for him to be home before I leave. Yuh see how his muddah worry. T'ank you for going to so much trouble.'

'Yuh better go now Tobias,' said Althea mildly, 'yuh be late for work.'

Tobias reached inside and grabbed a khaki satchel. He gave Althea a peck on the cheek and shook Miss Gladys's hand. We were silent, watching him jog down the corridor and get into the waiting lift.

Althea shifted her infant son to her other hip and tugged

Connie inside. He was only a fraction shorter than his mum, but she drew him to her and kissed his cheek. He looked down, embarrassed; still he nestled into the curve of her side.

'T'anks for seeing mi bwoy home,' said Althea. 'Nuh go all shy now, tell the nice lady t'anks.'

'Thank yuh mam,' said Connie.

'Yuh may call mi Miss Gladys,' she said, her accent relaxing into its usual rhythm. 'Mi hope we see yuh at our house again soon, but tell yuh muddah next time, nuh mek her fret.'

'Yes mam – I mean, Miss Gladys.'

'I'm Althea,' said Connie's mum. 'Mi very pleased to meet yuh. And who is this?' she added, her large, kohl-lined eyes resting on me.

'I'm Daphne. I'm in Connie's class at school.'

'Well mi pleased to meet yuh too sweetheart. She pretty innit Connie? She have good hair. Mi would gladly drill it in cornrow for yuh, t'read some bead in ah' the ends, mek yuh look even prettier than yuh do already.'

Althea was beaming at me and I looked down at my shoes to hide my glee. I heard Miss Gladys chuckle, her mirth genuine rather than polite. I liked Althea. I was sure Grandma liked her too.

After leaving the tower block, we linked arms and retraced our steps through the estate in a contented silence. I piped up when we crossed over Jamaica Road and started towards home.

'Connie's folks seem nice.'

'Yes. The muddah seem like a sweet woman.' I waited for Grandma to comment on Tobias, but she said nothing more.

'Were you really going to invite Connie to stay and eat with us?'

'Of course. Yuh *never* bring a friend home before.'

'He's not my friend. I'm just supposed to help him settle in.'

'Mi sure yuh the best person for the job.' Miss Gladys caught me rolling my eyes. 'What? It nuh nice to finally have another Black child in yuh class?'

'I suppose, but he was born in Jamaica and I was born here. We're different.'

Miss Gladys shook her head, a smile playing across her mouth.

'Grandma, what did Connie mean when he said Athea no land yet?'

Miss Gladys hesitated. Mrs Blake, who lived at number 55, was walking along the street towards us; my grandma nodded a greeting and Mrs Blake nodded back. When she passed us Miss Gladys peered over her shoulder, waiting until our neighbour was out of earshot.

'It's what dem say when a person nuh have the papers dem need to stay in the country.'

'Why d'you need papers for that?'

'Yuh just do, if yuh nuh born here.' We'd reached our gate, but before lifting the latch Miss Gladys turned to me. 'Yuh nuh fi tell anyone what Connie say to us about that. Promise me Daphne.'

Miss Gladys spoke in a low, sombre tone. I had more questions, but sensed now was not the time.

'All right. I promise.'

Mum was the last of the grown-ups to arrive home that evening; hauling herself into the kitchen just as Miss Gladys was dishing up supper. She sank down on one of the dining chairs, unhooking the wide elastic belt girdling her waist.

'That new ward sister, she facety yuh know! Mi nursing since she was a teenybopper, but she come tell me how fi fold sheets.'

'She prejudice?' asked Auntie Sybil.

'No, just badmind,' Mum replied.

'Come eat now Alma,' said Miss Gladys, 'yuh nuh have fi deal with her till Monday.'

Nobody ever sat in the front sitting room except on special occasions. Instead, the telly was positioned in the kitchen bay window and that half of the room had become more of a lounge. My cousins and I had already eaten. Kiplyn lay sprawled across the rug with his head propped up by his hands, Devon was draped across the armchair, while Marcia, Margery and me were all squeezed on the leather-like sofa. I was almost as quiet at home as I was at school and preferred listening to talking. 'Watch out fi Daphne, she's always attending,' Miss Gladys joked. 'She'll make a good news reporter. Or spy.' I liked the idea of being a journalist on a newspaper, finding things out and then people reading what I'd written. Mum's assessment of my listening skills was less flattering. 'Ah faas, she faas,' she said. 'And remember faas make Anansi climb too high and end up ah housetop!'

The grown-ups' conversation soon turned to the topic that had been on everyone's mind all week. Auntie Sybil had passed the burnt-out house on her way to the biscuit factory that morning, a police officer had been stationed outside. Uncle Earl had heard that specialist officers were carrying out forensic tests. The police commander in charge had been on the news, stating there was 'currently no evidence of a firebomb or any racist motive for the attack'.

'No evidence mi foot!' said Miss Gladys. 'Just look pan all the racist yout' round here? Wasn't it a likkle more than a month ago Michael Fields get chased by a group of dem bal' head boys?'

'They're called skinheads,' said Devon, shifting in the armchair so he could address the adults but still see the TV screen. He had turned sixteen last month and shot up in height. 'They knew it was Phil Barrett's gang, but when Mrs Fields went to the police station to report it, the cops were going on like it was Michael that was in the wrong. They even asked him how long he'd had his hair in dreadlocks—'

'Well mi nuh know why him locs-up him head, that's just ah ask for trouble,' said Uncle Earl flicking the ash from his cigarette. 'And why yuh ah listen to big people conversation?'

'Cos it affects us Pops innit?' said Marcia. 'Everyone knows there's loads of NF in the police and they'll protect their own. The bloody stinking pigs!'

'Eh-eh – wi nuh want that kind of talk here young lady!' snapped Auntie Sybil.

Marcia folded her arms and tutted.

'You know, *we* might have gone to that party,' said Margery, her tone reflective. 'I heard some of the teenagers jumped from the second-storey windows with their clothes alight. People were pouring water on them while they lay on the pavement.'

'Mi hear that too,' said Mum quietly.

Auntie Sybil exchanged looks with her husband. 'Well unnu nuh ah go to any party from now on,' she said. 'And mi nuh want yuh hanging about pan the street ah night-time neither, yuh hear?'

In unison my cousins mumbled, 'Yes, Mum.' Their eyes flitted across to one another. They were making a pact among themselves to go on with the business of being teenagers, never mind their anxious parents and racist white people. I wished that they would include me in their unspoken agreement, but I was just their little cousin.

'Anyway mi ah go win the pools this week,' said Uncle Earl, forcing a change of topic. 'Then mi can fix up this place and buy a piece ah land back ah yard for our retirement – or for when dem repatriate us, whichever come first.'

Auntie Sybil rose to clear the table. 'Eh-eh! Perhaps if yuh'd saved all the money yuh spen' on the pools and up ah Ladbrokes this past twenty-odd years, wi could have already fix up this house and buy land back home. The only good luck yuh ever had, Earlston Cameron Macintosh, was meeting me!'

Uncle Earl pulled her towards him, his arms tight around her waist. 'Well then that must mek mi the luckiest mon in the world!'

He kissed his wife's hand. Auntie Sybil gave a nonchalant toss of her head, although any pretence of being annoyed dissolved, along with her pout.

There was the loud scrape of a dining chair being pushed back and Mum carried dirty plates to the sink, the rubber soles of her black lace-ups squeaking as she walked. I noticed Miss Gladys was watching her and I thought I saw Mum's back stiffen, but she didn't turn around.

*

That night I lay for ages waiting for sleep to come. The alarm clock by Mum's side of the bed showed twenty past ten. Mum hadn't come upstairs yet. I slid my hand beneath my nightie, caressing my thigh and moving upwards. I knew boys touched their privates and I suspected that it wasn't a particularly ladylike thing for girls to do, but it calmed me. First, I ran my fingers through the curly, coarse hair that was beginning to cover my fanny, then I parted my legs and touched my crotch. I remembered the sensation that had fizzed through me in the swimming cubicle when Mark was staring. I felt that same pleasure stirring again; it was nice. Suddenly, I conjured Mark's face. I sat up abruptly, shaking my head, trying to dislodge the image. I decided to get up and make myself some warm milk to help me sleep.

All the bedroom doors on the first floor were shut; Auntie Sybil, Uncle Earl and my cousins had gone to bed. The light in the downstairs hallway was my guide along the chilly landing and down the stairs. The kettle was whistling but as I reached the kitchen door, its screeching was silenced. I heard Miss Gladys's voice.

'Wah yuh t'ink it's like for Daphne seeing yuh so vex all the time? Every night this week yuh come home with yuh face pout up.'

'Mi nuh must pout up when mi ah spend eight hours a day taking orders from a gyal nearly five years younger than mi, all because she ah State *Registered* Nurse – rather than *Enrolled*. Cha! Almost every Black nurse mi know is an SEN, dem funnel us down that path when we come here for training, now tell us we underqualified – even though we could run a ward every bit as good as the white gyaldem.'

'It nuh just work that make you vex,' said Miss Gladys. 'Nowadays it's whenever Earl and Sybil show a likkle affection to each other. Nuh shake yuh head at me Alma, mi see how yuh stay. Yuh t'ink mi nuh know what it's like to be lonely?'

I knew that I ought to either enter the room or go back to bed. I held my breath, conscious of how it would look if I were caught lingering at the door. This wasn't *attending while the big people ah talk*, this was eavesdropping: nosy, sneaky, *faas*.

'Huh! Between Dennis and Wishbone when yuh have time fi lonely?'

'Alma, mi ah widow longer than mi was a wife. Yuh daddy is still the finest person mi ever know. A real gentleman. But nuh nuttin' wrong with seeking comfort.'

Mum sighed. 'I'm sorry. Mi nuh judging yuh. Sybil neither. Unnu choose good men. Unlike the wretch mi have baby for. Mi should ah realise that if someone name "Easy", then there must be a good reason. Easy by name, easy by nature. Wutless man!'

I shivered. Mum had never mentioned my father by name before. Mostly he was never mentioned at all. I quietly exhaled, whispering *Easy*. Whatever Mum thought, I liked the name. It was mysterious. Cool.

'If yuh must know, mi buck up on that jack-arse the other day,' said Mum. 'Mi waiting for the bus and him pull up in him nice car ah grin him teet' at me.'

'He ask after him pickney?'

'Him did ask how she keeping, but mi nuh tell him nuttin.' Mi cuss him off with some bad word. All he can say before him drive away is *"Alma yuh hard-sah"*. Mi in uniform at the time and so it's lucky nobody report me for bad conduct.'

'Oh Alma ...' Miss Gladys's tone was weary. 'Yuh never stop and t'ink about Daphne? Wutless or not, him still her father. Yuh nuh t'ink it time she know about him?'

'No! Besides, she nuh interested. She never ask about him anymore, she understand him nuh part of our lives.'

'Huh! It's not that she nuh interested. She worried yuh t'ink her disloyal if she ask about him. Yuh need fi watch that yuh nuh strain her loyalty.'

Mum was silent. I sensed their conversation had come to an end. I stepped away as noiselessly as I could; then tiptoed back upstairs. I was now wide awake. Trying to imagine this man called *Ea-sy*.

3

The net curtains in the front sitting room rose up slightly as a draught slipped beneath the sash windows. I was only ever allowed in here on Saturdays, when I did the dusting, never on a Monday morning. Yet here I was, standing in front of the Bluespot gram, looking at Auntie Sybil's treasured photographs. Hidden behind snapshots of Marcia, Margery, Devon and Kiplyn, was a large gilt frame with a black-and-white picture of Sybil and Earl on their wedding day. This is what I was searching for, and there she was: Mum. Her bridesmaid's dress showing a fine neckline and a cinched waist made even more slender by the layers of crinoline under the skirt. She had on the highest of high-heeled shoes, but best of all, she was smiling. She looked like the sort of person whose face could slip into a smile effortlessly. I fancied that this was how she had smiled when she met the man called Easy. I picked up the photo and held it close, trying to remember if I'd ever seen Mum this joyful in real life.

'Put that down before yuh break it!' Mum was scowling in the doorway. 'Why you nuh gone ah school yet? Galang, before yuh late!'

I carefully returned the photograph to the gram and

stepped out of the room keeping my eyes down to avoid Mum's impatient glare. The image of her younger, happier face faded from my mind.

I only just managed to make it through the gates before the school bell went. Connie was ahead in the queue waiting to be let inside, but left his place to stand beside me. His parka was zipped up to his chin and he had on a pair of trousers that were a better fit than the ones he'd worn last Friday. He was still wearing the plimsolls.

'Yuh have a nice weekend?' he asked. 'How's Miss Gladys keeping?'

'She's fine. Thank you.'

I stood on my tiptoes, looking ahead and wondering when the line would begin to move. There was chuckling behind us. Glancing over my shoulder I saw Craig nudge Ted and point at Connie's plimsolls.

'Althea say I should give yuh this,' said Connie, holding out a plastic carrier bag. 'It's ackee! Mi bring a whole heap when mi come from Jamaica. Althea cook and freeze most of it. She say it dear over here so thought yuh might appreciate some. She ask if yuh can please bring back the Tupperware box. Yuh like ackee?'

I'd only ever had ackee once in my life. One Saturday afternoon, almost a year ago, Uncle Earl had shimmied into the kitchen smelling of rum, with a mischievous smile on his face. He placed two tins of ackee on the worktop. Auntie Sybil was furious, one tin apparently cost a 'blasted fortune', let alone two. She was even less impressed when he explained about his win on the horses.

Miss Gladys chuckled to herself, 'Eh-eh! Ackee in a tin.' The following morning, the smell of fried onions, pepper and thyme wafted from the kitchen, luring us from our beds. Miss Gladys had cooked the tinned ackee with saltfish, and served it with fried dumplings and plantain. My cousins and I marvelled at the buttery, creamy texture – trying and failing to describe the unique flavour – while the grown-ups ate in smiling silence. That was the only time I'd ever had ackee. And I loved it.

'Oi, what's that you got there?' asked Ted.

'Ackee, it's from Jamaica,' said Connie brightly. 'It's a fruit but we eat it like a vegetable.'

To my horror he held the bag open, inviting the boy to look inside.

'Ugh! Looks like frozen scrambled eggs,' said Ted. 'Don't you eat normal food?'

'This *is* normal food,' said Connie, his voice tinged with indignation. 'It's our food and I bring it as a present for her.'

'Nice present, frozen scrambled eggs,' said Craig.

Connie's smile dissolved. 'It's not scrambled egg. It's ackee.'

'Yes mon. It no scrambled egg mon,' said Ted in a mock Jamaican accent.

Connie drew himself up to his full height; so did Ted.

The line began to move. Without looking at Connie or the other two boys I snatched the bag and hurried into the building. Ted and Craig pursued me.

'Kunta Kinte's got his girlfriend a present,' said Ted.

'Yeah, he brung it over on the banana boat,' said Craig, laughing.

Their taunting continued all the way to our form room. I set my face like flint and tried to ignore them. In my mind, I was cursing Connie for bringing in the ackee, for showing it off in the playground and for wearing those stupid, bloody plimsolls.

'Why yuh walk off like that?' Connie whispered, sitting down beside me. I refused to look at him. 'Yuh so friendly and nice the other day after school, what make yuh act so boasy now?'

'Don't go calling me *boasy*. You were making a right show of yourself out in the playground with your flippin' ackee.' I turned to him. '*I* don't come here to socialise, or to be laughed at, I come here to learn!'

Connie's eyebrows arched. 'Well, Miss Daphne_ I can see now that I was wrong fi trouble you with my *flippin'* ackee. And I hate to drag you from yuh learning so p'raps I just go sit over there-sah!'

I turned away. 'It's a free country.'

With that, Connie took a seat on the opposite side of the room and I felt an unexpected scratch of dismay. I busied myself preparing for the lesson and shoved the carrier with the ackee in the bottom of my bag.

'Aye-aye here he comes,' Ted called out.

I looked up, then inhaled sharply, as Mark entered. Over the weekend he'd had his shaggy hair cropped close to his scalp, like his brother. I couldn't stop myself from staring as he joined his friends on the back row.

'You should have seen him on Saturday at the Den; he looked like a proper skin,' said Craig. 'I'm shaving mine after school.'

'It really suits you,' exclaimed Joanne Cole.

'Quite sexy as it goes,' said Michelle, with a wink.

'Come off it!' Mark's tone was more matter-of-fact than cocky as he leaned back in his seat and slowly ran a hand over his head, looking hard.

Our maths teacher, Miss Sayers, walked in and the lesson began. I spent the next fifty minutes trying to focus on algebra and ignore the heavy weight in my gut.

When the bell rang for morning break, Connie was out of the door before I'd had time to put on my coat. Outside, I sat on my usual bench and opened the *South London Star*. After skimming through the news, I turned to the letters page.

SIR, What a lot of nonsense is spoken about police brutality! Unless one is prepared to bury one's head in the sand, or happens to be associated with the lunatic fringes of the Left, one must face up to the fact that Blacks are the most criminally minded members of the community. That is the reason why they are brought more often into contact with the police. I am a socialist of many years standing; however, I face up to what is wrong with our society. The Special Patrol Unit should be commended for their sterling work.

Name and address withheld

I was always intrigued when I saw 'Name and address withheld'. I wondered who these people were and where they lived. Could they be people I knew?

'Phwoar . . . the lucky sod,' Craig said, laughing, as he and Ted wandered past my bench.

I looked up, inquisitive, scanning the playground and saw

Michelle coming out from behind the art block. She walked towards the drinking taps where Joanne was waiting, buttoning her coat as she went. Mark came trailing after her, wiping his mouth with the back of his hand. I shifted in my seat, pinched with agitation at the sight of them and annoyed with myself for being so. Mark wandered over to join his mates. Ted muttered something, then burst out laughing. Mark briefly grinned, then ran his palm over his scalp, like I'd seen him do a few times that morning. Once, he'd caught me staring and although I'd quickly looked away, at some point my eyes drifted over to him again. I wasn't sure why. I suppose I couldn't believe it was really him. The shaved head made him even more like Phil. *A proper skin.* I shuddered. Had he told his brother? 'This Black girl flashed me the other day, showed me her tits and her snatch!' I bet the sight of my skinny, black, naked body had amused him. No, most likely it had disgusted him. I made myself turn back to the paper.

SIR, I was disappointed by the way your newspaper reported last week's meeting, which was held to discuss a fund for relatives of the fire's victims. There were over 1,000 people present – a tremendous show of solidarity within the Black community – but rather than highlight this, you instead focused on the views of the Metropolitan Police, who keep stating how important it is to 'establish fact and combat fiction'. These are the facts as I see it. Racists have murdered eleven of our teenagers yet the police are doing nothing about it. Furthermore, when our young people go out they are stopped merely on 'suspicion' of wrongdoing. Black parents feel that our children are now neither safe on the streets nor in their own homes.

M. C. Thomas, London SE1

Marcia had been sneaking off to these meetings, telling Auntie Sybil that she was at the library. I wished that I could have gone too. I wondered what it would be like to go there as a reporter. I wondered if the *South London Star* had any Black reporters.

I spotted Connie standing with another group of lads from our year. Among them was a boy who labelled himself 'quarter-caste', and never associated with Black students. Connie was animated: gesticulating, smiling, yet this boy stood aloof with his hands in his pockets. He turned to his white friends and made some comment, nodding at Connie's plimsolls. They all laughed; Connie's face fell, and he walked away. I sighed inwardly. Miss Gladys was expecting me to help ease him into school life, but how was I supposed to help him if he didn't pay attention to how the white kids behaved, or other Black kids for that matter? So far he had made no effort to blend in and now he was finding out for himself. Nevertheless, I couldn't bear to watch. I buried myself in the paper. There was a letter in favour of the new Nationality Bill, 'because why should the children of foreigners be automatically entitled to British citizenship, just because they happen to be born in the UK?' I read another letter opposing the 'barmy proposal to build a Shakespearean-style theatre on the Southbank'. I was determined to ignore Connie. However, every time I blew on my fingers to warm them, I caught sight of him, ambling with his hands in his pockets, kicking at some loose pebbles on the tarmac.

It was 4 p.m. when I returned home. Miss Gladys's bedroom door was ajar and I heard the Singer's slow hum, then silence.

'What mek yuh stan' outside in the hallway, come greet mi nuh!'

Miss Gladys was sitting in the corner by the window. Hanging on the wall behind her in a wooden picture frame was the black-and-white photograph of Grandpa James. He was standing on the path of their front garden in Jamaica, playing the guitar left-handed. I recalled how a few days ago I'd heard Grandma say her late husband was still the finest person she'd ever known. I wondered if I'd ever feel that way about anyone. I always thought the story about how they met was so romantic.

An eighteen-year-old Miss Gladys was living in Mandeville and one evening she was waiting for a taxi; the driver who pulled up was a dashing twenty-two-year-old. On the journey they chatted and found they had things in common: they were both only children, both were orphans and neither of them liked living in the big town. When the driver remarked on the quality of the smock stitches on her blouse, the young Miss Gladys thought it was a chat-up line, which it was, but he also told her that he was a tailor by trade. This was his last night driving a taxi because he had finally saved enough to set himself up in business. He needed a good seamstress, perhaps they could work together. They did just that and over the course of a year they built a good reputation for fine suits and sturdy school uniforms. They also fell in love. Gladys and

James were happily married for nineteen years, until Grandpa was taken by pneumonia in the winter of '58. Miss Gladys said that she lost the love of her life, but somehow, through hard work and determination, managed to keep her business going. She remained the best seamstress in the district.

Two dozen or so denim miniskirts were piled on the ottoman at the foot of Miss Gladys's bed. She looked over her glasses at the white plastic carrier I was holding.

'What's that yuh have deh?'

'It's from that boy Connie and his mum.'

I handed over the bag and watched my grandma's face light up when her eyes fell on the contents in the clear plastic container.

'But Lord have mercy! Connie and him muddah sen' us this whole heap of ackee? Yuh see how it more plump and succulent than the ackee that come in the tin?' She looked at me and laughed. 'Yes mon, ah fi wi food dis!'

I turned to leave the room. 'I'll tell Connie you liked it.'

'We must can do better than that. Tell him to come over and eat it with us, him muddah too. It should keep till Saturday. What d'yuh t'ink?'

'Do we have to? It's not like he expects us to share it. He said it was a present.'

'Now Daphne, mi know yuh have good manners because mi help raise yuh, so mi sure yuh understand that it would be polite – as well as nice, to invite yuh friend to come and eat with us.'

'He's not my friend. He ain't even talking to me.'

'Nuh say *ain't*, say *isn't*. Whaap'm? Yuh quarrel?'

I told her what happened in the playground that morning,

how I'd scolded Connie and that now he wasn't speaking to me.

'Yuh mean to say Connie shame yuh ah school cos him bring yuh a gift that the white pickney laugh at, so yuh turn round and blame him fi dat? Cha!'

'Grandma, he just doesn't realise.'

I could feel tears brimming in the corners of my eyes. Blinking them back stung.

'Grandma, he's going to spoil everything. Everyone will think I'm just like him. They'll go back to calling me nig-nog and Sambo and wog.'

'Daphne yuh born ah England and yuh must never let dem badmind pickney say yuh nah belong 'ere. But that not fi say yuh cyaah be proud to be Jamaican too. Proud to be Black. Come now!'

I trudged over to her, bleary-eyed and buried my head in her lap. Miss Gladys allowed me a couple of minutes to rest there, stroking my head before she cupped my face in her hands, wanting my undivided attention.

'Yuh must never allow anyone to t'ink dem can rule yuh – whether dem Black or white. Even if yuh nuh feel mighty yuh must behave so. Duppy know who fi frighten, and who fi tell good night. Yuh understand?'

I nodded, but only because I knew there was no use arguing.

The next day I resolved to make up with Connie and invite him to eat with us on Saturday. But as I made my way over to his desk at the start of the history lesson, he put his bag on the empty seat beside him. I got the hump after that, and spent the rest of the week blanking him too, especially at break times. By Friday, we still hadn't spoken, so I decided I'd just tell Miss Gladys that Connie had made other plans.

All week I'd been following any news I could find about the house fire in New Cross. It was barely mentioned in the national papers now, and the local press's most recent report was just one column on the bottom of page two. On Friday lunchtime I sat absorbing the latest update, trying to figure out what to make of it.

FORENSICS POINT TO INSIDE JOB

... The forensic tests conclude that paint thinner had been sprinkled on the living room carpet, on the ground floor of the property. A group calling itself the New Cross Massacre Action Committee have challenged the forensic evidence and maintain that it was a racist attack, accusing the police of not cracking down on right-wing extremists. Over four hundred people gathered at a community centre last night, which has become a focal point for mourners and activists. Afterwards, they marched to demonstrate outside the burnt-out building. A Scotland Yard spokesman said, 'I don't like words like massacre. I believe that outside groups are using this tragedy for their own political ends.'

The death toll from the party has now risen to twelve.

Some of the newsprint was smudged, the paper stained from teabags and orange peel. I'd retrieved it from the bin where Miss Gladys had dashed it last night, fuming about what she called 'biased reporting'.

'Twelve Black pickney dead after some wretch set the house alight, and the police nuh want we fi call it a massacre. Then wah we fi call it?' she'd said.

I'd lain awake for hours in the darkness of the attic room, picturing the burnt-out house a few miles away. Wondering who was responsible for the arson. The massacre. And when they would be caught. I wondered what we would do if our house was set alight. Would I remember the instructions I'd seen in a government advertisement about fire? Shove pillows against the door to stop smoke from invading the room? Tie sheets together to make a rope? How could I make a rope long enough to reach the ground from our attic room? Would I survive if I jumped from the second storey? I remembered what Margery had said about the teenagers leaping from the upper windows of the New Cross house, their clothes alight. I thought about those trapped inside, unable to see. Unable to breathe.

I was deep in thought and didn't notice that Connie had come to stand next to me.

'Whapp'm Daphne? Yuh all right? I see you sit here ah gaze into space like somet'ing troubling you.'

'Oh. I'm fine,' I said, forcing a smile.

He looked down at the newspaper, twisting his head slightly so he could read the headline.

'One of Althea clients come round with that same newspaper last night. She was talking about all the young people that dead.'

I sighed. 'Yeah. Some of them were the same age as my cousins.'

'She say people are raising money to help the families meet dem funeral costs. Even prisoners in a jail called Wormwood Scrubs raise over fifty pounds, so Althea say she gonna organise a collection at the salon.'

'That's nice of her.'

'Mi t'ink so too,' said Connie. 'Tobias tell her to nuh bother give way her money cos she still owe him for mi plane fare, but she say she gwaan contribute anyway. Black people need to help each other.'

Connie smiled at me. I hoped this meant that we were friends again. I was surprised by a warm feeling in my tummy.

'Why yuh always ah sit here with the newspaper? You nuh feel the cold?'

'I was born here. I'm used to it.'

Connie's smile deepened, the dimple in his right cheek appeared. 'Suit yuself, I'm gonna keep walking,' he said, turning to move away.

I swallowed to moisten my suddenly dry throat. 'My grandma's cooking the ackee you gave us tomorrow. She said you . . . and Althea should come over and join us. About half elevenish for a sort of late breakfast, early lunch. Can you come?'

'Sure. I'd like that.'

'Good – oh watch out!'

Connie ducked to avoid the football that had been booted from the other end of the pitch. Mark was chasing, hoping to kick it back into play but it was too fast and so he left it to a boy from 1A for a throw-in. The boys from our class had been playing football against 1A all week. Their matches were ill-tempered with as many scuffles off the pitch as on it. The ball sailed past Mark again and he ran in pursuit, like the other boys travelling in waves back and forth across the pitch. Connie stood watching the game; I sat watching Mark.

Errol Morris, one of 1A's players, got the ball and began dribbling towards our goal. In a determined run, Mark appeared alongside Errol, barging him with his shoulder. The shove carried Errol towards the goalpost. I had to cover my eyes. Exclamations of 'Fucking hell!' echoed all around. I parted my fingers to peer at Errol who had collapsed to his knees, clutching his face and groaning. I followed the crowd of students swarming in to see if there was any blood. Then Mr Jones was on the scene, unravelling the clutch of bodies around the injured boy. Errol's brown skin was ashen and blood dripped from his nose. Mr Jones gently inspected the boy's injury with the tips of his fingers.

'All right sunshine, I think you'll live. Tilt your head forwards, that's it. Keep pinching the tip of your nose.' The teacher turned to Joanne Cole. 'Would you kindly take this fellow to the school office please?'

Grudgingly, Joanne escorted Errol across the playground, taking care to keep her arm extended so his blood wouldn't drip onto her coat sleeve.

Rob Hunt, a wiry lad from 1A, rounded on Mark. 'It's your fault, you fouled him!'

'It was a shoulder charge, dickhead,' said Mark.

'Watch it Barrett. I'll have none of that language,' said Mr Jones. 'What's the score?'

'Twenty-two all,' said a chorus of voices.

'Well, there's five minutes of break left,' said Mr Jones, producing his tin of Golden Virginia. 'Are you going to play or are you going to argue?'

'But sir, it's not fair, we're a man down,' said Rob.

His classmates joined in the protest while Mr Jones rolled a cigarette. As he licked the thin-gummed strip, his eyes grazed Connie, towering above us all.

'You boy! D'you play football?' he asked.

Connie surveyed the crowd of faces, lingering on Mark. 'Yes, sir. I do.'

'Then play alongside 1A.'

'He can't play for them, he's in our class!' Mark protested.

'I could send you off instead Barrett. Would you prefer that? Didn't think so. I'll be ref.'

All of us spectators got off the pitch so play could resume. The ball was placed in the centre and Connie passed it back to Rob. He ran with it before coming up against Mark who went in for a tackle, but Rob beat him and sent the ball to Connie. Rob ran up the wing for a return pass but Connie deftly feinted past one defender and then another, closing in on our class's goal. He glanced up before shooting, the keeper could only watch as the ball flew past him.

'Yes!' screamed Rob, punching the air.

Mark snatched the ball from the keeper and ran back to the centre spot, but before they could kick off again the bell went; lunchtime was over. Rob ran up to Connie, said something and they both laughed. Mark barged between them, red-faced and fuming.

'Your lot only won because of a lucky strike from that lanky jungle bunny in his spastic plimsolls!'

'Jungle bunny?' Connie scoffed. 'Just relax mon, it's only a game.'

'Don't tell me to relax!'

Mark lunged at Connie, shoving him in the chest. 'Piss off back where you came from, you fucking Black bastard.'

'Barrett! Headmaster's office, right now.'

Mr Jones's voice was colossal with fury, but it was Mark's words that were ringing in my ears. What he'd said, those words, the aggression: that whole image was Phil. But clearly some of it had to be Mark as well, and I'd just chosen not to see it. Mark stood motionless, his eyes widened as if some mist had cleared and we'd only now all come into view. He saw me and I shifted my gaze to the grey-black tarmac, biting my bottom lip. When I looked up again he was trudging off like a petulant toddler: head down, hands in pockets, shrugging away his mate's attempts to put a consoling arm around him.

'All of you back to class now,' said Mr Jones, regaining his composure. 'Mr Small . . .'

Connie stopped and turned around. 'Sir?'

'Come to football practice. Next Wednesday after school.'

'Yes, sir!' Connie replied. 'Thank you.'

He ran off to catch up with Rob and the other boys. He didn't look back. I traipsed towards the school building alone, suddenly feeling the cold.

4

It was Saturday morning and the scent of boiled salt cod was trickling into the hallway. Miss Gladys was standing by the stove with a ladle, ready to skim off the briny froth rising from the pan.

'Daphne darlin', come help me cook.'

I tutted, but went over to the worktop, where Miss Gladys had assembled scallions, bell peppers, tomatoes and thyme. The ackee was heaped in a colander. I caught the whiff of vinegar that had been sprinkled over it. Miss Gladys drained the saltfish and told me to slice the peppers. There were an assortment of blades with mismatched handles in a drawer beside the cooker. I lifted out the knife that I'd often seen Miss Gladys use for slicing carrots, chocho and such.

She reached over, spreading my thumb and my middle finger so they were gripping the green pepper. The knife slipped through the shiny skin, releasing a sweet smell.

'Mi remember the last time mi get yuh cousins to help with Sunday dinner. Marcia boil the peas till dem mash up and then Margery burn the rice.' She shook her head. 'If mi nuh know any better me'd say dem ah protest! Part of dem *women's lib*. Anyway, from what mi see of the way yuh slice up that pepper, mi gwaan make a cook out of yuh!'

Miss Gladys exhaled a chuckle.

'But isn't women's lib a good thing? I mean, look at Margaret Thatcher, she may never have become Prime Minister if she was doing housework all the time,' I said.

'Nuh mention that bloody woman to me!' Miss Gladys was slicing an onion into thin semi-circles, tears glinted in the corners of her eyes, but her gaze remained focused. 'She talk about how immigrants ah swamp British communities, and how dem must curb entry to Commonwealth citizens, even if dem family deh 'ere already – ah Black people she ah talk 'bout yuh know. Nuh all dem white folk ah flock here from Zimbabwe. Dem come here and land quick time.'

There was that word again. *Land.*

Miss Gladys continued, 'I want mi granddawtas to get dem education, I wasn't much older than yuh when mi force to leave school. But if Mrs Thatcher is what women's liberation look like then mi nuh want any part in it.'

Miss Gladys set the onion aside. I leaned in close, lowering my voice.

'Grandma, you know what Connie said to us, that his mum no land. Does that mean that he isn't either.'

Miss Gladys hesitated. 'Most likely dem come into the country legally, but overstay dem visa. If the authorities find out dem'll deport dem. Send dem home.'

'Is deport the same as repatriate? Like what the NF want to do to us?'

Miss Gladys kissed her teeth. 'Yuh muddah come here when Jamaica was still a colony; it was as a British subject she enter the country and she naturalised since then. I come after independence and take dual citizenship, and being born here mek yuh a British citizen – an English gyal. Nobody ah kick us out if we nuh want fi go!' She began picking the thyme leaves. 'But overstayers like Connie and him muddah . . . nuh have citizenship, that's why yuh nuh fi talk about dem situation. Nuh let nuttin' slip cos yuh never know who's listening. Nobody likes an informer – even if dem nuh mean to snitch.'

'I haven't said a word. Honest!'

Miss Gladys pinched my cheek.

'Look how wi ah cook and talk like big woman. This nuh nice eh?'

Her voice had softened and she moved about the kitchen at her usual, relaxed tempo. I nodded. *Big woman's talk.* Mature, comfortable, honest. I took a deep breath.

'Grandma, will you tell me about my father? About "Easy".'

The oil glugged a little faster as Miss Gladys poured it into the dutchie.

'Who say yuh father name suh?' I was silent. She looked at me. I shrugged. 'Mi nuh faas in ah yuh muddah business and neither should yuh.'

'But it's my business too.' There was more force in my voice than I'd expected, but I couldn't stop. 'I heard you talking about him the other night. I didn't mean to listen in but you were talking about me too. You want Mum to tell me about him, but she won't – you know she won't, so you should tell me.'

'It nuh mi place to talk to yuh about that man. I never know him. Yuh must talk to yuh muddah.'

'How am I supposed to ask her about him if she's always in a mood? Didn't she frighten him off the other day with her bad mood? I bet that's the reason they broke up. I bet she was moody – like she is all the time. And now she's gone and told him to go away again. I'll never know him, and it's just not fair!'

'What's not fair? Yuh have family around yuh, food for yuh belly and clothes pan yuh back. Yuh have stability and love – yet yuh come talk about how it nuh fair yuh nuh know some man who nuh bother look pan yuh in the eleven years since him leave!'

Miss Gladys rarely raised her voice, especially with me. I rolled my lips inwards, sealing them in order to prevent any more facetyness tumbling out.

'Heartbreak nuh like what pop stars sing about in dem songs. It's a whole heap more painful, and it tek time fi heal. Which is why Alma nuh like fi talk about it. Trust mi, yuh muddah love yuh, even if she nuh show it in the way yuh like.'

She lit the fire under the pot. We were silent. When the oil began to pop she tipped in the scallions, peppers, tomatoes and thyme; as their aromas slowly released themselves into the room, I saw her shoulders relax once more.

'Grandma, could you at least tell me why he's called Easy?'

Miss Gladys sighed. 'When Alma first write mi about him, she say him name Enoch, but that him never like it. He like it even less after that politician talk him foolishness about rivers of blood. So either him or him mandem start to call him by him initials: Enoch Zephaniah Ethan Edwards become Ezee. It sound fool-fool if yuh want my opinion.'

She stirred the vegetables silently, immersed in thought. I was thinking too. Enoch Zephaniah Ethan Edwards, an impressive array of names. I liked the sound of *Ezee* even more.

Connie arrived promptly at half-past eleven. He thanked Miss Gladys for inviting him over and said Althea would have liked to come too, but Saturday was the salon's busiest day.

His feet made a clomping sound as he crossed the room. I looked down and was surprised to see that he had on oxblood-coloured Dr. Martens. I'd only ever seen DMs in that colour on skinheads. At the end of Connie's slender, lanky body, they looked more comical than threatening, but they were much better than the plimsolls.

Uncle Earl usually sat at the head of the table, but when he, Auntie Sybil and Mum were out at work, Miss Gladys took his place. I always sat at the far end, where I could sometimes get away with propping a book up in front of me while I ate. Today, I was steered to the chair at Miss Gladys's right hand, opposite Connie who was seated on her left. My chest swelled at being elevated to the grown-up end of the table, although I was nervous about having a guest of my own come to the house. My cousins' mates would come by all the time, but then I wasn't sure if Connie and I were actually mates.

When Miss Gladys announced that I'd helped her to prepare the meal, Kiplyn immediately clasped his throat, pretending that he'd been poisoned.

'Stop it you!' I said, swatting him on the shoulder.

'Jeez . . . can't you take a joke?' said Kiplyn.

'Behave yuself.' Miss Gladys was smiling, but there was grit in her tone.

'I used to help my gramma cook ackee and saltfish all the time,' said Connie. He was looking at me. 'This tastes nice. Just like being back home.'

I smiled at my plate.

Between mouthfuls, Connie told us that he liked cooking but Althea didn't. On Sundays he'd usually help her cook meat with rice and peas, but during the week they tended to make meals that were 'quick and easy', sometimes his mother brought home takeaways. So far he'd tasted Chinese food, and fish and chips. Althea promised to buy an Indian curry for him to try one day.

'What d'you miss most about Jamaica?' I asked.

'Gramma and Papa.'

Connie's voice went quiet. Jarred by his sudden, solemn tone, I was anxious that I'd said the wrong thing. I looked at Miss Gladys for help.

'Yuh nuh hear from dem?' she asked.

'Gramma send a letter with the Christmas presents. But nuttin' more since then.'

Miss Gladys rested her hand on his. 'Nuh worry yuself. Yuh'll hear from dem soon. We grandmuddahs never stay quiet fi long.'

Connie managed a faint smile, which my grandma returned with her own wide grin.

'May I leave the table?' said Kiplyn. 'Football Focus is on and it's Arsenal-Chelsea today.'

Miss Gladys nodded. Kiplyn rose and switched the telly on, Devon followed, slumping himself onto the settee with his foot propped over the arm. Miss Gladys began to clear the plates; the twins and I followed her lead, leaving Connie marooned at the dinner table.

'D'yuh need a hand with the washing up?' he asked, his voice polite, faltering.

'No darlin', yuh is our guest, go watch the telly,' said Grandma. 'Daphne, leave the plates and go sit with him.'

Devon moved his feet to allow space for Connie on the

sofa. I went over and perched on the armchair, stiff and self-conscious; listening to Marcia and Margery clattering the plates in the sink with suspicious force. Their noisy protest lost on their brothers, absorbed by the TV.

'D'you like football?' asked Kiplyn, speaking more to the screen than to Connie. 'In't it all cricket in Jamaica?'

'Nah! Back home we play football everywhere,' said Connie. 'Bob Marley did love to play, before he get sick.'

They lapsed into a comfortable silence for a moment.

'What team d'you support? We're Arsenal,' said Kiplyn.

'Mi nuh know many of the English sides. I watch the football programme that come on Saturday nights, and see a brilliant Black player, what him name now . . . Cyrille . . . '

The footballer's name was on the tip of my tongue.

'Regis,' said Devon, cool and unhurried. 'He plays for West Bromwich Albion. Yeah, he's class in't he.'

'Brendon Batson plays for them too,' Kiplyn chipped in. 'They used to have another Black guy in that team, Laurie Cunningham, but he went to Real Madrid, they paid almost a million quid for him.'

I sat tense, looking for a way to enter their conversation. Connie was supposed to be *my* guest.

'You ever see dem play?'

'Nah. We've never been to a match. There are too many racist hooligans,' said Devon.

'Listen, I'm meeting my friend Lincoln and his brother Jerome for a kick-about in the park after this, come with me, it'd be better with four of us,' said Kiplyn.

'Yeah okay, t'anks,' said Connie. He turned to me. 'Yuh coming too, Daphne, right?'

Connie spoke as if including me was the most natural thing in the world.

'I was going to go to the library,' I said.

'Of course you were,' said Kiplyn, pretending to yawn.

'But I can put it off till next Saturday. I suppose '

Devon whistled. 'Wonders will never cease!'

'Good,' said Connie.

His smile was broad, all teeth, unguarded. I realised that he didn't want to be my friend. He *was* my friend. The boys continued chatting about footballers and fixtures while I relaxed into the armchair.

The crisp, February air nipped at my cheeks; I blew on my hands to warm them. Connie and Kiplyn began kicking the ball to each other as soon as we'd entered the park. They continued to pass it back and forth across the grass as we headed over to the football pitches. I thought how Connie was beginning to look like a regular kid from around our way. Yes, he was taller than average and in class that made him stick out a mile; yet here, outside of school, his height seemed less unusual. He moved with confidence. Happy in his frame. Happy in his skin.

Lincoln and Jerome hadn't arrived yet, so Connie and Kiplyn did keep-ups while they waited. Connie asked if I would keep score.

'Sure,' I said, thrilled to be included, yet trying not to appear too eager.

They were determined to outdo each other. While one boy stood with eyes on the football, juggling with his feet, his knees – and sometimes attempting to use his chest too – the other kept a light-hearted commentary, either admiring or dissing his opponent's skills. I joined in with the banter. For ages neither of them managed to keep the ball up for longer than eighteen kicks until Kiplyn made it to twenty-two. Exhilarated, he threw himself down on the grass, cheering and waving his arms.

'Beat that!' he shouted.

'Watch this now,' said Connie.

He winked at me. It made me want to giggle but Kiplyn was there, so I acted indifferent.

'Go on then,' I said.

Connie began kicking the ball back and forth between his left foot and his right, easily making it to ten. He tilted his left foot up and the ball landed on his knee. *Eleven, twelve, thirteen, fourteen.* Then back to his feet, *fifteen, sixteen, seventeen, eighteen.* Kiplyn and I were hypnotised by the ball, engrossed in our count. Then Connie suddenly stopped. As the ball rolled towards me, I heard the hollow sound of a slow handclap.

'Mi see yuh from over there. Mi never know yuh have such skills—'

I recognised the deep voice, the patwah with a South London twang, before turning to see Tobias loom towards us.

'—then mi never expect to buck up pan yuh in the park ah kick football.'

'I was at Daphne house,' Connie spoke cautiously. 'Althea say mi could go.'

Tobias was standing in front of Connie, dwarfing him. 'That's nice. Yuh finish yuh chores though before yuh go out?'

'Yes.'

'Cos yuh know when mi get back home mi ah go check.'

Connie kept his eyes level with Tobias's broad chest. He spoke in a murmur. 'Mi still have to dust the living room and put the peas to soak and—'

'So yuh nuh finish yuh chores but yuh out here ah play while yuh muddah and mi work fi keep yuh! What mi always ah tell yuh about responsibility?'

'Althea say mi could—'

The sound of the slap resonated, filling the wide-open space. Connie held his cheek in the palm of his hand.

'That was for chattin' back. For shaming me in front of yuh friend dem. Mi nuh gonna put up with no bad bruck bwoy in mi house. A young man should own up to him mistakes and expect to be corrected. Now get yuh backside home,' said Tobias.

He began walking away. Connie's shoulders slumped. I didn't know what to say. I thought that if he looked at me I might somehow be able to show that I felt for him, that I was on his side. Connie glanced at me, but only for a moment. His face was closed and without a word he turned and ran after Tobias.

'Bloody hell that was some lick – and in the face as well!' Kiplyn whistled, shaking his head. 'Honestly, I thought his dad was going to take off his belt then and there. Connie should have stayed quiet. I would have.'

'He wasn't answering back. All he said was that he had permission to come to our house today.' As I spoke, I realised my voice quivered. I paused and took a deep breath. 'And that man in't even his dad.'

'Don't matter! He's still a grown-up; you know how they stay when they even *think* you're giving them backchat.'

'Our grown-ups tells us off, we never get licks!'

'That's because Grandpa James didn't do that sort of discipline. Being a "real gentleman" and all of that. But trust me, what we saw just then was nothing. Lincoln's dad makes *them* fetch the belt to beat them with, his little brother Jerome is usually in tears before their dad has laid a finger on him ...'

While Kiplyn talked, my mind replayed the sound of Tobias's gigantic palm smacking Connie's face. I imagined the sting of the slap.

'I'm going home. I'm gonna tell Grandma,' I said.

'What do you expect our grandma to do about it? Firstly, it ain't any of her business, and secondly, she don't like backchat any more than that bloke.'

Kiplyn kissed his teeth like he always did with me, when he thought he'd made his point. But I know what I saw – even if I couldn't explain how I felt.

'Yeah, but he hit Connie really hard, and in the face as well. You said it yourself, it's not normal to hit a kid in the face—'

'Please! Every one of my friends get licks now and again, but it ain't something you sit and chat about! Trust me, you mention it to anyone – even Connie – then it will just make it embarrassing. If I was you, I'd keep my nose out.'

I'd never had any real friends before so had no idea how other kids were reprimanded at home. I thought about what Kiplyn said. Was it true that he would want to save face? Should I really ignore what I'd seen? We trudged back to Lime Grove, me silent as my cousin continued talking. But the more he insisted what had just happened was normal, the less normal I felt about what I had seen.

5

Mark Barrett was suspended. The rumour started in the playground on Monday before the morning bell, filtering down the line as we filed upstairs and along the corridor to the classroom. When Miss Sayers skipped over 'Barrett' during registration, all eyes drifted to where I was sitting, beside an empty chair. The roll call continued. Miss got to Connie Small but uttered his name as if she were talking to herself, made a mark in the register and then moved on to Keeley Tucker. I saw Craig whispering in Ted's ear. They probably thought Connie had cut school, afraid to face them after getting their mate into trouble. I knew that Connie wasn't frightened of them. I was worried that the reason he wasn't in class had something to do with Tobias.

As Miss Sayers closed the register there were three quick taps on the classroom door. Before waiting to be invited, Mrs Jennings, the school secretary, wafted in, the scent of Lily of the Valley trailing after her. She handed Miss Sayers a folded sheet of paper, which she studied.

'I see. Thank you, Mrs Jennings,' Miss said, refolding the letter and placing it in the side pocket of her culottes. Raising her voice she called out, 'All right, come in.'

The door pushed open and Mark entered, his navy anorak folded over his arm. Behind him was Connie, who politely stepped back to allow the school secretary to pass. Mark strolled towards his usual seat.

'No, not there,' said Miss Sayers. 'It seems you and Connie are to sit beside each other in every lesson for the rest of this week. Daphne, please go and sit next to Michelle.'

I looked at Connie. He shrugged. It was news to him too. Slowly, I gathered my things and headed for the empty chair beside Michelle; meanwhile, Mark stomped towards my now vacant seat. We managed to block each other in the narrow space between the row of desks; both stepping to the left, then to the right, like bad dancers at a disco. Mark's lips had vexed into a pale-pink line. He fixed me with his grey-blue eyes for a moment, then stood aside to let me pass. While I settled quietly into my new place, Mark slammed his bag down on the desk beside Connie, then scraped the chair's metal legs against the floor as he angled his seat away from him. Connie didn't flinch. He sat with his chin resting on interlaced fingers, waiting for the lesson to begin.

Connie and Mark missed the morning break; they were 'helping' Mr Jones tidy the sports cupboard. Fortunately at lunchtime I got a seat opposite Connie; it was the first time we'd had a chance to speak. He told me that Mr Jones had escorted him to the headmaster's office that morning, in order that they might sort out the 'bad business'. Mark was there with his father and had been made to apologise to Connie for the shove, and for calling him a Black bastard.

'He actually said sorry!'

'Cha! Him say it but him nuh mean it. Didn't he call me Sambo the other day? Him nuh apologize for that. Plus his dad pout up him mout' and moan about how the area where him born and bred will soon be overrun with foreigners and muggers like Brixton.' Connie pushed the stewed meat around his plate. 'Mi nuh know what dem serve us today but bwoy it's nasty.'

One of the dinner ladies was passing our table. She overheard Connie and pulled us up sharp.

'You two should count yourself lucky to be here, when there's all them like you starving in Africa. Think on,' she said, nodding sagely before walking away.

'Mi born ah Jamaica and since when that move to the African continent?'

'Yeah. Lewisham hospital's maternity ward isn't in Africa neither!' I added. 'Someone should get her an atlas – or maybe just the London A–Z.'

'Nice one!' said Connie, leaning towards me and melting into laughter.

I leaned in closer too, my forearms resting on the table. Sharing the joke – my joke. Ordinarily I never came up with wisecracks. I was never cheeky around grown-ups – I couldn't bear to get into trouble. While I knew it was unlikely the dinner lady had actually heard my facety remark, Connie did, and it made him laugh. I liked him seeing me that way.

'I'm relieved that you were just in the headmaster's office with Mark. When you weren't in class, I thought ... well, I thought it was because of ... your stepdad—'

'He's not my stepdad!' Connie shifted in his seat. 'Yuh no need fi worry 'bout him.'

He filled his mouth with another forkful of mashed potato, averting his eyes from me as he chewed. Was he irritated? No, embarrassed. Kiplyn was right. I'd said the wrong thing. I shuffled boiled swede from one side of my plate to the other.

'So, where is this Brixton with all the muggers?' asked Connie, the lightness in his voice sounding forced.

'Oh . . . it's not that far but you have to take two buses to get there from here. So we don't go that often – even though Grandma reckons the market is much better than the one near us, there are more stalls selling Caribbean food. D'you know, they've even got West Indian bakeries there, with actual ovens, so the hardo bread and the patties and stuff are really fresh. Grandma took me with her last Christmas to buy bun. We queued for ages.'

'What mi would give for a slice of bun right now!' said Connie, pushing his plate away.

'My cousin Devon and his mates hang out in Brixton most Saturdays, even though he's not supposed to. He likes the record shops there.'

I was enjoying being the authority on a place I'd only visited once. I was enjoying being able to talk about everyday things in my life with somebody else at school.

'Why yuh cousin nuh supposed to go to Brixton?'

I shrugged. 'Auntie Sybil says there's too much trouble. Muggings and that. Apparently it's so bad in Brixton that a special police squad has been brought in.'

'Special how?'

'They go around undercover. Grandma says it's so they can plant stolen goods on Black boys and then arrest them. That's really why Auntie doesn't want Devon to go there. Although he said the police around here are just as bad. The other day him and his mates were stopped and searched coming home from school. But he goes to Brixton anyway; he just doesn't tell Auntie. She thinks all his ska records come from Woolworths.'

Connie chuckled. I'd made him laugh again. Smiling, I went up to get pudding.

When Connie and I walked out of the dining hall, there were only twenty minutes of break time left. Rob and Errol spotted Connie sitting on the bench with me, and called over, inviting him to join in with their kick-about.

Connie turned to me. 'Is that all right?'

'Yeah, of course, suit yourself,' I said.

He jogged onto the football pitch. Mark was alone, leaning against the wall near the halfway line. He flung Connie a dirty look, but Connie ignored it. I wouldn't have done so if it were me. I would have hurled Mark's derision right back at him. What Connie said was true, he wasn't sorry at all. Mark still thought he was better than Connie. Better than all of us. Including me. I felt a sudden hollowness, in my chest, making my shoulders sag. Connie scored a goal and a couple of lads grunted their approval. Mark was now standing with his arms folded, but he looked less defiant, more like he was hugging himself against the cold. I gathered myself and opened the paper.

My eyes flitted over the headlines, not settling on any particular story. A petition to save the P4 bus route had attracted over three hundred signatures. Trade Unions were in talks with management in a bid to save 690 jobs at the brewery.

I turned the page and in the top left-hand corner was the headline:

DEATH TOLL FROM NEW CROSS
FIRE RISES TO THIRTEEN

The report was brief. It listed the names and ages of the three teenage women and the ten young men who had died. I found myself again thinking of Devon, Marcia, Margery and Kiplyn. I couldn't imagine my cousins going out to a birthday party and never coming home, never seeing them again.

'What are you looking at?'

I hadn't noticed that Mark had crossed the concourse. He was sitting on the low brick border around an empty flower bed, a few feet from my bench.

'Nothing,' I said, forcing myself to look down at my newspaper; the black letters a blurred mass in my unfocused gaze.

'Then what's that in your hands?'

His tone was neutral. Not teasing, not threatening.

'Oh, you mean this? It's the *South London Star.*'

He scanned me up and down. What was that look in his eye? I made myself stare back at him. His cheeks flushed, he broke off and flicked imaginary fluff from his trouser leg.

'Have you ever been in the paper?'

'No!' I laughed then stopped myself short. I didn't want to set him off.

'I've been in the paper. I was a Millwall mascot when I was a little 'un. Got me picture taken with Phil Walker. You know, central midfielder. Black guy.'

'Oh. That's . . . nice.'

I went back to the newspaper, trying to concentrate, but out of the corner of my eye I watched him. He was scraping the tip of his boot against the old lumps of chewing gum caked onto the tarmac.

'I ain't told anybody about . . . you know. The other day.'

Anxiety pinched, causing my body to tense; yet at the same time I felt a warm sensation radiate through my body.

'I ain't going to neither,' he continued.

Should I thank him? Should I pretend I didn't know what he was talking about? I didn't know what to say so I said nothing. He was looking at me again.

'Do you like being Black?'

'I love being Black,' I said, trying to flatten the tremor in my voice.

'But . . . if you could turn yourself white, would you do it?'

'No. Why?'

'I just wondered. I think you're pretty.'

I held in a gasp, my woollen gloves felt rough against my lips.

Mark ran a hand over his shaved head. This time watching him trace the outline of his scalp, I thought that he didn't look hard. He looked self-conscious.

'You don't believe me, do you?'

My tongue was fixed to the roof of my mouth.

'Forget I said it.'

He got up and walked away. I knew I heard him right, but it didn't make sense. I told myself to banish what he'd said to the back of my mind. Yet my skin prickled with feelings I didn't quite understand, a mixture of discomfort and delight.

6

At home time on Thursday, Connie caught up with me at the crossing. He was buzzing, delighted that he'd been selected to play in Saturday's match against Christopher Marlowe Comprehensive.

'Come, let's go buy a likkle somet'ing to celebrate.'

'I haven't got any money,' I said.

'Nuh worry, mi treat yuh. Mi have nearly two pounds.'

'Wow! The most pocket money I get is fifty pence a week.'

Connie shrugged. 'Ah nuh my pocket it come from. Mi tek it from Tobias.'

'You're mad! What if he finds out?'

'Mi take a likkle at a time and him nuh notice.' Connie kissed his teeth. 'Him nah notice a t'ing. Mi spit in the soup before mi serve it to him last week and him nyam it off same way!'

Connie chuckled, but rather than the smooth, easy laughter I'd grown used to, there was an edge to it, an undercurrent of coldness. Still, I was glad Connie had got his own back, so I forced myself to laugh along.

I took Connie to *Ben Stanley News & Tobacco*, which was on the corner of Lemon Street, beyond the south side of the park. It was a bit of a walk but it was worth it: Ben had the very best sweet selection. When we arrived, my neighbour, Mrs Blake, was at the counter and unfortunately for us she was in full flow. All the customers who had lived in the neighbourhood 'since the good old days', treated Ben's shop like a home from home. All Connie and I could do was wait, the aromas of sherbet, aniseed and mint making my mouth water.

'. . . my heart goes out to them parents. It's a bloomin' tragedy. But it's all this shouting outside police stations I can't abide. The Old Bill are right to question them youngsters who were at the party. I mean, where's the harm in that? I was saying this to Clement, my lodger, and he agreed with me. But then he's from St Kitts so in't as rowdy as them Jamaicans . . .'

Ben's gaze darted across to us and Mrs Blake finally glanced over her shoulder. She looked at Connie, raising one of the skinny hand-drawn lines that arched above her blue eyes.

'Cor, look at this one! Tall in't he?' she gushed, shifting her handbag to the other shoulder. 'Must have been raised in a bag of fertiliser eh?'

Connie looked down at his feet and tucked his hands into his coat pockets; he too had seen my neighbour guard her bag. I'd heard Devon and Kiplyn making jokes about how they adapted their behaviour in shops or on the street, especially around white ladies. I knew laughing it off was their way of dealing with the prejudice. Now I was seeing it for myself, I couldn't see anything funny about it at all.

'Listen, Ben, you know I come in for a natter as much as anything else,' said Mrs Blake. 'Serve them youngsters first. I don't mind.'

Flattening his accent, Connie asked for two Fantas and a

quarter pound of cola cubes. We were served, we paid and were heading to the door when Mrs Blake spoke up again.

'Don't you go eating all them sweets at once. You'll rot your lovely teeth. These youngsters have such nice teeth. Very white. I suppose you notice the whiteness more on account of them being . . . ' her words trailed off. She made a circular motion around her face with a finger, and mouthed the word 'Black' to Ben.

The shopkeeper nodded.

I'd known both of them for years and had always been polite and respectful. Even though I suspected they didn't appreciate it. I thought back to the dinner lady's scolding earlier in the week. All these little bits of racism I'd put up with day in, day out, for the sake of fitting in. I hadn't wanted to be noticed, but if I was, then I wanted to be seen as 'that good little Black girl'. Miss Gladys had said, 'Duppy know who fi frighten!' So, I stood up straight and looked these adults in the eye.

'Actually, these in't my teeth,' I said. Connie covered his mouth, stifling a snort. I became bolder. 'And his teeth are false and all!'

We hurried out of the shop and ran across the road into the park, laughing all the way. No doubt Mrs Blake would mention that I'd *given her sauce* next time she bumped into Miss Gladys on the street. Hopefully, Grandma would see the funny side, and the disrespect I'd shown towards an older person would never get back to Mum.

We sat on the benches by the bandstand, sucking sweets and looking out at the empty paddling pool.

'D'you suppose one day mi will begin to sound cockney like you and all dem other pickney ah school.'

'I don't speak like them! Grandma's really strict about us speaking what she calls Proper English. I only talk like the white kids when I have to.' Connie held out the bag of sweets. I took another, even though I already had one in my mouth. 'Grandma doesn't like us speaking Jamaican either; she reckons that it gives prejudiced people the chance to say we don't belong here. She says, "You English. You nar fi talk like we."'

'That is the worst Jamaican accent mi ever hear.'

Connie was laughing. There was that dimple in his right cheek; I wondered what it would feel like if I traced it with my finger. He was looking at me, his eyes lively and kind. I felt shy and looked away.

'Yuh say yuh muddah live here twenty years now She nuh go home in all that time?'

'No. Never had the money.'

'And yuh daddy?'

I hesitated. Connie knew what it was like not to have a dad. Even so, I looked at my hands, embarrassed.

'He left when I was small. I don't know where he is. I don't know anything about him really. Mum doesn't like talking about it. She gets upset. Actually more cross than upset. So, I don't ask.'

I couldn't think of anything else to say. My mouth felt raw from eating so much sugar. Connie pulled the crumpled paper bag out of his pocket and held it out in front of me. I looked across at him and he smiled. I took another sweet.

'D'you think you'll ever go back to Jamaica?' I asked.

'Yeah mon! Mi nuh intend to stay in dis cold for ever.

Besides, just before mi leave come here, Papa and mi finally gather all the parts we needed to build a bike. A racing one, with twenty-inch wheels, proper gears and t'ings. The main t'ing to find was the frame. It took ages to find that frame.'

I watched his smile die away. Then he gathered himself.

'Papa said he'll keep the parts safe till mi come home. Then we'll build it together. When mi go back yuh must come and visit.'

'I'd love to,' I whispered.

'Then it's a deal. Althea say we can go back and visit as soon as she gets t'ings sort out. She have to wait for Tobias to get him divorce. His wife run off and left him a few years back. He tell Althea that she and Kallai help him to love again. He say he wants to look after her. And when she marry him he'll get our papers sorted.'

He fell silent. Tobias's hulking figure and large hands filled my mind. I wondered if it occupied his too.

'Connie . . . did you tell Althea about the other day? You know, that Tobias slapped you?'

'She already know how him stay. She tell mi that him just need time to get used to mi. I'm not his son but he wants to raise me to be a good man. Tough, responsible . . . ' Connie trailed off, avoiding my eyes. 'Bwoy, the weather cold sah! Mi need to warm up a bit.'

He got up and began striding away, kicking a metal stopper from a Guinness bottle along the path in front of him. I walked quickly to catch up, wishing I'd kept my mouth shut.

We were halfway across the playing field before Connie spoke up again.

'So, yuh nuh curious about him?' he said.

'Who?'

'Yuh daddy?'

'I suppose so. A few weeks ago, I overheard Mum telling Grandma that she bumped into him on her way home from work. Apparently she had a right go at him.'

'Yuh mean yuh daddy live nearby and him never come look for yuh?'

'Well, if Mum sends him packing if he comes within ten feet of her then why would he?'

'True. But just because yuh muddah nuh want him near, it nuh mean that yuh can't meet him? It not fair how grown-ups t'ink dem should make all the decision for we. What could yuh muddah do if yuh just go look for him? If she see him recently then yuh must can find out where him live. What him name?'

'Enoch Zephaniah Ethan Edwards, but everyone calls him Ezee.'

'Rawtid! It shouldn't be too hard to find where him deh, not with a name like that.'

'But I'd get into so much trouble if Mum found out.'

Connie looked at me, his eyes wide. 'Yuh t'ink if my daddy deh a London somewhere mi would hesitate sah?'

We'd reached the edge of the park where the gates opened to Jamaica Road. It was beginning to grow dark and the internal light in the telephone box on the corner flickered before switching itself on.

'I bet yuh any money we can find him,' said Connie. 'Come.'

He headed towards the phone box. I followed, trotting to keep up with his strides. Nervous. Excited.

*

The pages of the directory were yellowed at the edges; I flicked through until I got to 'EDWARDS'. Connie leaned in. I felt his breath on the side of my face, and for a moment the phone box's stale tobacco smell gave way to the sugary scent of cola cubes. I scanned the entries. There it was: E. Z. E. Edwards. I gasped.

'Yuh find him?'

I nodded. 'But I can't just ring up out of the blue!'

'How else we go do it? C'mon. Yuh nuh have to say nothing. If him answer just hang up the phone. All we want to do at first is find him.'

As Connie read out the numbers, I slid my finger into each of the dial's big round slots, watching it spin back to its ready position. Butterflies crowded my stomach. The monotone sound was replaced by a steady hypnotic rhythm. Then the melody stopped abruptly.

'Hello.'

An urgent bleeping sound drowned out the voice – a woman's voice on the other end of the line. I fed the slot. I wasn't sure how much money it took to make the rapid notes stop. The phone guzzled the coins, and satisfied, the pips halted.

'Hello, who is it?'

She had the same sort of polite Jamaican voice Auntie Sybil used whenever she answered the phone. If this *was* Ezee's house then was she his wife? Were there children living there too? Their children. I could hear the woman saying 'hello' and growing impatient. I replaced the receiver, biting my bottom lip in disappointment.

'Well?'

'It was some woman. He won't want to know me! It's a stupid idea.'

Connie screwed his mouth to the side; he was thinking. 'Yuh ever hear the saying *wi run t'ings, t'ings nuh run wi?*'

I shook my head.

'It's what Althea say all the time. It mean that we can control how t'ings turn out. Our destiny she call it. Yuh nuh have fi look for yuh daddy if yuh t'ink it's too hard. But if yuh nuh even try, then yuh just letting t'ings run yuh.'

I wanted to tell him that I'd imagined Ezee pining for his long-lost daughter. It had never occurred to me that he had got on with life without me, until the moment I heard that woman's voice. I wanted to tell Connie all those things but instead I shrugged, told him I'd see him in the morning and shouldered the phone box door open.

On the way home, I thought about what Connie had said. According to Mum, Ezee was a 'wutless man', and in all these years he'd never come looking for me. Why should I waste my time trying to contact him? But then Mum had seen him recently and he'd asked after me. Rather than telling him anything, she'd cussed him off and sent him packing He did want to know me and I shouldn't let Mum – or this other woman – get in the way of that. Like Althea said, wi run t'ings, t'ings nuh run wi.

Christopher Marlowe Comprehensive had the best football teams in the borough and that Saturday morning they were beating us 1–0. Connie took another shot at their goal but the ball went wide. Phil Barrett and three of his skinhead mates began a slow handclap, while another one of the boys in their gang began grunting and jigging about with his arms curled upwards. They had been behaving that way since the match began, every time Connie touched the ball. Being a home game there was a good turnout from our school, yet apart from me, there were no other Black spectators. But then, apart from Connie there were no other Black boys on the team. My palms felt sweaty, despite the cold. I wiped them on my cords. I was determined to stay and support Connie, but I wondered how he could stand it. Mr Jones had gone over and had a word, but Phil stood his ground; it was a free country and he was entitled to come and watch his kid brother play. When Mark scored an equalizer with ten minutes left to play, the skinheads went wild.

All week at school, Mark had avoided the playground football matches. Instead, he and his mates, Ted and Craig, hung around with Phil's gang. I'd come across them on Wednesday lunchtime, on my way to use the girl's outside loo; they were sitting on the steps of the fire escape, listening to Two-tone on a cassette player. When I saw them I'd wavered, wondering if I ought to turn back, but I was desperate, so I hoped to slip by unnoticed. But Ted clocked me and, seizing the chance to impress the older lads, he started making monkey noises. Then Craig joined in.

I kept walking, shrinking closer to the wall. Then suddenly Mark spoke up, 'Shush you two! I like this one.' My eyes darted to where he was sitting but he looked away and made a show of turning up the volume. They all started nodding along to 'The Prince' by Madness. I hurried past, feeling humiliated yet relieved it hadn't been worse. Mark had stepped in; had he distracted them on purpose? Did that mean he really thought I was pretty? I quickly dismissed the thought, reminding myself of how shitty he'd been to Connie. They were still forced to sit next to each other in class and Mark continued to give Connie as wide a berth as possible. It was unlikely they would ever be friends. Nevertheless, I couldn't ignore the ripple of pleasure I still got from replaying the words "I think you're pretty" in my mind.

As the game meandered towards a draw, someone booted a long ball up the field. It bounced into the penalty area and the Christopher Marlowe goalkeeper ran out to claim it, but with his long, graceful stride, Connie bore down on him. They jumped at the same time, but even with his arms stretched, the goalie couldn't match Connie's height. He headed the ball over the goalkeeper and into the empty net. There was an eruption of cheers. The John Evelyn teammates celebrated, and a couple of them ran across to drape themselves around Connie's shoulders. He nodded his thanks as he gently shrugged them off and jogged back to his position, waiting for play to resume.

The score remained 2–1. After the final whistle, Connie sloped off to a nearby bench where jackets and sweaters were piled. I wandered over but stopped a few feet away, feeling out of place as the rest of the team arrived. They began pulling on tracksuits, their voices shrill with euphoria. While they all chattered, Connie had already donned his sweatshirt and trousers and was lacing up his boots, keeping his eyes fixed on his task. Mark slung his anorak on over his kit, but was loitering at the edge of the crowd.

'Good goal, Mark,' one boy said, in a toady, apple-polishing voice.

'Cheers,' said Mark, 'but I have to say, that last goal was quality.'

Connie looked up at him, surprised. I held my breath, disbelieving. Stubbornly hopeful.

'Come on, the lads are waiting,' Phil was shouting across to his little brother. 'I ain't got all day.'

Mark's face went rigid. When he spoke again, his tone was flat, deliberate. 'Nice header, Sambo.'

The other white boys shuffled uncomfortably, but nobody said a word. I watched Mark run off to join his brother. I still had some dumb hope that he'd look back, say that he didn't mean it. Connie snatched up the carrier bag with his kit. Some of the other teammates murmured goodbyes but Connie didn't reply.

We left the school playing fields and silently headed towards the main gates. I remembered how just a few weeks ago, I'd wanted Connie to follow the rules of the school pecking order. I'd told myself that he'd find out for himself that it was pointless to try and stand out among the white kids – or indeed, stand up to them. But I didn't feel at all vindicated. I was desperate to ease his pain.

'You know you're the best player on the team,' I said. 'They all know it too. Even Mark.'

Connie snorted. 'Mi nuh know how yuh put up with it, Daphne. How yuh can stand living in a country with white people calling yuh monkey, jungle bunny, Sambo and go on like dem better than yuh?'

'Mark just says those things. He's an idiot. He's pathetic, confused even.'

'How him *confused?*'

The thought of telling Connie about Mark's behaviour, the things he had said to me flitted through my mind. But how could I tell Connie that Mark Barrett, the racist, fancied me, without coming clean about how he made me feel? How I'd felt flattered to have the attention of one of the popular boys. And me, a Black girl, how special did that make me? But I knew that even if Mark really did like me, he was ashamed of liking me. Now I was ashamed of myself for trying to see the good in him, for hoping he was different from Phil.

Connie kissed his teeth. 'Althea gwaan like this is the promised land, like the street dem paved with gold, when all mi see here is spit and dog shit. I wish Gramma and Papa would send for mi. I just wanna go home.'

'You mean, to go back to Jamaica for good?' I said, my voice more alarmed than I'd expected.

Connie didn't answer. I thought about what it must be like for him living in a new country, with a new family, attending a new school. We walked on in silence, I daren't speak in case I said the wrong thing again. He had only been here a relatively short time but I'd already grown so used to him being around.

We'd left the school grounds and were standing at the crossing on main road before Connie spoke again.

'Come make we go to the shop and buy a can of Fanta.'

'Oh God, Connie. You've not been stealing from Tobias again, have you?'

'Ah nah teef mi teef it! Him owe it to mi for all the work mi do cooking, cleaning, and minding Kallai when dem go out with him friends.' He straightened up, pushing his shoulders back, as though snapping himself out of the gloom. 'Besides, it's not just for mi to spend on drink and sweets. Mi bring a likkle more so we can call yuh daddy again. Unless yuh nuh want to.'

A smile, unbidden, spread across my face. I was so touched that he had thought of me. 'Of course I do. I just don't want to get you into trouble.'

He'd been pouting but now his mouth slipped into a timid grin. 'Yuh nuh need fi worry, I'm always very careful.'

I was pleased to see Connie's bad mood was lifting. I also felt a sweet buzz at the prospect of trying Ezee's number again.

If the woman answered then I'd hang up straight away. In my mind I counted each time the signal bleeped into my ear. I got to seven.

'Hell-oh.'

This time a man was on the other end of the line. I was startled by the pips and I fumbled to get the coin into the slot. There was a gentle chinking sound as Connie's money dropped into the cashbox.

'Hello.' My voice was little more than a squeak. 'Is this . . . are you Ezee?'

'Yes. Ezee speaking.'

A rich baritone voice, smooth and melodic. I sighed into the receiver. I couldn't say another word.

'Hello? Who is this?'

I slammed the phone down so suddenly that it took me a minute to register what I had done. Straightaway I lifted the receiver again but it was too late. I'd ended the call.

'Was it him?'

'Yes. It was him.'

Connie was talking but I wasn't paying attention. I could only hear Ezee's voice. It was a nice voice. Manly. I wondered what he looked like.

'Are yuh listening?'

'What? No. Sorry what did you say?'

'That it's best yuh tell him who yuh are face-to-face. Where is SE14?'

'I've no idea. We could go to the library and look in the *A–Z*. If it's not far then maybe we could go now, we've still got some of your money left, haven't we?'

Connie frowned. 'We have plenty money left, but mi nuh have the time today. Sorry. Mi promise Althea that the football nuh go interfere with the chores mi have to do ah Saturday daytime. Mi already stay out longer than mi did plan. Here, yuh better have this. Mi usually spend what mi take. Best not fi get caught with it.'

Holding my hand, Connie poured out the assorted copper and silver he had left, then gently closed my fingers around the coins. My hand rested in his warm grasp for a moment longer before he let go.

'Thanks, Connie.'

'Sure t'ing.'

A chill breeze carried the sound of the Millwall fans chanting at the Den and the smell of biscuit dough from the Peek Freans factory. The weight of the mixed coins caused the left side of my coat to droop a little. There had to be at least a quid, maybe more. It was the most money I'd ever had all at once, and Connie had trusted it to me. I felt happy to have a best friend.

7

Connie and I agreed at school the following Monday that we would go and search for Ezee's house on Saturday. All week I found myself drifting off during lessons, replaying Ezee's voice in my head and trying to imagine what he looked like. I'd fantasised about him seeing me in the street and recognising me in an instant.

At 2 p.m. on Saturday afternoon we caught the 53 from Deptford Broadway. Mums loaded with crying children and supermarket carrier bags sat among pensioners whose pulley baskets crowded the bottom deck. Connie and I scrambled upstairs, swaying through plumes of cigarette smoke, and found two empty seats close at the front. I placed the bus ticket between the pages of the *London A–Z*, marking our destination.

There had been two copies of the *A–Z* in the public library's reference section. After thumbing through the index I found the page number and grid reference for the street where Mr E. Z. E. Edwards lived. Thick black lines – railway tracks – skirted a network of streets close to the Old Kent Road. I stared hard at the page and then spotted it. I laughed out loud, elated, until I saw the librarian watching. Pointedly he cleared his throat and gestured to the sign stating 'QUIET PLEASE'.

'It nuh look far from here, I bet we could get there and back in an hour,' said Connie. 'To think, him in the same part of London all this time and he nuh come look for yuh.'

He was right; Ezee's street looked tantalisingly close. He might have easily dropped by Lime Grove. Then, perhaps he had, secretly. Who's to say he hadn't spied me from afar?

'I told you before, my mum gave him a tongue lashing last time she saw him. Maybe she turned him off,' I said. 'Let's go and find him. I'll get a pen and paper from the librarian, so we can copy the map.'

'Nuh bother with that.'

Connie looked over his shoulder before slipping the *A–Z* into his anorak pocket. He moseyed towards the exit and I trailed after him, promising myself that I'd bring the book right back, the next time I came to the library.

'This is New Cross Road. Change here for New Cross train station.' The bus conductress's big voice carried over both decks of the bus. I opened the book to see how much further we had to go. Connie nudged my arm.

'Look,' he whispered, pointing across the road.

Among the row of tall terraced houses one stood out. Scorched brickwork surrounded the blank spaces where glass used to be. Charred holes, pitiless, like hollowed-out eyes. I'd seen this house so many times on the news and in the paper, but I'd never seen the devastation in real life. The bus lingered at the stop while passengers got on and off. Connie and I gazed across at the building that was once a home. I'd heard that there was soon to be a big demonstration through town. Miss Gladys had been handed a leaflet at the market by the New Cross Massacre Action Committee who'd been mentioned in the newspaper. Right now a group of people were gathered outside the house. They stood leaning on each other, weeping.

'Mind your backs. Next stop, Marquis of Granby.'

The conductress signalled to the driver and the bus heaved away from the curb. Connie and I craned our necks, keeping our eyes on the house and the mourners outside, until it was out of sight.

The bus meandered along the busy main roads. It had looked like no distance at all on the map, but it felt as though we had been travelling for ages. Finally, we reached a stop on the Old Kent Road where the railway line spanned the noisy six-lane street. We got off the bus, following the directions in the A–Z, past rows of partly demolished houses, cordoned off by graffiti-covered fencing. One statement in big bold letters declared **LABOUR LOVES BLACKS VOTE NF**. No one batted an eyelid at us as we passed by, but there didn't seem to be many Black people about. We walked quickly, not slackening our pace until we turned into a lane off the busy main road. Between the rows of terraced houses was a newsagent, a hairdressers, a TV repair shop, a sub-post office and then a hardware store. I felt the tension in my shoulders ease. It was all so ordinary, just like the streets around Lime Grove.

'Yuh nervous?' asked Connie.

'Yeah. Excited though as well.'

He winked at me. My smile grew wider.

*

We skulked to the top end of the street, peeking around the corner, trying to decide what to do next.

'Which house him live?' said Connie.

'Number 14.'

'How about we just go see what him house lock like. We could walk down to the end of the street and back again.'

'Oh . . . I don't know . . .'

Connie took my hand. 'Come.'

My heart was thudding in my chest but I walked as casually as I could manage, glancing at the two-storey terraced houses. There were only four cars in the street. Connie whistled, slowing his relaxed pace down almost to a stop.

'Look at that,' he said, nodding his head towards a navy blue car parked up ahead. 'A BMW 2002. That's the sort of car me'd like. Yuh t'ink it belong to him?'

'Maybe. Mum said he likes flash cars.'

I could feel my shoulders tensing up again as we drew up to number 14. Unlike the neighbours' net curtains the ones that hung in its front room were heavy with lace. Pale blue stays allowed the curtains to drape sumptuously yet leave just enough of the window uncovered to draw in a passer-by. I always thought the purpose of nets was to prevent the people outside looking in; Miss Gladys would have said, 'Wah mek dem ah flass sah?' I thought about the woman who'd answered the phone that first time. These were her curtains: showy, proud. The front door opened and a man stepped onto the pavement. His voice was raised, continuing a conversation he was having with someone inside. I shivered as the deep, dulcet sound carried along the street.

'Mi did tell yuh Manny want mi fi look at him clutch today

so nuh make up yuh face! Nuh bother cook for mi neither. We'll probably head to Shadrach's after that. All right? Likkle more.'

He slammed the door and stepped off the pavement. He walked down the middle of the street with his head high and his shoulders swaying to a rhythm only he could hear.

A delightful warmth crept from my neck up to my cheeks. This was Ezee. My father. I stared, willing him to sense the connection between us, to turn around and see me, his long-lost daughter.

But he didn't. He turned the corner and was gone. I set off after him.

'Where yuh going?' said Connie.

'It's him. C'mon.'

We spotted Ezee further ahead and followed him down the road, then along quiet backstreets that eventually led to the same train lines that ran across the Old Kent Road. Here, the arches beneath the railway bridge were lock-ups. Above the tall metal gates was a sign painted on weather-beaten wood 'Ezee Auto Repairs'. We watched as he opened the padlock, pulled out the chain tethering the metal gates together and disappeared inside. A train thundered on the tracks overhead, then it was quiet. We loitered behind a parked transit van and waited for a few minutes. Then a few minutes more. I began to feel a little cold. I wished he'd noticed me.

'It's getting late,' Connie said. 'We need to head back.'

'I thought you said Tobias wouldn't miss you because he's on lates.'

'Yes, but mi still need to get home before him leave. Mi nuh want to give him any excuse to be vexed with mi. Yuh daddy nuh doing nuttin' now except fix him friend car. We can come back next week.'

'We'll just stay five more minutes then we'll head home. Okay?'

Another train went by. As the rattle of the carriages faded away, I heard the click-clack of heels on the cobblestones coming from the top of the road. A woman wearing a knee-length denim skirt and a black leather coat was coming down the lane. Her hair was braided with beads at the ends. She looked like Pattie Boulaye, except she wore large brown specs that she took off and placed in her shoulder bag. She drew back the bolt and started to push at the gate; the scraping of metal on stone alerted Ezee.

'Yuh reach!'

'Yeah. Sorry mi late,' the woman said.

'Yuh worth the wait. Mi ah come now.'

Ezee muttered something to the woman while he fiddled with the padlock and she laughed. I saw him slip his arm around her waist as they set off back up the lane. I gazed after them as they walked away, even after they'd turned the corner and were out of sight.

'She nuh look like someone named Manny to mi,' said Connie.

'She's probably a friend,' I snapped.

Connie raised an eyebrow. 'Anyway, him gone now so come nuh.'

He was already moving off towards the main road. I yanked my eyes away from the corner, trotting to catch up with him. Glad that I'd finally seen Ezee. But wishing that he had seen me.

8

'It look like it ah go rain all day.'

Miss Gladys was peering through the curtains at the patch of slate-grey sky, visible from the kitchen window. It was Monday and my grandma was dressed down in a plain roll-neck jumper and navy blue cords. She had yet to don one of her wigs. I wondered if it was because she couldn't decide whether it was worth risking a good wig in bad weather, or if she was uncertain which one she should wear to a demonstration.

My cousins exchanged glances across the breakfast table; we knew that Grandma wasn't addressing any of us. She was trying to chip away at Sybil's silence. Mum was leaning against the kitchen counter, cradling the teacup in her hands. She looked weary after her night shift and could have done with going straight to bed, but instead she hung around, poised like a referee on Saturday TV wrestling. All weekend there had been words about the protest. Miss Gladys was set on going, but Auntie Sybil was against her taking part. She reminded Grandma of the National Front march through New Cross in 1977. Hundreds of anti-racists had come out to counter the demonstration and a huge fight ensued – mainly between the anti-racists and the police. Over one hundred people were injured and twice as many were arrested. Sybil feared this time the NF would be the ones out in force, hell-bent on breaking up the protest. She turned to Miss Gladys with a hand on her hip.

'Yuh know some people ah say this Massacre Action Committee are communists. Dem just ah use the fire to stir up trouble with the police. True mi know coppers like that Special Patrol Group can't be trusted. But the fire is different. These police say dem committed to finding the culprits.'

Miss Gladys shook her head. 'Whether it's racists cause it, or the fire start some other way, how come the authorities drag dem foot with the investigation? How come neither the Prime Minister nor the Queen send any condolence to the families? Mi nuh expect yuh to go demonstrate today – yuh have fi work, Earl have fi work and Alma just get back from work. But mi nuh working today, and although mi is an ol' lady mi still have two good feet, so mi ah go march.'

Sybil grunted, then sighed. 'Just mek sure yuh nuh cuss off any policeman, mi nuh want fi have to come bail yuh out if yuh get arrested.'

My cousins laughed.

'Imagine Grandma arrested for cussing a police officer!'

'Knocking him out with her handbag more like!'

'Hush yuh mouth and hurry up, or yuh be late for school,' said Sybil. 'And make sure unnu come straight home after-wards yuh hear, mi nuh want yuh pan the street tonight.'

Chairs were pushed back as my cousins rose, piling their bowls into the sink before departing to gather their school things. Mum poured herself another cup of tea and took a seat at the table. She glanced across at me. She had that penetrating expression on her face, eyes narrowed, mouth pulled to the side.

'Yuh nuh finish yuh breakfast yet, Daphne. Yuh sickening for anyt'ing?'

'No, no,' I said, scraping up the remnants of cereal, keeping my eyes down. I was convinced that Mum would be able to tell that I'd been secretly spying on Ezee just by looking at me.

'Well, nuh dawdle or yuh'll be late too . . .' Mum trailed off into a yawn.

'Yuh better galang ah yuh bed, Alma,' said Miss Gladys.

Mum nodded. 'It was a long night. And at the end of mi shift an old man mess up himself, but him say him nuh want my *effing dirty black hands* to clean him.'

'Eh-eh! Mi would have just lef' him deh,' said Auntie Sybil.

Mum sighed. 'Most likely him proud and feel ashamed, so just lash out.' I had put my bowl in the sink and was heading out of the room. 'Daphne. Mi nuh want yuh to linger in the library after school today either. Come straight home yuh hear?'

Although Mum spoke with her usual abruptness, there was a softness in her expression. It reminded me of the way she used to look at me, when I was very young. Back then, it always made me feel safe. This time it made me feel guilty.

'Yes, Mum,' I said and hurried from the room.

I took the stairs two at a time. As I turned onto the landing, I saw Devon leaning through the doorway to the girls' room, speaking in hushed tones. He stopped when he heard my tread and looked over his shoulder.

'It's all right, it's only Daphne. Look, if you just do your coat up nobody's going to see your uniform.'

I peered inside. Margery was hiding schoolbooks under her bed, while Marcia was stuffing jeans and a bulky jumper into her bag.

'That's not the point, stupid. I don't want to wear the flippin' uniform through town,' she said.

'Can I remind you it's a political protest not a fashion show?'

'Shut up, Devon,' the twins said in unison.

'D'you mean you guys are going on the march?' I said, straining to keep my excitement to a whisper.

'Of course. We've got to stand up to racists,' said Margery.

'—and not just those in the NF, but the police, the government, the whole bloody system,' said Marcia.

This was different from all the other times Devon, Marcia and Margery had sneaked out behind their parents' backs. Before, it was just so they could buy records in Brixton, stay out late or meet up with guys – standard teenage things. But this was my cousins standing up for their rights. For our rights. I was brimming with admiration.

'Can I come too?'

'Nah, you're too young,' said Devon.

'I put up with prejudice at school all the time. I can stand up to racism too.'

'Devon's right,' said Margery. 'There'll be other marches, Daphne. Trust me, this is just the start.'

'Here, some white guy from the Anti-Nazi League was handing these out in the street the other day, you can have it. Wear it today as a show of solidarity – but don't let our mums see.'

Marcia handed me a little yellow badge with a red arrow, the words in bold black type read 'Stop the NF Nazis!' I pinned it to my cardigan, then buttoned my blazer. I was thrilled to be in my cousins' confidence and proud of being part of something important.

I couldn't wait to tell Connie about my cousins bunking school to go on the march, but my excitement palled when I saw his face. The bruise around his left eye was barely visible unless you looked closely. He kept the hood of his parka zipped up tight while we waited to be let into class, but I could see the taint on his smooth skin, partially covered by his thick eyebrows. I knew Connie wouldn't want to talk about it in front of the other kids, so I said 'hello' and pretended I hadn't seen the mark. In class, Connie sat with his elbow on the desk and rested his hand against the side of his face.

The injury went unnoticed for most of the morning lessons until Miss Sayers, handing out worksheets, commented that Connie looked as if he'd 'been in the wars'. Her tone had that note of inquiry grown-ups often have when their statements are really questions. Connie brushed away her observation with a polite, breezy air, saying that he'd tripped getting out of the bath. Our teacher looked thoughtful and nodded but didn't ask any more probing questions. I felt guilty. We'd stayed out later on Saturday than he'd wanted to because I'd insisted. If Tobias had hit Connie for coming back late, then I was to blame. I longed for the rain to stop so that we would be allowed out at break time and I could talk to Connie in private.

It was still raining at lunchtime and when I didn't see

Connie in the dinner hall or the 1st Year's common room,
I went to look for him in the library. Connie wasn't there
either. I sighed. With only ten minutes left before lessons
restarted, I decided to peruse the books in the senior section. The windows on this side of the library faced the park
and beyond. I looked out through the rain-spotted panes
and thought about Miss Gladys, my cousins and the other
marchers out in the gloomy weather. I wondered where they
were now: the Houses of Parliament? Downing Street? Hyde
Park? I'd only ever seen those places in books or on the telly;
now *my* cousins and *my* grandma were marching through
London, down those important streets with hundreds, perhaps thousands of other Black people. I tried to imagine what
a thousand Black people would look like. Auntie Sybil was
worried about the NF attacking them, but I felt sure they
would be safe. I tilted the badge up so I could admire it. So
I could feel ... what was that word Marcia used? *Solidarity.*
I took it off my cardigan and repinned it to the lapel of my
blazer. Next time, I'd be on the march too.

I picked up a copy of *1984.* I knew I wouldn't be allowed
to borrow a senior book, but I could probably get through the
first chapter before the bell went. I headed to a secluded spot,
at the far end of the library, but when I got there I saw Craig
and Ted leaning over the desk in that corner. They looked
up, flustered and furtive; Craig was trying to conceal a pair
of compasses in the palm of his hand.

'What you looking at? Piss off,' he hissed.

I straightened up, trying not to look intimidated. I wouldn't
scurry away like a frightened mouse. Not today.

'Aye-aye, what's that you got on your blazer?' said Ted, his top lip curled to a sneer. 'It's one of them Anti-Nazi League badges, innit?'

'Stop the NF Nazis. Who's gonna do that then? You?' said Craig.

'All us Black people. And white people who ain't prejudiced like you. There are Black people in town right now, standing up for our rights.'

My words came out in bursts. I was trying to disguise the tremble in my voice.

'What rights?' Craig said. 'You lot shouldn't even be here. I bet some of our boys have gone into town today an' all. They'll be sticking up for our country. Stopping all them noisy coons from mugging people and making trouble.'

My faced flushed with anger. 'We're not coons! And they're not mugging or making trouble. They're marching because thirteen Black teenagers were murdered and the police and white people like you couldn't care less. Like their lives don't matter.'

Ted walked up to me; my heart was pounding. I was scared he'd hit me, but I was rooted to the spot. He leaned in, then forced a soft but nasty laugh.

'A bunch of dead wogs don't matter to me.'

He knocked my shoulder with his as he pushed past and Craig trailed after him sniggering like Muttley.

I went over to look at the desk, feeling heavy with dread, knowing I'd hate what I saw. They had etched NF and a swastika in the dark gloss finish. It was bad enough seeing these threats daubed on walls in the streets, but it made me feel sick to see it written in a place that I enjoyed coming to. Somewhere I had felt safe. So much for *duppy know who fi frighten*. I'd stood up to them, but it still felt like they'd won.

I slammed *1984* down on the table. I needed to cover up their vandalism. I reached for another book off the shelf and slammed it down too, then covered that book with another.

'You taking out *all* them books?'

I turned around and saw Mark standing at the end of the stack. He was looking at me, amused.

'If you're after your mates, you've just missed them,' I spat.

'I weren't. As it goes.'

'So you'll be looking for your brother then – oh no, I forgot, he's in town today, in't he? Gone to stick up for your country by fighting all them *noisy coons*.'

He folded his arms. 'What's got your knickers in a twist?'

'This!' I said, shoving the books aside and pointing at the desk.

Mark peered at the marks, then he shrugged. 'They can be idiots sometimes.'

'And you're an idiot for hanging out with them. And I'm an idiot for thinking you ain't just like them.'

'I ain't like them,' Mark said, his voice quiet. 'You know that, don't you?'

He looked at me like he did that day in the playground, when he told me that I was pretty. But he wasn't surprised by what his mates had done, nor the vile names they always used for Black people: wog, coon, Sambo. He'd directed that particular slur to Connie on two separate occasions – passing it off as a joke, when he knew full well it was an insult. Connie was my friend. I felt my eyes pricking but I would not cry in front of him. The bell sounded, marking the end of lunchtime.

'I can't like you. I hate you. Just leave me alone,' I said, then quickly walked away.

*

By home time, the rain had stopped. A damp, musty smell infused the air, but streaks of sunlight slid through the clouds, making the tarmac glisten. I pushed my way through the crowded gates and ran to catch up with Connie, tapping him on the back. He spun around, skittish like a hare.

'Oh Daphne, it's yuh.'

'Yeah. You never said goodbye. I've barely seen you all day – outside of lessons I mean. Are you all right?'

In the sunshine the bruise above his eye looked angrier than before. I knew that it hadn't been an accident. I lowered my voice.

'Connie, how did you really hurt your eye?'

He looked around carefully, as if checking whether anyone had heard. 'Can yuh walk with mi?'

I knew Mum wanted me home directly after school. After my run-in with Ted and Craig I was worried about other racists hanging about, narked by the demo in London, looking for someone to pick on. But this was the first time Connie and I had been alone all day. I was determined to show him that I cared about him and he could trust me.

'Sure. Let's go.'

We walked among the stream of kids meandering through the estate, the flow of bodies thinning as they dispersed in different directions. When we reached the estate's shopping precinct, I broke the silence.

'Was it because we were late back on Saturday?'

He shook his head. 'No, mi get home in good time. It happen yesterday.'

'It was Tobias, wasn't it? Was Althea there? Did she stick up for you?'

'Is them quarrel cause it. One of her private clients come round with t'ree pickney, say she want Althea to do dem hair. As soon as dem lef' Tobias get in a rage and cuss about how she turn the place into a *blasted crèche*. I tell him not to shout at mi muddah. He call mi a facety likkle Mamma's bwoy and t'ump mi.'

Connie spoke in a matter-of-fact tone. When he finally turned to look at me I kept my expression neutral, I didn't want to embarrass him by looking worried or upset.

'Althea run between us when she see him draw him hand again. Him calm down when she give him the £30 the woman pay her. He even praise me for standing up to him, say mi behave like a "proper man".'

Connie scoffed, his eyes fixed on the path ahead. 'Him act all lovey-dovey after that, and lead Althea to dem room.'

Without warning, I pictured Althea and Tobias naked in bed. I blushed, thinking about the two of them together, like that.

Connie continued, 'That's how dem stay when dem make up after a fight. He'll act nice for the next few days now. Probably come home with a present – perfume, a new top or some shoes. Somet'ing she can wear when dem go out and he'll brag to everyone about how him buy it fi 'er.'

We were nearing the entrance to Hibbert Court. Connie slowed down.

'Let's just sit here for a bit,' he said, veering off towards a brutal slab of grey concrete fashioned into a bench.

I checked my watch; it was ten past four. I sighed and followed him, sitting down on the hard, cold seat overlooking a patch of green.

'Althea has a Prince Charles and Lady Di tea towel pin up on the kitchen wall. Last night she tell mi she and Tobias are as happy together as the two of dem, but at the moment Tobias's work is giving him stress. His friend has been put on suspension after punching a foreman who'd called him a "fucking lazy nigger". All the other foremen at the plant say a suspension is too lenient and are threatening to strike, unless the Black man is sacked. She say that Tobias never meant to fly off the handle. That he's a good man.'

I noticed his hands had clenched into fists. He did too and buried them in the pockets of his parka. It was the most he had ever said about his home life. I thought about how from time to time, Mum, Earl and Sybil would come back from the hospital, the train station and the biscuit factory, pissed off about treatment from racist colleagues, but I couldn't recall any of them ever lashing out against us. Did Althea really think it was okay?

Although it wasn't yet dark, the lights on the walkway above began to flicker. I blew on my fingers to warm them.

'Yuh can come up. If you want,' said Connie. 'Mi nuh know what mood he will be in, but him act better if we have company.'

'I'm sorry but I have to go home. Mum wanted me to come back straight after school. I'm late as it is.' I touched Connie's forearm, his coat sleeve was still damp. He lay his hand on mine but didn't look at me. 'Will you be all right?'

'Yeah mon!' He managed a smile. 'See yuh in the morning.'

I looked back twice as I walked away; instead of going inside Connie remained on the bench. I could still hear the lightness he'd forced into his voice. I steeled myself and kept walking.

It was quarter to five when I turned into our street. Mum was waiting by the front gate; she folded her arms when she saw me.

'Yuh nuh remember me tell yuh to come straight home after school? Where yuh deh till now? Why on today of all days yuh decide to disobey me?'

I wanted to tell her about Connie's bruise, how I thought I owed it to my friend to try and help him, just like he helped me on Saturday, and has been helping me all these past weeks. But I knew I couldn't.

'I'm sorry. I forgot,' I said.

Mum grabbed my arm and tugged me inside 'Devon, Marcia and Margery nuh come home yet neither. Kaplyn own up that dem went on the march. Everyone ah' do dem own t'ing today and nuh listen to dem parents.'

Mum continued scolding, calling me irresponsible, telling me how selfish I'd been not to consider how worried she would be. It didn't feel like she'd been fretting at all. When Althea had been worried about Connie that time Miss Gladys and I had walked him home, she'd spoken to him in a calm, warm voice. Not like this. Once upon a time I would lean against Mum's chest, feeling the notes as she sang *Chi Chi Bud Oh* to me. Now all she ever did was tell me what to do.

She was interrupted when the front door opened and in stepped Miss Gladys. Marcia, Margery and Devon crowded into the hallway after her, noisy and exhilarant. Their hubbub brought Auntie Sybil out of the kitchen. She was so pleased to see them she forgot to be angry.

'Mi bump into dem outside the community centre near where the march start,' said Miss Gladys. 'Dem walk with mi the whole way. Mi know dem shouldn't have been deceitful, but mi proud of the way dem behave today.'

'There were loads of young people there,' said Devon. 'We passed some secondary schools on the route and some of the pupils even climbed over the gates to join us. It was amazing.'

'Dem make banners with the names and faces of the thirteen youngsters,' said Miss Gladys. 'It make yuh heart sad. But this will show the nation that these were real flesh-and-blood people that perish in the fire, nuh just numbers.'

'Wi hear there was some trouble ah Blackfriars,' said Auntie Sybil.

'Yes, it was because there was a line of police with shields and stuff trying to stop the demo from going down Fleet Street, but they broke through and the march carried on,' said Marcia. 'All these journalists were hanging out of their office windows, probably thinking what the hell are all these Black people doing here.'

'Probably never seen so many Black people before in their lives,' said Margery.

'Maybe it'll be on the news,' Kiplyn said.

We hardly ever saw Black people on telly; now the local news bulletin showed thousands of people just like us occupying the important parts of London. My cousins began speaking over each other, looking to see if they could spot themselves on the screen. Nobody noticed me slip away, sneaking along the hallway to the front sitting room where I quietly lifted the telephone receiver. There were five beeps before the call was answered. It was the woman. I was disappointed. I wanted to hear Ezee's voice, not hers. I placed my finger down on the hook switch, and ended the call. I could hear the others in the kitchen, still excited and talking loud. I dialled the other number I'd memorised. I knew I'd have to be quick. While my eyes were fixed on the door, my hand was gripping the receiver; feeling excited, feeling sick

The beeps seemed to go on for ages, but then his easy-going voice sang into the phone, 'Hello, Ezee Auto Repairs.' I shivered, unable to speak, just listening. He said 'hello' a couple of times, sounding irritated. I hung up. I didn't want him to be annoyed with me, but I could never imagine him raising that cool, relaxed voice.

Not like Mum. She had tried to prevent me from knowing him and I'd disobeyed her. But I no longer felt guilty, I was glad.

9

Connie and I stood outside the entrance to Brixton tube station waiting for Althea's friend Valerie Dunne. When Connie had telephoned that Saturday morning I'd assumed it was to plan another trip to the Old Kent Road. But instead he told me that Althea was taking him to Brixton and I was invited too. He sounded so excited, and so much happier than he had been at school all week. Part of me wanted to go and spy on my dad again. Instead, I decided that I'd try and sneak a phone call to Ezee later.

Four young white people had erected a table close to where we were standing. A woman was collecting signatures for some sort of petition, while three blokes milled about with newspapers draped over their arms. A man with curly hair approached us; he had an Anti-Nazi League badge attached to his lapel and a solemn expression on his face.

'Copy of the *Socialist Worker*?' he said. 'Read all about the march last Monday. Thirteen dead and nothing said!'

My cousins had chanted those same words when they came home, excited after the march. People had come from as far off as Birmingham and Manchester. According to the police, around five thousand people had joined the protest; others said it was closer to twenty thousand. I'd held my head high when I went into school the next day, proud that my family had been a part of what they were calling The Black People's Day of Action, until break time when Michelle and Joanne barred my way to the girls' loo.

'Sod off nig-nog, go and piss somewhere else,' said Joanne. 'You lot wanna take over, marching up in London and moaning about living here.'

'Yeah! Smashing things up and robbing shops. Why don't you fuck off. Go back to swinging in the trees. Leave more jobs for us white people,' said Michelle.

I knew they were talking about the march, but their version of events sounded so different from what my cousins had told me. I made a point of going to the library after school and saw how what I considered to be a momentous day had been reported in the main newspapers. According to those reports, the police had used riot shields and truncheons to quell a rampaging mob of two hundred Black youths who broke away from the main demonstration. Three policemen were injured; two were knocked unconscious by flying bricks and bottles when youths 'ran amok' in Blackfriars Road. The mob smashed shop windows in Fleet Street and looted a jewellers. The police arrested twenty youths. I walked home from the library disconsolate. Why was there so little mention of all the other thousands who peacefully made it to Speakers' Corner, or the reasons for the march in the first place?

The *Socialist Worker* guy was persistent. He told Althea the paper was only 10p if she was unwaged or perhaps on strike. Althea was rolling the pushchair back and forth, trying to lull

Kallai to sleep. She had been so chatty the last time I met her, but today she seemed distracted. Her tone with the young man was polite but impatient.

'Well, perhaps you could sign our petition to the Home Secretary calling on him to ban the march the NF are planning past the house where thirteen teenagers died.'

'No! No thank you. I don't want me name on anyt'ing like that—'

'Whaap'm, Althea! Girl yuh look fine.'

The nicotine-drenched voice was as deep as a man's, but I saw a tall, light-skinned woman sashaying towards us. Her leopard-print coat was unbuttoned, revealing a black roll-neck sweater and two gold chains draped over her bosom. Her tight blue jeans were tucked into white stiletto heeled boots.

'Valerie!'

Althea wilted in Valerie's tight embrace. When they drew apart she sniffed and blinked her eyes rapidly.

Valerie spoke softly, 'Sorry mi late. Greville drive so slow it would have been quicker if mi did walk. Ah months now mi nuh hear from yuh, mi glad yuh finally call.'

Up close I could see that Valerie was older than she looked at first glance. She was more Mum's age than Althea's. Now she was rubbing Althea's coat sleeve affectionately.

'So, at last yuh tell that dragon Mrs Samuels to stick her job up her pom-pom. Good. That woman gwaan like she nuh come here as an immigrant too. She turn round ah exploit her workers. Better yuh strike out pan yuh own.'

Althea sighed, 'Mi know but . . .'

Valerie patted Althea's arm. 'But nuttin'. Cha! Yuh nuh remember what yuh always say? *Wi run t'ings, t'ings nuh run wi.*' Hearing this saying again made me smile. Althea nodded. Valerie lowered her voice to continue. 'Mi assume *him* nuh know yuh leave the salon yet? Seen as yuh only walk out this morning.' Althea shook her head. 'I hope him being sweet to yuh, else him will have fi answer to me. Mi nuh suppose there's any news on him divorce yet neither.'

Althea's eyes darted across to us and Valerie took the hint. She turned to Connie, producing a wide smile. 'So this is yuh first born. Look how him handsome! Who's this, yuh girlfriend?'

'No,' Connie mumbled, his eyes down, bashful. 'This is Daphne, mi school friend.'

'Please to meet unnu. Mi work with yuh muddah when mi did hairdressing. She's the best stylist mi know.'

'Yuh say yuh know where mi can get a good deal on supplies. Mi never get mi last pay,' said Althea.

'We'll go to Eden Hair and Beauty. Mi know the shopkeeper, Sanjay; him like fi haggle and mi like fi flirt so we should get a good price. But first mek wi go ah Wimpy, get a cup of tea.' She winked at us. 'And a burger for unnu. My treat.'

'Please Miss Valerie, Daphne know a place that sells patties. Can we have that instead of a burger?'

'Yuh too long-eye! Valerie offer yuh burger and yuh come beg-beg patty instead. Crayven pickney!'

Connie cast his eyes to the ground again, this time chastened. I instinctively looked down as well, as though I'd also been lashed by the ticking-off.

'Nuh worry about it, Althea. If him nuh want burger it's no problem.' Valerie's tone was light and composed. She brought a red leather purse from her handbag and handed Connie a fiver. 'Here, gwaan go buy patty for yuh and yuh friend.'

'Valerie, that's too much!'

'Yuh nah hear mi say it's my treat? Besides, when dem gone wi can have a proper talk.'

'Mi nuh know Valerie. Mi hear all kind a t'ings ah go dung round 'ere,' said Althea.

'It will be all right,' said Connie. 'Daphne come 'ere with her grandma. We shan't get lost.'

'Mi nuh t'ink anyone will bother dem. Just nuh go any-where near the Front Line, yuh know where m'ah talk 'bout?' asked Valerie.

I nodded, although I wasn't sure where she meant. I felt too embarrassed to admit it after Connie had made a big deal about me knowing the area.

'All right, meet us back 'ere outside the underground in one hour, yuh understand?' said Althea.

She smiled at Connie, trying to make up for snapping at him before. I knew what it was like to have your head bitten off for no good reason, but my mum would never try to make friends with me afterwards. Connie was lucky to have a mum like Althea. I looked at him, he was smiling back, but it wasn't his real smile.

We somehow found the bakery Miss Gladys had taken me to, and queued for twenty minutes just to get through the door. It was worth it – the patties were spicy and delicious. We strolled along the streets, munching and sipping Lilt. I saw as many white people as Black people passing by. Every week the local paper printed letters from victims who had been mugged in Brixton by Black men in broad daylight, yet nobody looked particularly frightened.

'Look over deh,' said Connie, pausing to finish his last mouthful of pastry. 'Is that the record shop yuh cousin go to?'

I knew we were supposed to be heading back to the tube station to wait for Althea, but I was excited to see one of the places Devon sloped off to on Saturday afternoons. We crossed the road and peered between the posters of Black Power activists and album sleeves that covered the windows. The shop door was closed but the reggae beats from within pulsated through the glass and into the street. I cupped my hands around my eyes for a better view inside, wondering if I might spot Devon and his mates, but I couldn't see him.

'Shall we go in?' asked Connie. 'We still have some time before we need to meet up with Althea.'

'Dunno. We haven't got any money and I can't see any kids our age in there.'

'Mi nuh see why we can't just go and look.'

Connie went inside and I trailed after him, sticking close by, trying not to look out of place, even though nobody was paying us any attention. A group of teenagers were gathered around the counter where a turntable was playing a reggae tune I'd not heard before. Several people in the shop were nodding to the beat while they skimmed through the twelve-inch discs in the racks. Connie began flicking through a section called 'ROOTS'. I was nervous about touching the LPs, all

pristine and protected in their plastic sleeves. At home I was
never allowed within a mile of Devon's records, and Uncle
Earl's precious collection of Blue Beat and Rocksteady were
also out of bounds. But I could hardly just stand there with
my hands in my coat pockets, I'd look even more out of place.
I turned to the crate marked 'LOVERS' and began copying
what everyone else was doing, except rather than looking at
the track lists, I was admiring the girl singers posed on their
album covers: imagining myself with Janet Kay's hairstyles
and Carroll Thompson's clothes and makeup.

'Raas! Look wah go down out deh!'

A youth standing next to me was pointing outside. I
couldn't see, a poster of Black Uhuru blocked my view, but
I heard the thud against the windowpane, followed by a
muffled cry. A chill slipped into me as the atmosphere in the
shop turned hostile.

'Babylon fuckers,' another customer shouted, 'they're all
over him. Come!'

Everyone, including Connie, surged towards the door.

'Connie wait – we need to go, we shouldn't even be here!'
My voice sounded small, strangled by panic.

Connie didn't answer – perhaps he didn't hear me, he was
swept up in the crowd. Most of the customers were shouting
now, throwing out cuss words in Jamaican and English as
they bundled out of the shop. Connie was the only person I
knew here. I had to get to him and we had to go, something
bad was happening. The pavement was thick with bodies.
I held my breath as I stumbled through the people in front
of me, dodging elbows, my face rubbing against the sleeves
of khaki and polyester anoraks. I couldn't find Connie so I

kept pressing forward, then there was nobody in front of me, except for a young guy, pinned against the shop front by two white men dressed in jeans and leather bomber jackets. I froze.

One of the men was dark haired, the other was blond, both wore big black shoes on their feet. Chunky shoes; ready for agro. The young guy kicked out, wrenching himself free from the dark-haired man's grip, but was tackled and brought down by the blond. The guy attempted to get up again, but then both white blokes started kicking him. He lay on the pavement a few feet from me, curled up like a baby. I could see the veins on the backs of his hands, taut from being clasped around his head, desperately shielding himself from the blows of those big shoes. The white men ordered him to 'stay down'. He began to whimper. All this must have happened in seconds, but it felt like I was watching it in slow motion. I kept thinking *please, please stop.* I began to back away. But everyone around me was taller than I was, their bodies forming a solid wall that loomed over me, blocking my escape. I looked around at their faces, all of them strained with fury, the pitch of their anger was piercing. I covered my ears, but could still hear them shouting.

'What kind of fuckery is this?' said a Rasta in a leather tam.

'Leave the bwoy alone!' cried an elderly woman. 'Yuh gonna kill him!'

'Stand back. This is police business,' the blond officer shouted while his partner handcuffed the young man on the ground.

I looked away, fighting back confused, frightened tears. Then spying a gap, I managed to squeeze myself between two blokes. I told myself I wouldn't cry as I pushed through the mass of people, swallowing my emotion. I'd find Connie and we'd get away, we shouldn't even be here. But then the crowd began heaving this way and that, jostled by the sudden swarm of uniformed officers surging through, insisting that everyone disperse. A blue flashing light glinted in the corner of my eye, a police wagon had pulled up too. The guy was peeled off the pavement. I could see now how young he was, probably a couple of years older than Devon. They dragged him over to the waiting Black Maria; his body was limp.

The elderly woman turned to the dark-haired officer. 'The force you have used here was excessive and unnecessary.'

'Move along now, madam. If you don't step away, I'll be forced to arrest you.'

'Arrest her for what?' said a young woman. 'What she done except point out what you lot just did to the yout'?'

They and a few others continued to argue, but most of the people began to move away, although still agitated by what they had seen. I shivered, fumbling to button up my coat. A hand touched my elbow making me jump.

'Where were you? Are you all right?' said Connie.

'I . . . I couldn't find you. I . . . '

No more words came. My teeth began to chatter. It was so cold. Connie took off his scarf and wrapped it around my neck. I caught the scent of cocoa butter on his hands. Then I felt his arm around my shoulder, drawing me close.

'I'm sorry. C'mon. Let's go,' he whispered.

Slowly, silently, we retraced our steps back to the entrance of Brixton tube. Althea and Valerie arrived soon after, animated and thrilled about the good deal they had managed to negotiate on hair and beauty supplies. Althea asked if we'd had a nice lunch. Connie managed to utter, 'Yes. T'ank you.' All I could do was nod.

10

The following Saturday afternoon, I was lazing in front of the new colour telly Uncle Earl had recently hired. The wrestling was on; Mick McManus knocked Catweazle to the floor and manoeuvred him into a single-leg submission.

'Hold 'im Mick, hold 'im down!' said Auntie Sybil, who was sitting in the armchair with a plate on her lap, picking out stones from the rice grains.

The bell signalled the end of the bout and the South East London wrestler was strutting around like a cockerel, when the telephone began to ring.

'Daphne darlin', go answer the phone for mi.'

I hauled myself up from the settee and scurried to the front sitting room; Mum and Miss Gladys were coming through the door with shopping bags.

'Is that the telephone?'

'Yes, I'm just getting it.'

'If it's Zippy Matthews ah ring about her curtains, tell her mi call her back,' said Miss Gladys.

I dived for the phone, sweeping the receiver from the cradle.

'Hello . . .'

I recognised the rich, deep voice on the other end of the line, but instead of the usual thrill, I felt alarm. I slammed the phone down.

'Why yuh hang up?' Miss Gladys called from the hallway. 'Who was it?'

'Nobody . . . I mean, it was nothing,' I blurted.

Mum peered around the door, one of her eyebrows raised. 'Was it one of dem heavy breathers?'

'No. I don't know.'

I jumped as the phone started ringing again. I looked at it, then looked at Mum. I wanted it to stop, but I daren't pick up the receiver. I couldn't move.

'Let mi show you how to deal with dem perverts,' said Mum, marching into the room and sweeping up the phone.

'Hello . . . hello . . . what you mean who's this? You must know who it is you call . . . Yes. This *is* Alma Johnson, how you know me name? . . . Ezee!'

Mum turned her back to me and lowered her voice.

'How yuh get this number? And why yuh call here? Mi nuh business with yuh, mi na'eve know where yuh live, so why would *I* be telephoning yuh home, or yuh garage?'

I stood there, unable to run because Miss Gladys was standing in the doorway. Mum was silent, listening to Ezee. Finally, she turned and faced me.

'So the operator confirm it . . . Two or t'ree nuisance calls a week for the past month . . . '

I looked down at Auntie Sybil's best rug, concentrating on the swirling brown and orange pattern, willing myself not to cry.

'Nuh worry yuself,' Mum continued. 'Mi ah go deal with it.'

She slammed the phone down. I braced for the blasting that I knew was coming my way.

'D'yuh have anyt'ing to say, Daphne?'

Mum and Miss Gladys were both looking at me. I wanted to tell them that every time I had called Ezee I thought I'd have the courage to speak, but I hadn't dared to. I was content to just hear his voice. I wanted to tell them that it wasn't my fault I'd kept calling him. That if anyone was to blame, it was Mum.

'He's my daddy, isn't he?'

'How yuh know he's yuh daddy?'

I knew that I'd have to admit to eavesdropping on the conversation she'd had with Miss Gladys. My troubles would multiply.

'It was me,' said Miss Gladys. 'I tell her him name when she asked a couple months ago. Mi never tell her to call him on no phone though. She figure that part out for herself because she's determined, and as yuh can see, she want fi know her father.'

'So that makes it all right? Running up Sybil and Earl's phone bill? Causing a nuisance? She lucky me nuh box 'er 'cross the room.'

I started to cry. Miss Gladys came over and pulled me to her chest.

Mum continued, 'Him come asking why it is mi ah call him house, like as if mi want anyt'ing to do with him! Instead, mi find out it's mi dawta ah chase after him. Mi feel so shamed.'

'Mi nuh understand why *you* feel shame Alma! Him is the one who should feel shame. Him eleven-year-old dawta show more initiative than him. He left it fi 'er to go look for him when him should be the one ah look fi 'er. And yuh Alma, yuh part responsible in dis too! Daphne has a right fi know who him is. Now yuh have fi decide how yuh want fi proceed. Wah yuh gwaan put first? Daphne or yuh pride?'

Mum walked out of the room. I listened to her march up the stairs, trudge along the landing and slam the attic door. I looked at Miss Gladys.

'It'll be all right. Yuh muddah just going to spend a likkle time with 'er pride, before she have fi set it aside.'

For the next three days, Mum's manner was icy. When she spoke, her words were blunt. But by Wednesday she had lapsed into a melancholy silence. Miss Gladys assured me that everything would be all right, but I was beginning to doubt her. While Mum's brusqueness was tough, it was no more than I'd expected. This solemn quiet made me feel guilty. No, more than that, it made me sad for Mum as well as for myself.

It was a warm Saturday afternoon and we'd broken up for the Easter holidays. Connie had come to the park for a kick-about with Kiplyn and his friends. When the others went off to buy drinks, Connie came and slumped onto the bench beside me.

'What's in the news today, Miss Daphne? Read mi somet'ing.'

'Well there's a letter here about Brixton. Listen to this: Dear Sir, as one who has been robbed by a Black youth, I take great exception to last week's letter by N. R. Bell of Deptford, which stated that "racial tension in this country is not caused by the number of Black faces, but by the number of racists". It is not racist to point out where we can see things going wrong in our own land. The sooner parents, race-relation officers and the army of do-gooders start to instil discipline in Black youths the better. – Name and address withheld.'

I looked up from the page. Connie was sitting with one leg bent across the other, using a wooden lolly stick to prise stones from the grip soles of his boots.

'Why d'you ask me to read if you weren't going to listen?'

'I was listening. How come the t'ing we see happen in Brixton was never reported in the paper?'

It was the first time either of us had mentioned the beating we'd witnessed three weeks ago. I'd thought about it since, picturing the man on the ground, his hands clasped tight around his head, those sounds he made. I could see the image swimming towards me again, feel the tightness gripping my chest. I took a long, deep breath, then another, trying to compose myself.

'We should write a letter and send it to the newspaper. Write about what we saw,' said Connie.

'Don't be silly. They don't print letters from kids.'

'How dem fi know? We could write a letter as good as the one yuh just read, only from our point of view.'

It was tempting. I liked the idea of writing something and having it printed in the paper. I wondered if Marcia would let me use her typewriter.

'Okay. How should we start it?'

Connie uncrossed his leg and relaxed back in his seat. 'Mi nuh know. We'll figure it out later. Can yuh read the star signs now?'

I rolled my eyes.

'Ah gwaan nuh! Who nuh want fi know dem future? Althea and mi always read our star signs. We like the one in the *TV Times* best.'

I couldn't imagine Mum and me ever sitting down together doing anything, let alone reading horoscopes.

I read out the predictions for Sagittarius, Connie's sign. Apparently Saturn was rising which meant romance, while Mars would bring a boost in self-belief.

'It's a bit vague, innit?'

Connie shrugged. 'Read Leo, that's Althea's sign.'

'Okay ... Leo: Mercury set up second chances for you, especially in career terms. The moon could get money flowing faster your way. You could also discover why love can be special – but challenging.'

'Now that one's exactly right! Althea have a steady run of clients since she leave the salon, even Tobias is pleased. Although him vexed about the wages she leave when she walk out on Mrs Samuels. Him been nagging her to go back and get it from her.'

'Is it a lot of money?'

'Mi nuh know the amount. Althea always earn the most tips out of all the gyal deh, which was why Mrs Samuels never like her. Anyway, yesterday she decide that Tobias is right, and it's the principle that matters more than the cash.'

'So, she's going to get the money Mrs Samuels owes her?'

'Ahuh. Althea's going to the salon later. I'm going with her for moral support. She promised to buy an Indian takeaway afterwards. What's yuh horoscope say?'

'I'm not reading my horoscope. It's nonsense.'

Connie pulled the paper from my grasp and looked down at the page.

'Gemini ... here it is: Life has presented you with lots of challenges recently but you have weathered the storms. Mars

contacts Venus in your love chart, so look out for new rela-
tionships. Hmm . . . I wonder what it means.'

'It don't mean nothing. I bet most times they make it up.'

Connie looked thoughtful. 'Some t'ings just need time to
make sense. There's a woman over there waving at yuh.'

I looked in the direction where he was pointing and saw
Mum standing on the path at the edge of the field.

'It's my mum.'

'She still have yuh under heavy manners?'

I exhaled through my lips. 'I better see what she wants. Bye
Connie, happy Easter.'

I picked up my things and hurried over. When I reached
her, Mum turned and began walking towards the exit that
led to Jamaica Road.

'Where are we going?' I asked.

'To see yuh father. I called him last night and tell him why
yuh was bothering him. He wants to meet yuh.'

'Really? I'm going to meet him today – now? Oh my God.'

'Nuh need for blasphemy. As Mamma say, yuh entitled to
make up yuh own mind about him.'

I was finally getting to meet Ezee. I would see him and he
would see me. I wished I'd had a chance to change into some
nicer clothes. I ran my hand over my hair to press down the
tufts that had come loose. I caught my reflection in the shop
windows we walked past. My face was beaming.

The café had red-and-white checked tablecloths and smelled
of fried eggs and bacon. It was deserted except for an old man
smoking a fag and sipping his tea from the saucer. There was
no sign of Ezee. Mum asked for two glasses of water and we

sat beside each other, facing the door. Ten minutes went by. I wondered if Mum had ever come here before. It didn't look like her sort of place, but then I'd never pictured her anywhere except at home. Even when I thought of her at the hospital, I tended to imagine scenes from the TV show *Angels* rather than Mum's day-to-day work. The café was most likely Ezee's idea.

Mum kept taking little sips from the tumbler and looking at her watch. She kissed her teeth.

'Mi should have realised that when him say four o'clock it was BMT not GMT he mean,' said Mum.

'What's BMT?' I asked.

'Black Man Time. We give him five minutes more,' Mum said, speaking more to herself than to me.

Another ten minutes went by. Then the café door opened and Ezee stepped inside. He wore blue jeans and a brown cord jacket, which had a fleece collar that looked like rice pudding. He was wider and taller than I remembered. His heavy-lidded eyes grew wide when they fell on me. I felt my chest rise.

'So at last yuh reach,' said Mum.

Ezee shook his head. I had never seen anyone look at Mum like that, charmed and exasperated at the same time. 'Yuh nuh remember that mi move smooth?'

In this enclosed space I could feel the rumble of his voice vibrating in my chest.

'Move smooth mi foot! Daphne, this is Enoch Edwards.'

'Everybody call me Ezee.'

Mum cut her eye past him. 'Is Enoch the name yuh use when yuh first introduce yuself to mi. This is yuh father.'

His eyes settled on me again. A glimmer of gold appeared in each corner of his smile.

'So Daphne, mi nah go get no hug from yuh?' he said.

I looked at Mum. A single nod told me I had her permission so I got up and took a small step towards him. Ezee swooped forward and folded me in his arms. I hadn't realised that I was holding my breath until I exhaled, sinking into his embrace. My head came up past his chest, and the gold chain that hung loosely around his wrist made a jingling sound at my ear. I held him tighter and inhaled the smell of cigarettes and the musky scent of his cologne.

He pulled away and held me at arm's length.

'What a pretty young lady,' he said. 'Now if mi not mistaken, it's yuh birthday at the end of next month.' I nodded. 'Me'll be in Jamaica then. Mi have some business to take care of, so here . . . get yuself somet'ing nice.'

He produced a paper bundle from his trouser pocket. I gasped as he handed me a £20 note!

'Eh-eh! Let *me* hold on to this,' Mum said, plucking the cash from my hand.

Ezee winked at me. 'Yuh muddah ah go squirrel it away in some savings account.'

'Or maybe buy a frame to put it in,' said Mum.

I sipped the cream soda Ezee ordered for me and watched him put three sugars in his coffee. Mum leant on the table with her chin resting in the palm of her hand, as though she was bored. But I noticed her eyes were alert; she was ready to continue sparring with my father at any moment. He asked me about school. I told him everything I'd learnt that year, my nerves making me talk. I spoke about the books I'd read recently, the foods I liked, even what my favourite TV programmes were. I wanted him to like me. He sat back in his chair smiling, taking long drags on his cigarette. When I finally ran out of words, he leaned forward. I sat up straight, ready for his appraisal.

'Yuh intelligent,' he said. 'Mi expect yuh to study hard at school so yuh can go to university.'

'Ah so me tell her . . .' Mum muttered.

'. . . make twice the effort, and nuh let anybody keep yuh down,' he continued.

My dad thought I was pretty and clever. My heart soared.

Mum made a show of looking at her watch.

'We have to go now,' she said. 'Mi have another early shift in the morning.'

Outside the café, Ezee hugged me. His neat beard scratched against my cheek; then I felt him kiss the top of my head. I wanted to watch him walk away but Mum was already heading up the street.

'Well, yuh like him?'

I paused before answering. 'I don't really know him yet.'

Mum's eyes were fixed on the way ahead as she steamed along the pavement. She shrugged with an air of indifference, but her tone was rigid with indignation.

'Yuh should know him have other pickney. Probably a dozen or more, knowing him. Mi nuh know how that mawga Assyrian him live with put up with it for so long. Still for all of that, mi nuh going to stand in the way if yuh want fi see him. He's yuh father and mi cyaah change that. But mi nuh go friend up with 'im, yuh understand?'

I nodded, even though Mum wasn't looking. Again, it was like she was speaking more to herself than to me. There were so many things I wanted to ask her. When would I see Ezee again? Would we always meet at that café? Who were these *other pickney*? I wondered what they looked like, if I'd ever meet them, if Ezee thought they were as clever as me. I also wondered who the *mawga Assyrian* was too – she must be the one behind those show-off curtains.

The number 1 was pulling up at the bus stop ahead of us and Connie leapt off before it came to a standstill. It was a nice surprise. I could tell him about Ezee. Without his encouragement I might never have got up the nerve to look for my dad. I watched Connie pick his little brother up. He smiled as he jiggled Kallai on his hip. I was too far away to actually see the dint in his cheek, but I imagined it, and some impulse made me brush my index finger with my thumb.

Althea was unfolding the pushchair and she spotted Mum and me approaching.

'Look, Connie, it's yuh friend. Hello Daphne. Yuh good?'

'I'm very well, thank you. Mum this is Connie from school, his brother Kallai and his mum Mrs ... Miss ... I mean ... Althea,' I said.

Connie mumbled 'howdeedo' while Althea chuckled.

'This likkle gyal so sweet. Is yuh 'er muddah?'

'Yes I am. You are?'

'Althea Small. Nice to meet yuh ...?'

Mum summoned her polite smile. 'Alma Johnson. Nice to meet you too. You shopping?'

'Nah, mi ah go to mi old workplace, mi have some business to tek care of. But it looks like we ah walk the same way,' said Althea. 'Yuh know now mi meet yuh, mi can see where Daphne get her good hair from.'

I noticed the corners of Mum's lips stiffen, the way they did when she was trying to prevent her smile from fading.

We all turned into Dockyard Row and saw that two police cars blocked the far end of the narrow side street. A crowd had gathered along both sides of the road; gawking, pointing, muttering.

'Why all these people jus' stand up 'pan the street?' said Mum, annoyed, but I could tell she was curious.

As we drew closer to the assembly, Althea froze, staring. My eyes followed the path of her gaze over to where four women were sitting on the grimy pavement outside 'Blades Hair Salon'. Their hands were cuffed and their heads hung low, their eyes probably set on the big black shoes worn by the five policemen standing guard. The shop door was open and a middle-aged woman with a large Afro was being pulled from the building. Unlike the women who sat quiet, this woman was bucking and swearing under the humiliation.

'Mi ah naturalised British citizen, a respectable business-woman. Wah the backside dem status have fi do with mi!'

Althea gasped. Connie touched her hand.

'Why is there police in Mrs Samuels's salon? Althea, what's happening?'

Connie sounded frantic, his eyes were wide. Mum looked at Mrs Samuels, then looked back at Althea.

'Yuh know her?' Mum whispered.

Althea opened her mouth but no words came out. Now a police van with blackout windows was backing into the street.

Mum grasped Althea's elbow and leaned in close. Her voice was solemn.

'Stay calm. Nuh turn and run, nuh draw any attention. We

all just ah cross over the road here and walk down the other side of the street. Nice and easy. We just two women ah walk home with dem pickney. We nuh business in any of dis.'

Mum tugged and Althea began to move, her high heels thudding, rather than clicking, along the pavement. I looked back. The police began yanking the women off the ground and jostling them into the van. Mrs Samuels railed against the officers and onlookers.

'Get yuh hands off mi and mind yuh bloodclat manners! Wah yuh all ah look at? Nuh look pon mi!'

Althea seemed to shrink at the sound of her former boss's cries, slumping even further over Kallai's pushchair, keeping her head down. Mum slipped her arm through Althea's, mumbled something and they began walking a little quicker. We squeezed behind the bystanders and followed them. I glanced at Connie who was walking with his shoulders stooped as he hurried along the street. There was none of the usual grace and confidence to his movement, just the caution and worry of a twelve-year-old boy. I reached out, the back of my hand knocking against his knuckles, before sliding it tentatively into his palm. I felt his fingers close around my hand, holding it tight.

Althea gulped white rum from the tiny glass she held in both hands.

'There, yuh look better already,' said Miss Gladys. 'When yuh first walk t'rough the door yuh did favour ghost. Yuh too Alma. Mi knew unnu needed somet'ing stronger than tea.'

Althea turned to Mum. 'T'ank yuh. Mi never t'ought that mi could catch 'fraid sah. Mi nuh know what would have happened if . . . '

Mum, Auntie Sybil and Miss Gladys all nodded. Althea took another sip.

'Mi babyfather and mi plan fi marry, but him nuh divorce yet. Him ex run off. Him nuh know where she deh.'

Mum leaned across the table, speaking quietly. 'Does anyone at the salon know which part yuh live?'

'No. Mi friendly with the gyaldem but wi nuh really friends. And Mrs Samuels never keep anyt'ing on paper for all of wi who work deh that come from yard. She say it was for our own good, but it did suit her too.'

'All the same, better yuh steer clear of the High Street for a while, till t'ings die down,' said Mum.

Connie had barely spoken a word all the way home. He now sat with his attention fixed on the telly, but I could tell that he wasn't really watching it. His expression was blank; he was miles away.

'Eh-eh, look pan the time. Earl will soon be home and we na'eve feed the pickney yet,' said Auntie Sybil.

'Wi better get out of yuh way,' said Althea, rising from the table. 'Come Connie, let's go home. Put Kallai to bed.'

'Why unnu nuh stay and eat with us?' said Miss Gladys. 'Mi cook some soup earlier. We can have that and send the pickney-dem to the chip shop as a treat.'

Althea looked hesitant.

'Please stay,' said Mum. 'Yuh very welcome.'

'Okay,' said Althea, and she smiled for the first time since we got home. 'T'anks, that would be nice.'

Connie and I were sent to the chip shop to order for ourselves and the cousins. The park gates had already closed, so we had to take the long way around to get back onto Jamaica Road.

'Are you okay?' I asked.

He exhaled deeply, shaking his head. 'I was scared, Daphne. What if dem did catch Althea? What if dem catch me?'

'They didn't though. You're safe now. Althea will get her papers sorted soon,' I said, forcing a bright tone. 'I bet she and Tobias get married by the end of this year. And didn't she tell you that the first thing she'd do is go back to Jamaica for a visit? You'll get to see your grandparents and build that bike. *And* you get to stay here, no questions asked. Once them papers are sorted, everything will be okay.'

Tears gathered in his eyes and he wiped them away with the back of his hand. The optimism I'd manufactured dissolved in an instant. I looked away, not wanting to see him sad, then timidly threaded my arm through his.

'I was scared too.' I broke off to clear my throat. 'I really want you to stay here. I really like you. You're the best friend I've ever had.'

Connie didn't look at me, but I felt his arm squeeze mine. 'Yuh my best friend too, Daphne,' he said.

The Albion Family Fish Bar was busy but Mr Mustafa and his grandson worked briskly while bantering with their customers. Connie hadn't said a word and rather than attempt conversation in a crowded shop, I thought it best to leave him be. The smell of salt mixed with malt vinegar and the sound of sizzling batter was tantalising; my belly rumbled but I didn't mind the wait, it was a welcome pause. I found myself wondering what Ezee was doing, and if he was thinking about me. I hadn't had the chance to tell Connie about meeting him yet. We could talk about it on the way home. Perhaps it might lift his mood. As we moved up the queue, I noticed a black minivan pulling up outside. There were at least five white blokes in the vehicle, but only the man in the front passenger seat got out. I scanned his blue jeans, his brown leather jacket, the big black shoes on his feet. Shoes similar to those worn by the policemen standing guard over the women at the hair salon. A jolt of fear took my breath away. Were they still rounding up overstayers? Had they spotted us walking past the hairdressers and sent these plainclothes coppers to find us? The man blustered into the chip shop and settled himself next to the till, rather than joining the end of the line.

'All right Mehmet, how's tricks?'

'Officer Price, long time no see. What can I get you?' said Mr Mustafa.

'We'll have cod and chips twice, one saveloy and chips, one battered sausage, have you got any steak and kidney?'

I exhaled, swallowing to dislodge the lump in my throat. I turned to Connie, but he was looking past me, staring at the man and biting his bottom lip. Officer Price cast a glance at all of us waiting in the line and Connie immediately looked at the floor. The cop spread his elbows out along the counter, taking up the space. I looked at his thick neck, crew-cut hair, the wide, pinky-white face; those shoes. My mind flashed back to the young Black man curled and helpless on the ground. Despite the heat in the takeaway, a chill slipped over my skin. Earl, Sybil, even Mum believed that though there were a 'few rotten apples', the Met Police force were there to help us, and so were entitled to our respect and obedience. But I couldn't deny the feelings bubbling within. From what

I'd witnessed recently, it seemed to me that these people were not on our side. In fact, they didn't even like us.

The shop door opened and another white man in jeans and leather leaned inside.

'We've got a shout from the yard. Urgent assistance,' he said. 'All available units to make their way to Brixton, the natives are restless.'

'We best go sort them out. Hopefully, we'll be back later Mehmet.'

My eyes followed the man out of the shop. A blue light had now been attached to the roof of the van.

'Thank God, they're going,' Connie breathed.

'Yeah. Bloody stinking pigs,' I whispered.

When we reached the head of the queue, Mr Mustafa was all smiles, asking what he could get me, his 'favourite little customer'. I recited our order, but the chip shop's smells were no longer appetising, they made me feel sick.

When we got back, the house was quiet.

'Grub's up! The servings are massive. Mr Mustafa's practically given us an extra portion for free.'

Nobody responded. Perhaps they didn't hear. But it was unusual for Kiplyn and Devon not to come thundering downstairs when there were chips to be doled out. Apart from the murmur of the TV down the hallway, all was still. I looked up at Connie. He shrugged.

'Maybe yuh cousin dem gone out,' he said.

I frowned. That seemed unlikely, and I was about to tell him so, when in the distance I heard a siren wail. My mouth felt dry. I kicked off my shoes and hurried to the kitchen. I needed a drink. I needed to know what was going on. Where was everybody?

I nudged open the door and was relieved to see Devon and Kiplyn sitting on the settee. Like everyone else, they were staring at the telly, mesmerised by the images on screen. There, in vivid technicolor, was a police van like the one I'd just seen outside the chippy. It had been turned on its side and set ablaze; the orange flames were tall, angry and dazzling against the black smoke that billowed from the wreckage. The broadcast then cut to pictures of young Black men throwing bricks, stones and glass bottles. I blinked, scarcely able to take in what I was seeing.

'What madness is this?' said Mum. 'It look like Northern Ireland, not Brixton. It look like war.'

'That's Brixton!' I said, sinking onto the settee.

'Ah nuh madness ah gwaan deh, Alma,' said Miss Gladys quietly. 'What we ah see deh is rage. What we seeing is an uprising.'

Dozens of police officers armed with long plastic shields were attempting to move against the crowds. But every time they inched forward, they were pushed back by makeshift missiles falling on them like rain. They looked clownish in their pointy hats and stiff tunics, running for cover. Outnumbered. Their pale faces shocked and frightened. I told myself this was comeuppance for all the Black boys they'd kicked in over the years. That it was about time. Yet I couldn't muster a genuine sense of triumph, there was a hollow feeling inside. Was it dread?

'T'ings nuh gonna be the same after this,' said Miss Gladys. 'T'ings nuh gonna be the same at all.'

1985

11

Yards of white ribbon criss-crossed the ceiling of the Marsh Town Community Centre. Althea and Tobias sat at the centre of the top table, in front of a specially made banner; the embroidered letters on an ivory satin background proclaimed:

Two

become

One

Althea's skin glowed, her eyes were bright; she hadn't stopped smiling since she left the registry office. I supposed that this is what people meant when they said the bride looked radiant. Connie was sitting at her right side, shuffling food around his plate.

'Kallai, get up off the floor!'

Tobias's voice carried across the hall, cutting above the chinking of cutlery and the hum of conversations. Connie rose from the table and walked over to his brother. He'd spent most of the last five weeks of the summer holidays playing football with the other boys on the estate, and as a result his skin had grown darker, almost concealing the downy hair above his top lip. He had always included me when he was out with the lads, but this summer, he had stopped asking. In the black suit he looked older than sixteen, he looked taller too. And handsome.

Kallai emerged from beneath the table where the wedding gifts were piled high. His trousers were dusty at the knees. Connie crouched down, speaking to him in a low voice, while gently brushing away the fluff with a serviette. He held up his hands and the six-year-old balled his fists, jabbing at his big brother's open palms. One-two, one-two, the kid had a determined expression on his face. In a deft move, Connie moved his left hand away and Kallai, unbalanced, toppled into his arms, laughing. Connie smiled. It was the first genuine smile I'd seen from him all day. He took Kallai's hand and they walked back to their table, just as a three-tiered wedding cake was being wheeled out to a round of applause.

'Tobias's Auntie Sissy do a good job, it nuh look like she make it in a hurry,' said Valerie Dunne, her raspy voice bringing my attention back to our table. 'Mi did doubt this wedding would ever happen, but Althea get what she want at last. It's a pity her mamma and papa nuh able to mek it over here.'

'Yes mam, dem miss a beautiful ceremony,' said Valerie's husband Greville. The dapperly dressed senior citizen tapped the end of his cigarette on a silver case.

Tobias's big hand covered Althea's so that it seemed they were both holding the knife. Althea giggled with joy, with nerves. A flash went off as one of Tobias's friends took a picture of the happy couple.

After five years of engagement, the actual wedding

ceremony had come together with only three months' preparation. It was at the end of May that Tobias made the surprise announcement, his decree absolute had come through. Not only that, he'd been to the town hall and fixed a date for the ceremony; he and Althea would be married by the end of the summer.

The past few weeks leading up to the wedding had been a whirlwind. Connie said that he had never seen Althea so happy, and Tobias was more chilled, too. At the beginning of the year, things had gotten so heated between Connie and Tobias that Connie had ended up spending the night on the settee at my house. But for the last twelve weeks, Tobias had been the picture of a perfect husband, without a single flare-up. I watched him fork a morsel of the rich dark cake and lovingly feed it to Althea. The romantic gesture prompted an exhalation of *Ahhh*s from the wedding guests. This was so different from the Tobias who would fly into a rage if the towels in the airing cupboard were not piled neatly, or if a tablespoon was accidentally placed where the dessert spoons went. But Connie never spoke about home life much. From what I'd glimpsed over the years, I understood that it was bearable when Tobias was appeased, so Althea and Connie anticipated the things Tobias wouldn't like, and largely avoided doing them. They walked a tightrope, carefully negotiating around his moods. They shielded each other from the harsh words and the blows, when inevitably, Tobias would find fault with something they hadn't foreseen. When Connie opened up, I mostly just listened and tried not to ask too many questions. I did once ask him how Althea could love a man like Tobias. Connie scoffed, 'It's more than love, mi t'ink she enchanted.'

As Althea fed a little of the wedding cake to Tobias, Connie's expression hardened.

'Yuh watching how the love birds ah gwaan, Daphne? Or is it Connie yuh ah gaze pan?' Valerie added a wink. 'Him good-looking, innit. Nuttin' like a wedding to mek love bloom.'

I sipped some juice, hoping it would help cool the heat rising to my face. 'We're best friends, Miss Valerie,' I mumbled.

'And who better yuh ah go find for a future life partner than a good-looking bwoy who's yuh best friend too!'

She nudged my arm and burst into her rusty laugh. Dalton Bustamante saved me from having to respond – Busta was Tobias's best man. He was clinking a spoon against his glass.

'Ladies and gentlemen, it's time now for the speeches. We'll hear from the groom in a likkle while, but first mi want to read the messages that send from the people who can't be here.'

Busta picked up the first telegram and began reading in a dogged monotone, but my eyes drifted back to Connie. Over the years, he'd grown in popularity at school, especially among the girls. We'd got our exam results a week ago; I got seven As, and a B. Connie only took six O-levels; apart from his A in Maths, the other results were Bs and Cs, but he was pleased with his grades. I was sure he could have done as well as me, if he hadn't been so distracted. In the past year he had gone out with Dionne Brown and Monica Saunders. Neither of those girls talked to me; they thought I was stuck up and boring. I didn't care because they were the sort of girls Miss Gladys would have called 'force-ripe'; but I'd overhear their giggled conversations in the girls' loo about how good Connie was at kissing and how far they had gone with him.

It bothered me that even though I knew more about Connie than they did, they knew him in a different way. There were even some white girls that fancied him, although as far as I knew he'd never got off with any of them. As for the boys Connie hung out with, it was obvious that they mostly put up with me because they liked Connie so much. Still, I was the only one that had been invited to the wedding, which I took as proof of the special status I still held. I preferred it when it was just the two of us.

During Busta's readings, a couple more of Tobias's friends had been going around the hall topping up the adult guests' glasses with fizzy wine.

'Now, ladies and gentlemen,' said the best man, 'before we get to my speech, I want you all to put yuh hands together for the man of the hour, Tobias Beckford.'

Everybody clapped except Connie, whose hand remained clasped around the glass in front of him. Tobias rose, his face grave.

'Many of yuh here know about the heartbreak mi went t'rough all those years ago,' Tobias continued. 'I never t'ought I'd find happiness again. But then this wonderful woman walked into mi life.'

A solemn hush descended across the room as Tobias spoke about how he and Althea fell in love and how long they'd waited to be together as *man and wife*. He faltered, his chest rising and falling as though fighting to contain emotion. Althea took his hand, murmured something sweet and loving. The audience was rapt. I was too. Seeing the two of them like this was beguiling. Tobias recovered himself.

'I'd always wanted a family and this is what I have because

of you. I promise to raise the boys – both our sons – to be proper, respectable men. And I will strive to make you happy and never, ever let you go. I want everyone here to be up-standing and raise a toast . . . '

There was a rumble as chairs were scraped back and every-one stood. Connie was among the last to stand, his movement sullen, reluctant, without looking in the bride and groom's direction. Tobias raised his glass high.

'To Althea, my beautiful wife.'

We chorused: 'To Althea.'

At 6 p.m., the dining tables were pushed back against the wall and reset for the buffet. The black-and-white tiled floor now provided ample space for the small children to run around, as well as a place for the adults to wine up. Tobias's cousin Clive set up the sound system and soon Dennis Brown was singing about the money in his pocket. I made my way over to Connie who was standing alone near the kitchen service counter that someone had turned into a makeshift bar. It was so loud it was impossible to chat, so Connie and I stood and listened. Ordinarily we would have rolled our eyes at these old-time tunes; neither of us listened to reggae much anymore. Connie was into rap and I was captivated by Prince. But these reggae classics were infectious and I found myself swaying to the beats.

There were whoops as Althea entered the room. She had changed out of her white lace and was now dressed in a crim-son gown with sequins and a slit that came up to her thigh. She swayed to the centre of the dance floor, bathing in the attention; Tobias handed his cigarette to Busta and swaggered towards her. 'A Good Thing Going' was faded down and the intro to 'Hopelessly In Love' sang out of the speakers. I began to dance from side to side, transported back to 1981.

'Ladies and gentlemen,' said Clive, speaking through a microphone. 'Mr and Mrs Tobias Beckford are about to take to the floor for their first dance.'

Tobias placed his hands on Althea's hips. The two of them swayed to the rhythm, their bodies melding, the moves slow; more tender than sexual. It was stirring to see them together like that. Althea always told Connie that they would be a proper family after she married Tobias. After his speech, it felt like this really could be the start of a new chapter. By the second verse, other couples began joining in, dancing close-up. I turned to Connie, feeling coy, feeling hopeful. But he put his glass down on the counter and pushed towards the exit, disrupting the flow of wedding guests drifting towards the dance floor.

I found him sitting alone on a wall opposite the community centre's entrance.

'Are you going to stay out here all night?'

'I ain't expecting yuh to tan here,' he said, in the half cockney–half patwah way he spoke these days. 'Go back inside. Enjoy the party.'

'I came to find you because I could see that you're not exactly having a great time. So don't act like I'm just like all the other people at this wedding.'

'Sorry.'

He loosened his tie and undid the top button of his shirt. I sat beside him, catching the scent of Sta-Sof-Fro. He didn't use DAX anymore.

'Listen, if nothing else, at least now Althea can apply for her stay, which means you can too. Isn't that worth celebrating?'

'Ah suppose so.'

'Come on! You'll become a British citizen, you'll be eligible to play for England should Bobby Robson come calling.' I detected a hint of a smile. 'You might have to stop cheering on the West Indies at cricket though.'

'That might be teking t'ings a bit far.'

He grinned, his ebony eyes brilliant. For a moment, I glimpsed my outline reflected in the pupils. It brought to mind a line from a poem Miss O'Mahoney had asked me to read out in English last term: *My face in thine eye, thine in mine appears.*

Jean Adebambo's 'Paradise' was playing inside, and her singing became louder for a moment as the main door swung open. Tobias came out with a cigarette in his hand. He walked towards us and Connie's smile evaporated.

'See this now! Looks like Althea and me aren't the only lovebirds in the place. Come back inside and me'll ask Clive to play some slow jams just for unnu.'

Connie stood up. 'We're good out here t'anks.'

Tobias turned to me. 'Yuh having a nice time, Daphne?'

'Yes. Thank you.' I groped for more to say. 'It was a lovely wedding. Althea looks beautiful. Congratulations. I hope you'll both be very happy.'

'That's nice of yuh to say so, Daphne,' said Tobias bowing from the neck in mock humility. 'Yuh nuh gonna congratulate mi too?'

'Con-gra-tulations,' said Connie, his tone snide.

Tobias flicked his cigarette away. 'T'anks. Now come back inside, show yuh muddah how happy yuh are for we.'

'In a likkle while. When dem change the music up a bit.'

Tobias raised an eyebrow. 'Somet'ing wrong with the music dem ah play?'

'No these tunes are great . . . classics,' I said, speaking rapidly, sensing danger.

'Glad to hear yuh know good music, Daphne. Somet'ing with a melody,' said Tobias, staring at Connie. Most the music him listen to sound like the record stuck.'

'That's because it's not old people's music,' Connie muttered.

Tobias produced a humourless chuckle. 'Yuh come with yuh facety self, telling mi that mi too old to know what good music is. Is that why yuh out here? Sulking about the music as well as the wedding?'

'No!'

'Yuh t'ink mi nuh see yuh? Going around all day with yuh face vex.'

He was standing close to Connie now. They were both tall, but Connie's slender frame was no match for Tobias's brawn.

'Mi well aware of how much yuh want to ruin this day. Spoil our happiness. But it nuh go work. And if yuh nuh like the way t'ings are now, then yuh nuh have fi stay.'

'What yuh mean mi nuh have fi stay? Yuh nuh just marry mi muddah.'

'That's right. Since Kallai born him name Beckford, now yuh muddah take the name Beckford too. Is yuh one in ah mi yard name Small. Yuh one.'

Tobias and Connie stared at each other. 'One Dance Won't Do' by Audrey Hall seeped out of the community centre. Busta was leaning at the entrance with a glass in his hand.

'Come nuh, Tobias! Yuh wife send me to look for you.'

'Mi just ah come now,' said Tobias, strolling towards the community centre. 'Lord, mi just love the sound of the word *wife.*'

The door closed and the music became muffled and indistinct once more.

'Connie, are you—'

'Yeah, yeah,' Connie jumped in, batting away my concern with a casual wave. 'It nuh nuttin'. He'll have forgotten all about it in five minutes.'

I nodded, even though I could see that Tobias's spell of good behaviour had come to an end. Connie knew it too. He slumped back down on the wall.

'Daphne, will it be all right if mi stay at yours tonight?'

I leaned over and hugged him. 'Yes, Connie. Of course you can.'

Mum and I moved to the Marsh Town Estate three years ago, into one of the maisonettes in Merchant House. It was nice to finally have my own room, but I missed the bustle and the noise at 59 Lime Grove. And, with fewer people around, Mum and I tended to bump up against each other more. Thankfully, Miss Gladys often visited.

It was half-eleven when Connie and I got back and Mum was already asleep. The bedclothes Connie used the last time he stayed over were still stashed behind the living room door. He wished me good night, so I left him to make up the sofa himself. After pouring myself a cup of hot chocolate, I started upstairs, tiptoeing softly on the runner. I paused halfway. Connie had left the living room door ajar and hadn't completely closed the curtains. Peering through the gap, I could see him stretching. The orange lights from the walkway of the flats opposite filtered into the gloom, illuminating his shoulders, the muscles in his arms and the arch of his long spine. I stayed there, watching. He stood up and took off his trousers; he wore tight black underpants. Cocoa slopped into the saucer as I hurried to my room. In bed, I pictured Connie half naked on the sofa directly below, reimagining the curve of his arse. I rolled onto my back, my middle finger resting against my clit, making small circles. I closed my eyes, gradually increasing pressure, visualising Connie in bed beside me and his finger where mine was. I felt the familiar rise followed by a shiver. I rolled onto my side, my cheek finding a cool spot on the pillow, and fell into a satisfied sleep.

12

'There! What yuh think?'

Althea angled the mirror so I could see what she had done with my hair. It was Friday afternoon, the last day of the summer holidays, and I'd bumped into her outside Londis that morning. Nowadays, the bulk of Althea's clients wanted curly perms or relaxers, but she still liked to experiment with what she called 'natural styles'. Apparently my hair was perfect for a look she wanted to try out, so I'd agreed to model for her. I hadn't seen Connie since the wedding a week ago. The next morning, he had got up and left before I went downstairs. We'd spoken a couple of times on the phone since then, but Connie was monosyllabic. Everything was 'fine'. Letting Althea do my hair was an excuse to go to his house; when I arrived, I discovered that he had left the flat after breakfast. I sat there for three hours, but Connie never reappeared.

'D'yuh like it?' Althea pressed.

'It's really nice. Thanks.'

'A Black woman's hair is her beauty; this style suits a pretty young woman like you.'

I'd kept my hair natural more out of necessity than

principle; Mum wasn't prepared to fork out for me to get it treated every six weeks. Usually I'd blow-dry my hair until it was practically kink-free, and then slick it back with mousse. I thought it made me look stylish, like Sade; I hadn't drilled my hair in cornrows for years. Althea began taking pictures from different angles with her Instamatic camera.

'Mi gonna apply to get a grant from that enterprise allowance scheme, then I'll open up a salon specialising in natural hair. But first, mi have to get mi stay – "leave to remain" dem call it. After we get that, then we can apply for 'naturalisation".' Althea chuckled. 'I tell yuh Daphne, I was nagging Tobias to fill out that Home Office form the day after we marry! Because Connie is under eighteen him class as a dependent so it's only the one form wi need.'

'Couldn't you fill it out yourself?'

'Nah, the spouse with the UK citizenship is the one that has to make the application. Besides, Tobias is better at that sort of t'ing. Him buy a copy of wi marriage certificate and post it off with the form this morning.'

'So in a few weeks you and Connie will have leave to remain,' I said, cheered by the information, flattered that Althea was confiding in me.

'Ah nuh so it go! T'ings will tek a likkle while yet honey. Valerie tell mi that when she first send in her application it take six weeks for the Home Office to get back to her, and all the letter say was "we have received your application".' Althea sighed, 'Still, wi on the road to citizenship at last. Mi long fi see Mamma and Papa. And dem will be so proud if mi go back ah yard as a fully fledged businesswoman.'

I smiled. Althea's ambition reminded me of Ezee; my dad

was enterprising too. He had a good business, he always drove nice cars and went back to Jamaica every year. Mum hadn't softened her stance towards my father, but she mostly held her tongue whenever I mentioned him. I called Ezee most weeks, and over the past four years we would meet up once a month, although from time to time it would slip to every couple of months, depending on how busy he was.

Ezee had been in Jamaica on business since June, but a week ago Miss Gladys said she saw Audrey Henry, Ezee's common-law wife, shopping in Morley's department store in Brixton. When I realised he was back, I telephoned and asked if we could meet. I wished that for once he'd have called me and that I hadn't had to do the chasing. But then he was so effusive on the phone – inviting me over for a takeaway and promising to give me some money – that I quickly forgot to be annoyed. I was going to show off my hair to him when I saw him that evening.

Kallai had been quietly absorbed by the telly while Althea braided my hair. Now, he came over and picked up a couple of the photographs she had placed on the coffee table, smiling as images of my hair in close-up appeared before his eyes.

'Put it down darlin',' said Althea. 'Mammy need the pictures for her portfolio and mi nuh want them spoiled. Daphne, yuh want a cold drink? We have cream soda, ginger beer, squash . . . '

'Ginger beer please.' I held up the mirror so I could look at my hair again; the tiny tight braids were beginning to pinch my scalp. I could hear Althea opening the fridge and getting glasses from the cupboards and called to her, 'D'you know when Connie's due back?'

'Nah. Him probably playing football. Making the most of him free time before school start on Monday.'

Althea came back and handed me the drink, just as the front door slammed. I turned, hoping to see Connie but instead Tobias walked in, frowning. Althea stood to attention.

'Hello darlin'. Mi never expect yuh this early.'

'It wasn't planned. One man get suspended for not taking him card to the supervisor after him clock on, and so the bloody shop stewards tell us all fi walk off. We gwaan lose part of today's pay because of some facety white man. Yet the other day, when my man Leroy get sanction for going to the toilet without permission dem raas union men nuh lift a finger.'

Althea was now hovering between the living room and the kitchen doorway. 'Yuh want a cuppa tea? Or mi can start dinner now.'

'Tea, please,' said Tobias. 'Mi nuh in any rush fi eat.'

He collapsed onto the sofa and Kallai nestled under his arm. Althea exhaled before retreating to the kitchen.

'So, yuh all set for next week?' Tobias's question was more of a statement, nevertheless I dutifully nodded. 'Staying on at school, getting A-levels, very impressive. Unnu need all the qualifications yuh can get, to have a chance of any sort of job these days, let alone a decent job. Yuh must work hard.'

His gaze was drilling into me.

'I'll do my best.' I sipped the ginger beer, both hands clasped around the cold glass.

'Yuh know, I was eleven when mi parents send for mi. Back home I was one of the brightest students in mi class. Yet when mi come here the teachers say that my Jamaican education wouldn't be up to the standard of the grammar school. That I'd be out of my league. My father always defer to the white mandem. So him send me to the secondary modern instead.'

Althea had come and stood in the kitchen doorway while Tobias was talking. He switched from looking at me to looking at her.

'Unnu have the chance to get proper qualifications, not like my friends and me. We never get anywhere near the ordinary-level certificate, let alone advanced. Dem just shove us in the lowest group for everyt'ing, then steer us towards manual labour. We never get a chance to be soft like my stepson.'

'Connie know how lucky he is.' Althea's tone was bold at first, but then faltered. 'Him grateful for the opportunity. Innit, Daphne?'

'Then where him deh?' said Tobias. 'Hanging out pan street, when him should be here ah read him book and helping around the house. If after these two years him end up on the dole, him will have fi leave mi yard, cos mi nuh go work at that plant, putting up with all dem racists to support no layabout here.'

Althea opened her mouth, but then closed it. I drained the glass of ginger beer. The cold fizz scorched the back of my throat.

'I should probably head to my dad's now,' I said, carefully placing the tumbler on the heart-shaped coaster. 'Thanks for doing my hair.'

Althea followed me into the tiny hallway, closing the living room door behind us. 'Nuh go out of yuh way or anyt'ing, but if yuh see Connie where dem play football, please tell him to come home. Me'd like him here.'

I nodded. 'If I see him, I'll tell him.'

The back entrance to Hibbert Court opened onto a meagre lawn. I walked along the strip of bald earth made by pedestrians cutting across the grass, rather than following the path around it. Pablo Gad's 'Hard Times' blared out from a balcony above, its bass bouncing off the pebbledash of the flats opposite. The scent of fried fish wafted from a kitchen window as I cut down Dreadnought Close. Sounds and smells that had become common on the estate over the last four years, and that had led to many white families requesting transfers. Mum's housing application had risen up the council's waiting list because of the exodus. This shifting demographic had started to change our school too; together with the kids that travelled in from the south of the borough – black and brown faces now made up around a quarter of the students at John Evelyn Comprehensive. Even so, while there were more Black girls to nod to in the corridor, I still didn't have a close girlfriend at school. I was never any good at small talk and my tendency to be quiet and studious in class was often mistaken for superiority, or that I was 'boasy'. Only Connie seemed to understand my seriousness and appreciate it. Instead of taking the path to the bus stop, I set off in the opposite direction.

A ten-foot, chain-link fence surrounded the patch of asphalt everyone called the cage. I could see Connie through the plastic coated mesh, concentrating on his keep-ups. He was alone except for some guy who was standing with his back to me. A proper match must have been played earlier, as Connie was wearing football shorts rather than jeans, and his companion wore tracksuit bottoms and a hoodie. I walked up and stood waiting by the fence, my nose peeping through one of the diamond-shaped holes. Connie's eyes darted across to me for a split second. He miskicked, sending the ball rolling towards the edge of the enclosure.

'Something catch your eye?' teased the other youth.

Connie nodded to where I was standing and the youth turned around. I found myself looking straight at Mark Barrett. I was astonished to see him standing there chatting easily with Connie. I was astonished to see him on the estate, full stop. His family were among the first wave of white flight, but rather than moving to Downham, Eltham or Thamesmead, they'd only gone to South Bermondsey, a few miles down the road. He still attended John Evelyn, but when the tutor groups were shuffled after our first end-of-year assessments, Mark and his friends were moved to a different class to Connie and me. By the end of the third year, we were set according to the subjects we'd chosen as well as ability. After that, I spent the next two years concentrating on my O-levels, and I only saw Mark in passing. Over the years, he, Craig, Ted and the other lads they hung out with, had swapped their Dr. Martens for designer trainers and wore Pierre Cardin roll necks under jumpers by Gabicci, Pringle or Lyle & Scott. They tended to keep to themselves and I mostly kept my eyes down whenever I saw him in the school corridors. Mostly, but not always. I was wholly unprepared to see him here.

'Whaap'm, Daphne,' said Connie. 'Yuh looking for me?'

'Yeah ... no ... I was sort of passing. I'm off to see Ezee.'

Connie tied his tracksuit top around his waist and gathered his kit. Mark was walking towards the fence. Towards me. Since last year, he'd allowed his hair to grow back and his face had become more angled, less boyish. I also noted those full, pale lips and those grey-blue eyes. There was a tickle in my throat and I swallowed rapidly to soothe it. As he approached, I wondered what he wanted from me. Then he bent down and picked up the football; it had settled on a drain cover near to where I was standing.

'All right?' he said.

'Yeah. All right,' I said, nodding.

'So you live here now?'

'Yeah I do.'

I wasn't sure if I ought to say more. I didn't know what else to say.

'Your hair looks nice.'

'Oh, thanks,' I said, running my fingertips over the braids. Althea's words came back to me: 'a Black woman's hair is her beauty'. Would someone like Mark think this style made me look pretty? I quickly looked away. Connie had joined me on the other side of the cage and I made a show of greeting him with a gush of smiles.

'See you then,' Connie said to Mark.

'Not if I see you first,' Mark replied, deadpan except for a small smirk.

Connie and I set off but when we reached the corner I glanced back. Mark was still standing in the cage, watching us.

'What's going on?' I said.

'What d'yuh mean?'

'*Him* hanging around here. Playing football. With *you*!'

'Hmm ... Ah was surprised to see him here too, the first time.'

'What d'you mean "the first time"?'

'He's been coming here since the summer start. Him grandmuddah live in one of dem flats down at the Longshore. When he visit her, he come by here too and join in if we having a kick-about.'

'What? You never said! Why on earth are you playing football with him? He's still a bloody racist isn't he, or am I missing something?'

Connie shrugged. 'He's good at football.'

I must have looked dumbfounded because Connie began to laugh.

'But ... but ... how the bloody hell can you like him?' I stammered, flustered, somehow annoyed with myself.

'I never say mi like him! It's him who turn up here – mi never go look for him! Cha! Apart from when we play in the school team, we nuh have nuttin' to do with each other.'

'I'm sure Mark's brother would kick off if he knew he was mixing with you.'

'That's Mark's problem. Mi nuh business with that. What's it to you anyway?'

'Nothing. Him coming round here after his family moved off the estate like they were too good for us just pisses me off, I suppose.'

We arrived at the square beneath Hibbert Court where our paths would separate. Connie seemed to hesitate.

'I've not seen you since Sunday,' I said. 'I missed you.'

'Mi been playing football and t'ings, hanging out at Errol's ...' Connie trailed off into a shrug.

'Have things been okay with Tobias?'

He grinned but it looked more like a grimace. 'I'm on mi best behaviour so it's all right for now.'

'Well, just so you know, Tobias is home already. Apparently there was a walkout at work. He's pretty grumpy. You know yuh can talk to me, right?'

'Thanks Daphne, it nuh nuttin' mi can't handle. See yuh Monday, yeah?'

I sighed. 'Okay. See you soon.'

The 53 ambled along New Cross Road, stopping and starting because of the weight of traffic. I sat looking out of the window, thinking that if Ezee gave me a tenner, or maybe even fifteen quid, then I'd go to Greenwich Market on Sunday. A few weeks ago, I'd seen a lovely '40s tea dress there, and the second-hand paperback stalls were always worth a browse. The bus pulled up across the street from 439 New Cross Road. There was now no trace of the fire that had devastated the house in 1981. The bricks had been cleaned up; the sash windows replaced with clear, clean glass, that on a day like this reflected back blue sky. The council had converted the tall terraced house into flats, but four years on from the tragedy, the building remained empty. Nobody wanted to live there.

Back in April 1981, a jury at the coroner's court delivered an open verdict. The police investigation into the fire had been scaled back from fifty to only two officers. Meanwhile, relatives and friends were still grieving and the survivors were still traumatised; one so much so that he had taken his own life two years later. He was twenty-one years old. A couple of days ago, I'd read the Director of Public Prosecutions had ruled there was 'insufficient evidence to charge anyone with any offences'. The criminal case into the deaths of the thirteen young people was now officially closed. When I first started reading the papers it was because I'd wanted to know more about the things grown-ups talked about; I was fed up with being treated like a kid all the time. Since turning sixteen last May, I'd often remind Mum and Miss Gladys that I was well on my way to becoming an adult. But looking at the house across the road reminded me that I was now the same age as several of those who died in that fire, and that sixteen is no age at all.

The bus had finally reached the Old Kent Road. I rang the bell and hurried downstairs.

Audrey stood in the doorway with her arms folded. Her long brown-black hair was tied in a ponytail and three months of Jamaican sunshine had tanned her pale skin, darkening her freckles. I'd always thought there was something witchy, rather than refined, about Audrey's features; her top lip curled upwards, as if something permanently displeased her.

'Hello Audrey,' I said, forcing politeness. 'How was your holiday?'

'Fine, thank you.'

'Ezee said I should come over. For dinner.'

She walked inside, leaving the front door open.

'Him gone to the Chinese. Go sit in the living room till him come,' she said.

A beaded curtain hung across the kitchen doorway; she swept it back with a flourish and disappeared.

I perched on a corner of their beige leather couch with my hands in my lap. Whenever I came by, Audrey spoke to me like that. Sometimes I'd think up stinging remarks I could chuck back at her, if I ever plucked up the courage. But I didn't want to give her an excuse to claim that I'd been badly brought up. I also didn't want Ezee to think I was a pain. I looked at the gallery of pictures of her on the living room walls. The large black-and-white print from the 1970s dominated the space above the fireplace; it had Audrey wearing the *Miss Black and Beautiful* crown and sash, sitting between the two, darker-skinned runners-up. There were studio poses of her from her modelling days in evening gowns, pictures of her with Ezee when the two of them were younger, nearly always posing beside a flash car. I had to admit that they still looked good together in pictures, even though Audrey smiled less in the more recent photos. Just last year she had a picture taken on a beach in Jamaica looking elegant in her bathing suit and sarong. I let slip to Mum that I thought she was in great shape for a woman her age. Mum kissed her teeth. 'Well mi suppose that's one advantage of being barren.'

I'd given Ezee several photographs of me over the years; he'd always accepted them with enthusiasm, but had never put any of them up. In fact, there were no pictures of any of Ezee's children on display. On the one hand, I was curious to know what they looked like. On the other, I had to admit, deep down, I didn't want to see them. I liked to imagine that I was his only child; they were out of sight and out of mind. I imagined that was how Audrey liked it too.

After fifteen minutes, the front door opened and Ezee came in, boasting that he'd bought the biggest banquet on the menu. I called out to him from the living room. His complexion looked lush after weeks of sunshine.

'Wah gwaan, sugar dumpling. Nuh just tan deh, come hug mi nuh!'

I almost ran into him. Ezee held me tight and I felt my gloom lifting.

'Yuh miss mi?'

I nodded.

'Audrey in the kitchen? She getting yuh refreshment or anyt'ing?'

I looked down. 'I dunno. Maybe?'

'Give mi a moment,' he said, in a flat tone. 'Put on the TV. Mek yuself at home.'

I switched the telly on but kept the volume low, wanting to hear what Ezee and Audrey were saying in the kitchen.

'She come all the way over here and yuh na'eve offer her a cup ah water? Cha! Wah gwaan wi yuh?'

'She's your guest – not mine!' said Audrey, her tone sharp as a blade.

'Yes, and this is my house, so yuh can show my dawta some hospitality.'

I heard footsteps crinkling the plastic strip that covered the carpet from the kitchen to the sitting room, then Audrey appeared in the doorway.

'The table lay and the food set out. Yuh *welcome* to come t'rough,' she said.

'Thank you,' I said, pulling my face into a smile.

Audrey picked at the food, then pushed her plate away after a few bites. She lit a Consulate and sat smoking it through her elegant black holder; she took long drags, flicking the ash with a flourish. Ezee ignored her, so I did too. He spoke about his trip to Jamaica while we ate. The Jamaica Ezee talked about felt alive and vivid, not stuck in the past like when Mum talked about it.

'You better take me next time you go,' I said, smiling – though only half joking.

Ezee kept busy surveying the dishes on the table, opting for more fried rice. 'Sure, mi can do that. Perhaps next spring, it could be yuh birthday present.'

'Oh my God, really!'

Ezee raised an eyebrow and grinned. 'Yuh understand mi nuh promising nuttin'. But . . . we'll see.'

'That's yuh get-out clause innit,' Audrey muttered. 'Wah yuh know about promises?'

Ezee reached over and took Audrey's hand. 'I know mi promised never to leave yuh.'

Audrey went to tug her hand away but Ezee held on, clasping it between both of his large palms.

'Maybe one of these days mi will end up leaving yuh,' she said. Her voice was weary.

Ezee kissed her hand. I averted my eyes, hating to see my father pandering to her sulky ways. I was relieved when Audrey got up and fetched him another beer from the fridge.

At 8 p.m., Ezee offered to drive me home. His latest BMW was parked directly outside his house, but he gestured for me to follow him towards a tatty-looking Triumph Stag.

'Mi know Audrey have her moods, but yuh must know that's because she jealous of yuh. Jealousy is the most unattractive trait a woman can have, and nuttin' will turn man against yuh quicker than if yuh jealous of him and him pickney. Mi sorry to say, but that was what mash up yuh muddah and mi. Never succumb to jealousy, Daphne, it only cause destruction and hurt.'

I'd never thought that Audrey, with her nice house, her nice holidays, her nice hair and fine complexion could ever be jealous of me. It made me glad. I was also thrilled by the way Ezee had spoken to me. He had never been so open before. He wanted me to be a part of his life – whether his common-law wife liked it or not. I settled myself in the front passenger seat. Ezee lit a cigarette and I opened the dashboard ashtray for him.

'T'ank yuh darlin'. I'm going down to Brighton at the end ah next month, to do a part exchange on this. Yuh want to come? We can mek it a likkle day trip.'

I couldn't believe my ears. This was the first time Ezee had ever asked me to meet up with him, and not just that – we'd be spending the day together.

'I'd love to!'

'Good. Yuh can bring yuh lanky boyfriend too.'

'He's not my boyfriend.'

Ezee winked at me. 'Oh and before mi forget. Here . . . ' He handed me two tenners and a fiver. 'Get yuself somet'ing nice.'

On the drive home I kept glancing across at Ezee, admiring how he reclined in his seat, driving with one hand on the steering wheel. I sat drinking in his handsome profile, feeling too happy to speak.

13

It was Monday, the first day of the new school year, and Connie and I were walking along Jamaica Road. The 141 arrived at the bus stop and among the students who got off was Chantelle Williams. She was wearing black-lace tights beneath a short pencil skirt, with a shiny-satin blouse tucked into the waistband; her bone-straight hair was slicked back and silky smooth. Chantelle gave Connie the side-eye and whispered to her mates, Precious Arnold and Marlene Drake; then they all looked him up and down. Connie took his hands out of his pockets and straightened up, his pace slowing to a saunter as we passed by.

'My cousin Marcia said the lower sixth is a bit of a doss, but I reckon it will fly by,' I said, making my voice as loud and breezy as I could. 'This time next year we'll be prepping for the A-level mocks and then it'll be the real thing. I hear most university English courses won't even look at you without an A and two Bs.'

'Sure. But wi nuh need to stress this year,' said Connie, glancing back over his shoulder at the girls. 'Wi need to make time for some fun as well.'

I tutted. We hadn't even arrived yet and he was already losing focus. I rolled my eyes, but maybe Connie had a point – maybe I should be a little less uptight. I decided to hold my tongue.

We continued towards the gates, Connie tapping fists with his bredren and nodding greetings to the white boys he was friendly with. Mark Barrett was leaning against the wall by the entrance, sharing a fag with Craig and Ted. Since last Friday, he'd kept popping into my head; I was bothered by him coming back to the estate, playing football with Connie, complimenting my hair. So arrogant. Still, Mark wasn't any sort of acquaintance. I wasn't about to let on to him. I set my face to neutral. Yet as we drew nearer I tripped on a loose paving, lurching forward. Luckily Connie caught my elbow, steadying me. I glanced over in Mark's direction, conscious that he might have seen. He was pulling on his ciggie, looking at me. Connie didn't acknowledge Mark at all.

'Whapp'm, Con!' Errol Morris had spotted us, came up and slapped Connie on the shoulder. He was with one of Connie's other good friends, Omar Walker.

'I got the new Kurtis Blow album on Saturday. Here, I taped it for you,' said Omar.

'Wicked! T'anks mon.'

Errol leaned into Connie. 'I've just seen Chantelle Williams. Bwoy, she's looking fine . . . '

The three of them laughed and strode on ahead. I followed but I couldn't help peering over my shoulder. Mark was still looking in our direction. Looking at me.

The time passed quickly and soon we were three weeks into the new term. I'd volunteered to help out in the library; it would look good on future university applications. Also, with Connie playing football and no one else to hang out with, it had become my routine to spend almost every break time there anyway, and as a sixth-former I was finally allowed to borrow from the senior's section. There, among D. H. Lawrence, Thomas Hardy and Virginia Woolf, were writers I'd never heard of before: Nella Larsen and Ntozake Shange, Joan Riley and Toni Morrison, to name only a few. That first day, I took home *The Unbelonging* and read it in one sitting. The main character, Hyacinth, reminded me of Mum, how she still called Jamaica home, even after all these years. I was moved to tears and burned with anger at the way Hyacinth was treated. It made me think of all the racism Mum had endured since she'd arrived here. When she slept, exhausted after a long shift, did her dreams take her back to the garden at 1½ Spring View? I might have asked her, had she not started nagging me about some chores or other.

After *The Unbelonging* I was eager for more; *Sula*, *Passing* and *Sassafrass, Cypress & Indigo* were among the many books I had devoured in the last fortnight. I saw myself in these stories. It was thrilling. I wanted to thrust these books into my classmates' hands, but didn't want to come on too strong. So, instead I set about rearranging the library shelves, putting books by the likes of Buchi Emecheta, Alice Walker and others, with their covers facing outwards. Or displaying them in prominent positions, like the table beside the issue desk. These novels had made me feel visible, maybe they would speak to other young women like me. In the past, immersing myself in books had always been an escape, a good way to conceal the fact I didn't really fit in; I wasn't reading these books in order to run away from the world, but to be more in it.

It was Friday morning and I had a free period. I sat in one

of the easy chairs reading *The Women of Brewster Place*, when I sensed a body coming toward me.

'Hey Daphne, how's it going? Yuh good?'

I looked up from my book and into cat-like eyes, heavy with mascara and liquid liner. Chantelle Williams was in my history class but had never spoken to me directly, although once she'd clocked my 'Free Nelson Mandela' badge, and had given me a Black Power salute. She and her besties, Precious and Marlene, slipped from South London slang to patwah with ease. They were vivacious, loud, sexy and cool; and commanded the attention of most of the boys in the sixth form. And now Chantelle was coming to speak to me. I was determined to make myself easy-going and sociable.

'Yeah, thanks. Just ... chilling. You good?'

'Feelin' irie. I was hoping to run into you. I wanted to ask about Connie; is he your fella? It's just that I see you with him sometimes. I thought you might be—'

'No!'

Chantelle raised an eyebrow at my fast reply. I faked a smile.

'We're just friends.'

'Good. Then, I beg you give him this note. I was going to get one of my girls to do it, but seein' as you know him, it would be better coming from you.'

Chantelle handed me a peach-coloured envelope with Connie's name written in loopy blue biro. Precious and Marlene came bursting into the library.

'Cheers Daphne, likkle more. Hail up sistren, unnu reach at last!'

Chantelle sashayed away to join her mates, leaving me alone, feeling vexed and small. The envelope wreaked of perfume.

I noticed the flap had merely been tucked into the back; it was unsealed. I glanced across to the magazine racks where Chantelle had picked up the newest issue of *Smash Hits*. She and her mates were busy rapping 'White Lines'. I slid the note from the envelope, carefully concealing it in the leaves of my book. The more I read, the more incensed I became.

'Are you gonna come and watch the match later?'

Connie and I were sitting outside the chippy on the High Street having lunch.

'Why? Haven't you already got enough cheerleaders?'

Connie frowned. 'Yuh in a mood about somet'ing?'

I reached into the side pocket of my bag and handed him the note. 'Here. It's from that girl, Chantelle.'

He sniffed the envelope. 'Poison.'

'Typical! Everyone is wearing that scent,' I said.

Connie pulled out the letter and began reading it.

He glanced at me, then slid the letter inside his blazer and looked down. Was it to hide embarrassment? No, most probably it was elation.

'I didn't know you knew her.'

'She and her gyaldem are into rap too. Her place has become a bit of a hangout, after school as her muddah work shifts at some nursing home.'

'So, how long have you been . . . seeing each other?'

'I'm not seeing her. Not really. It's casual.'

'From what I hear she might want to make things official.'

Connie's neutral expression dissolved. 'Yuh read mi letter?'

'No! I just heard her going on about you to her mates. It explains why I've not seen you around much.'

Connie didn't respond; he just sat there eating his chips, probably lost in some reverie about stupid Chantelle and her *longing to kiss his eyelids.*

'So, d'you like her then or what?'

'Yeah. She's cool.'

Suddenly, the chips turned into a bland mush on my tongue. 'She's prettier than that girl Barbara or Sandra or whatever her name was . . .'

'I like girls, I ain't gonna lie. And yeah I think Chantelle is pretty.' Connie looked at me. 'Although I'd say that yuh as pretty as she.'

'Yeah, right . . .'

'Why yuh never believe me when I say these things?'

'It's what you say to all the girls,' I said, hearing the acid in my voice. Connie heard it too.

'Mi nuh saying it because mi say it to others girls. Mi saying it cos it's true. I always t'ought so.' I looked at him. 'It's just that. Yuh know. We're friends innit. Best friends. Why risk spoiling that?'

I got up and dumped my chips in the bin. 'Why, indeed.'

On the way back to school, I reminded myself of Ezee's warning. How unattractive a jealous woman was, how nothing would turn a man against you quicker than jealousy. I didn't think of Connie and Chantelle getting off with each other, or even just kissing. I wondered what they talked about. Would he have told *her* about his life back home in Jamaica? His dreams of returning one day? Might he have even told her about Tobias and why he hated being at home? Or that he and Althea nuh land? But even that would be over soon, as Tobias had sent in their papers. They would get an initial acknowledgement in a couple of weeks and could get their stay by the end of the year. Be that as it may, I felt certain that Connie wouldn't have told Chantelle; that was *our* secret. Because I was still his best friend.

At half-three the corridors were thronged with students shouting, laughing and making plans for the weekend; by quarter-to-four the sounds had faded. I wouldn't go and watch the football match but I was in no hurry to go home; I knew the school library would stay open for another hour. Light flooded in through the large windows on the far end of the stacks. Although it was almost the end of September, the weather was still fine and bright. Single wooden desks were shoved up against the wall at the side of the library. 'SILENT STUDY ONLY' was printed on cards, BluTacked beside each one. I picked up the local paper and took a seat, scanning the headlines.

UNEMPLOYMENT UP 7.6% IN SOUTH LONDON: 83,000 ON THE DOLE

PETITION TO SAVE THE 189 BUS ROUTE GATHERS 1,000 SIGNATURES

RATE PAYERS TO FOOT THE BILL FOR REMOVAL OF RACIST STICKERS

My attention was snagged by the last article about the British National Party stickers that were being plastered around the neighbourhood. A load of them had appeared on the lampposts and road signs in the streets around our school, ever since the riots in Handsworth. For the last fortnight, the national press had run articles about 'inner-city anarchy' and 'arsonist terror' along with photographs of young Black men armed with Molotov cocktails.

Four years ago, the Government commissioned Lord Scarman to hold an enquiry into the Brixton riots; they wanted him to find reasons for the 'serious disorder' and to make recommendations so it wouldn't happen again. The Scarman report talked about the abuse of 'stop and search', and admitted that the Black community felt alienated from British society. The MP Enoch Powell argued that the Black community felt alienated because it was alien, and many people agreed with him. Little had changed for Black people in the four years since the Scarman report was published, yet following the riots in Handsworth, Enoch Powell renewed his call for repatriation; the stickers appeared after that. We'd been warned not to touch them, as razor blades had been attached to the underside.

I'd begun reading the article when Mr Jones walked into the library, his booming voice cutting through the silence.

' . . . you may well be here voluntarily, but we expect all of the students who signed up to stay on in this sixth form to give a hundred per cent commitment to their studies. So far you are falling well short, my lad. You're wasting your time and ours.'

I looked up, interested to see who would emerge from be-tween the stacks, and came face-to-face with Mark. At first he started, then tucked his hands in the pockets of his Sergio Tacchini tracksuit jacket and strode, cool and casual, towards one of the desks.

The teacher placed two textbooks down. 'According to Ms

Binney, you've missed three assignments. So you will sit here until you've drafted an essay on—' he scanned the pages of a past exam paper, 'number seven: The macroeconomic causes of poverty in the UK.'

Mark sat back in his chair, hard-faced.

Mr Jones's tone softened. 'Nobody wants to throw you off the course. God knows the dole queues are long enough. This is for your own good. D'you understand?'

'Yes, sir.'

'Good. If you sit here in silence and focus for the next sixty minutes, you'll have it done. Then everyone's happy.'

I watched Mr Jones leave the library, then Mark turned to me.

'Don't say hello or nothing.'

'All right, I won't,' I said, staring at the *News in Brief* and not taking in a word.

'Still reading the newspapers in your spare time? You're such a bloody boffin.'

I wanted to laugh. Such a benign insult, considering the words I knew tripped easily off his tongue.

'I like to know what's happening in the world. I'd rather be a boffin than go around knowing . . . fuck all.'

He grinned. 'That ain't very friendly.'

I shrugged, feeling bold. 'We ain't friends.'

I turned the page, even though I hadn't read it. I could just get up and leave. But something pinned me to my seat.

'What subjects are you doing?' he asked.

'English, history and German. You're doing economics?'

'You surprised? Did you think I'd be on some Youth Training Scheme?'

'I didn't give it any thought at all. How is it? Economics?'

'Boring, but it beats signing on. Geography's better. Ted and Craig are doing retakes.'

Silence.

'You in't watching your boyfriend play football then?'

'Obviously not, as I'm here. And actually he isn't my boyfriend. You not playing in the match then?'

'Obviously not, as I'm here.' Soft creases appeared around his mouth. 'I should be playing, but that Welsh arsehole left me off the team and marched me up here.'

'You got something against the Welsh?' My tone was curt.

'No, just arseholes.' His smile grew. 'Still, they should win easily against Saint Nicks. He's a good player your mate. He's *almost* as good as me.'

'You can see the football pitch from here, you know,' I said. 'From the reference section.'

'How d'you know?'

Now I smiled. 'I'm a *boffin* in't I? I come here a lot.'

Mark stood up. 'Show us then.'

I led him through the stillness of the library, hearing his soft tread behind me, sensing his eyes as they moved from my neck, down the curve of my spine to my backside. A cool sensation prickled my skin, making the hair on my arms bristle. In the narrow room where the *Encyclopaedia Britannica* were shelved, we stood at the window, barely three feet apart, gazing at a far-off field where indistinguishable dots in red bibs were playing against other dots dressed in blue. Out of the corner of my eye, I watched Mark angle his body towards me. I realised that I was holding my breath.

'So all this time I thought you were up here studying, when actually you were watching me play.'

I exhaled, chuckling softly. 'God, you don't half fancy yourself.'

I could feel the heat of his stare. My heart was hammering against my chest, but I kept my eyes on the football pitch.

'Nah . . . you know that I fancy you.'

I couldn't keep looking out of the window, it was useless to even try. My eyes grazed Mark's hands resting on the sill. I wondered what it would feel like when we touched. Slowly, I turned to face him.

'Come here,' he whispered.

'No, you come here.'

I couldn't believe what I'd said, but Mark stepped forward, reaching for me, finding my waist. I wrapped my arms over his shoulders, like I'd seen other girls do. His lips were soft against mine. I watched his eyes close, then I closed mine. I felt his tongue gently move into my mouth and I felt my jaw slacken, electrified by my first proper kiss. His hands settled on the base of my spine for a moment, before sliding down until they were resting on my backside, then he was kissing my neck. His hair had a fresh smell of citrus and honey, unreal but pleasing and heady. His hand moved up, caressing my side, finding my breast, his fingers gently tugging at the buttons of my blouse. My hand burrowed beneath the waistband of his tracksuit top, searching for his skin. Suddenly, I could hear the library trolley's squeaky wheels. Mr Stoddart, the librarian, was re-shelving books. I opened my eyes, and the spell was broken.

'What?'

I nodded towards the main library.

'Oh. Yeah. Right.'

Mark stepped back. I straightened my blouse.

'I'm coming down the estate next Saturday, visiting me nana. D'you wanna meet up with me?'

'What? I mean . . . I dunno. This is pretty weird, right?'

He shrugged. 'What's weird about it?'

I let out a short laugh. 'Come on! What d'you think your mates would say if they saw us just then. Or even standing here talking like we are now?'

His scowl appeared. 'What would your lot say?'

'Well, it's not like *my lot* go around plastering the streets with stickers. Like you and your brother and all your mates.'

'That weren't me.'

'Really! Or just not that time?'

He nodded. 'Fair play. I've done things, said things, I ain't proud of.' He broke off to look out the window. 'Look, I like you all right? And you like me an' all. Don't you?'

The back of his hand brushed against mine. My shoulders relaxed. I took a step towards him, pressing my lips against his. I allowed my tongue to roam, tracing the outline of his mouth and tasting cigarettes and Juicy Fruit. There was that sound of the library trolley again. It was getting closer. I broke off from kissing.

'Quick, hide,' I said, ducking behind a shelf just as Mr Stoddart turned the corner.

'What are you doing in here?'

Mark cleared his throat. 'Watching the football, sir.'

'Mr Jones told you to stay put,' said Mr Stoddart.

'Actually, he said I should stay silent. He didn't say nothing about staying put.'

'I'll have none of that cheek. Get yourself back to that desk. In fact, as you can't be trusted, I shall escort you myself.'

Mark flashed a grin at me before following Mr Stoddart back to the main library. I sneaked out of the reference room, wiping my mouth with the back of my hand, enjoying how my fingers tingled.

The fine weather had brought a laid-back vibe to the estate. There were people chilling on the communal landings, soaking up the September evening. I'd walked home in a daze, replaying what happened in the library with Mark. Did he really like me or was this some elabourate hoax? It felt real. I went back to relishing the encounter and wondering if he was thinking about me too. A couple of boys were practising wheelies around the shopping precinct and a group of men had already assembled outside the British Sailor, even though the pub wasn't due to open for another hour. The sound of an argument cut through the sunshine. Tobias stormed out of the minimarket carrying a plastic carrier bag in each hand, both of them bulging with shopping.

'Ten p for a fucking plastic bag!' he shouted.

I skulked behind a community information board, trying not to be noticed. 'Fucking daylight robbery. No wonder Idi Amin run unnu backside from Uganda, bloodsuckers ah get rich off the backs of Black people.'

Althea emerged, laden with another bag of shopping, Kallai trailing behind her. Tobias was muttering to himself and then he rounded on Althea.

'And you! Yuh just hand up mi hard-earn money, when we

could get all of this cheaper from the supermarket. Yuh t'ink
money grow pan tree?'

'Wah yuh expect mi fi do?' Althea's voice was more stri-
dent than I'd ever heard. 'How mi fi go ah Co-op or the
market street to buy food when mi have clients all day today
and all tomorrow. Yuh forget mi work too? It nuh just yuh
money wi ah spend!'

Tobias kissed his teeth and stomped on ahead. After five
or six steps the handle of one of his carriers gave way. The
bag slipped from his grasp, spilling its contents onto the pavement. I ducked into the launderette and watched through the
window, waiting for them to move on.

'Mi did tell yuh to bring the strong bags from home but
yuh never bother. Instead, yuh let the damn coolie man
charge me ten p for this rubbish!' He picked up one of the
cans that had fallen on the ground and flung it at Althea,
missing her head by inches. The BMX boys ceased their antics
and watched, mute, while Tobias continued flinging groceries.
Tins of baked beans and packets of saltfish flew past his wife,
or landed close to her feet.

'Yuh beg mi to come shopping with yuh because yuh
fucking lazy-arse son nuh around to help with the chores!
Where him deh?'

I was frozen, disbelieving. The men outside the pub stopped
their chat. Kallai crouched behind his mother and began to
cry. Althea seemed to finally come to herself. She stooped and
slowly began to pick up the cans and packets, placing them in
her own, already bulging carrier bag. Tobias marched away,
leaving the bag on the ground where it fell. Shamefaced, I
walked over to Althea, picking up groceries as I went.

'Oh. T'ank yuh, Daphne.' Althea affected a cheery tone, but her hands were shaking.

'Are you all right?'

'Yes, of course. It nuh nuttin'.'

I recalled how Connie would often say the exact same thing. 'I'll get the other bag and help you carry it back,' I said.

'No, mi can manage. Come Kallai, stop crying now and help with dis.'

Kallai wiped his eyes with his sleeve.

'Althea, I'm not trying to be nosy or anything, but will you be all right . . . when you get home I mean?'

She was about to say something, but then her gaze slid past me. I looked over my shoulder and saw Connie standing outside Ladbrokes. He had seen it all. Althea took a step towards him but Connie was shaking his head and backing away. Althea called out to him but Connie turned and fled.

Just after six, there was a knock at the door. I opened it and found Connie on the landing. I snibbed the latch and stepped outside. We leaned against the railings, our arms resting against the cool metal crossbar.

'Where have you been?'

'I walk t'rough the estate till mi reach the river. Then I just sat there.'

I waited for Connie to say something else but he remained silent.

'Althea was shaking. There's no way Tobias can pass that off as an ordinary row – not after going off on one like that. And in public, where people could see!'

'So him mask slip, but what difference it make if people

see? Nobody step in. All them big men ah stand up outside the pub, dem just watch! And me. I just stood there too.'

'I didn't do anything neither. It's not only up to you to protect your mum.'

'Then who will? The police?' Connie looked away. His hands were clasped together, the fingers tightly interlaced. 'The thing is, Daphne, I saw what was happening and I couldn't move. I was frightened. Now I feel so shame.'

'Bloody hell Connie, I know the licks that man has given you over the years. None of this is your fault! Let's talk to Mum about it, Grandma too. Maybe we could call Valerie as well. She hates Tobias. If we get all Althea's friends together then we could figure something out. Okay, so you can't go to the police, but there must be something we can do . . . '

Connie continued to look out over the estate rather than at me.

'What yuh don't understand Daphne, what I can't understand, is that she loves him. Plus, Althea come here for a better life. She's too close to getting all that to walk away now. Three days ago, we get an acknowledgement from the Home Office, confirming Althea's application. In a few months' time she'll get her stay, then mi can get mine too. Then I can leave, get mi own place, or better still, go home to Jamaica. Tobias won't be able to control me anymore. But till then . . . '

Connie weakened. I stretched my arm over his shoulder, inhaling the cocoa butter on his skin. My mind flitted to Mark, and was held for a moment by the memory of having been so close to him that I'd smelled that unfamiliar, yet sweet scent of his hair. I pushed the thoughts away.

'Listen. Stay here with us for as long as you like. I'll talk to

Mum, she'll understand. I'm supposed to be going to Brighton tomorrow. You could come too. Don't go back there.'

'Yuh make it sound easy.'

'Wi run t'ings, t'ings nuh run wi,' I said, with a lightness I didn't feel.

Connie put on a grin. 'Yuh still have the worse Jamaican accent mi ever hear.'

Miss Gladys was sitting at the kitchen table, pouring Carnation into her coffee cup. She had come over to discuss plans for the 'likkle party' next Saturday, to celebrate Mum's fortieth birthday. Mum held up a compact and was applying lipstick, her hair was out and she'd tonged the ends so they curled up. She never usually put this much effort into her appearance when she met up with work friends. She looked nice. I gestured Connie towards the remaining seat at the table, while I took a jug of sorrel from the fridge.

'Long time since mi see yuh young man. How yuh keep-ing?' asked Miss Gladys.

'Good, thanks.'

My Grandma observed Connie with serious eyes, but smiled warmly. 'Glad to hear it. Now, Daphne, mi hear yuh father teking yuh on a day trip tomorrow. What time him picking you up?'

'I'm meeting him outside East India House at nine.'

Mum tutted. 'Mi nuh know why him can't collect yuh where yuh actually live.'

'He said he'd get lost if he had to fiddle through the estate. Don't be so down on him.'

The letterbox banged twice.

'Mi nuh down on him,' said Mum, squeezing past Connie on her way to the front door. 'Mi just pointing out how him stay.'

From the kitchen, we heard Mum say, 'Oh hello, Althea. Yuh like to come in? Connie's here too.'

'Mi guess this is where him deh. In future, me'd prefer it if yuh send him home rather than let him to cotch here day and night. Connie have t'ings to do at home and him never there to help mi. Yuh letting him turn him back on his responsibilities.'

I hadn't heard this spikiness from Althea before. Connie sighed at the ceiling.

'Wah yuh ah talk about Althea? Connie nuh come by for weeks now.' Mum was trying to stay calm, but her accent was starting to poke through. 'And I wouldn't know what responsibilites you mean. Cha! Yuh ah gwaan like him is a man when him just a yout'.'

'Nuh tell me how fi raise my bwoy. A yout' need to learn respect. He wouldn't run away from his obligations if he never have dis place to run to all the time. To yuh open door, yuh open larder and most probably yuh dawta's open legs!'

The chair scraped the lino as Connie sprang up. Miss Gladys and I hurried after him as he marched into the hallway.

'That's enough!' he said, pushing past Mum and stepping onto the landing. 'Nuh talk 'bout Daphne that way! And nuh come around Miss Alma house and bawl at her. Yuh act just like him, is him send yuh here? After him shame yuh pan the street earlier.'

'Yuh facety wretch!'

The slap was swift and precise. Connie absorbed the blow, but I saw his fist clench.

'Stop this foolishness now!' Miss Gladys's voice ricocheted along the landing.

She stepped outside, putting herself between Connie and Althea; Mum followed her, the two of them forming a barrier of wide hips and big bosoms against Althea's tall but skinny frame. The neighbours were peeking through curtains, others had come out on their doorsteps to get a better view. The severe expression on Althea's face melted.

'Yuh my boy. I love yuh. I need yuh. Please nuh run from mi.'

'Come inside and let's sort dis out properly, in private,' said Miss Gladys, putting her arm around Althea's slender waist and guiding her inside. Her shoulders hunched as she leaned against my grandma's stout body.

Connie and I were sent to the living room, while the big women talked in the kitchen. The news was on; a Black pastor in Birmingham was being asked whether the police force's campaign to recruit more Black officers would help ease racial tensions. I wondered aloud what our mothers were talking about in the kitchen, but Connie just shrugged. I wanted to say something wise and helpful, like characters in novels did, but couldn't think of anything. Eventually, the living room door opened and Althea entered, offering us a nervous smile. She told me I was wanted in the kitchen. When I left the room, Althea shut the door tight behind me.

In the kitchen, Mum was putting away a quarter bottle of Wray & Nephew.

'Mi t'ink it's best if Connie nuh sleep here overnight anymore. It's what him stepfather want, and it look like what works for him is best for dem all.'

'But, I was going to ask you if he could stay with us. He's so unhappy at their place, and did Althea tell you what Tobias did down at the shopping precinct? We should be getting her to leave him too if you ask me.'

'It's none of our business. Nuh trouble trouble till trouble trouble yuh!'

'Well Alma, mi agree with Daphne. Yuh know as well as I do that wi shouldn't let neither one of dem go back to dat deh place.'

'Mamma, there's nothing we can do.' Mum lowered her voice. 'One minute she tell us how Tobias treat her, then in the next minute she say how him regret what him did. And pride himself on dem being a respectable family—'

'—respectable mi back foot! Mi known men like him. He just want dem under his control.'

There was a tap on the kitchen door before Althea entered.

'We're going now. T'anks for yuh ... understanding. Daphne, I just want to apologise. What mi say before. It was ugly.'

'It's okay. You were angry,' I said. 'My dad's taking me to Brighton tomorrow. Can Connie come too? It's a really fun place to let off steam.'

'Mi nuh know ...' said Althea.

'Please, I'd really like him to. I'll be outside East India House at nine,' I said, talking to Althea but looking at Connie.

'We'll see,' he said.

14

'I wasn't expecting Calabash Bay or nothing, but I thought there would at least be some sand!'

Connie kicked up the shingle with the toe of his trainers as he crunched along Brighton Beach, sending a cascade of pebbles down to the shoreline. Tobias had apparently been so full of remorse on Friday night that Althea was able to persuade him to let Connie come on the trip. I trudged along the beach beside him. I was disappointed too. I looked out at the forlorn West Pier, still awaiting restoration to former glory. It was hard to imagine its abandoned walkways and the dour, deserted ballroom ever being a fun place to hang out. The shops along the promenade looked faded and weary. The Grand Hotel still had part of its front blown off after the IRA bomb attack; the sight of it made me shudder. I'd been looking forward to this day trip, and none of it was as I had imagined. But the biggest letdown was the fact that Ezee had dropped us off, then disappeared.

That morning, he'd picked us up as arranged on the edge of the estate. I heard the swing of the Skatalites horn section before the car turned the corner, and when the Triumph Stag came into view I saw that it had been resprayed; the canary yellow finish gleamed in the morning sunshine and I felt my chest swell. We fiddled through South London with the sunroof down, briefly popping up in Brixton as we followed the A23 to the motorway. Ezee, in his black wraparound sunglasses, had one hand on the steering wheel, while the other was holding a cigarette. But when we arrived in Brighton, he left us at the seafront.

'Unnu nuh need me. Go amuse yuself, while mi go take care of business.'

'But I thought I'd be spending the day with you.'

'Yuh nuh want fi stand up in a garage while mi haggle over money. Plus if it nuh work out there's another dealer mi could go see. Here tek dis,' he'd said, handing me two tenners. 'Go have some fun. Meet mi back here at half-four.'

His voice was laid-back and his words were so reasonable I had no way of protesting without looking like a baby. But I was sure he'd said it was supposed to be a day trip. Our day trip. I'd imagined us shopping on the Lanes and visiting the Royal Pavillion. Doing whatever it was dads did with their teenage daughters. Would Ezee have left me here alone if Connie hadn't come? Maybe it had been a mistake to invite him.

A couple of white-haired ladies were wading into the greeny-blue sea. As the cold water reached their waists, their high-pitched gasps were carried on the breeze, but they urged each other on. I wondered if they were day-trippers too, determined to enjoy themselves.

'Dem must want frostbite,' Connie remarked.

'I've never swum in the sea before. I should have brought a cossie.'

The bustier of the two women plunged in, crying out again,

but laughing too. Her friend followed and soon both women were off, swimming elegant breaststrokes, their heads aloft like swans. I took off my sandals; there was the odd sharp pebble but mostly the stones moulded around my bare soles.

'I'm going for a paddle. Coming?'

'Yuh must be mad!'

I wobbled off, leaving my bag and Connie behind. I paused at the water's edge, waiting for the first wave, and let out a yelp when the cold water enveloped my toes. I felt my feet sink a little deeper as the current shifted the pebbles before receding. I was here at the seaside. I would enjoy this day out – and I'd never tell Mum that Ezee abandoned me. I waded out further, bracing myself against the chill, the waves reaching as high as my knees. When I looked back, I saw that Connie had taken off his trainers and turned up his jeans; he was inspecting the water as it rolled onto the shore. Ezee may have gone, but I still had Connie. It was rare these days to have him to myself.

He called out to me, 'Yuh know close up this water looks brown.'

'That's just because of the stones; c'mon, it's not that cold.'

He took a step forward, then he jumped backwards. 'Ahh – yuh lie. It's bloody freezing!'

I threw my head back and cackled. 'The look on your face was priceless.'

'Well then let me see the look on yuh face when all yuh clothes wet up with cold water ... '

He charged at me, kicking up seawater. I shrieked with alarm, and glee.

*

We shared the small towel I'd brought and lazed on the beach, waiting for the sun's rays to dry our damp clothes. After a while, I rolled onto my front, propping myself on my elbows. Connie's shirt got soaked, so he lay in his vest, the back of his head resting in his hands; with elbows bent, the strip of muscle in his biceps expanded. He had his eyes closed and there was a half-smile on his face. He looked more relaxed than I'd seen him in ages. My gaze lingered over his mouth and I wondered what it would feel like to kiss him. How different would it feel to kissing Mark? Sensing my stare, Connie opened his eyes. I felt my breath catch. I was half convinced that he'd heard my thoughts.

'Erm ... I'm dry now,' I stammered. 'And I'm starving. Let's go and get fish and chips.'

We spent the rest of the afternoon at the Palace Pier on fairground rides that flung us about so it felt that we were flying above the sea, hanging around the arcades playing *Space Invaders* and losing more money than we won on the penny pushers. It felt like those days when we were young, hanging out in the park across the road from 59 Lime Grove; just me and him, happy in our world. After four, we headed back along the seafront, to the square where we were to meet Ezee. Connie was carrying a big stick of pink rock he had bought for Kallai.

'Thanks for today. This was really and truly the best way mi could have spend mi last Saturday of freedom. After this mi will have to stay home more, so Tobias can't find fault. I have no idea how mi gonna break it to Chantelle.'

It was the first time he'd mentioned her all day. I flicked an imaginary wasp from my arm. 'I suppose Althea doesn't know about Chantelle. I mean, if she thought you'd been staying over at my house for the past few weeks ... '

'She know now.'

Connie's tone was dry. I remembered Althea's apology.

'What did she say?'

'At first she say mi too young and mi nuh responsible yet and all of that. But then she relax. She tell mi to make sure mi treat mi girlfriend with respect and that I must buy condoms, cos she nuh ready to be Granny Althea yet.'

'She's got a point,' I said, kicking an empty Coke can into the gutter.

'Daphne. We are okay now, aren't we?'

'Yeah. Sure we are Connie. We're friends.' I pulled my mouth into a smile; I didn't care that he could see it was false. 'I've got some news of my own, as it goes. Yesterday, Mark Barrett snogged me in the library.'

Connie let out a one-syllable laugh that sounded more like a cry. 'What? Yuh joking! Him na'eve like Black people.'

'Well he seems to like me.'

'And yuh only just ah tell me now? Baxide! That is proper madness. What yuh do after him kiss yuh?'

'Why d'you wanna know? I don't recall asking you for details about Chantelle.'

'What? Yuh mean ... Yuh like him?'

Connie stopped smiling.

'I've known him for a long time. I don't think he's like the others.'

Connie made a humming sound under his breath. I suddenly felt foolish and exposed.

'I never say anything about who you get off with so don't go judging me! And don't go telling anyone neither.'

Connie kissed his teeth. 'Please! Nobody would believe me. Mi cyaah believe it miself.'

He pushed ahead and I let him go, stubbornly sticking to my own pace.

Ezee had closed the roof of the Triumph Stag and was perched slantways on the bonnet, smoking.

'So, you didn't do your deal then? With the car?' I asked, trying not to sound sulky even though I was still a little pissed off with him for leaving me earlier.

'Nah . . . it never work out. But mi catch up with a friend mi have down here, so it wasn't all a waste of time,' he said, tossing the cigarette butt onto the road.

'That's okay then,' I said with a touch of sarcasm so slight that Ezee didn't appear to notice.

I settled down in the front seat; there was a faint smell of perfume. I sniffed again, slowly recognising the rich, heavy fragrance. Poison.

I looked at Ezee, but he was focusing on the road. Questions swamped my mind. I opened my mouth, but I couldn't make myself speak. Instead, I rolled the window down; once we got going the smell would surely fade. Ezee steered his car through the Brighton streets and we were soon on the motorway heading to South London, but the scent lingered. Neither Ezee nor Connie seemed to notice it. Perhaps because it was a fragrance they both liked. I found it cloying and heavy. I sat there unable to stop myself stewing over the questions I wanted to put to Ezee, but was too afraid to ask: Who was this friend? Why had he really invited me to Brighton? Had it been so he could spend the day with her, rather than with me?

'Put some music on for mi darlin'.'

I switched on the radio and got static, so turned the dial, ears pinned back for a station I recognised. The aerial tuned in halfway through a news bulletin:

'Scotland Yard have issued a statement on the accidental shooting at a house in Normandy Road this morning. Members of the press were told that at 7 a.m. armed police officers arrived with a warrant to search the premises. While they were there, a woman was accidentally shot by a police officer. She was immediately taken to St Thomas's Hospital ...'

The commentary turned into hiss as the station went out of range.

'Yuh nah go get any decent stations out here. Put on one of the cassettes mi have deh,' said Ezee.

He lit another cigarette and out of habit I pulled open the dashboard ashtray for him. A slim white cigarette butt with a dark purple stain around it protruded from the mass of brown fag ends. I looked at Ezee. He briefly glanced down, tapping ash from the end of his cigarette. Then his gaze moved up to me, and a wry smile formed on his face.

'I'm gonna be busy for the next few weeks now so mi nuh know when next mi go see yuh. But I'll call. Okay babylove?'

He was still smiling, coercing me into cheeriness. Mum's words wormed their way into my head, 'Ezee by name, easy by nature.' I looked away, grabbing a tape and thrusting it into the cassette deck. While Marcia Griffiths filled the silence for the next ninety minutes, I stared out of the window, trying to unsee that lipstick-soiled cigarette end.

Connie woke from his doze when two police cars overtook us on Brixton Hill.

'They're in a hurry,' he said, leaning forward so his head was poking between the two front seats.

I sat up straight, craning my neck in order to see where the cops were going. The police cars had already disappeared from view, but I saw the traffic ahead of us beginning to slow down. Vehicles were suddenly switching lanes, creating a din of car horns. A Ford Fiesta nipped out in front of us, almost colliding with the Triumph; Ezee slammed his brakes and I was flung forward, then yanked back by the seat belt.

He leaned out of his window. 'What yuh nuh see me here? Use yuh damn mirror. Cha!'

'There must have been an accident or something,' I said, rubbing my chest.

Ezee wouldn't be soothed. 'Man nearly scratch up mi motor with him ugly car.'

Brixton seemed busier than I thought it would be at this time of day. I'd assumed the shops and the markets would pretty much have closed by now, yet there were still so many people on the street. Older people, as well as men and women in their twenties and thirties; several were standing in groups, they were gesticulating, agitated. My stomach turned as I wondered what they were doing.

'What's going on with all these people?' I said.

'Mi nuh know. And mi nuh know what time mi ah get home this evening,' Ezee grunted.

I glanced at Connie. He seemed unconcerned, more pre-occupied with stretching his long limbs as far as he could in the cramped back seat. I kept looking out of the windows as we pressed through the congestion and finally I could see the reason for the traffic jam – and the Brixtonians' vexation.

Two police cars and two vans were parked in a horizonal line across the street, effectively cordoning off part of Brixton's town centre. I sat up in my seat. Around ten metres further up the road, I could see the backs of two groups of officers clad in dark suits and helmets; they were carrying long plastic shields. One group was slowly proceeding down the left-hand side of the street, while the other moved in from the right. About sixty or maybe seventy metres ahead of them, a car was on fire, grey-black smoke billowing into the sunset sky. The burning vehicle was being used as a barricade by a group of people who were hurling missiles at the riot cops.

'Rhaatid! Ah wah gwaan deh?' breathed Connie.

'Some damn foolishness,' said Ezee. 'Mek wi get out of it quick time.'

Ezee was no longer lounging in his seat; he was sitting up-right, gripping the steering wheel with both hands. He eased into a space on the right and then turned into Coldharbour Lane. There were spectators gathered along the pavement here too. I wound my window down and leaned out as far as the seat belt would allow, hoping that I might catch the gist of what was going on, why the police were out in such force. Somebody shouted, 'bloodclaat murderers!' then another voice – a woman's – cried out, 'fuck Babylon!' We had just passed the railway bridge when the car in front of us, a tan-coloured Ford Cortina, came to an abrupt halt. I looked past the Cortina and saw the reason it had stopped dead. Sixty metres away was a pack of guys, and they were walking towards us. There were around a dozen at the core, striding down the middle of the road, but more people were joining the group every few yards. Their numbers were swelling before my eyes, soon they were thirty or forty strong. They were armed with sticks, bricks, even dustbin lids. Shouting cusses, angry and defiant, their cries mingling with the howl of police sirens that seemed to be coming from all around. Some in the crowd had covered their faces with masks or scarves, many of the others hadn't bothered. I could see how young some of them were – only a year or so older than me! There were even a few white faces among the group. They were a rag-tag bunch, but all of them had come ready for a fight. Anxiety knotted my stomach, yet I couldn't take my eyes off them. I'd never seen anything like it in real life; it felt like a movie.

The noise of the Cortina's engine shook me from my reverie. The car screeched as the driver, a white man, speedily executed a three-point turn.

'Christ!' I cried out, jumping in my seat, as the Cortina swerved wide, almost ploughing into us in its haste to head back up the lane. Aghast, I twisted in my seat and watched the car speed off up the road, just as a bank of flashing blue lights appeared. Police vans were pulling up about twenty metres behind us and officers in riot gear burst onto the street. They looked sinister in their dark helmets, their protective visors obscuring their faces. Quickly, they began spreading themselves across the road, locking their plastic shields together like an armadillo shell.

'Close yuh window and lock the door,' Ezee barked.

I cranked the lever, all the while still gazing at the rear-view mirror, at the police getting into formation. Then my eyes darted to the windscreen, seeing the crowd draw nearer. Suddenly, three youths broke away from the throng. They were running towards us; a lit rag hung from the bottles they clasped. My heart skipped a beat. My first thought was that these missiles were not meant for us, but then, what if they were? These people didn't know us. They might want to do us harm. I covered my face with my hands, yet couldn't resist peeking through the gaps in my fingers. I held my breath as I watched them each hurl their missiles. The bottles flew past our car, there was a shrill sound, the shattering of glass, then three explosions of red and orange as the fire bombs landed behind us, and six metres in front of the cops. I was stunned, transfixed by the glow, more vibrant than you ever saw on TV – but then the miasma of burning and the smell of petrol began leaking through the closed car windows. It all felt unreal. I covered my nose and mouth with the palm of my hand. I could hear Connie coughing behind me. I leaned forward in my set, finding a hanky, which I pressed to my face. I grabbed the towel from my bag and passed it back to Connie. Through the haze of smoke I could see the cops retreating from the flames, shuffling backwards in unison.

Ezee had shifted the gear into reverse, ready to make a getaway like the man in the Cortina, but now tufts of fire licked the tarmac behind us. Ezee calmly moved back to first. He wound his window down and leaned out.

'What are you doing?' I cried.

'Shush, quiet now!'

Keeping his left hand on the steering wheel, he gently eased the car forward, while he held his right hand out of the window, his palm open as though in surrender – or offering a high five.

'It's just me and mi dawta and her friend in the car – we wanna come t'rough . . . we just ah go home,' he shouted.

A guy in navy tracky bottoms and a motorcycle helmet came striding out ahead of the others, wielding a table leg as though it were a baseball bat. He made a beeline for my side of the car. I sat rigid, breathing slowly as he bent down and peered at me through the windscreen. I jumped as he slapped the car bonnet with the palm of his hand, *bang, bang*, before continuing on past us. The others followed, intent in their stride, yet the column parted, allowing us passage.

Ezee wound his window again, and placed both hands on the wheel, breathing steadily. I watched mesmerised as bodies brushed past the car, some so close I could see the wear on their jeans and the scuff marks on their elbows. Ezee kept inching slowly forward and in a few seconds, the crowd had moved on and we were through.

A group of spectators were gathered on the pavement ahead. Ezee drove past them, then pulled up at the curb.

'Stay there,' he said, ducking out of the car.

Through the mirror, I saw him walk back to the onlookers. He was talking to them – no doubt asking what the hell was going on. Then he too stood at the side of the road, eyes glued on the skirmish between the young men and the police.

Quietly, I opened the car door.

'Where yuh going?' asked Connie. 'Didn't yuh daddy just tell yuh to tan?'

I didn't answer him. I couldn't explain. I just needed to get out of the car. I wanted to see what was going on so I stepped out. Now wave upon wave of the youths were hurling their sticks, bricks and bottles. I could hear shouting, cussing and the dull thudding sound of debris hitting the coppers' plastic shields. I moved away from the car, walking, captivated, to the middle of the road where I could better see. The clash was scrappy, yet synchronised. As one surge ebbed away, another rush of bodies came, mounting a fresh assault. The police edged their way along, moving in a steady, coordinated crawl but were held back by the rain of missiles. I could still feel the knot in my belly but it wasn't fear, it was more like suspense. I didn't need to wait long, as some more youths came out of a side street, a few yards away from me. They were pushing a large cylinder dustbin, like the ones at the bottom of our rubbish chutes, only this one was alight. I could feel my pulse racing as they sent it rolling down the road where it tipped off the curb and turned over, the burning contents strewn across the street.

'Daphne! Mi tell you to tan in the car. Yuh muddah would skin mi alive if anyt'ing happened to yuh. Get back there now!'

'What's going on? Why is this happening?'

'The damn police raid a house this morning and shoot an innocent Black woman in her back.'

We got into the car and Ezee set off up the street. I kept looking back until we turned onto Loughborough Junction and then I saw no more. I sat back in the seat, my mind buzzing as it replayed the scenes. I knew we had to come away, but part of me had wanted to stay – not because I wanted to take part, but because I needed to see how it would unfold. I wanted to get home as quickly as possible; it would be all over the TV news, but unlike the other reports I'd seen on the telly, this one would feel different – because this time I'd witnessed the events, firsthand.

*

For once, Ezee followed the maze of roads through the estate that eventually led to Merchant House. He deposited us in the car park outside the flats before screeching off in his car, having muttered something about how late it was and that Audrey would be worried that he'd run off and left her. Mum must have been spying from the window because she came out onto the landing, calling down for Connie and me to come up quickly.

'Have you seen what's happening in Brixton?' I said as I drew near to where she was waiting for us. 'There were police everywhere. We were there at the start of one of the clashes, it was surreal—'

'All right, calm yuself.' Mum cut across me, even more terse than usual.

I felt deflated by her lack of concern. I crossed my arms, pissed off.

'Come, quickly now, you too Connie.'

'Actually Miss Alma mi better get back. Althea must be at home worried.'

'Connie mi telling yuh to come with me. Will unnu just do as mi say?'

Confused, we followed Mum inside. Althea was standing in the hallway. There was a bruise beneath her left eye.

'What did he do to yuh?' Connie spoke in a low growl I'd never heard before.

'Calm yuself. Kallai's in the living room and mi need yuh to stay calm.'

Althea placed a hand on the newel post, as if to steady herself.

'Wi quarrel and him storm off. Mi cyaah take no more. Mi gather up a couple t'ings and walk out. Mi lef' him.'

15

Connie's closest friends knew his stepfather was a bully, but it was never openly discussed. They knew never to expect to be invited to Connie's home nor to telephone the flat after 6 p.m. They also knew that if a fresh bruise appeared then he might not be able to hang out much after school or at weekends. I remembered what Kiplyn had told me years ago, how everyone gets licks, and it wasn't something boys would sit around chatting about. Even so, I was troubled by the fact Connie told no one else at school that Althea had left Tobias. It seemed such a weight to carry alone. But he continued with his usual happy-go-lucky manner. He'd even bunked off a couple of lessons to go over to Chantelle's flat while her mum was working day shifts. It was only when the two of us were alone that he was silent and sullen. He nipped at me when I suggested confiding in Mr Jones, our head of year. These moods vexed me, but I didn't push him to open up, wary that he might just withdraw further. Meanwhile, we all knew that Tobias might turn up at any time. He had already left flowers on the doorstep on two separate occasions, each time with a note asking for forgiveness and begging Althea to come home. She had thrown the first bouquet in the bin, but had hung on to the second bunch, which she took upstairs, avoiding Connie's glower. Mum watched with puckered brows and sighed heavily when Althea left the room. Later at bedtime, when we were alone, I ventured to ask what she was thinking.

'Just that mi lose count of the amount of times mi see women on the ward who say dem bruised cos dem meet in an "accident". Then likkle after this, a man will turn up with cheap flowers, mumbling apologies.'

'If it gets to that stage – being hospitalised – then surely the women don't go back!' I said.

'Huh! Yuh be surprised,' said Mum. 'From now on we nuh open the door without checking first. To him, Althea is a possession. Him all charm now but it won't last.'

I rose at half-seven on Saturday morning, driven out of Mum's bed by her gentle snoring and craving a moment to myself. 'Raspberry Beret' was playing on the radio. I turned the volume up a notch, nodding in time with the beat as I poured hot water into a mug. My schoolbooks were piled on the kitchen table, where I'd been doing my homework for the last six days, since Althea and Kallai now occupied my bedroom. While the tea bag steeped, I picked up *Wuthering Heights* and took out the sheet of lined paper I'd hidden between the leaves. My eyes flickered towards the closed kitchen door before I unfolded the note and re-read it.

Meet me here at 3 p.m., Saturday. Mark.

Below these words was a hand-drawn map with directions to a place called Waterman's Way, which was marked with an asterisk. I'd found the message in my locker on Friday at home time. Mark and I hadn't spoken all week. I'd seen him in the common room at break times, but was careful not to stare. Finding his note I felt a spark of excitement at the thought of kissing and touching him, rather than just looking. I slipped the note back between the pages of the book. Prince's vocals faded out and the broadcast cut to the news headlines.

'The Home Secretary, Douglas Hurd, has rejected a call from the Labour leader, Neil Kinnock, for a public inquiry into the shooting of Mrs Cherry Groce at her home in Brixton. In the past seven days there have been violent clashes between youths and the police in Peckham, South London, and in Toxteth, Liverpool. Community leaders fear that there could be further unrest . . .'

I turned the radio down, yawning as I dropped a dripping teabag in the sink. A shadow blocked the daylight coming into the kitchen window and I looked up. It was the postman pulling the next bundle from his bag. He moved on. I heard our letterbox clang and envelopes fall to the floor. The hot tea burned my top lip so I left it to cool and went to pick up the mail. Connie was sitting on the bottom step putting on his trainers; he started when he saw me.

'Oh. Yuh up early.'

'So are you. Where are you sneaking off to?'

Connie tugged his laces, pulling them tight. 'Ah nuh sneak mi sneaking. I just have t'ings to do.'

'Where are you going?'

'Mi gonna go get our t'ings. If Kallai had more of him toys then maybe he'd settle, then we could all get some sleep ah night-time. Yuh see how Althea stay. It's like she gone into a trance. She barely eat nor speak and nuh set foot outside since she come here. All she do is gaze pan dem blasted flowers he send.'

'Althea's scared. And confused. Tobias is using his charm to woo her back.'

'Yuh t'ink mi nuh know that!'

We both glanced up the stairs. Mum, Althea and Kallai slept on undisturbed.

'Sorry.'

'It's fine,' I muttered.

'No mi sorry, honestly—'

'I told you it's fine.' I crossed my arms, holding my elbows. Connie tried again.

'Yuh know all dem years Althea wait for Tobias to get a divorce, believing that him nuh know where him wife was. Well, it turn out he always knew she was living in Reading. Valerie hear it from a customer who know one of the woman's cousins. This first wife wanted to divorce *him*, but Tobias make her wait just to spite her for leaving him. And all the while, Althea sit in igorance ah wait for him to marry her and make her a citizen.'

I winced at the thought of Tobias controlling the lives of two different grown women, making them abide by his will. Connie continued talking, saying that he'd appreciated everything Mum and I had done for them, but he was the man of the family so had to step up.

'Mi already call Valerie and tell her what happened. She say we must stay with her and Greville. Dem gonna collect us tomorrow morning.' He manufactured a grin. 'And if we ah go live all the way ah Brockley then mi want mi t'ings.'

'If Tobias is there he'll beat the living daylights out of you.'

'He's on the early shift. He should have left for work already, so now is mi best chance.'

I looked in Connie's eyes. It was the first genuine emotion I'd seen from him all week. It was the first time he'd allowed me to be close to him.

'All right, but I'm coming with you.'

Connie was kneeling outside the flat, looking through the letterbox. Satisfied, he slowly closed the cover and slipped his key into the deadlock. The click of the mortice seemed louder than usual. I hooked my thumbs in the front pockets of my jeans, feigning calm, and followed Connie inside.

The venetian blinds hanging over the living room windows were partly open; weak daylight filtered in, casting horizontal shadows across the furniture. Althea's ornaments were all evenly placed on the shelving unit; *Black Hair & Beauty*, *Black Tress* and *Ebony* lay in a fan shape on the coffee table. Everything neat and ordered.

Tobias's bedroom door was ajar. Connie pushed it with his index finger and it creaked open further. The curtains were open, the bed was made, every drawer in the dressing table was closed. Althea had packed in a hurry, yet here, just like the living room, there was no evidence that she had left at all.

Connie left me to pack Althea's things; I pulled a suitcase down from the top of the wardrobe and placed it onto the pristine bedcover. I grabbed some underwear from the drawers, then packed tops, jumpers, skirts and jeans, trying to find the ones I'd seen her wear before. I reached for a warm-looking winter jacket, hanging at the back of the wardrobe. When I lifted it from the rail, I saw Althea's wedding dress behind it, draped in clear cellophane. I slipped my hand beneath the plastic wrapping, gliding my fingers across the silk, tracing the beading and lace on the bodice. I remembered how beautiful she had looked. How happy and full of hope. That was just six weeks ago. I shoved the wedding dress to the back of the wardrobe and closed the door on it.

Connie was in the sitting room, rooting around at the back of the sideboard.

'I'm done,' I said. 'Let's get out of here.'

'There's just one last thing . . . '

From behind Althea's best china, Connie pulled out an old Lipton tea caddy. He opened the tin and pulled out a mixture of bank notes.

'Don't! Tobias will go mad.'

Connie kissed his teeth. He rolled up the notes and put them in the front pocket of his jeans.

'This cash belongs to Althea and him teef it from her, say him saving it for a "rainy day".'

He replaced the lid, crouched down again and was about to put the tin back in its hiding place when he paused. He got up and instead, set the empty yellow caddy down in plain view on the sideboard.

'Now we can go,' he said.

Althea gasped at the sight of the cash Connie placed on the kitchen table. 'Come here, let mi hug yuh,' she said.

Connie stepped into Althea's embrace but rather than hugging him, she seemed to crumble in his arms. He stood there, holding her. When Althea peeled herself from Connie's chest, her eyes were moist. She gathered herself, turning to Mum, who was leaning against the worktop.

'Alma, mi really appreciate yuh letting all of wi stay here this week. Yuh must let mi give yuh somet'ing for wi keep. Especially as mi understand it's yuh birthday tomorrow and mi nuh get yuh anyt'ing.'

'It's not necessary. You'll need that money to get yuself sorted.'

Althea frowned. 'Yuh still having yuh party tonight?'

'Well . . . it was too late to cancel. It's not really a party, it's just a few friends. Mi nuh expect it to go on late.'

'Then let mi do yuh hair fi yuh. Mek yuh look stunning fi yuh guests.'

'Oh . . . thanks.' Mum looked surprised and touched. 'I can't remember the last time someone did mi hair fi mi.'

'I'll go upstairs now, see what yuh bring for mi and Kallai,' said Althea, suddenly self-conscious.

Mum waited until Althea was safely out of earshot.

'Whose idea was it to sneak back to Tobias's this morning?'

'Mine, Miss Alma,' said Connie.

'You're a good son. Mi see how much yuh muddah rely on yuh, and yuh nuh want fi let her down, but it was a foolish thing to do. That place nuh safe for yuh muddah, it nuh safe for you – and it certainly nuh safe for my daughter.'

'I wasn't about to let Connie go there on his own—'

'No Daphne, yuh muddah's right. I'm sorry, Miss Alma. I'll go check on Althea. Excuse me.'

I tried to make Connie look at me but he left the room, with his eyes down. Shut off to me once more.

'Thanks, Mum. We try and help the situation and all you can do is criticise.'

'Mi nuh need any facetyness from you, my girl. Tobias Beckford is dangerous, and all of wi need to steer clear of him.'

The sultry September weather had departed and wan grey clouds spread across the afternoon sky; it definitely felt like October. I buttoned my jacket, telling myself it was often cooler on the Longshore. It was the breath of the Thames, not my nerves. I'd pressed my hair and curled the ends, a style achieved with Mum's electric tongs and half a can of Luster's spray. My eyes were lined with blue-black kohl and mascara. I'd snuck out while Althea was busy doing Mum's hair in the living room and Connie was upstairs packing, ready for Valerie in the morning. I told myself that I'd stay out for thirty minutes, an hour at the very most. That way, if they asked me where I'd been, I could just say that I fancied some air.

The tide was out and old car tyres lay washed up on the stony beach. Seagulls were picking at the litter along the shoreline. I followed the directions and eventually found Waterman's Way, a cobble-stoned alley that wriggled between a derelict warehouse, and a high brick wall where 'SMASH THE BNP' was scrawled in white paint. My nerves turned to worry. It was a dismal place for a rendezvous; what if this date was a joke after all? I thought about turning back, but then I spotted Mark at the end of the narrow passage, pacing back and forth. He was waiting for me. I strolled towards him with a spring in my step.

'I weren't sure you'd come; I'm glad you're here.'

This coyness was new. I made an exaggerated show of looking at the surroundings.

'Yeah, I am as well. This is a really nice dead end you've invited me to.'

He laughed and a thrill ran through me.

'Stick with me and I'll take you to all the nice places.'

Mark began descending the watermen's stairs. I hesitated, looking at the moss-covered stone, the damp green line, high up the embankment walls, marking the height of the tide when the river was full. Mark retraced his steps and took my hand.

'It's safe. Trust me.'

His fingers closed around my palm; the touch was warm and assured. My trepedation faded away, and I followed him down the old stone steps.

Moments later, I was walking along the strand looking up at the empty warehouses on the bankside. There was no one else around and no traffic noise, only the sound of the Thames gently lapping against the shore and our feet tramping along the pebbles. I felt a strange charge being this close to the river. This close to Mark. Three weathered wooden planks stood upright and tall in the silt and shingle. They were all that remained of a jetty, but from a distance they looked like they'd arisen straight from the riverbed.

'These old buildings are massive; you can really see how tall they are from here. I wonder what will happen to them now.'

'There's even bigger ones over there,' said Mark, nodding towards the Isle of Dogs. 'My grandad was a docker. His dad too. Back in the day, they used to bring all sorts through Millwall, stuff from all over the Empire. But that's all gone now.'

My hand slackened. 'You sad about the docks or the Empire?' I asked, hoping I sounded more cheeky than frosty.

He shrugged. 'Neither I suppose. Things change.'

We stopped on the shoreline. Mark let go of my hand as he bent down to pick up one of the flat stones. He threw it and the stone skipped across the water six times before sinking beneath the murky brown surface.

'Impressive,' I said.

'Yeah, not bad.'

'God, you're modest in't you!'

'Not sure what I'd do with modesty.'

I rolled my eyes, hoping that it made me look nonchalant.

'It's easy. You have a go. I'll show you.' He handed me a flat grey stone. 'Hold it with your thumb and your middle finger; now sort of hook your index finger around the edge.'

He moved behind me, his chest snug against my back. He was still holding my hand, gently guiding it into a throwing position.

'Now, try and snap your wrist when you throw; keep your arm low.'

He stepped back but I could still sense the warmth of his hand and his mouth by my ear. I released the stone. It flew in the air for about two metres before dropping straight into the river.

'That was so rubbish!' I said, laughing.

'Nah. It's just practice,' said Mark. 'When I was younger, me and Phil used to see who could get their stones to go the furthest or bounce the most. Phil said he reckoned if I tried hard enough I could get mine to reach the island. I was so determined to show him that I could. I must have been about seven before I realised he was pulling my leg!'

He laughed and I politely joined in, before trailing off into silence. My wariness returned; I could feel it thickening the air. Mark chose another stone and sent it across the face of the Thames.

'It's funny. You and Phil joking about. Doing ordinary things. I didn't think he could be like that. So . . . normal.'

Mark looked at me. 'What d'you mean?'

I shifted from one foot to the other, crunching the pebbles. 'To me, your brother is just . . . scary. You know, cos of the things he says about Black people. And the sort of things he's done.'

'Well, all that don't stop him from being normal,' said Mark, turning away from me. 'Phil has his views. He's patriotic. It don't make him a monster.'

'Patriotic? Is that what you call it?' I couldn't believe what I was hearing. 'My dad, my uncle, my cousins – in fact, all the Black men I know ain't muggers, and rapists and murderers. They ain't the *monsters* people like your brother say they are. And we ain't monkeys neither!'

Mark picked up a larger stone and flung it overarm into the river. It made a satisfying splash.

'Look, not everyone in my family is racist. But the ones that are, are still my family.'

'Sure. I understand. I think I should go now.'

He reached for me, catching my sleeve. 'Listen. I'm sorry. Let's just not talk about me family.'

'What? I'm supposed to pretend they don't exist?'

'For fuck's sake, all I mean is that there's no point cos I can't change any of that.' He sighed. 'I can't change the fact that I really like you neither. We could both go home with the 'ump now or we could make up. I'm for making up. What d'you say?'

I wanted to laugh in his face, to ask him how he could expect me to ignore his racist brother: the things he said, and did, like it was nothing. In fact, how was I supposed to brush aside the shitty things Mark had come out with too? Referring to Connie as Sambo like it was a joke – calling Connie a Black bastard that time when he'd pissed him off. What on earth was I doing here with him? But then, wasn't he taking a massive risk being here with me? And the fact that he was here meant something. After all, how could a racist white boy fancy a Black girl?

'D'you really like me?'

'Yeah. I *reeeally* do.' Mark pulled me towards him and slipped his arms around my waist. 'And you like me too.'

'How d'you know?' I asked, my tone flat and serious.

'You're here, in't you?' he said, smiling.

It was after five when I arrived back home. Kallai was sitting at the kitchen table; a plate with the remnants of beans on toast was in front of him and he was rapping along with The Sugarhill Gang.

Connie was at the worktop, pouring a glass of milk. He looked me up and down before he spoke. 'Yuh been out a long time.'

'I just went for a walk,' I said.

'I know all the words to 'Rapper's Delight' now Daffeny. D'you wanna hear?'

'Sure thing Kallai, but maybe later yeah?'

Connie placed the milk on the table and Kallai made a face. 'Can't I have lemonade?'

'Yuh could, but then yuh won't grow big and strong like me,' said Connie, pulling back his T-shirt sleeve and flexing his biceps.

'And like Daddy. He's got big muscles too.'

Connie didn't answer. Kallai gulped down the milk, draining the glass.

'Good boy. Go and start running you bath. I'll be up in a minute.'

Connie took Kallai's dishes to the sink, averting his eyes from me. 'So where d'yuh go?'

'Just around the estate. Down to the Longshore.'

'D'yuh see anyone yuh know?'

Indignation jabbed me. 'I might have done. So what?'

Connie let out a noise, half-sigh, half-groan. 'Yuh want to carry on with yuh likkle Romeo and Juliet t'ing that's up to yuh, innit. It nuh have nuttin' to do with mi.'

'No it doesn't. Just like how you bunking lessons to go over to Chantelle's has nothing to do with me.'

He tutted, turning his back to me, and began washing the dishes. The letterbox banged. This caller had a heavy hand. I remembered the yellow tin Connie had left on the sideboard. He looked at me.

'I'll go,' he said, making for the kitchen door.

'We'll both go,' I replied.

But Mum was already there, peering through the peephole. She hurried to unlock the door.

'Hello, you're early,' she said to a clean-shaven white man, trying to suppress the gleam in her voice.

The man was tall. He had ears that stuck out and a nose that looked like it had once been broken; he bowed slightly as he extended his enormous right hand.

'Hello, I'm Colin. You must be Daphne; I've heard a lot about you. Don't worry though, it's all good,' he said, winking.

I wondered why he was being so assiduously matey. I didn't feel like shaking hands, but I did it anyway. Out of the corner of my eye, I was sure I saw Mum's shoulders relax. Connie excused himself and went upstairs to give Kallai a bath. I sloped off to the kitchen, leaving the door ajar just enough so I could peek into the hallway.

'Nice hairdo,' said Colin.

'Thank you,' said Mum, bashful, touching the side of her head.

'I thought I'd come early and lend a hand. I've brought snacks, I've brought drinks and I've also got a pressie, but you'll have to give me a kiss first.'

I managed to muffle a gasp with my sleeve. Mum shyly pulled Colin towards her and they kissed. I knew I ought not to be watching, but I couldn't tear my eyes away. Ten minutes ago I had no idea Mum even had a fella, and I'd certainly never seen her kiss a man before. Afterwards, her face was sunny.

'Daphne, you finish yuh homework yet?'

I paused a moment before opening the kitchen door. 'Yeah, but I—'

'Ah-ah, mi nuh want to hear any *but*. These are mi last few hours as a thirty-nine-year-old woman. Let's get ready for mi party!'

*

At around seven thirty, Mum's' other work friends arrived. Each one of them brought a guest and a bottle. Instead of filtering into the living room where I'd set out bowls of nuts and crisps, they all stood around the kitchen, eating Twiglets straight from the packet, and gushing over Mum's new hairstyle. Althea had plaited wide cornrows that went straight back and were tied in a bun at the nape of Mum's neck, giving her an elegant profile. A couple of the white women exclaimed that she didn't look anywhere near forty.

'Well you know, Black don't crack,' said Mum, making all these people laugh. I couldn't remember ever seeing my mother this playful.

Miss Gladys came with Wishbone, one of her 'gentlemen friends', and her pals Claudia and Rufus. She ordered everyone except Connie and me out of the kitchen while she warmed the food she'd brought.

'How yuh muddah keeping?' Miss Gladys asked Connie.

'She's a likkle better today.'

'That's good. And *yuh*?'

'I'm all right t'anks,' came his stock reply.

Miss Gladys remained silent, allowing him space to say more, but Connie said nothing. He kept his eyes focused on washing the rice, although he fumbled over the task, spilling a few grains into the sink.

Uncle Earl poked his head around the door.

'Just the person mi ah look for. Young man mi have an important job fi yuh.' He flourished a battered LP carry case. 'Come put on some of the tunes mi 'ave 'ere. Since mi know Alma, her music taste has always been more Jim Reeves than Jimmy Cliff!'

Connie dried his hands and followed my uncle out of the kitchen.

'How him really doing?' Miss Gladys asked me.

'I don't know. At school he strains every muscle to act normal. No one there knows anything about it. Then when we're alone, he's all moody and morose. It's a bit annoying if I'm honest.'

Miss Gladys chuckled, but I could tell she wasn't amused.

'Sounds to mi like maybe yuh need a likkle less honesty and a bit more understanding. Him dealing with more than a boy him age should ever have fi deal with. And to mi it sounds like the only person him able to be himself with right now is yuh – which is why him nuh put up any pretence.'

'I know he's got a lot on his plate now, but what if it's not just that? All these years he's been putting up with Tobias, he's had to be tough. I worry that it's making him hard inside too and I just hadn't noticed before. I dunno. I really wish he'd talk to me, like he used to.'

'Yuh need to be patient. Unnu have always been close. He'll open up to yuh when him ready, and when he does, just make sure yuh listen.'

She tugged at my cheeks, dislodging my pout. The intro to Nicky Thomas's 'Have a Little Faith' oozed from the speakers in the living room and a cheer went up. The party had begun.

Althea made a brief appearance but largely stuck to the kitchen to serve food alongside Miss Gladys. Nobody commented on the livid bruise around her left eye. At 10 p.m. she took Kallai upstairs and Mum insisted that the music be turned down. Now it hummed in the background while people clustered in groups, chatting and laughing. The aroma of curry goat mingled with the smell of cigarettes and rum. After giving each of Miss Gladys's friends a rundown of how I was doing at school, I escaped the funk in the living room and joined Connie. Gregory Isaacs's voice filtered into the hallway; Mum's friends cheered and turned the volume back up. Colin started crooning along to the lyrics of 'Night Nurse'.

'So he and yuh muddah are dating?' asked Connie, breaking the silence between us.

'I suppose. I heard Grandma telling Wishbone earlier that there are plenty of male nurses nowadays. She also said, "him white, but him nice".'

'He seems it. D'yuh think she'd say the same t'ing about your fella?'

'I don't suppose she'll ever meet Mark, because he's not my fella,' I said.

'What is he then?'

I tutted and got up. Connie reached out, touching my arm. 'I'm sorry, Daphne. Can we call a truce?'

I remained standing, leaning against the wall. 'I suppose so.'

Connie sat forward, as though trying to bridge the distance between us. He spoke softly. 'Yuh muddah sound really happy. Colin makes her more relaxed.'

'He's a bit of a wally though. Compared to Ezee.'

'Then maybe yuh shouldn't compare Colin to Ezee. Maybe yuh should compare him to Tobias. Living in that flat . . . it was stifling. But now mi can breathe. Mi starting to feel safe.'

Mum joined in with the singing, her voice flat, yet earnest. Connie chuckled, the sound was deep and unguarded. It felt like he had come back to me and made me smile. The song faded and there was a gap in the music while Uncle Earl selected another record. We could hear people shouting out requests, then Carroll Thompson's voice sauntered from the living room.

'"I'm So Sorry". Seems appropriate for us,' said Connie. 'T'anks for being there for mi. Yuh mi best friend. I don't wanna lose what we have. But . . . I don't know.' He looked at me. His eyes were bright, but serious. Then he stood up and held out his hand. 'Will yuh dance with mi?'

I thought of the way Mark had held out his hand earlier, when he led me down the steps to the strand. I couldn't move.

'Nah. I'm not sure I can face the living room, with all them oldies,' I said.

'We nuh need to go in the living room, we can just stay here.'

Connie took my hand, gently tugging me away from the wall. I was standing close, looking up at him. I felt his arm hook around my waist and he began to sway. I was lulled by the music and the scent of his skin. I found myself leaning into him, closing my eyes. There was a knock at the door and I sprang back.

'Sorry. I should get that,' I said, a brutal heat rising to my cheeks. Mum bustled out of the living room and intercepted me.

'It's probably the neighbours ah complain about the singing. Let mi deal with this.'

She unhooked the chain, opened the door, and gasped. There was Tobias, with his crooked grin.

'Yuh having a likkle party? Mi nuh mean to gatecrash but I need a word with mi wife.'

'Althea is asleep,' said Mum. 'Why don't yuh come back tomorrow?'

She moved to close the door, but Tobias put a hand out.

'Mi here now. Mi never put off till tomorrow what mi can do today,' he said.

Connie took a step towards the door and I pressed my hand against his chest to restrain him.

'We don't want no trouble now, mate,' said Colin, coming down the hallway from the living room. He stood beside Mum.

Tobias looked him up and down. 'Mi nuh know you, so mi nuh know how mi can be your *mate*.'

'Wah yuh want?' said Mum, finding some steel.

'Nuttin' from you, missus. Mi want fi talk to mi wife. Mi see she come by my place earlier so mi just bringing her something she left behind.'

Tobias wasn't shouting but his voice was loud. He picked up a black bin liner that was slumped at his feet, turning it upside down. Jagged fragments of white silk and beading fluttered onto the landing. A lump came to my throat.

'Oh, mi never see you there before,' said Tobias.

At first I thought he was talking to Connie, but when I turned around it was Althea, who had come downstairs.

'Is it because yuh love mi so much that yuh tear up mi wedding dress and bring the pieces here?' Althea's voice wavered, but at least she was talking back. 'Yuh want mi to tell all the people here why me walk out last Saturday?'

'What's there to tell? We quarrel over some stupidness and since then I apologise, but yuh too stubborn to meet me halfway. I left yuh alone, giving yuh time to cool off, so we could work t'ings out. But instead yuh and yuh good-for-nuttin' bwoy come to mi yard and take the t'ings mi give yuh, and teef mi money too. Why yuh want to break my heart?'

'Tobias, yuh know mi love yuh! Is yuh make t'ings hard—'

'Mi nuh interested in anyt'ing yuh have fi say. Hear mi now – there's two of us in this marriage and it nuh just yuh one that gets to say when it's over. If anything it will be the other way round. Yuh need me. But mi nuh go chase after yuh no more. I'm just gonna wait till you to run back to me, cos time longer than rope – and mi have all the time in the world!'

'Nuh come to mi door again or I'll call the police,' said Mum.

Tobias was already walking away but Connie made for the door. I grabbed his arm but he shook me off and stepped outside.

'T'ank yuh for the way yuh behave just now.' Connie's voice carried along the landing after Tobias. 'Althea sees who yuh are. Everyone sees who yuh really are. We're done with yuh.'

Tobias kept walking and didn't look back. In fact, to me it looked almost as though he was scurrying away, back to the neatly ordered cage he'd emerged from. He had lost his cool and embarrassed himself. His public mask had slipped and Althea had stood up to him, sort of. He expected her to come crawling back to him and I knew neither Connie, nor Valerie nor I, would ever let that happen.

16

Double German was my last lesson on Thursday afternoon. The aural practice tapes had worn thin with overuse, which made the actors speak agonisingly slowly. Although I willed myself to focus on the exercises, my mind refused to obey. My eyes strayed out of the classroom window, to where Mr Sweeny, the caretaker, was cleaning graffiti off an outside wall. He'd been at it for the past hour and had managed to erase the first three letters. What remained said:

---GERS OUT

It had been startling to see, but not wholly unexpected after the furore that followed the riots on Broadwater Farm in Tottenham. The images broadcast on Sunday night's news-flash, showed parts of the North London housing estate in flames, and police officers in a pitched battle with youths. The report cut to a snapshot of a woman with a neat Afro and a winning smile; the voice-over briefly stating that Mrs Cynthia Jarrett, a mother of five, had died of a heart attack that started during a police raid at her home on Saturday afternoon. I was dazed. How could it be that within the space of a week, one Black woman had been left with serious injuries and another had died following police raids on their homes? The news report gave little information about why the police invaded Mrs Jarrett's home. Instead, it focused on the unrest. I hoped there might be more information in the morning newspapers. However, the next day, the main story in the press and TV news was the brutal murder of a policeman, set upon by rioters. All week, the press and the public's outrage grew.

Everyone knew who'd daubed the message on the wall. When I'd arrived at school that morning, I saw Mark and his friends leaning against the railings opposite the gates. Ted had gone back to shaving his head, but all of their pale, pinched faces twisted up into a scowl whenever the Black students passed by. Some white girls had attached themselves to the group. They all clustered together, sharing cigarettes, laughing loudly. Of course, Mark blanked me like he'd done all week. I knew it was because he was with his friends. I fingered the edge of the envelope in my pocket that I had planned to post through his locker. I had written a note with a new time and place for us to meet. But after seeing the graffiti – and Julie Carter whispering in his ear – I tore the letter up and threw it away, appalled with myself for having written it in the first place.

Mr Sweeny had finally managed to scrub away the second 'G' when the bell rang, marking the end of the school day.

There were a mass of bodies in the ground-floor corridor. Connie and I wove through the crowd of students packing bags and slamming locker doors. Craig and Ted were lounging on one of the window ledges, and as we passed, Ted looked up from the newspaper he was reading.

'Off to start a fire and loot some shops?'

'What you on about?' asked Connie.

'Us whites ain't safe in our own country no more,' said Ted, brandishing the paper he had been looking at.

BULLDOG
PAPER OF THE YOUNG NATIONAL FRONT

'Handsworth, Brixton, Tottenham, them riots were just the start,' said Ted. 'There's gangs of coons attacking whites all over our country now.'

Errol, Omar and a couple of Connie's other friends were standing at their lockers, further along the corridor. They stopped what they were doing and looked on, alert, their bodies shifting; I couldn't tell if they were getting ready to fight or flee. Mark squeezed past them. Julie Carter was with him, chatting avidly. He clocked me but kept his expression carefully neutral. I cut my eye past him and turned to Ted.

'It's all bullshit.'

I could hardly believe that I'd spoken aloud. Ted fixed his gaze on me, surprised, amused almost.

'Just because you read it in that rag, it doesn't mean that it's true.' I tried to keep my voice even, despite the nerves rising up from my belly, constricting my throat. 'Does it mention Cherry Groce? Or Cynthia Jarrett? What the police did to them?'

Ted jumped down from the ledge and stood barring my way. 'It mentions PC Blakelock, how he was killed in the line of duty, butchered by niggers.'

He loomed over me. Up close his scalp was still flecked with ginger.

'Back off.' Connie stepped forward, he more than matched Ted in height.

'Fuck off back where you come from, Sambo,' said Ted.

'What about me? I was born here,' I said. 'I'm British.'

'What's all this then?' Mark had pressed his way through the crowd. He leaned into Ted speaking in a low, reasonable tone. 'You don't wanna go starting nothing here. Jones is already on your case.'

'Mate, are you with the skins or the fucking Blacks?' spat Ted.

'*Mate*, d'you seriously wanna get expelled for starting on a girl?' said Mark.

Ted smirked. 'What girl? D'you mean this fucking ape?'

'Jesus, Ted!'

'What?' said Ted, amused, and slightly curious.

I could almost hear the cogs whirring in Mark's head, his eyes flickering to me then back to his friend. I could feel my eyes stinging, but there was no way I'd let those hot, angry tears flow in front of them.

'Arsehole!' I hissed, pushing my way between him and Mark. But then Craig got down from the ledge. Blocking my way. The fat he had in the first year had solidified, making him imposing, even though he was the shortest in the gang.

'Get out of the way,' said Connie.

'Make me, you Black bastard,' he said, shoving Connie's shoulder.

Without any of the usual posturing or preamble, Connie punched Craig in the jaw. Craig staggered, shocked and disgusted at being caught off guard. Then he launched himself at Connie, the force of his body slamming them into the lockers.

Crowds surged forwards and I was jostled out of the way by those eager to get a better view of the fight. I could hear slaps and swearing. My heart was racing as I pushed and shoved my way back between the spectators. Craig was poised, ready with a punch, but before he swung Mark steamed in.

'Leave it!' he demanded, pushing Craig back.

Mr Jones appeared, barging his way through the onlookers.

'What's going on here?'

'Nothing,' said Mark.

Mr Jones surveyed Craig as the youth straightened his jacket, glowering at everyone. Then he scanned Connie: dishevelled, rubbing his knuckles. 'Evans? Small? Do *you* have anything to say?'

'Nothing, sir,' the pair mumbled.

'How predictable. Well unless you and everyone else loitering here wants a suspension right now, I suggest you make your way off school premises.'

The teacher remained in the corridor while the crowds ebbed away. I watched Mark and his mates wander off. The Black students hung back until Connie and I joined the exodus and together we cautiously walked to the gate. When we got there, a group of around twelve Black students were waiting for us. Word had already got around.

'Glad you boxed that ugly white boy in his stupid mouth'; 'Fucking dickhead racists'; 'What about Daphne, eh? We all thought she was so quiet, now she ah gwaan like Katherine Cleaver, all she needs is the 'fro!'; 'Yeah, big up sistah!'

I'd never felt so brave, or so popular. Although I was well aware they wouldn't be nearly as impressed with me if they knew I'd been hanging out with Mark. I wish I knew what it was I saw in him, even now. He'd tried to stop Ted and Craig by cajoling them, but he hadn't called out their racism. He hadn't actually stuck up for me. Connie was also quiet, brushing away the admiration of everyone in the group. His other friends still had no idea that he was now taking two buses to travel in from Valerie's house in Brockley. He was keeping up his sunny performance, but I could tell it required effort. Chantelle invited him back to hers, but Connie said he had to pick Kallai up from after-school club. He gave her a quick kiss, then walked off alone. He didn't say goodbye to me.

I stopped at Londis on my way back through the estate to pick up some groceries for Mum. An elderly woman was paying Mr Sharma, the shopkeeper, for her goods in change, holding each coin up to within an inch of her spectacles before laying it down on the counter.

Mr Sharma had installed an automatic alert, which bleeped every time somebody entered the store. The note sounded and I looked over: there was Mark. His face lifted with surprise. I spun away, gripping the wire handle of the shopping basket. I needed something to do. Early editions of the evening paper were stacked by the till. I picked up a copy and placed it in my basket. Finally the old lady shuffled away; Mark opened the door for her.

'T'ank yuh darlin',' she said.

Mr Sharma began to ring up my shopping. Mark came and stood beside me.

'Can I have a word?'

I looked away.

'That will be £3.65,' said Mr Sharma.

I handed over a fiver and waited for my change.

'Will you wait for me outside?' asked Mark.

'I dunno.' I turned towards him, finding the edge falling away from my awkwardness. 'What would be the point?'

There was a searching look in his eyes, but I wasn't having it. I set my mouth in a pout. Mark exhaled, exasperated, and wandered off down the tinned goods aisle.

I left the mini-market in a strop. Mark couldn't just expect a cosy chat after what had happened at school. For fuck's sake, Ted Butcher called me an ape, and he had just stood there because he didn't want to give himself away. Anger gripped me once more; I shouldn't let him get off that easily. If he wanted a chat, then bring it on.

Mark was coming out of the shop; a plastic bag dangled from his wrist.

'I thought you'd gone,' he said.

'Well as you've risked life and limb to come to this dangerous neighbourhood I thought I'd better hang around; see what you want. After all, ain't this the sort of place you read about in *Bulldog*?'

'I don't read *Bulldog*. Actually, I come down here to get some bits for Nana; she's been poorly. But I'm glad I've seen you. I weren't sure how I'd get in touch. Can we talk then?'

A guy walked past us on his way into the shop. I vaguely knew him as he used to hang out with my cousin Kiplyn. His eyes narrowed as he gave Mark the once-over, then greeted me with a terse upward nod. What must Mark and I have looked like, standing there together?

'Not here.'

I marched around the corner where an alleyway ran behind the parade of shops. We needed to be out of sight, but only got as far as the back of the chippy. I couldn't hold back any longer.

'How can you stand them? Craig and that lot? How can you just stand by and listen to that vile crap they come out with?'

'They're my mates,' said Mark, guarded.

'Nice mates!'

'You don't know them.'

'Well, I don't like what I know about them,' I said, my voice rising.

Mark frowned; it made him look hard. 'Well from what I saw it was your mate that started it. "Mild Mannered Connie" throwing his weight around.'

'After *your* mate called him a Black bastard! And Connie was standing up for me which is more than you did. Look, I don't even know what I'm doing here discussing this with you, it's fucking stupid. You blanked me all week because you were with your racist friends, and now you're sticking up for them!' I kissed my teeth and pushed past him.

'I was the one what broke up the bloody fight!' Mark shouted after me. 'And got proper slagged for doing it.'

'Oh dear, call you a nigger lover, did they? Well boo fucking hoo! Maybe Julie Carter can whisper you sweet nothings and make it better.'

'You can talk! Like you ain't always cosying up with your mate Connie. I mean, what is it with you two? Are you just fucking me about?'

I stopped and turned around. 'What d'you mean fucking you about? You're the one whose friends would have a fit if they saw us together. Along with your dad and your brother and your nana.'

'For your information Nana gets on with everyone. It was her neighbour Osborne who rang and told us she was ill. So don't go accusing Nana of being prejudiced against Blacks when she ain't.'

'Ted called me an ape. Do you have any idea how that makes me feel?'

Mark walked over to me. 'Look, I'm sorry for the way that lot acted before.'

'It's not just before; they're racist all the time! Why on earth are you apologising for them?'

I folded my arms, but remained where I was. I couldn't bring myself to leave. Not yet. I needed to know whose side he was on.

'I ain't apologising for them. They couldn't care less. I'm apologising to you because I didn't do nothing about it. I let him get away with calling you ... that. I'm ashamed of myself and I'm sorry.' His shoulders dropped, he spoke softly, 'For fuck's sake Daphne, don't you know how I feel about you? I think you're gorgeous.'

My stomach jumped. I pressed my arms tighter across my chest.

'I just don't understand how they can be your mates.' My voice was uneven. 'Have you ever gone out ... with your brother. To beat up Black people?'

'No.'

'Would you?'

He grinned. 'I'm a lover not a fighter.'

I allowed him to draw me close. The kiss was brief, more like a peck, but he kept his arms wrapped around my waist.

'So, are you with the skins or the Blacks?' I asked.

'I'm with you.'

I felt his hands resting on my lower back. Heavy and secure. I liked it. I liked him. 'Can you stay out for a bit? Please?' he asked.

I finally smiled at him and nodded.

I arrived home forty minutes later, dumped the groceries on the kitchen table and switched the kettle on. While waiting for it to boil, I unfolded the evening paper.

GROCE FAMILY MUST WAIT
FOR DPP DECISION

The family of Mrs Cherry Groce, who was shot by police during a raid on her home, are still waiting to find out if charges will be brought against the police officer, who has been suspended on full pay. The Black community have called for the officer to be charged with attempted murder. A spokesman for the Metropolitan branch of the Police Federation warned that policemen licensed to carry firearms may hand in their authorisation if the DPP decide to file charges against their member after what they argue was simply a tragic accident.

The newspaper had printed a picture of Mrs Groce on her wedding day. She appeared poised and dignified. It reminded me of the photograph of Auntie Sybil I used to polish on Saturday mornings. When I thought of armed officers, I pictured news footage from South Africa, the United States, and Northern Ireland. Until now, I never realised how often the Metropolitan Police raided ordinary people's houses; that you could be innocent, yet shot in your own home. For days the papers had all detailed the violence in the streets and the appalling murder of PC Keith Blakelock. But wasn't the shooting of a woman in front of her children an unthinkable act too?

I flicked to the letters page and scanned the readers' comments. There were demands to bring in the SAS next time the 'Blacks went on the rampage', calls for 'us Blacks' to 'stop moaning' and 'assimilate to white society'. I read every letter, wondering if this was really what everyone thought, or if this showed the newspaper's bias. Then I came to a letter at the bottom of the page.

Dear Sir, I have lived in England for nearly 30 years and believe that the vast majority of white British people have no understanding of the deep psychological impact their racism has had on Black British-born young people over the past decades. In my opinion, and indeed in my experiences, racism is rampant in British society today. It is institutional as expressed in our immigration and nationality laws, educational institutions, churches, press and media, trade unions, political parties and in every social and economic aspect that touches the lives of Britain's Black citizens. Until something is done to address these issues, I fear Black British youths will forever feel like outsiders and there will be more unrest.

I re-read the letter. The word 'institutional' stood out. I'd only ever thought of racism as name-calling, threats, or physical attacks. But this letter was saying that racism had breadth and scope, that it was around us all the time. It was about more than prejudice and intolerance, it was about power as well.

Mum came into the kitchen dressed for work. I was surprised to see Miss Gladys with her.

'I didn't realise you were here,' I said, putting down the paper.

'Mamma was just helping me change the sheets. She's staying here tonight while I'm at work.'

'Mum it's been almost a week; I don't think Tobias will come around now ...'

'Daphne, mi nuh care what yuh think, that man is unpredictable. Mi nuh like having to go back on night shifts so soon after what happen last weekend. At least this way mi know yuh safe.'

'I don't need a babysitter!'

'Eh-eh! After mi nuh come here to babysit!' said Miss Gladys, taking a seat at the table. 'Earl ah set up him domino school in the front room this evening; the house will be full of him British Rail mandem. Mi here for a likkle peace and quiet. Mi gonna fry some snapper.'

'Escovitch?' I said, already sensing the malty, peppery aroma.

Miss Gladys winked. 'Of course!'

There were three loud knocks on the front door. People usually dropped the letterbox; we were unaccustomed to knocks. Miss Gladys and I followed Mum to the hallway.

She put the safety chain on, shifting so her body remained behind the door.

'Good evening, I'm Sergeant Wallace and this is WPC Maxwell.'

'What do you want?' said Mum, trying to control the surprise in her voice. My mind strayed to the newspaper article I'd just read.

'We're looking for a Althea Beckford, or perhaps you know her as Althea Small.'

'She doesn't live here. It's only me and my daughter live here.'

'And you are?'

Mum hesitated. 'Alma Johnson.'

'Mrs Johnson, we have reason to believe Althea Beckford is here. You could get into serious trouble if you don't co-operate with us. We could discuss the matter now or I could come back with a warrant to search the property. You wouldn't want that now, would you?'

Sergeant Wallace was heavyset as well as tall; he sank deep into the armchair, his knees rising high up in front of him. Constable Maxwell remained on her feet, standing in the doorway with a flinty expression on her face. I sat in between Miss Gladys and Mum on the settee. It felt as though the living room walls and the ceiling had moved in by several feet.

'So you say that Mrs Beckford and her two sons stayed here for a week, but left five days ago,' said Sergeant Wallace.

'Althea turned up on my doorstep in a distressed state. She was having trouble with her husband. She never told me what it was about. She said he'd hit her. I could see her face was bruised, so I allowed her to stay here.'

I noticed how Mum was using her 'English' voice, and like Miss Gladys, it signalled that she was no pushover, or that at least, she was not prepared to let her trepidation show.

Sergeant Wallace continued, 'The matter we are looking into concerns Mrs Beckford's immigration status. An anonymous source claims that she came to this country from Jamaica in 1978 on a six-month tourist visa and overstayed, thus making her an illegal immigrant. It's alleged that she subsequently brought her eldest son to this country; although he is still a minor, he too is here illegally.'

I tried to slow my breathing but my mind was running in all directions. There was no way the police would have this much information from some anonymous source. But surely not even Tobias would turn informant. Surely not. But my mind jumped back to what he had said on Saturday night. About expecting Althea to come running back to him – that she needed him.

'I understand that she is married to a UK citizen,' said Mum pointedly.

'Unless he has applied for her to remain in the country, Mrs Beckford is an illegal immigrant. We went to an address in Hibbert Court before coming here. There was nobody home and the neighbours say the place has been empty for the past few days.'

WPC Maxwell chipped in. 'You do know that you can get into serious trouble if you knowingly withhold information about an illegal immigrant from the authorities? Were you aware of Althea's immigration status when you allowed her to stay with you?'

Mum had maintained eye contact with the police officers until that moment; now she looked down, speaking to her lap.

'It was my view that Althea needed to be somewhere safe. I let her stay here because in my job I see many women who end up in hospital beds because they had no safe place to run to when their husbands and boyfriends beat them.' Mum looked up, her eyes fixed on the female officer. 'Perhaps I should have called the police on her husband the night he hit his wife, but from what I see, you police don't interfere in "domestic affairs".'

A pink spot appeared in Officer Maxwell's cheek, but then her jaw stiffened. Sergeant Wallace shifted in his seat and cleared his throat.

'Perhaps when we question Mrs Beckford we will be able to establish if there is any truth to the information we have been given. Of course, if there is, then Mrs Beckford has the option to leave the country of her own accord. In many ways that would be better for her and her eldest son. If she doesn't, then she will be served with a notice of deportation. She will be forcibly removed from the country and barred from re-entering.'

My spine tensed as a shiver ran down it.

'I'll mention it, if I see her again,' said Mum.

The officers left a card with their contact details on the coffee table. After fastening the front door behind them, Mum let out a sigh that sounded like a groan. I'd followed her into the hall. Connie had scrawled Valerie's contact details on the pad by the telephone. I had to warn him that the police were looking for them. The dial tone droned on and on; there was no answer. I replaced the receiver and grabbed my jacket from the coat rack.

'Where yuh going?' asked Mum, grabbing my arm.

'To Valerie's.'

'What? Yuh nuh think that dem "anonymous informant" hasn't already given dem her address too? Trust me, that will be the next place the police ah go to and yuh can't get there quicker than dem.'

'I have to try!' I said, my voice pleading.

'It's best we nuh give the police reason to think we are any more involved in dis. Yuh nuh hear dem? "Illegal immigration", "knowingly withholding information from the authorities". I could lose mi job. Lord, all this trouble wi getting dragged into!'

'Of course! No trouble trouble, till trouble trouble you,' I muttered sarcastically.

'Nuh use that tone with mi—'

'Unnu need fi calm down,' said Miss Gladys. 'Daphne, there's nuh no need for any facetyness, yuh muddah have a point. But Alma, mi proud of the way yuh face down the police just now. Yuh give dem a few more facts dem should know. You have fi remember that dis isn't Althea's fault. She needs help.'

Mum was shaking her head slowly and she sighed when Miss Gladys finished. Her bag was hanging from the newel post. She hesitated for a moment, then dug a fiver from the inside pocket.

'Take this. Get a minicab from the place on the High Street.'

'Thanks, Mum. I'm sorry if I was rude. It's just that I'm so upset—'

'And yuh t'ink yuh the only one who's upset. Cha! Mi have to get to work,' said Mum, turning away and putting on her coat.

The cab driver tapped the steering wheel in time with the soca playing on the radio. I could feel the agitation within me rising like mercury whenever we stopped at a red light. My mind strayed back to Mum, the way she had spoken to the police officers and the fact she had given me my cab fare. Then I remembered how she cut me off when I'd tried to apologise; I couldn't think about that now. I needed to focus on Connie.

At last, we turned off Lewisham Way and were fiddling through the backstreets of Brockley. Once we turned into Adelaide Avenue, I kept my eyes peeled on the house numbers. As we drew near a wide Edwardian house, my mouth dried.

There, parked across the road, was a police car, and Althea was being led towards it by WPC Maxwell. Kallai ran out of the house and down the front path. Connie caught up with him at the gate, tugging him back and then holding him while the little boy wept. Valerie came out too. She was shouting to Althea, telling her that she would get to the police station as soon as she could. I saw Althea put her face in her hands; then the car drove away. I sat in the back of the taxi, helpless while all this happened in front of me. After so many years, the secret was out, and it wasn't down to a careless remark Connie made at school, or because Althea had been caught up in a raid at work. It was all Tobias, I was sure of it. Althea had had the temerity to leave him, so he would now get her – and Connie – deported. Hateful, spiteful man.

*

At 10.30 p.m., the telephone rang for the second time that evening. On hearing the telephone's first chime, Connie had sprinted to the hall to answer. There had been no news since 8 p.m., when Valerie called to tell us that Althea would be interviewed under caution, so had decided to wait for the duty solicitor. She assured Connie that Althea would be back soon, that he should try not to worry. Connie reheated some leftover mutton curry, but none of us could eat. After busying himself clearing away the food and washing the plates, he was still unable to settle. He was agitated, trying not to allow his simmering anger to boil over in front of Kallai. But as the light faded from the sky, the heat of his rage waned, leaving apprehension.

Kallai had fretted and cried himself into exhaustion; he now lay curled up on the sofa in the back part of the sitting room. He'd stirred when the phone rang, snoring gently. I covered him with a crochet quilt that was draped over one of the armchairs. The call was brief. When Connie returned to the sitting room he said that it was Miss Gladys who had offered words of sympathy and comfort, but gently insisted that it was time for me to come home; she had ordered a cab to pick me up.

'I'm gonna call her back right now and tell her I'm staying,' I said, making for the hall.

'No.' Connie sidestepped so he was standing in my way. 'All we're doing here is waiting. Go home and rest.'

'I'm happy to sit and wait with you.'

'Are you? I can't stand it!' Connie's voice went up. He glanced at Kallai, but the little boy slept on. 'What if they don't release her? When will they come for me? What will happen to Kallai when they throw us out of the country? Will he have to stay here, with that . . . bastard? I can't stand this, Daphne. I just can't.'

My mind was a whirr, casting about for the right words to say. Connie was staring, as if pleading with me to make things better, but my thoughts only echoed Connie's own fears. I remembered the raid on the salon years ago. We'd grown so close since then; if the authorities took him away would I ever get to see him again? I couldn't find the right words, so I hugged him. Connie inhaled, raising his chest and shoulders, then breathed out slowly, his body enfolding mine. I held him tight. This was better than words. This is what he needed. I didn't ever want to lose this closeness.

The sound of a car horn beeping outside broke the spell. Connie immediately pulled away from me, clearing his throat.

'Your cab's outside. You better go. I'll call you tomorrow if there's news.'

17

Connie was absent at registration the following morning. Errol was the first to ask me if I knew where he was. He was on the team sheet for the match against The Mariners Eleven later, a tough fixture, so it was odd that Connie wasn't in. I said that I hadn't seen him and suggested that he'd probably just overslept. Chantelle joined in; she'd phoned his flat last night and there had been no answer, wasn't that odd too?

'That *is* strange I guess,' I said, keeping my tone as even as I could. 'Perhaps their phone is out of order.'

Chantelle's eyes narrowed. I fished out a novel I was reading and flicked through the pages to find my place, refusing to look up until the bell rang, summoning us to first period.

All morning during lessons, I was unable to stop thinking the worst, picturing coppers arriving at Valerie's house and carting Connie away. For all I knew, he and Althea might already be booked on a one-way flight to Jamaica. By lunchtime I'd had enough. I had to find out what was going on.

Greville Dunne ushered me into the large kitchen at the rear of the ground floor. I'd never bunked off before in my life and had been sick with worry on the journey to Brockley, yet the old gent behaved like it was perfectly normal for me to turn up in the middle of the day. He'd greeted me with a hearty 'Howdeedo', pulling up his bright red braces and rolling down his shirtsleeves – on account of 'having company'. Red pea soup was bubbling on the stove, and two bowls were already set on the table. He got another from the cupboard and told me to grab myself a spoon. Valerie would be down in a minute; she'd just taken Althea something to eat.

'Wi run her a bath and when she get back from the station and tan in it for almost an hour. Then she sleep and she sleep till now,' said Greville, bringing the pot to the table. 'Connie sleep through him alarm too and nuh wake till gone eleven. Then quick time him dress and leave the house. Him say something about an important match later. Yuh nuh see him?'

'No! So I've missed him. I've been really worried, thinking all sorts. I better head back to school.'

'Where's the fire? Yuh can eat first! After all yuh tek two bus to come here,' said Greville. 'Yuh young folk always in a rush. Sit down nuh!'

'Erm. Okay. Thank you,' I said, feeling soothed and told off at the same time.

I perched myself in the nearest seat and Greville ladled a hefty portion of soup into my bowl. The food smelled delicious, but I sat rigid in my chair, eager for news rather than sustenance.

The door was nudged open and Valerie backed inside, carrying a tray. I sprang up and held the door for her.

'Althea say she nuh hungry – Oh hello, Daphne, nice to see yuh. Connie's not here though. Unnu probably pass each other on the bus!'

'Looks that way. I came over because I was worried. So, they let Althea go. Is she okay? What happens now?'

'Calm down darlin'. There's nuttin' to fret about – at least not as far as the police are concerned,' Valerie said, placing the tray on the worktop.

'How come?' I asked, thankful yet bewildered.

Valerie kissed her teeth. 'Tobias turned up at the police station! Say him want to make a statement about "the malicious allegations against his wife".'

'Seriously?'

'Yeah! Apparently Althea leaving had hurt him so bad that he's been off work. But being in the flat alone was making him blue so he'd been staying with Busta since Saturday. He claim that it was only when he swing by to check him post that one of the neighbours inform him that the police were looking for Althea. So he "set aside his hurt feeling" and came to clear her.'

'What a man love drama sah!' Greville interjected, shaking his head.

'Drama and attention! Anyhow, he confirm that he made an application to the Home Office for her and bring the acknowledgement letter to prove it. The police dem let her go.'

My chest felt tight. Bloody Tobias, grassing them up and then painting himself as the hero.

Valerie continued, 'Connie was so relieved when Althea walk through the door, but then he get mad when he hear what happened. He kept saying, "it was him who inform on us. I know it was him!"'

'That may be so,' Greville chipped in, 'but I say to him, "son, wi all suspect it was yuh stepdaddy – but wi cyaah prove it".'

Valerie nodded. 'Tobias nuh want people to think he inform on his own wife; he care too much about him public appearance plus he knows how everyone hates a grass. He say that probably it was one of Althea's ex-clients that report her. Or a rival hairstylist.'

'I don't believe a word of it,' I said. 'I'm not surprised Connie's furious.'

Valerie nodded. 'But as Greville say, we cyaah prove anything.'

I stirred the soup. I had no appetite. Valerie had lapsed into a glum silence; she was pushing the peas about in her bowl. Only Greville was eating.

'Well . . . I suppose if we look on the bright side, Tobias has snookered himself.' Valerie gave me a quizzical look. 'I mean, if his plan was to get them banged up and deported, then it's failed. By wanting to save face, he's been forced to admit that he's applied to the Home Office for Althea to stay here. He can't go back on it now, or else everyone will know *he* caused them to get deported.'

'She's a bright gyal,' said Greville. 'She make a good point.'

I smiled at him, my angry feelings abating a little. However, Valerie was shaking her head.

'Men like Tobias play a long game, and you must remember that him have a trump card: the fact that Althea still loves him. Last night she thank him for coming down to the station and him just walk off! Didn't say a word to her, throwing the thanks back in her face. That hurt her a lot. If yuh ask me that's what she upstairs ah brood pan.'

'But she's better off without him. In a few months she'll realise that, I'm sure.'

'A few months yuh say,' said Valerie, finally pushing her bowl away. 'Let's just see where we are at the end of next week.'

The top deck of the 47 was deserted except for two women who were sitting towards the back. One had long cornrows decorated with beads; the other wore an African print head-scarf, tied at the front with a knot. They were seated across the aisle from one another, lounging with their feet dangling off the end of the chairs. They were chatting about the bust of Nelson Mandela that was soon to be unveiled on the Southbank. I'd read that notice in the newspaper too, apparently when Margaret Thatcher was asked if she would ever visit the statue, her answer was a firm 'no'.

I sank into one of the empty seats at the very front, where I used to like sitting when I was a child. This was the second of the two buses I needed to get back from Valerie's house and the streets were more congested around here. I leaned my head against the glass, looking out of the window, feeling the vibration of the engine as the bus meandered along. A couple of blokes swigging from bottles of strong cider were sitting on the steps of the doss-house and the stallholders on Market Street were packing up for the day. I was feeling very differently on the way back from Valerie's, compared to how I felt on the way there. Nobody had come for Connie and Althea was home. They were safe. I hated the fact that Tobias would get away with knocking Althea about, just as he'd got away with hitting Connie for years. I was sure once the shock of last night calmed down, Althea would begin to see Tobias more clearly – it certainly didn't sound like he'd be wooing her with flowers anytime soon – so whatever lingering affection Althea had for him would surely melt like snow. I didn't get why Valerie was being so negative, just like Mum. Althea was stronger than they all thought. After all, hadn't she always said, 'wi run t'ings, t'ings nuh run wi?'

The bus didn't go down Jamaica Road, so I got off on the east side of Marsh Town and cut through the estate. It was just after 3 p.m. and the match started at half-past. It was unlikely I'd catch Connie before kick off but there would be time to talk afterwards; he could off-load his thoughts about Tobias turning up and acting the saviour. A caretaker was using strong bleach to swill the stairwell of Tea Clipper House. I veered off the path to get away from the smell, cutting across the scrappy lawn in front of the building. An old man stood on the grass feeding stale bread to the pigeons and from an open window I could hear a woman warbling a gospel hymn a cappella. I could also hear someone calling my name. I turned and saw Mark Barrett coming up a few yards behind me, carrying a sports bag on his shoulder. He glanced around, probably checking there was nobody about that might know him, and then jogged over to me.

'This is a surprise.'

'Seein' as I live on the estate, it can only be half a surprise,' I said, teasing, trying to sound smart.

'God, you're a bloody prover!' he said. 'I mean that it's nice to see you.'

We were standing about three feet apart. Hardly close enough to arouse suspicion. Except to the people that knew us. I thought, *what if his friends happened upon us right now?*

What would the Black students I knew think? My next thought was, did I even care? The last twenty-four hours had been fraught; it was nice to be distracted. I wanted him to kiss me and I wasn't sure how to ask. I wondered if he knew what I was thinking. I needed to say something.

'Visiting your nana?'

'Yeah, picking up my kit; she washed it for me.'

I raised my eyebrows.

'What? She likes doing it!' said Mark. 'You coming to watch the match then?'

'Yeah. I thought I might. Especially if it means seeing you in your kit all washed and pristine! Plus I hear it's an important fixture.'

'Yeah, the Mariners are cocky bastards. Be nice to bring them down a peg or two. I hope your mate's feeling up for it.'

'Why shouldn't he be?' I asked, turning away slightly.

Mark eyed me keenly.

'I was in the common room earlier and overheard some of the Black lads talking. Saying they knew his stepdad was an arsehole, but had no idea about the whole immigration thing. Is it true? That Connie's an illegal?'

'Don't talk about my friend like that! And for your information, he and his mum came here legally. They've applied to the Home Office to get permission to stay. They'll probably hear back in a few weeks. But I suppose you'll run and tell Ted and Craig, so they can daub "Connie go home" on the school walls, rather than just "Niggers Out".'

'I imagine when the lads hear about it, they're gonna have a few things to say, but I ain't saying I agree with them. So I don't know why you're jumping on me.'

I looked at Mark and he paused, pulling himself up.

'Don't get me wrong. We're never gonna be blood brothers or nothing, but Connie's ... well, he's decent. He's a good football player and all. I hope he gets to stay.'

I opened my mouth but couldn't think of a reply. I was taken aback and relieved.

Mark looked sheepish. 'What? I'm not just saying it.'

'I believe you. It's just, you surprise me.'

His familiar grin appeared. 'It's better than boring you. I'm supposed to be meeting Phil later.'

I flinched, but tried to disguise it by fiddling with the strap of my bag. Even so, Mark noticed the way I'd recoiled.

'I can put him off until six-ish if you can meet me.'

Connie was firmly back in the forefront of my mind. After all that had happened, now this – his private business becoming common knowledge. He would definitely want to talk things over with me.

'I dunno. I might be busy.'

A flicker of disappointment crossed Mark's face, but he managed a shrug.

'You got a pen?'

I nodded.

'Give it here,' he said.

'Do you want some paper too?' I asked, handing him a Berol marker.

'Nah,' he said, gently catching my fingers.

The tip of the pen tickled as he wrote seven numbers on the back of my hand. I could smell the Orbit on his breath.

'That's the number of the phone box on the Longshore. I'll be waiting there at quarter-to-five. Call me if you're coming.'

Mark was still holding my hand. He pulled me towards him and kissed my mouth. Right there, in the open space. My head was spinning but at the same time I felt peaceful. When I opened my eyes, Mark was smiling at me.

The two teams were warming up on the pitch when I arrived at the sports field. Mark had gone on ahead of me so he wouldn't be late and also so we wouldn't be seen together. I reminded myself not to stare at him. Connie was on the far side of the pitch, stretching out. Errol ran over and bumped fists with him before jogging off to the stands. I noticed that Omar, Emmanuel and a few of Connie's other friends had shown up, when normally they didn't follow the football. Clearly, it was Connie they had come to support. Rather than joining them by the home-side goal, I found a spot on the halfway line, so I could see both ends of play.

'Hi Daphne. Yuh good?'

The voice came from behind me. I turned and saw Chantelle strolling up.

'Yeah thanks. You?'

Chantelle replied with a nod, then stood beside me.

Connie had finished warming up and looked over in our direction. He waved and in unison, Chantelle and I waved back. I immediately felt embarrassed; was he waving to me or her? Chantelle glanced at me. I let my hand drop and put it in my pocket.

The match began. Twenty minutes of play went by before Chantelle broke the silence between us.

'You weren't in history. It's not like you to bunk lessons.'

'There was something important I had to do,' I said.

She turned to face me. 'It's all right, Daphne. I know you went to look for Connie and I know the reason why. Connie's told me everything. About his mum, his stepdad, the immigration thing.'

'What? He told *you*?' I felt my temper rising, so she was the culprit. 'And you've been spreading it around?'

'No! When Connie opened up to me I just couldn't believe he'd been shouldering so much for so long, which is why I got him to tell his boys too. I think them lot should be more open with each other. Don't you think? That way he's got all our support.'

'I've actually been telling him that for ages,' I said curtly.

'He told me that you've been amazing. Really strong. But it's better now things are out in the open. That way we can *all* be there for him.'

Chantelle had a point. But hearing her say it annoyed me for reasons I didn't understand. I let her statement hang in the air and went back to watching the game.

Connie took a shot on goal, but it hit the post. The home crowd groaned. The opposition cleared it, but only as far as Mark, who struck with his left foot and the ball flew past the Mariners' keeper. There were cheers from the crowd and backslapping among the players; Connie and Mark exchanged a desultory high five. As he jogged back to his start position, Mark cast a glance in my direction. The look brought back the memory of his mouth against mine and I pressed my lips together to revive the sensation. Play resumed and after a few minutes, Chantelle spoke up again.

'You know I was surprised that you and Connie had never got together. Seein' as unnu close like bench an' batty.'

Despite her casual tone, there was a definite bite in her voice. My mind jumped back to when Connie and I briefly danced together at Mum's birthday party, then flashed to last night, the feelings I had when I held him close. Had Connie made some sort of confession to Chantelle when he opened up to her? I couldn't tell if she was goading me into admitting that I had feelings for Connie.

'We're just friends,' I said firmly.

'I know. What I'm saying is that it always seemed as though you really liked him, and to be honest, I felt a bit threatened.' She lowered her voice. 'But I don't now. Cos from what I see, it's the white boys you *really* like.'

At first I was aghast, then quickly forced a scoff.

'I don't know what it is you *think* you see, but you're talking crap.'

Chantelle's eyes widened. 'Luvvie, my auntie lives in Tea Clipper House, and what I *actually* saw from her balcony was you and Mark Barrett kissing.'

My stomach dropped. Alarmed, I looked around, checking that nobody heard.

She continued, 'You do know his brother is a racist psycho.'

'Yes!' I hissed. 'But Mark isn't.'

'Really? Don't his good friends refer to Black people as wogs and niggers? Didn't they call Connie – your best friend, a Black bastard yesterday?'

I folded my arms, holding myself in. 'Mark isn't like them.'

Chantelle kissed her teeth. 'D'you seriously want to be his little trophy? Does he say, "I don't like Blacks but you're all right?" Or worse, does he call you Brown Sugar? Girl, why are you fooling yourself?'

'I'm not fooling myself, and I'm not your *girl*—' I said through clenched teeth.

'Too right! You act so white. Just listen to the way you talk. D'you want to be called a sell-out? A coconut?'

The word felt like a kick in the ribs. I could feel my limbs sag.

'I'm telling you – warning you – what they'll say if people find out about you and him.'

I couldn't speak. I couldn't trust my voice not to betray how much her words had upset me.

'Personally, I think you're mad to like him. You'll never be a normal couple. But I ain't gonna say nothing. I just thought I should have a word.'

Chantelle folded her arms, satisfied that her point had been made.

'Well you've done that now,' I managed to say, before turning and walking away.

Although staying to watch the match was the last thing I wanted to do, I didn't want to give Chantelle the pleasure of driving me off the field. I found a spot on the other side of the pitch, away from Chantelle, away from Connie's friends, away from the white spectators too. Was I really a sell out? A traitor to my race? I was enormously proud of my blackness. But then, what business does a proud Black woman have kissing a white lad from a notoriously racist family? I wanted the match to be over. I needed to talk to Connie. He was the only person who really understood me. I'd been there for him, now I needed him. He'd show Chantelle that she was out of order.

The match ended in a one-all draw. Chantelle stood with

Omar and Emmanuel for the entire second half; now they were clapping loudly, shouting Connie's name. He waved his thanks, but then came over to where I was standing. I couldn't see Chantelle's face clearly, but I hoped that she was livid.

'Hi Daphne, glad to see yuh. I wasn't sure you'd come.'

'I was worried when you weren't around this morning so I went to Valerie's at lunchtime. We somehow missed each other! How are you?'

'Okay, considering all that has happened. I played crap today though.'

'You did well to play at all!'

Connie shrugged. 'To be honest, I just needed the distraction.'

'I hear you told Chantelle and everyone. About what's been going on,' I said.

Connie nodded. 'Chantelle was mad that I never confided in her before, but we chatted about it. She's cool now. Telling the others was easy after that. I'm lucky to have so many good friends. Especially you.'

A smile broke out across my face. Sod Chantelle and the others. Connie and I were solid.

'I couldn't believe what Valerie told me about Tobias, the wretch!'

Connie grimaced. 'I don't want to talk about him.'

'Oh. Fair enough. Well come back to mine and we can just hang.'

'Actually, I'm going over to Chantelle's now. Her mum's at work. And ... well, I just need to relax, you know. Behave like a normal, ordinary yout'. D'yuh understand?'

'Yeah. Sure.' Connie shuffled his feet, perhaps wondering

how to take his leave, as my heart sank. 'You should make tracks,' I added.

'Yeah. Thanks for everything. You've been great these past few weeks. I couldn't ask for a better friend.'

'Best friends, yeah?'

'Yeah,' he whispered.

I tramped off the playing fields and out of school, kicking at the loose shingle along Jamaica Road. I was feeling properly pissed off. We were so very close last night, but he didn't want to be with me now. He wanted to be a 'normal, ordinary yout' – which as far as I could see meant shagging bloody Chantelle Williams. He'd been through a lot these past weeks but hadn't I been there at his side? Trying to support him? I'd reached the entrance of the estate; there was a telephone box outside the East India House flats. I didn't have to be alone. I could be a normal, ordinary yout' too – I didn't care what Chantelle thought. As Althea said, 'wi run t'ings, t'ings nuh run wi'. I looked at my watch; it was 4.45 p.m.

Cradling the receiver between my ear and my shoulder, I dialled the numbers written on the back of my hand. The dial tone purred three times, four times, five, then:

'Hello.'

The voice on the other end was drowned out by the bleeps. I didn't have any change for the slot – I'd have to speak quickly.

'Mark? It's Daphne. I'm on my way.'

18

My alarm went off at 7 a.m.; I reached over and pressed the stop button just as the bleeps were becoming urgent. Mark's eyes flickered, he rolled over, laying his arm across my body. Two months had passed and although we'd been having sex for the last four weeks, this was the first time we had ever spent the whole night together.

'Come on, wake up. My mum's shift finishes in half an hour. If she comes straight home she'll be back at half-eight.'

Mark's eyes opened. 'That's ages away,' he whispered, kissing my shoulder. His hand slid beneath the covers.

Our bodies were already pressed tight in my narrow bed, but I shuffled the few inches closer, kissing his neck and reaching for his cock. Mark slipped his hands between my thighs. I rolled onto my back and closed my eyes, no longer thinking about the time ticking away; I wanted a repeat of the night before. From the start, it had felt different from those other occasions. We lounged on the settee for ages, chatting and joking, before he leaned in to kiss me. By the time we got upstairs, we were both turned on, yet curiously slowed down. I didn't feel under pressure to just get to it. I watched him undress, enjoying the leanness of his body.

I shivered with an exquisite anticipation as he took off my clothes, allowing myself to enjoy him looking at me. I trusted him, despite everything. I didn't writhe around, panting like women did in the raunchy scenes on *Dynasty*. Joy came as a quiet, intense rush rather than a theatrical moan. It was the first orgasm I'd had with Mark. Afterwards, I found myself wondering if one day we could bring our relationship out in the open, but quickly decided there were far too many obstacles.

Downstairs, the phone started to ring. I groaned.

'Just leave it.'

'I can't, it's probably Mum.'

I slung on my dressing gown and hurried downstairs.

'Hello?'

'Daphne?'

'Connie!' I lowered my voice. 'D'you know what time it is?'

'Yeah. Sorry, it's just I'm not going in to school today and I wanted to catch you before you headed out. I need a favour. Well Althea does . . .'

In the background I could make out Althea's voice getting louder, telling Kallai to 'eat the blasted cereal'.

'Hold on a minute, Daphne,' said Connie. He muffled the receiver but I could still hear his voice, soothing, patient. 'Nuh make him eat the cereal if he don't want it. I'll cook him some cornmeal porridge. Go back to bed and mi bring yuh some tea.'

Connie uncovered the mouthpiece. 'Hello, Daphne. Yuh still there?'

'Yeah, go ahead.'

'Althea has a trial at a salon tomorrow, dem pay cash and

with Christmas coming, we need all the extra money we can get.'

'But Valerie isn't charging you to stay with her.'

'I know. She and Greville have been great. Before dem go on their vacation last week, dem buy a whole heap of food and presents for us. But Althea and me feel we should contribute. Althea has her portfolio but it's like she's lost confidence; if dem can see her in action I'm sure she will impress dem. Could yuh come and model for her? It would be tomorrow morning. Yuh know how she works fast; she'd be done by lunchtime.'

'Yes, of course. Anything to help.'

Connie released a deep sigh. 'T'anks. Althea's been a bit stressed lately; we still nuh hear anyt'ing from immigration since she called a fortnight ago. She said they told her there was a backlog after some strike.'

'Oh Connie. I'm sorry. This waiting must be awful.'

I listened to Connie's breathing, expecting him to respond to what I'd said. Instead, he changed the subject.

'It's easier if you just meet Althea there. It's Nubian Roots off Camberwell Road. Come by the takeaway after. We'll have lunch. It'll be good to see you.'

Mark was sitting up, waiting for my return. He patted the bed, but my mind was still with Connie. I tugged my dressing gown closed. Suddenly, I felt uncomfortable rather than sexy.

'It was Mum. She'll be on her way back soon.'

He looked at me funny. Had he heard the phone conversation? He rose slowly and began to dress.

'Meet me in Leicester Square later. We'll go to the

pictures.' He spoke as though he were issuing a dare, rather than an invitation.

'Why would I do that?' I said, giving him the side-eye.

'Cos it's Christmas next week and we won't get to meet up then. And well . . . it'll be nice to go out. Properly.'

'Miss Tempest is looking at Blake's poetry in this afternoon's lesson.'

Mark rolled his eyes. 'You do realise it's the last day of term. Nobody will even notice if you ain't in. Go on, you know you really want to . . . '

'What I really want is the exam practise, so next year I can get 2 As and a B, and study English Lit at either Bristol, Durham or Manchester.'

'You're such a swot. It's one of the things I love about you.'

My pulse skipped.

Mark looked away. 'Well, you know what I mean.'

He laughed. It wasn't a proper laugh but I laughed too. Then I kissed him.

'If I'm gonna go skiving with you this afternoon, I'd better get some work done now. So, you need to be on your way,' I said.

The traffic crawled all the way from Elephant and Castle, and when the bus reached Parliament it ground to a halt. On the square, there was a group of people unfurling a banner calling for sanctions against South Africa; there was another, separate bunch with placards pledging support for the Women at Greenham Common. I'd come into central London last month, when I joined Marcia, and thousands of others who marched from Herne Hill to Hyde Park, in solidarity with the Cherry Groce Support Campaign and the Cynthia Jarrett Defence Committee.

It was the first time I had ever taken part in a protest. At first I was nervous, fearful of losing Marcia and her boyfriend, Kwame, in the crowd, worried that there would be trouble with the police or from far right groups. But once we began marching – chanting in unison – all my nerves dissolved. I was surrounded by people passionate about justice. I was involved, I was making noise! It was exhilarating. Connie had wanted to come on the demo too, but these days his weekends were spent juggling his part-time job at Valerie's takeaway with looking after Kallai. While I didn't expect Mark to show up for the protest, I hadn't thought he would get so narked when I told him why it was so important for me to go. After that quarrel, there was a tacit understanding that we should avoid discussing certain topics. We both wanted to keep seeing each other, and I thought that by spending time together, Mark would start to see things differently. It was fun. It was exciting. There was what he'd said this morning. Last night it did feel as though things between us had shifted. I felt close to him. But was I ready to say those words to myself, let alone say them out loud? I'd bought Mark a Christmas present I found at Greenwich Market, a bootleg tape of The Specials' gig at the Hammersmith Palais in 1980. Up ahead, I saw the traffic had begun moving again. I sat up in my seat, urging the bus forward.

'In't it lovely just doing fuck all,' said Mark. 'This is proper skiving.'

It was after the movie and we'd left the hustle of tourists

in Leicester Square and Christmas shoppers tramping up the Haymarket. We had held hands as we wandered down the Mall, the charm bracelet Mark had given me, an excellent charity shop find, hanging loosely around my wrist. Now we were lying beneath a tree in St James's Park, looking up at the grey sky through the bare branches. My head was propped against Mark's stomach, feeling his body move every time he spoke.

'You can't even skive when you're on the dole, they're on your back so much. Craig's joining the army, thinks he'll get to learn a trade. Most likely he'll end up squatting behind some garden hedge in Londonderry, dodging bullets.'

I hated it when he mentioned his friends. I rolled onto my side so I could see him better; he remained on his back looking past me.

'Why don't you apply to a Poly? You can get in with two A-levels.'

'Nah, that in't me.'

'It could be.'

Mark shifted his head so he was looking at me. 'D'you know what I've always fancied doing as a job? Don't laugh . . . being a fireman.'

'Why would I laugh?'

'It's the sort of thing you say when you're a kid. Anyway, now they're getting more Black people and women to apply, so . . .'

'What d'you mean *so* . . .?' I said, hearing the edge in my tone.

'So, it will be harder for people like me to get in.'

I sat up and fiddled with the love heart charm on the bracelet.

'What now?' Mark said.

'Why did you say that?'

He sat up. 'Well it's true, ain't it? It's what the bloody GLC are doing. It was in the paper.'

'The *Sun*, I presume.'

'Might have been.'

'I don't suppose they mentioned that every fire brigade in London is pretty much made up of white blokes. The GLC ain't trying to let other people in just to spite you, it's about . . . providing equal opportunity.'

'Right. D'you know you sound like some loony lefty?'

'Yeah. And you sound just like your mates and your brother.'

'Here we go. How is it racist to point out that it's gonna be harder for me to get the jobs I want, if they're gonna be offering preferential treatment to Blacks and women? How is that equality?'

'Well you wouldn't understand inequality, because you've been ahead of some of us since birth.'

I knew it was a weak retort, but I didn't feel like having a reasoned discussion. It seemed so plain to me that society was racist and things needed to change. Mark wasn't thick, why was he still not able to see this?

Mark lit a cigarette. He was looking out across the grass at the people walking along the paths, while I kept my eyes facing the lake. I could feel the pleasure of the day evaporating.

'I told Nana about you last week. She wants to meet you.'

'What? Really? How did I even come up?'

Mark shrugged. 'We've always been close. She just come out with it, asked me if I had a girlfriend yet and I said yes.'

'You actually said girlfriend?'

'Yeah, I did as it goes. I said she was a right clever clogs, calls second-hand stuff "vintage", a bit of a weirdo really.' I slapped Mark's arm. He laughed; it made me smile. 'I also said she was gorgeous. Then I said, she's Black.'

I gasped, 'What did she say to that?'

'Nothing. I told you before, Nana in't prejudiced. Not like Grandad, he was proper racist. Him and his workmates from down the docks went out on strike for Enoch Powell. Him and Nana never got on; they only married because she got pregnant. She kicked him out years ago.' Mark tugged on his cigarette, tilted his neck and slowly blew the smoke into the air. 'Dad's always on at her to move off the estate, says there are no "decent whites" left there now. Only slappers with half-caste children.'

'So you'd never tell your dad or Phil about me then,' I said, dryly.

Mark scoffed, 'Only if I wanted a fucking slap. Then a lecture. Then another slap!' He flicked ash from his cigarette before crushing it into the ground. 'They hate Blacks, and Asians, and Jews and Fenians, and West Ham. It's fucking stifling.'

He trailed off into silence. His usual cheeky self-assuredness had gone. An uncomfortable feeling was niggling its way to the front of my mind. Chantelle had said it. 'You'll never be a normal couple.' I didn't want it to be true; I wanted to be closer to Mark.

'I'm sorry about your dad and Phil. I like the sound of your nana and I'd love to meet her. She'd get on with my grandma. She likes the bloke Mum goes out with. She's not bothered about him being white cos he makes Mum happy. Looks like we can at least rely on Miss Gladys and your nana to help the course of true love run smoothly . . . '

Mark looked up. He was staring at me. I realised what I'd said and quickly continued.

'Well, true *lust* rather than true love . . . '

He stroked my face with the tips of his fingers. It was an honest, tender touch.

'D'you think, maybe it's both?' he asked.

I gazed into his eyes; I felt warm and light. 'Could be,' I said.

19

Kallai was sitting on a sofa beneath a framed poster of Haile Selassie. The large 'I am 7' badge was still pinned to his pullover, even though his birthday was a month ago. He was playing with the Transformer 'Auntie Valerie' had given him, while Althea plaited my hair. She gave me a copy of *Chic* magazine to flick through but I was more interested in looking around. I'd never been to the hairdressers before – and most salons were not like Nubian Roots. Here, there was no hair straightening nor Jheri curl solution. The clients at all of the six workstations were either having their Afros braided into intricate cornrows or their dreadlocks treated, retwisted and styled. I liked the idea of having dreadlocks but Mum was dead against it, saying that if I had locs then I could kiss goodbye to job prospects and expect loads of police harassment Even so, I watched in awe as a woman of Miss Gladys's age prepared to wash her hair, removing her headscarf then unfurling silver-grey dreadlocks that almost reached the floor. Behind me one of the stylists and his client, an older Dread, were reasoning on Black history, discussing what they'd read in *Staying Power* and *The Black Jacobins*; I made a note to look these books up next time I went to the library. I imagined this was the sort of place Althea would love to own someday. I watched her through the mirror while she worked, concentration etched on her face. She hadn't spoken much. It was warm in the salon and when she pushed back her sleeves, I noticed how skinny her wrists were. Nevertheless, her fingers were dexterous as usual and the style she'd given me, a beautiful criss-cross of plaits building from the nape of my neck to the crown of my head, trumpeted her skill and flair. Kallai came over to us.

'I'm bored now, Mammy. When will I get my treat?'

'Soon. Hush yuh mout' now,' Althea commanded.

A petite woman, whose crinkly locs were tied up with kente cloth, came and stood next to Althea, greeting me with a smile.

'Blessing, sis. That style really bring out the empress in yuh.' She turned to Althea. 'May I have a word?'

'Yes ... yes ... of course,' Althea stammered.

She followed the lady to a room at the back of the shop.

Kallai was tugging at my sleeve. 'Daffeny, what do you like best about Optimus?'

'I don't know. I like his colour. He's a shiny red truck and then he's a shiny red robot. That's pretty cool.'

'I like his gun best. Megatron is a tank, so it's got an even better gun than Optimus.' I nodded, distractedly admiring my hair.

Kallai continued, 'I'm getting Megatron later. Daddy's bringing it for me.'

Suddenly, Kallai had my full attention. 'Your daddy? Later? What do you mean Kallai?'

'My friend Malachi has got Megatron too, so we'll both have the same, we'll be able to do battles ...'

Kallai was absorbed in conversation with himself. I looked up and saw that Althea was coming back towards us.

'Imani really liked the way I did yuh hair. She told me to come back tomorrow and then I'll work next week too – well, until Christmas Eve. T'ank you fi modelling for me this morning,' said Althea.

'Not at all. Thank you,' I said, forcing a smile.

When we were outside I asked Althea if she was heading home, as we would be able to ride together as far as New Cross Gate. I watched her eyes drift to the side, then downwards.

'No. Mi have some errands to do. Mi see yuh likkle more. Happy Christmas.'

Althea took Kallai's hand and set off, her shoulders stooped, walking so quickly that the kid was trotting to keep up. A 171 was heading up the street; I'd easily catch it if I ran to the next bus stop, but instead I stood, watching Althea. She'd reached the corner of the road and was standing outside a pub. I saw her push open the doors and go inside. As far as I knew, hardly any Black people, let alone Black women, ever went into pubs in South East London by themselves, especially with children in tow. The 171 lumbered past and I walked hesitantly towards the Dew Drop Tavern.

Althea had gone in through the entrance with 'saloon' written in loopy gold writing. A frosted glass panel in the door made it impossible to see in, so I went around to the side of the building. Peering through the green stained glass that ran along the bottom of the panes, I could see this part of the pub was deserted, except for two elderly Black men who were leaning against the bar. A photo of Merlene Ottey with her Olympic bronze medal was on a shelf behind the optics post, along with a Jamaican flag. A pub run by Black people – fancy that. There was no sign of Althea and Kallai.

I moved along the outside of the building. I felt uneasy spying on her like this, but I told myself I was acting out of concern. Passing the entrance to the 'lounge' I peeked in again. A light-skinned bartender with a receding hairline was behind the bar serving a tall man. Even though the man had his back to the window, his build, his hair, even his jacket, were familiar to me. It was Tobias. In disbelief, I watched him pick up two glasses, carrying one in each hand. I craned my neck to follow him, stepping to the next window where I caught sight of Althea. She was sitting at a table watching Kallai unwrap a present, the Megatron Transformer. Tobias sat down beside them and Kallai gave his father a hug. They made a charming group, a happy family, without a care in the world. Althea's gaze shifted. She shrank when her eyes locked with mine. Tobias turned and stared too, a slanted grin appeared beneath his moustache. My heart thudded against my chest as I spun on my heel and hurried to the bus stop, wishing that I could unsee what I'd just witnessed. Connie was probably mopping the takeaway floor at this very moment, wondering how Althea had got on at the salon and trying to remain strong in the face of all their worries. Yet here was Althea sitting cosy with the violent man she had fled from.

'Daphne, wait!' I quickened my pace. 'Daphne, please!' The hitch in Althea's tone arrested me. I waited for her to catch up before I went on the attack.

'What are you doing with him?'

'By *him*, I suppose yuh mean mi pickney father? My husband? What mi doing here is my business, who yuh t'ink yuh is?'

'I'm your friend and I'm telling you that man is no good for you.'

'Friend? How are we friends when mi a big woman and yuh jus' a young gyal? What yuh know about life? How yuh fi understand what it is to love somebody – even when yuh know it's bad fi yuh?'

I felt myself shrink. Althea looked away and when she spoke again, her voice was low and plaintive.

'It nuh just that. I haven't told Connie, but ... they've paused mi application. Tobias called and tell me a week ago. The Home Office are investigating us.'

'What does that mean?'

'Mi and Tobias have to be interviewed. They suspect mi marriage is a sham. Wi have to prove to dem that wi really are a couple. If mi get deported, how yuh think mi ah go live? No job, no money, cotching at mi daddy yard. Tobias will divorce mi and want custody of Kallai. D'yuh t'ink mi want him to stay here, to grow up without mi? Yuh nuh understand what it would do to him – to me. My marriage may not be ideal, but it was never a sham, not to me. I want to save mi family.'

'What about Connie? He's your family too. He wouldn't want you to get back with Tobias – even if it meant you could stay. There has to be another way. If Connie knew, he'd be telling you the same thing as me.'

'Nuh tell him.'

I blinked at Althea. 'If you're seriously planning to get back with Tobias then he'll have to know, and it's better he knows now.'

She grabbed my arm. 'Yuh must can see the pressure him under trying to stay strong. It shouldn't be that way for no seventeen-year-old. Don't give him more stress when nuttin' nuh decide yet. If Tobias will take mi back, then I'll talk to him, but for now Daphne, I'm asking yuh please nuh tell him. Promise mi.'

The mascara on her lashes had clumped together in the corners. She looked weary. I felt sorry for her. Mum had always said, 'Yuh too faas and ah faas make anansi de ah house top'. I'd chosen to meddle and now I was tangled in the affairs I'd crawled into.

One Love Caribbean Cuisine was primarily a takeaway, but Valerie had squeezed tables into the L-shaped space between the door and the serving counter for any customers who wanted to linger and chat. When I arrived, the lunchtime rush had slowed to a trickle, only a stout guy in council overalls was eating in. Blossom, Valerie's head cook and bottle washer, changed the tape from reggae to soca; she began picking up plates and empty bottles of Supermalt, wiggling her hips as she went. Connie appeared from the kitchen carrying two soup bowls balanced on dinner plates. He sat down opposite me.

'Yuh hair looks nice. So it went all right at the salon? Althea's okay?'

'Yeah. Fine,' I said, halving a dumpling with the edge of my spoon, remembering to smile.

'It's good to see yuh. Yuh like the soup? It's the first time I get to cook here.'

The soup's aroma took me back to the Saturday dinner times of my childhood, when Miss Gladys would throw together a soup while watching the wrestling on TV. Then it had always been a comfort, but the beautiful flavours Connie had cooked up were tasteless on my lying tongue. Connie slouched with his elbows and forearms on the table, hunched over the bowl. I sat upright in my seat, tense.

'Yuh all set for Christmas?' Connie said, breaking the silence.

'Nah. You?'

'I've planned what I'm cooking. I got a Knight Rider Car for Kallai and Chantelle used her Boots staff discount to get bath t'ings and talc for Althea.'

'I thought you two had broken up? Are you back together now?'

'No, me and her are just friends.' Connie's tone was abrupt, then he softened. 'She understands that I have enough to deal with right now.'

'Oh. I see.'

'Speaking of presents . . . ' He rummaged in the front pocket of his apron and pulled out a small package, wrapped in tissue paper. 'Merry Christmas.'

'Gosh. I thought we weren't doing presents. I haven't got you anything.'

'That doesn't matter to me. Well open it nuh!' said Connie shifting in his seat, looking bashful.

I tore open the wrapping; inside was a C90 cassette.

'Greville have some fabulous records in him collection,' said Connie. 'And his music centre have Dolby so it sound crisp.'

I turned it over; the tracks were listed in Connie's neat hand, a mixture of old-school soul and the classic lovers' tunes he knew I liked. So much time and thought. So much love. It made me ache.

'It's lovely. Thank you.'

Blossom came over and handed Connie an envelope with his wages that she said included a Christmas bonus; Connie looked proud and also relieved.

'Yuh deserve it, but nuh spend it all in one place. I'll set everyt'ing here in order, galaag and have some fun with yuh nice friend here.'

She winked at us.

I gulped down a piece of chocho. 'Oh, I actually need to go after this ... Mum's got a heap of chores for me to do in the house.'

'D'yuh have to rush off?' Connie asked. 'I mean ... I hardly see yuh anymore. I tell yuh what, Errol lend me his bike till New Year in exchange for calculus tuition. We could go to the old park. I'll take yuh home after. If yuh like. Please.'

I stirred the soup, playing for time, but I couldn't think up an excuse.

'Okay,' I said, prizing out a smile.

I sat sideways on the crossbar and Connie leant over me. Neither of us spoke as he cycled along the backstreets towards Marsh Town. I wondered if Althea was still with Tobias. When would she tell Connie about their immigration application? How could I just stay silent? As we neared the park, Connie swerved around a pothole; I yelped and clung tighter to the handlebar.

'Careful! I don't want to end up in casualty.'

Connie swerved again, despite the smooth road. Then again. I looked over my shoulder at him; he began to chuckle. I poked my tongue out at him as he laughed. I hadn't seen that dimple denting his cheek for ages. It was lovely to see. I knew then that I wouldn't say a word. Not today.

We hardly ever came to the park now. It seemed smaller and shabbier than it did when we were young. We sat on a bench looking out onto the grass, where white lines marked out the football pitches. Connie took a can of Nurishment from his bag and we sat sharing the drink.

'Somet'ing's wrong. Althea hasn't been herself for ages now, but these last two weeks she's been jumpy and bad tempered. What she said about the application being stuck in a backlog . . . I dunno, she's hiding something. Makes me uneasy. Although I can't remember the last time mi never felt uneasy.'

He tried to smile but it was too great an effort. I reached over and placed my hand on his, holding it tight. He didn't react.

'The other day I found meself t'inking that mi could just hand meself over to immigration, let dem send mi back. At least that way me'd have some control over the situation. Better that than waiting.'

I wanted to come clean and tell him about the application and Althea's foolish, desperate plan. But I knew that he would hate it. He'd be angry. My tongue stuck rigid to the roof of my mouth. Instead, I caressed his cheek with the back of my fingers. His skin was warm. Connie caught my hand.

'I'm sorry. That was wrong,' I said, drawing back, flustered.

He held on to my hand and brought it back to his face. I felt myself kissing his temple. Soft, light kisses. He tilted his face towards me. I paused, watchful, waiting for permission. I kissed his forehead again, then the bridge of his nose, then his mouth. I pressed my lips against his, coaxing them to open. My tongue tasted the vanilla in his mouth from the drink, his arms tightened around me and I felt myself melting into him.

'Oi, stop that!'

We sprang apart, looking around. A man was calling to his German shepherd, but the dog ignored him, too busy bothering squirrels up a sycamore tree.

'Let's walk,' I said, scrambling up from the bench.

We strode along beneath the avenue of plane trees, walking either side of the bike, the click of its gears punctuating the silence.

Connie paused. 'This is awkward innit? It was out of order. Me kissing yuh.'

I kept my eyes fixed straight ahead. 'I kissed you first, didn't I? I dunno what came over me. I'm the one who is being out of order, to you. To Mark. Christ! As if things weren't complicated enough with him already.'

'Yuh nuh have to tell him. And I won't say nothing. It was just a kiss.' Connie glanced at me. 'It's not that we likely to do it again. Is it? Yuh with Mark and anyway, this is the way it is with us.'

Connie carried on speaking but I was only half listening. I liked Mark, but until just now, I hadn't really thought about him at all. I didn't want to do anything that would hurt Mark, but I was already hurting Connie by not telling him about Tobias. All these bloody secrets. I needed to get away.

I cut in over Connie, 'Let's leave it eh? It shouldn't have happened. I ought to get back home.'

Connie frowned at me. 'All right.'

We'd left the park and were heading along the road towards the estate.

'There's no need for you to come any further,' I said.

Connie sighed. 'This is just weird now. And I don't want it to be like that between us. It's bad enough that Althea and me haven't been getting on.'

I fiddled with the strap of my bag, the mention of Althea adding to my unease. Connie didn't seem to notice.

'With Althea I only want what is right for her, but she is so distant and moody nowadays. Sometimes it's like I'm the adult and she is the child. It's tiring.'

I directed my gaze to the pavement while Connie continued.

'Your muddah is strict, but she's there for yuh – Miss Gladys too. Although mi love Althea, there's been times when I haven't been able to say the same. The only person who's always been there for mi since mi come ah England is yuh, Daphne. And I'm sorry to make t'ings tricky, but I wanted to kiss yuh.'

I finally made myself look at his open, honest face. He was so dear to me. 'Connie, I have to tell you ... '

The shrill blast of a siren cut me off. A police squad car pulled up alongside us, the copper on the passenger side bellowed from the window.

'Stop right there!'

'Who, us?' said Connie.

'Yeah, you.'

The police officers got out of their car. They were tall, taller than Connie and broader across the shoulders and chest. I sensed Connie tensing up. I was tense too, even though I knew we hadn't been doing anything wrong.

'Can you tell me what you're doing around here?' said the dark-haired officer with bushy eyebrows. It didn't seem like he was talking to both of us – he was only looking at Connie.

'We're going home,' I said.

'D'you live around here?' he said, his eyes still riveted on Connie.

'Yes. I live over there, on the estate,' I said, speaking louder.

'And you? D'you live on the estate too?' asked the other officer. He was close to our age, his skin still bore the marks left from acne scars.

'No. I live in Brockley,' said Connie, warily, flattening the Jamaican from his voice.

'Well you're a long way from home, aren't you?' he said.

'Is there a problem, officer?' asked Connie.

'We're asking the questions here. Turn around, put your hands against the wall. Legs apart.'

Connie moved slowly, more stunned than defiant. The young policeman shoved him towards the wall and he stumbled, causing the bike to clatter to the ground. Instinct made me move towards Connie.

The copper barked at me, 'Stay there, you. Don't move.'

I stopped dead. He was looming over me. I'd heard about what the police could do if they felt like it – I'd seen it with my own eyes. We hadn't done anything and I hated them for stopping us and treating Connie this way. I hated that they were able to make me so bloody compliant. I clasped my hands in front of me, to hide how much they were shaking. The officer turned back to Connie.

'Somebody matching your description was seen fleeing from a burglary on a bike,' he said.

'Whoever it is, it's not me,' said Connie, resentment edging into his voice. 'I've been at work, then I was with her.'

'What's this?' The officer had found Connie's envelope.

'That's my wages. I earned it.'

He turned Connie around so he was facing him, pinning him forcefully against the wall with his arm.

'You've earned fifty quid? Pull the other one.'

'It's true. Leave him alone!' I said.

The officer ignored me. 'I want your full name and address,' he said.

'Cornelius,' Connie mumbled.

'Like from *Planet of the Apes*? Cornelius what?' Connie hesitated. 'Can't remember your name? Can you remember where you live? Or is that back in Africa?'

The policeman leaned in further, pressing against Connie's chest, but still he didn't reply. If they knew his full name, they'd be able to check his immigration status. Any trouble with the law would negatively affect his application for leave to remain.

'Look, c'mon. I haven't done nothing,' said Connie, gasping.

'All right, you're nicked.' The dark-haired policeman began pulling him towards the car.

'Wait! You can't do this!' I said. 'He hasn't done anything.'

'Step back unless you want to be arrested too,' said the other officer as they bundled Connie into the back seat.

'But where are you taking him?'

'Asylum Road, to help us with our enquiries.'

The car pulled away and I was left on the pavement with the bike lying on its side. My mind was a roar, trying to process what the fuck had just happened. I had to tell Althea. I ran across the road to a graffiti-covered phone box, hoping the telephone worked. I stabbed at the buttons and waited for Althea to pick up. I counted twelve rings; there was nobody there. I shivered, suddenly feeling very cold. Could she still be with Tobias? The pub was miles away but perhaps I could ring and see if she was there. Then it dawned on me. I re-inserted the coin and slowly typed another phone number. A voice growled down the receiver.

'Tobias?'

'Yeah. Who is this?

'It's Daphne.' I took a breath to compose myself. 'I need to speak to Althea. Please. It's important. Connie's been arrested.'

'What! When?'

'Just now. He was seeing me home and the police pulled up out of nowhere.'

Tobias was silent.

'Hello? Are you still there?'

'Tell me what happened. Nuh leave anyt'ing out.'

The desk officer at Asylum Road Police Station looked Tobias up and down.

'I'm afraid I cannot give out information about anyone who's been detained without their permission, unless you are a solicitor. Been to law school have you?'

Tobias exhaled through his lips. 'I know you have me step-son in custody. He's seventeen years old and if you're holding him for questioning, then it's his right to have a parent or guardian present. This girl was there when he was arrested; she saw the whole thing.'

While Tobias was speaking, I noticed how his patwah had crept back, his South London accent was genial and direct. He sounded like one of them.

He leaned into the glass panel. 'I know me rights and his rights too. You can't bring him in 'ere and hold him because you suspect him of this, that or whatever. You need concrete evidence that he's committed a crime, or was about to commit a crime. So, either you release him and send him out here to me, or let me in there to see him. I ain't leaving this spot till you do one of them things.'

The police officer tutted but took up his biro. 'What was the name?'

Tobias smirked. 'Cornelius Small, that's S M A double L . . .'

Connie looked dishevelled when he was finally brought into the foyer, but at least he didn't seem hurt. I hurried over and held him tight, pressing the side of my face against his chest. I could feel the muscles in his upper arms go rigid. Glancing up, I saw that he was looking over my head. At Tobias.

'Come, mi nuh have all evening,' said Tobias, walking towards the door.

Heavy-footed, Connie allowed me to tug him across the foyer and out of the building; then he shook my hand away.

'Wah yuh doing here?' he asked, glaring at Tobias.

'It was me,' I said. 'I rang Althea when you got arrested. Somebody had to come and get you out.'

'Yeah but what's *he* doing here? Where's Althea?' Connie was looking at me, his brow knotted, his eyes darkened. I bit my lip. 'What's going on?'

Tobias was smiling. 'What? Yuh good friend nuh tell yuh she see me and yuh muddah together earlier? The Home Office want to interview us. Probably because of that trouble a couple of months ago when someone inform pan unnu. Now dem suspect the marriage is a fraud.'

Connie was shaking his head while Tobias continued, relishing the moment.

'But it's good in a way. We've been sorting t'rough our differences. She realise she still loves me and beg for me to tek her back. After all, I couldn't go to any government interview and just pretend, that wouldn't be right. And I'm an honest man. So, just like how me save yuh from the police tonight, me gwaan save yuh from deportation too. Yuh best remember it and be grateful. Now get in the car.'

Tobias got into his Ford Granada and started the engine, but Connie remained where he was, looking at the ground. Silent.

'Althea made me promise not to say anything. I wanted to tell you. I was going to.'

I reached for his hand but he snatched it away. There were tears in his eyes.

'I don't want to hear what you were going to do. You're supposed to be my friend, but you kept this from me. How could you?'

Connie followed Tobias to the car. I started to cry.

'I'm sorry,' I called after him, trying to get him to turn back to me, but they drove off, leaving me alone on the pavement. 'I'm sorry,' I said again, to no one.

20

It was 3 p.m. on Sunday when I stepped out of the lift onto the eighteenth floor of Hibbert Court. I walked along the dimly lit corridor, rehearsing the lines I'd prepared. The words I'd wanted to say to Connie since Friday night. Earlier, I'd travelled over to Adelaide Avenue, but the house was locked up tight. Through partially drawn curtains I could see a forlorn Christmas tree standing lopsided in the bay window; bare except for the odd strand of lametta still draped over the plastic branches. Connie, Althea and Kallai had already moved out. So I headed back to the estate.

Althea opened the door as wide as the length of the chain. Her plaits hung loose around her face and there were hollows under her eyes.

'Connie's not here.'

'Are you just saying that cos he doesn't want to see me?' I asked.

The door closed, I heard the rattle of the chain, then Althea was standing before me, in shapeless, grey jogging bottoms and a sweatshirt with *Relax* printed across the front. She wandered off and I followed her into the sitting room.

'Yuh satisfied? Him not here, all right?' she said.

'I'm sorry. It's just that we've not spoken since Saturday. I know he's angry with me, but I must see him.' I sounded pathetic.

Althea folded her arms across her chest. 'Him vexed with me as well.'

'No wonder, we've both betrayed him.'

Althea bristled. 'Mi never betray him. I am doing what is best for all of us. So we have the best chance of staying 'ere and staying together. Tobias wants that too. He's changed, he really has – despite what Connie t'ink.'

'Oh come on, Althea! Men like Tobias don't just change. I know you're scared that without him you'll get deported. But you're acting like this is all a fresh start. Think about what it will mean if you stay with him.'

Althea was shaking her head. 'Listen, darlin', it's all right for yuh. Yuh English. It's all right for Valerie too; she find a nice pensioner husband, she marry quick time and naturalised like that,' she said, clicking her fingers. 'Mi live here nearly eight years now; if mi deported then everyt'ing me work for would just dissolve like butter in the sun. Yuh t'ink life is simple. And love is all hearts and flowers. Well let mi tell yuh sweet'eart sometimes it's hard, and sometimes it's about sacrifice – especially when yuh have pickney.'

I suddenly felt very small. I looked down at the carpet. 'I'm sorry I bothered you. Please tell Connie I came by. Tell him I'm thinking of him,' I said.

Rather than being able to make amends, all I'd achieved was to make myself more wretched. The lift stopped on the sixteenth floor. I managed to suppress a sob as the doors opened and a woman stepped inside. She was followed by two boys and a little girl with Ghana twists, all still in their church-going clothes. The children gazed at me, but the woman told them off for staring. As the lift made its laboured descent, I stood there willing myself not to cry. I thought of Mark. He might be at his nan's; it was Sunday after all. I knew that I shouldn't just turn up out of the blue, but I was so anxious to see him. True, Connie had been at the forefront of my mind for the past two days, but it was like he said – this is the way it was with us. We'd always be best friends, nothing more. Now I needed to feel Mark's arms around me, hear him tell me that it would all be okay. I didn't want to think about the last two days. I wanted to be with someone who wasn't angry with me. I wanted my boyfriend.

The white lady standing in the doorway had platinum-coloured hair, held back from her face by the tortoiseshell combs lodged above each ear. The gold chain hung around her neck said BERYL in block capitals. I could hear laughter coming from inside. Suddenly, I felt frightened, what if the whole Barrett family were gathered there? Perhaps they were all visiting Nana as it was so close to Christmas.

'Sorry ... I think I'm in the wrong place ... sorry,' I stuttered, turning to leave.

'Is it Daphne?' I nodded, unable to trust my voice. 'Would you like to come in?'

There was a peal of laughter from inside the flat.

'No. I don't know. Is Mark there please?'

'Yes dear. Other than him, it's strictly friends inside – not family. If that's what's worrying you.'

Beryl turned to call inside but Mark had appeared behind her.

'I heard your voice. What are you doing here Daphne?'

'I'm sorry to just call round like this. But I wanted to see you.'

Beryl made an *ahem* sound. 'I'll give you some privacy,' she said.

Mark grabbed his coat and we walked across to the riverbank.

'Nana's got the neighbours over; they've been on Snowballs since lunchtime. She'll be playing Slade and that bloody Shakin' Stevens song any minute now.'

I tried to smile but couldn't. I looked down at the paving stones.

Mark placed his hand beneath my chin, lifting my face towards his.

'Daphne, what's wrong?'

'I've fucked up. I've fucked everything up . . . '

'What d'you mean? God . . . you're not . . . you know . . . ' he trailed off, biting his lower lip.

'No, Mark. I'm not pregnant.'

A look of relief broke out across his face. 'Oh. Good. Well, what is it then? C'mon, love, tell me.'

'It's Connie. We've really fallen out. He's so angry with me. I don't know what to do.'

A shadow crossed Mark's face. I felt his arm go slack. 'Oh. Right,' he said.

'Shall I tell you what happened or what?'

Mark stepped away from me. 'If you want.'

'Yeah I do want. I'm upset. This is really important to me.

I've let him down badly; now I feel dreadful and can't make it right. Don't you care?'

'Would you care if I fell out with Craig?'

I hesitated. 'Probably not, but then your friendship with Craig Evans is different from my friendship with Connie.'

'Really? How is it different?' said Mark. 'Is it because I don't actually fancy Craig?' I felt my breath skip; it took my speech away with it. Mark's expression hardened. 'You do realise that you're supposed to say: "I don't fancy Connie".'

I looked away so I didn't have to look at him. The weak sunlight shone on the river, reflecting the buildings on the Isle of Dogs in the green-brown water.

'Is there something you want to tell me?' Mark's voice was quiet. 'Have you fucked him?'

'What? No!'

'Have you ever kissed him?'

A lie was frozen on my tongue. I remained silent.

Mark stepped away, shocked, crushed. He was quiet for a moment, then he turned on me, eyes flashing with hurt and anger.

'So all of that "we're just friends" was a load of bollocks, weren't it? I bet you and him have been having a right laugh at me, in't you.'

'No, it isn't like that.'

'How is it then?'

'I don't know!' I said, tears welling in my eyes. 'It was just one kiss.'

'Fuck . . . This is all I need . . . ' Mark brought a hand to his eyes. I touched his arm and he shook it off. 'Just leave me all right. Just go.'

'No, please – I hate this. I didn't come here to row with you.'

I took his hand, holding it tight. Mark looked at me; he was shaking his head.

'You need to go.'

His eyes glided over my shoulder so I turned around. The man coming towards us was the same height as Mark; he had the same angular features but wore his hair shorter. I dropped Mark's hand like a stone. Phil Barrett slowed, but kept on walking, looking from Mark to me then back to Mark again. A sneer calcified in a thin pink line across his face. I wanted to run. Mark had told me to go, but I couldn't move. I didn't want to leave him on his own with Phil – although what the hell could I do if they had a fight? I slid my hand into my coat pocket and grasped my keys. I could feel my heart pounding.

'What's all this then?' asked Phil, his gaze still fixed on Mark.

'Nothing.' Mark's tone was flat. I couldn't gauge any emotion.

I felt a shiver. What did he mean by 'nothing'? Was I *nothing* to him now I'd kissed Connie? I held the keys between my fingers in my pocket, then made a fist.

'Nothing? That's not what it looks like,' said Phil.

'What's it look like?' Mark snapped back.

Phil was stone-faced, 'Like someone's gone and got themselves cunt-stuck. Like someone don't care about our family name. Like someone's a *fucking disgrace*—'

'Fuck you,' Mark spat.

Phil's eyes flashed. Had Mark ever stood up to his brother before? I held my breath. Phil recovered his composure, his sneer returned. Rather than turning his head, he regarded me through his side-eye. 'On your way home love?'

Mark sidestepped, partially shielding me. 'Yeah she is. Leave her be.'

'Or what?'

'—just leave. Her. Alone.'

Phil turned his head and looked me up and down. 'Mind how you go,' he said. Then he leaned into Mark as he pushed past him. 'You're an embarrassment.'

Mark seemed dazed. He exhaled, shaking his head, not meeting my eyes.

'Mark, I—'

'Don't ... just don't. Leave me alone, Daphne. I don't wanna see you anymore.'

Mark turned away and I watched him go. He didn't look back.

Once he had disappeared inside Beryl's house, I slumped against the wall, pressing my forearms against the concrete, feeling the rough texture through the sleeves of my jacket. I stared out across the river, wiping my eyes with the back of my hand. It wasn't enough. I screamed 'Fuuuck' over and over again, until my throat was raw.

The bath water had grown tepid, so I lay as still as I could, trying not to disturb what little warmth there was left in the tub. 'See the Day' by Dee C. Lee had faded out, and I thought about heaving myself out of the bath. It was Christmas Eve and I hadn't seen nor heard from Mark. I'd dropped a note through his nana's letterbox, telling him I was sorry and pleading for him to call so I knew he was all right. No call came and there was no reply to my letter. I hadn't been able to reach Connie either. When I last rang him, he'd refused to come to the phone and I was too discouraged to just go and see him.

I could hear Mum calling me from downstairs. Most likely Grandma had arrived and was ready to start cooking. It was rare for Mum to get the whole of Christmas Day off work, so since moving onto the estate, it had become tradition for Miss Gladys to stay at ours on Christmas Eve. Then I'd have company on Christmas morning before heading to Lime Grove for the big family gathering. For the past three years, Miss Gladys would turn up with sprats, which we'd eat with Hardo bread. We'd wrap presents then settle down to watch whatever evening movie was on the telly. Since the age of twelve, I was always allowed a bottle of Babycham, which as far as Miss Gladys was concerned wasn't really alcohol. I loved the festive hustle and bustle at Lime Grove, but I'd always look forward to our cosy Christmas Eve more. This Christmas, I didn't feel very jolly. Everything was spoiled. I got out of the bath, fed up with myself for feeling this way, and mad with Mark and Connie. I knew I had let them both down and made mistakes, but I thought they cared enough about me that we could work through this.

I took my time drying off, moisturising and getting dressed, before I made my way to the kitchen. Mum was standing over the kettle, willing it to come to the boil. I took some juice from the fridge and poured myself a glass.

'I thought Grandma was here; I heard you calling me before.'

'Then why yuh nuh answer? Good manners nuh cost nuttin' you know.'

I slammed the fridge door, making Mum start.

'I did tell you that I was going to have a bath. But I suppose with your boyfriend coming over tomorrow night your mind was elsewhere.'

Mum turned away, pinched by my insolence but clearly not looking for a fight. She poured water into her mug. 'Yuh father rang while you were in the bath. Inviting yuh to him house this evening. Something about a Chinese takeaway.'

'He's not in Jamaica?'

'Obviously not.'

We'd spoken on the phone twice since the Brighton trip, but this was the first time I'd get to see him.

'What time did he say to go over?'

'Yuh know yuh nuh have to drop everyt'ing and go see him just because him summon yuh.' She tutted. 'Yuh forget it's Christmas Eve? Mamma will be here in a little while. And for once in a blue moon I'll be around for most of Christmas and the whole of Boxing Day. If you want yuh can make time for Ezee after that.'

'Why can't I just go and see him this evening? I've not seen him for over two months. And I need to get out for a few hours.'

'Eh eh! After nobody force yuh to spend the last two days lock up in yuh room. Yuh nuh help Mamma with the groceries, nor go with her to the bakery. You've been wrapped up in yuself, till now all of a sudden yuh "need to get out" – just because him call.'

'You don't care about my life or what I'm dealing with. You have no idea what kind of stress I'm under!'

'Then why yuh nuh tell me?'

The look Connie gave me the night Tobias got him released from custody came to mind; the way Mark didn't look back when he walked away clouded my vision. 'You wouldn't understand.'

'Huh! And Enoch Edwards does? Because him know yuh so well, and him care so much about yuh?'

'He understands more than you do. He's lived more life than you have, and I'd rather be like him than old and boring and moany and bitter like you.'

'Just wah gwaan 'ere?' The kitchen door had opened and a scowling Miss Gladys entered the room. 'Mi come ready to cook and drink mi Baileys but it look like mi gonna have fi turn referee.'

Mum kissed her teeth. 'Yuh needn't have bothered coming – Daphne wants to have Chinese tonight – with her father.'

'Oh … I see.' Hurt flashed across Miss Gladys's face but she quickly gathered herself. 'Well, it has been a while since she last see him. I'll cook anyway and we can eat together in the morning.'

'Why should yuh have to change up all yuh plans? Who the hell eats takeaway on Christmas Eve? This is typical Ezee – inconsiderate. But of course yuh nuh see that do yuh, Daphne. Him nuh boring and moany like me. Him nuh old. Well let mi tell yuh darlin', him older than me, him just nuh bother to grow up.'

'God! Why are you still so jealous of him?'

'I think unnu need fi calm down—' said Miss Gladys.

'Ah nuh jealous, mi jealous. Mi just know how him stay,'

said Mum leaning against the worktop, folding her arms. 'But gwaan! Suit yuself.'

'Thanks. I will,' I shouted, storming from the room.

Ezee tugged me inside, wrapping me in a big, warm hug. The smell of his cologne and the jingle of his wrist chain made me feel like a little girl again. I looked up at him. I wondered if I could tell him how I'd really been feeling these past days. But Ezee was smiling down at me, in that way he did when he wanted me to join in with his good mood. I set the thought aside and I plastered on a smile. He released me from the hug and clapped his hands.

'Let's eat, mi starving. Then after that, I'll give you yuh present.'

Ezee drove the conversation at the table, while Audrey kept to monosyllables, her manner terse as usual. Eventually, Ezee asked me a question.

'How's yuh friend? The lanky one from yard?'

My unhappiness came washing over me. I lay my fork down.

'I didn't want to say before, because it was a secret. He and his mum are overstayers. His stepfather applied for leave to remain on their behalf, but I just heard that the application has been paused. It's really worrying. Althea and Tobias have to attend an interview.'

'Uh-huh, dem got it in for Jamaicans right now, yuh know. Blaming us for everyt'ing from unemployment to the riots,' said Ezee.

'Cha! It's bad for all Black people,' Audrey muttered, stabbing prawns with her fork.

'True, but certain countries nuh in favour right now,' said

Ezee. 'That's why when people send dem application into the Home Office dem should make sure dem forms are correct. A friend of mine know a guy who work at the Immigration Reporting centre who'll fill out the form for yuh. Him charge a couple hundred but at least then it's done right.'

'But if he really wants to help other Black people, why charge at all?' I asked.

'Two hundred pounds is cheap. Mi read in the paper last week about a white couple charging African students a thousand pounds a time to marry dem dawta. The gyal only nineteen and she married more times than Elizabeth Taylor. The judge send she, the parents to prison. But there'll be others ready fi exploit the desperate.'

'Ezee ... Dad, if the worst happens and Connie gets deported, you have to take me with you on your next trip to Jamaica. I'd hate never to see him again.'

I was looking at Ezee but he was carefully studying the array of foil containers on the table. I waited for a response.

Audrey sat forward. 'Yuh gonna tell her?' Ezee ignored her; he spooned more rice onto his plate. 'Then perhaps mi should tell her, seen as yuh too—'

'Tell me what?' I asked.

Finally, Ezee turned and faced me. 'The t'ing is, mi nuh planning on going home for a likkle while.'

'What about in the spring? You said we might go for my birthday?'

'Mi never yuh promise anyt'ing,' said Ezee.

I pushed my plate away, almost knocking over a sauce bottle.

'Why yuh pout up yuh mouth?' said Ezee. 'Mi nuh just

buy yuh a nice dinner and all of a sudden yuh vex. Jamaica nah go nowhere yuh know.'

'Jesus, Ezee!' said Audrey reaching for her fags.

'Don't start! Yuh say that mi should tell her face-to-face rather than on the phone, isn't that what mi doing?'

'Only because mi force yuh! And now yuh act like she in the wrong when it's yuh. Why yuh nuh just tell her the truth? Why yuh nuh tell her about the likkle eight-year-old dawta yuh send for? That yuh bringing one of yuh outside children to come live with yuh. After yuh promise mi yuh never would!'

'I don't understand,' I said slowly.

Audrey raised her eyes to the ceiling. 'Lawd! How can somebody that read so much book and newspaper and all dat, still be so naïve? All this time yuh t'ought it was just holiday why him go to Jamaica so often? That him taking care of business?' She paused to cackle. 'Yes, mon, him business is the pickney him have out there. T'ree – that me know of, but most likely more, innit Ezee? Jamaica, London, Brighton, everywhere yuh go yuh run around after gyal some barely older than she.'

'Hush yuh mout'.'

'Why should I? I keep mi mouth closed and mi look the other way till mi sick and tired of it. Yuh know, as far as mi concerned yuh can gwaan and nuh come back.'

'What? Yuh nuh want mi fi leave yuh! Who'd have yuh now?'

Tears glistened in Audrey's eyes.

'Is it true?' I said.

Ezee was shaking his head; his tone was impatient. 'Yuh

know mi have other children and mi love unnu – equally. Yuh gwaan let Audrey jealous temper spoil the evening?'

He was leaning towards me. There was that cajoling look again, urging me not to dwell on anything uncomfortable. I stared at him, hearing Mum's voice in my head, 'Ezee by name, easy by nature'.

'How many are there? How many kids have you actually got?'

'None of yuh business. Mi nuh answer to yuh! Mi nuh answer to neither of yuh.'

His chair tipped over as he pushed it back, crashing against the floor. He dashed the dinner plate into the bin and walked out, slamming the front door. Leaving me alone with Audrey.

'Do you know how many children he has?' I whispered.

Audrey dabbed her eyes with a serviette, scrabbling to compose herself once more.

'At one time mi reckon it was nine, with five different women. But now mi nuh know for sure. This one name Matilda. Tilda for short. Her muddah working in America but nuh land. The grandmuddah think the gyal will be better off here. With her daddy.'

I got up. I felt cold and sick. 'I'm going.'

Audrey looked at me, surprised. 'Yuh want a lift? I can drive yuh in mi Honda.'

'No, I'll take the bus. I need some air.'

'Did he give yuh the cheque already? Yuh Christmas present?'

'I don't want it,' I said, tugging on my coat. Audrey was still seated. I looked at her across the table littered with takeaway boxes and dirty plates.

'Why are you going along with it?'

Audrey sank back in her seat. 'Him right about one t'ing. Who'd have me now?'

It was dark along the Old Kent Road. A 53 pulled up at the stop, but I continued walking, trying to make sense of my feelings. I kept thinking why her? Why does Ezee want this girl to live with him here? Out of all of us, what's so bloody special about her? I ended up walking all the way home. It was almost 9 p.m. by the time I arrived. Mum and Miss Gladys flurried from the kitchen. They stood with hands on hips, their foreheads puckered with worry.

'Is what time yuh call this?' said Mum. 'You left yuh father's house nearly two hours ago, where you been till now?'

'Has Ezee been here? Was he looking for me?'

'No, that Cindy Breakspeare look-alike phone here to check yuh reach home safe. She said Ezee upset yuh.'

'I suppose Audrey told you about the daughter he's bringing over to come and live with him.'

Miss Gladys nodded. 'She mention somet'ing about it.'

Mum folded her arms. 'Yuh nuh remember me tell yuh that him have children spread here, there and everywhere? So him bringing this likkle gyal over to come live with him. Good! It's about time him take some responsibility for him pickney-dem.'

'D'you know she's eight years old? I didn't even get to meet him until I was nearly twelve, and since then I've made do with seeing him, what? Once every two months if I'm lucky? I get that you don't like Ezee, but I'm trying my hardest to have a relationship with my father and I get no support off you. Now I'm probably gonna get even less of his time because of this kid that for some reason he thinks is so special that she should come and live with him.'

'Nuh tell me yuh jealous!' said Mum, raising her eyebrows, exaggerating shock.

The fury that had been building all the way home brewed within me, pushing up to the surface. All the anger and upset I'd been holding in for the past two days suddenly exploded out of me.

'Yes I am! I am angry and so jealous of this little girl, because if it wasn't for you and all your bitching and nagging, Ezee might never have left us in the first place and I would have the same relationship with him that this little girl is gonna have. It could have been me, but it's not. And it's all *your* fault.'

Mum stiffened, her jawline taut, except for a muscle pulsing.

'I'm late for work. Mamma, I've made up Daphne's bed for you. She'll sleep on the settee.'

Mum kept her eyes trained on the floor as she put on her coat, hat and scarf. I stood watching; waiting for an outburst of some sort. Perhaps she would slam the front door. Instead, she closed it gently with a click. Miss Gladys had a face like granite.

'She started it—'

'No, Daphne.' My grandma raised her palm, cutting me off. She stepped past me without another word. I was left alone in the hallway. I hid my face in my hands and wept.

I woke the next morning with my side numb and my legs feeling cramped. I rolled onto my back and stretched, letting my feet dangle off the arm of the settee. Daylight trickled through a gap in the curtains and I saw that half a dozen packages in shiny red wrapping were piled beneath the Christmas tree. Miss Gladys must have sneaked in and placed them there while I slept. I felt a wave of shame as fragments of the row I'd had the night before came back to me. How was I going to make amends?

There were three knocks on the living room door, then Mum entered. I pulled my legs up to my chest, hugging my knees under the blanket.

'I got back from work early. Colin gave me a lift. I've made some tea. D'you want some?'

'Yes, please. Thanks.'

Mum took a step inside the room. She kept one hand on the door handle while she rubbed the other against her sky-blue uniform.

'I think we need to talk. I mean, I think I need to talk to you. Can I come in?'

I nodded. At first, she took a step towards the armchair, then changed her mind and came over to the settee. I scooped up some of the covers and Mum settled into the space, sinking into the sofa. The A-line dress rode up above her knees; she wriggled, shifting her legs to the side and tugging down the stiff fabric. When she finally looked up from her lap, she and I were properly face-to-face. Her eyes were red around the rims. I looked away and started picking at some loose stitching on the quilt.

'Daphne, last night I upset you. I'm ... I'm sorry.'

There was no blunt edge to her voice.

'But mi haven't just come to apologise. I've decided ... no, I realised that mi need to tell yuh some t'ings. About yuh father and me, and what went on back then. Mi nuh telling yuh any of this because mi want yuh to dislike him; yuh have to make up yuh own mind about him, and what yuh can expect from him. But I want yuh to understand why him still make mi so angry.'

She paused, gazing at the light from the window. When she spoke again it was as though she'd been transported back to the 1960s when she and Sybil first arrived in London. She told me how homesick they were at first, but quickly made new friends – not just Jamaicans, but Bajans and Trinidadians too.

'And then there were the parties ... bwoy, mi did have fun. The work was hard, the English people were as cold as the weather, but come the weekend we'd lively up ourselves.'

Ezee was always at the parties she went to. He'd come over in the '50s, his skills as a mechanic got him a job at London Transport, then later at a garage in Chelsea. By the late '60s he had his own workshop and enough work to employ two other mechanics. Ezee was handsome and supremely confident. He knew how to make Mum laugh. I tried to conceal my shock when Mum told me she knew that he was seeing other women; she also knew about the wife and children he had living in Penge.

'Bet yuh never knew yuh muddah so slack eh? But when yuh with him, Ezee has this way of making yuh feel that yuh are all him want in this world. It went on like that for almost a year; then two t'ings happened and everyt'ing changed. First, him wife decide she was going to divorce him, and of all the dozens of women she could have put in her petition, it was my name she find out and use.'

'And the second thing?' I asked.

Mum looked at me. 'I find out that mi pregnant. And me, a nurse. How mi could be so careless! But mi tell meself that it didn't matter. Ezee was getting a divorce, he would be free. I asked him to move into mi bedsit with me. He say no, not until him divorce come t'rough. Mi never want to be a nuisance. I told meself to trust him.

'Four months after yuh born mi hear that some woman ah Norwood had had a pickney for him too. A son. We quarrelled. Mi tell him that see'n' as my name was being dragged t'rough the divorce courts, he should stop all him nonsense with other women and be with me. With us. If all he was prepared to give was just a day here or there, then him should leave and nuh come back. He kiss him teet' and tell mi that "nuttin' mek a woman more unattractive than jealousy".' I shuddered on hearing Mum recite Ezee's often repeated refrain. 'He say him was going to give me time to cool off. He went. Mi never see hide nor hair of him again till over one year later.'

'Did he go and live with the woman in Norwood?'

'No. Little after this mi hear him shack up with the one him still with now. The beauty queen.'

I rubbed my arms to smooth away the goose bumps. Mum had never been this way with me before, so open and honest.

Mum continued. Feeling angry and ashamed, she shut herself away for two, maybe even three weeks – she lost track of time and the days became a blur. She didn't remember leaving her bedsit, let alone entering the grocer's. She had no idea why Spam, herrings and packets of instant mash – the sort of things she'd never eat, let alone steal – had been tossed into my pram. In her exhausted, altered state she had been oblivious to everything – and then she was under arrest.

'Fortunately, the shopkeeper didn't press charges. Say she did suffer with the baby blues too. That same day, Earl move us into dem house and Sybil write to Mamma. Two months later, Mamma sell off 1½ Spring View, the home she and Daddy work so hard to build, in order to get the money to come here and help look after yuh – and me.'

Mum's hands were clasped. I reached out and rested my hands on hers.

'I should never have said those things to you last night. I'm sorry.'

Mum shook her head. 'Ezee turns his face away from the consequences his actions have on the people around him. And I'm guilty of the same sort of t'ing. I allowed the hardness that built up when he left to come between you and me, when you are the most important t'ing in my life. And while I've gone out of my way to be practical and keep yuh from harm, I haven't always shown you enough love. And more than anything else, mi sorry for that.'

I was seven the last time Mum and I had made up with a hug after quarrelling. While I couldn't remember why we had argued, I still remembered the warmth of her breasts against the side of my head and feeling the softness of her belly pressing against my chest. Now I was grown, I felt her wide, warm body lean into me and her chin slot itself over my shoulder; it was a true embrace. I inhaled the scent of her body lotion and felt calm for the first time in days.

21

Instead of returning to my classes after lunch, I headed out of the school gates. If anyone were to ask me where I was going, I would just say that I had a stomach-ache. It was partly true, after all. The dull ache in my chest had lasted the entire Christmas break. I thought about Mark and I thought about Connie and how my relationship with both of them was broken. Now it was the new year. I'd braced myself to meet them on the first day back at school, but neither of them appeared that day. It was all around the sixth form that Mark had had a fight with Phil, although nobody knew what had caused the brothers to fall out. Some said that Mark had gone off to stay with his nana's family down in Kent until things calmed down at home. When I heard this I hoped it was true. I wanted Mark to be safe, even though it now seemed less likely that we would make up, and that we really were through. While the rumours about Mark were rife, there had been no news of Connie at all. Nobody had seen him nor spoken to him all Christmas, and there was no sick note sent into school that day, nor the day after that. By Thursday, I decided it was time to act.

I knocked on the door, but there was no answer. I crouched down to lift the letterbox flap.

'Can I help you?' said a middle-aged white woman. A mixed race child dozed in the buggy she was pushing; Co-op carrier bags dangled from the handles.

I sprang up, and the letterbox banged shut.

'I'm a friend of the family. I go to the same sixth form as Connie. I was just wondering where he was. I thought his mum might be home.'

'I saw the bloke and the missus leave around half-eleven this morning. Dressed up smart. I said to meself they've either got a funeral or a court appearance. I see the tall boy and the little 'un over at the adventure playground when I was coming back from the supermarket, or at least they were there twenty minutes ago.'

'Thanks.

I started to walk back towards the lift when the woman called after me.

'How well d'you know them?'

'I've known Connie for years.'

She pulled her mouth to one side. 'I'd stay clear if I were you. You seem like a nice girl and they're trouble.'

As I came around the corner, I saw Kallai on one of the tyre-swings, imploring Connie to push him.

'You're big now. You can swing yuself,' said Connie.

'But you make it go higher,' said Kallai. 'Please . . . '

Connie pulled back the tyre until it was chest height, then with a big shove he sent it swinging forwards. Kallai hooted with delight. Connie was smiling too, until he noticed me. I forced my legs to carry on towards him.

'Look it's Daffeny. Hey Daffeny, I'm skipping school!'

'I wouldn't go shouting about it, Kallai. Hello, Connie. I called at the flat. Your neighbour said you might be here.' Connie ignored me. 'Can we talk? Please.'

He gave the swing another push, then stepped away, leaving momentum to do the rest.

'What yuh want Daphne?'

His curt tone brought a lump to my throat.

'I want ... I want for us to be friends. I'm sorry I didn't tell you about Althea and Tobias. It was wrong to keep it from you.'

'If yuh knew it was wrong then why did yuh do it?' Connie's voice quivered with the betrayal he felt. Heat rushed to my face.

The swing had slowed. Kallai jumped off and ran across to the big fort-like structure. Connie was waiting for my reply.

My words came out in bursts. 'I don't know. Because Althea asked me to. Because she said she would tell you herself. Because I thought that if I told you about seeing them together that it would make things worse for you—'

'As opposed to how good t'ings are for mi now? Being back there with him lording it all over mi, and Althea going along with it, as if she never had any cause to leave him in the first place.'

Connie slumped onto the vacant tyre-seat, looking defeated.

'They're at the immigration place today, for the interview. Last night, Althea was picking out photographs of her and Tobias together, wedding pictures, pictures of she, him and Kallai when he was first born. Tobias said it will show that they're a genuine, devoted family it'd be cruel to separate.'

I looked down at the ground. Connie continued, his voice heavy with scorn.

'You should have seen him last night, drilling her on what to say and what not to say. Picking out what she should wear. All the time telling her that if it doesn't work then they'll deport her and there's no way Kallai would go with her because his son is a British citizen. Tobias is loving this. He's got Althea where he wants her.'

'Maybe for now. But Althea is strong. She'll only put up with all this until she gets her stay. And if she gets to stay then it means that you will too. And, I want that more than anything.'

A thick silence massed between us. Kallai had reached the top of the fort; he was shouting down to us and waving. We both waved back to him.

I turned to face Connie. 'I've missed you.'

He sighed. 'I've missed you too.'

Kallai came hurtling down a zip wire, screaming his head off and laughing. When he reached the end, the line jerked back and Kallai landed bottom first on the soft ground.

'Yuh all right Kallai?' asked Connie, stretching his hand out and pulling the little boy up.

'Yeah, that was great! I want some crisps. Can we go to the shop?'

'Sorry likkle man, I ain't got no money. There's biscuits at home.'

Connie turned to me. 'Yuh can come back to the flat for a bit? If yuh like. I can't tell what sort of mood they'll be in, but you know they always behave better when we have company. Or are yuh meeting up with Mark?'

I paused. I wanted to tell him that Mark and I were finished. I wanted to ask him why he'd kissed me that day. But Connie yawned. This wasn't the right time.

'No, I'm not meeting Mark. I'd like to come back with you,' I said.

'Okay. Kallai, where's your scarf?'

'I left it at the top of the fort.'

Connie gave a playful groan. 'Wait here while I go fetch it.'

'Was it nice having a day off school?' I asked Kallai.

'Not really. Connie was a bit blue. Mammy has an important meeting. She told me that if it goes well then everything will be all right. I hope so, cos I don't want her and daddy to argue anymore. I get scared. When I tell Connie, he covers my ears with his hands,' said Kallai. 'I don't like it when Connie is sad. I really love him.'

'I love Connie, too,' I sighed, unable to stop the words escaping.

Kallai looked up at me. 'That's good,' he said.

'So yuh reach,' said Althea, placing a bottle of rum back inside the cabinet, and then clearing mugs from the coffee table. 'Nice to see you, Daphne. Happy New Year.' She smiled, but not with her eyes.

Rather than her usual cornrows or twists, Althea's hair was brushed back and tamed with a dowdy banana clip. She was dressed in a grey skirt and white blouse with a high collar. Sombre, serious clothes. The plain gold wedding band was the only item of jewellery Althea had on. No bangles, no beads. All her personality was buried beneath the trappings of respectability and good character, as Tobias had ordered.

'How d'yuh get on?' asked Connie.

'They'll let us know in a couple of weeks,' said Althea. 'Kallai, go to you room and play darlin'. Yuh breddah will bring yuh some snacks in a likkle while.'

The little boy withdrew, but Connie stayed behind. Tobias was standing by the sideboard, a short glass tumbler in one hand while he gesticulated with the other, his large open palm cutting through the air like a switch.

'Tell me exactly what you said when they asked the names of my family?'

'I name dem everyone from yuh auntie, uncles, cousins, second cousins and half brothers.'

'But did you tell dem which ones came to the wedding?'

'I told them exactly what you tell me to tell dem. I answered all dem questions. Please let me rest mi mind. Mi cyaah cope with any more stress now.'

Althea went into the kitchen. We heard the cups clanking in the washbasin while Tobias continued taking bites out of her.

'These details are important. Our answers have to match. Dem looking to catch yuh out and if dem find even the tiniest fault, then it nuh gonna be me that gets kicked out of the country. And like I said before, yuh nuh taking my son with you.'

'Yuh nuh hear she say she stressed? Just stop now, leave her alone!' Connie said.

'Who asked yuh? This is big people conversation. Galang and see to yuh breddah,' snapped Tobias, marching into the kitchen and kicking away the wedge stopper so the door swung closed.

'Go and make sure Kallai's all right,' said Connie.

'I'm not leaving you.'

'I'll be all right. See to Kallai.' Connie's tone was urgent.

I took a step towards the bedroom when we heard a high-pitched groan.

'Althea!'

Connie ran to the kitchen and I ran after him. When he flung the door open we saw Althea in the far corner beside the larder cupboard, clutching her middle, wheezing; Tobias was standing over her, his hand still balled in a fist. When he turned his bulk towards us, Connie charged, shoving him square in the chest. Tobias staggered; he grabbed the table and steadied himself. He was still blocking the way to Althea.

'So yuh a big man now?' said Tobias, mocking Connie.

'Stay away from her yuh bastard,' said Connie, his body tense, poised to strike again.

Tobias raised himself up to his full height, despite whatever pain he felt in his chest. His voice was thick, 'Or what?'

'Fucking leave her alone or I'll kill yuh.' Connie's voice was shrill with fury.

Tobias's laugh was deep. 'Come nuh!'

Connie took a swing; Tobias swerved, and caught Connie's fist in his hand. I screamed as I saw his other hand whip through the air and smack Connie hard across the face. Connie reeled and grabbed the worktop for support. Tobias was laughing; the sound jangled in my ears. I held my head. I couldn't move or speak. Until I saw the carving knife. Connie must have grabbed it off the wall beside the cooker. I watched the smile on Tobias's face freeze.

'Connie, put it down,' I said, trying to suppress the panic creeping into my voice. I'd never seen him this way before.

Althea, still slumped against the larder, had got some of her breath back; now she was sobbing. I saw his hand tighten around the handle of the knife. He was edging toward Tobias.

'Connie, please put down the knife.' My voice was high, pleading. I finally snared his attention; then I realised he wasn't looking at me, he was looking at the doorway. I turned around and saw Kallai standing there, clutching a Batman action figure to his chest. Connie dropped the weapon. He staggered past me and then Kallai, lurching towards the front door.

By the time I'd collected myself, Connie had reached the staircase at the end of the corridor.

'Wait!' My voice bounced off the hard walls.

He didn't stop and so I started running too. The stink of the rubbish chute infused with the faint smell of weed on the staircase. The blood pounding in my ears dulled the sound all around, except my footsteps stamping the concrete steps. I called out again, but Connie kept moving. I hurried down another two flights, grabbing the bannister to stop myself tumbling over. I could feel a stitch coming on and my legs were shaking.

'For God's sake, Connie. Stop!'

I found him slumped on the flight of stairs between the tenth and the eleventh floor with his elbows on his knees, his head in his hands.

'Didn't you see what just happened?'

'Yes. I know it was horrible. Come back to mine, stay with us – at least until things calm down.'

'I can't. I live here. According to the Home Office application my address is *that* flat,' he said, stabbing the air. 'You know that even if we get our stay, nothing will really change. Tobias is going to be like this for ever and because Althea will never leave him, I am stuck right here!'

I touched his shoulder and he shrugged me off. His cold glare drilled into me. I didn't know he could look at me that way.

'Don't pretend to be on my side. If yuh were, yuh would have told me Althea was planning to go back to him. But yuh didn't. So just leave me alone. I'm done with you.'

The words hit me like a slap, stunning me for a moment before a bitter sting radiated through my body. Connie got up and continued down the stairs, and I sat there listening as the echo of his footsteps grew fainter and fainter until there was nothing at all.

1989

22

The Oak Tree was a back street pub on the Camberwell-Brixton border. At weekends between 9 p.m. and 10.30 p.m. you could buy weed from a guy named Marcus. I was with my friends, Fliss, Clancie and Sue; we had all returned home from our universities that week. I'd completed my second year at Manchester and a long summer in London stretched out in front of me. The plan was to score, then head to Omar and Emmanuel's; their house parties were legendary. Between us, we'd pooled enough to purchase an eighth, and as I scanned the room for a man matching Marcus's description, I caught sight of Connie. He was facing away from me but I recognised his straight posture, his usual high-top fade haircut, the sound of his laugh. He was wearing a black T-shirt and dark blue jeans; a record case was on the floor by his feet. I'd last seen him a few months ago on Good Friday; I'd stopped at the bakery to buy an Easter bun, and he and some girl were coming out of the shop with patties. The sight of him stung – we hadn't been close for such a long time, but it still hurt. This time, seeing him was only half a surprise – of course he'd be going to Omar and Emmanuel's too.

'He's over there,' said Fliss, nudging my arm.

'What? Who?'

'Marcus, of course. Clancie and me will go see him. Sue's bagged us a table. Can you get a round and we'll pay you back?'

There was a crowd at the bar, but my eyes kept drifting over to Connie. He was with Errol, a girl in a red halterneck, another girl wearing a Def Jam hoodie and two more guys. They were probably friends from his course. As usual, Connie seemed composed. Content.

He and Althea got their indefinite leave to remain in 1986, and by the time we sat for our A-levels the following year, Connie had his citizenship. He had only applied to London colleges and accepted an offer to study computer science at the local Poly. He'd joked that the student allowance from the state was now so paltry it would be cheaper to live at home. Also, that he needed to stay close to Althea so she could keep his hair trim, 'the gyaldem are used to me looking fly'. It was obvious to me that the real reason he wanted to stay close was in order to watch over Althea, but I kept this thought to myself. Connie didn't really confide in me since the fight with Tobias. We'd made up, but the spark that I'd felt between us in the run-up to that Christmas never ignited. We were friends and nothing more. Whenever we hung out together, it was as part of a group, always sociable, but no longer intimate.

With only thirty students enrolled in the upper sixth, we all began mixing more and the old cliques seemed to dissolve. I'd got chatting to Fliss after an English lesson. We both applied to study at Leeds and she invited me over to her house so we could prepare for the interview. Fliss hailed from the more affluent neighbourhood close to the Heath and her house was huge. Most of the rooms had shelves crammed with books, hardback as well as paperback ones, and there was no TV in their living room; that was confined to the basement. At first I'd worried that we wouldn't have enough to say to each other outside of school, but we'd talked and talked. After that I fell in with her crowd – they all thought my vintage clothes, my taste in music, even the fact I lived on the estate was 'cool'. They might not have thought it was so cool if they actually lived there, but I wasn't complaining. It was great to finally have my own group of friends; I found that I was also growing in confidence, so much so that I eventually told Fliss that I'd dated Mark Barrett. She was in awe. She said that she'd always thought he was 'edgy and interesting', like Matt Dillon in *The Outsiders*, but even as a white person, she was terrified of his friends and family. I'd agreed that Phil was scary, but Mark was different – most of the time he'd just made me laugh.

Mark never returned to school after we split up. I was sorry that he quit. I was sorry not to see him again. I had made such a mess of it all – I wondered if things might have turned out differently if I'd had Fliss to talk to at the time. Still, I couldn't bring myself to tell my new friends how I felt about Connie. There was nothing 'cool' about the depths of my longing. It was easier when I was in Manchester. There, I wrote for the student paper and got involved with demos against Alton's Anti-Abortion Bill and Tory plans to replace student grants with loans. I couldn't afford to travel home that often, but everyone sent each other letters or at least postcards. I'd heard through the grapevine that Connie was involved with the Poly's football team and the Black student society; he was a resident DJ at the Student Union's club nights. His circle of friends was wide and varied, and of course there were the gyaldem.

The girl in the red halterneck was pretty. Her extensions had that freshly done look. She was sitting beside Connie and turned her body towards him when she talked, rather than addressing the group. I decided that I'd get these drinks then make a hasty retreat to where my friends were before he could see me. The pub was busy and there were only two people behind the bar. The customers ahead of me kept ordering rounds of drinks that seemed to take ages to mix and serve. I saw Connie get up from his stool; I hunched over the bar, tapping the edge of a beer mat against the counter. Connie came and stood at the opposite corner; he saw me and his mouth fell open; he then hurried to twist his surprise into a smile. I hadn't been able to afford to get my braids redone, so I had scooped my hair up into a bushy Mohican with a little spilling forward like an Afro-quiff. I'd applied a little gel to the baby hairs at my temples and added some finger waves. I was going for a Whitney vibe with a dash of Ella Fitzgerald, but wasn't sure I'd really pulled it off. Connie's reaction didn't boost my confidence. He nodded and I nodded back, then I waved like an idiot. I could feel sweat beading my hairline – that was sure to kill the finger waves! Connie was walking over to my side of the bar. I took out a tenner and leaned into the counter, hoping that would snag the barman's attention so I could get served quickly.

'I didn't know yuh return already.'

'Yeah, I got back yesterday. Fliss and that lot are going interrailing. But I've gotta find a job.'

I rubbed the sweat from my hand against my jeans, wondering what to say next. Connie was silent too, then:

'You've done your hair differently,' he said. 'Yuh had extensions at Easter.'

'I fancied a change,' I said, touching the side of my head.

Connie nodded. 'It's nice. Really suits you.'

At last, the barman came over and I ordered four halves of lager. Connie hovered while my drinks were served.

'So, have there been many good end-of-term parties?' My voice was light. False.

Connie shrugged. 'A few so-so gatherings, people sitting around chatting with a tape deck in the corner. Yuh coming to Emmanuel and Omar's? I'm DJ-ing.'

'That's where we're heading. Maybe see you there later.'

'Yeah. That will be good.'

'Connie Tall! Wah a go waan?'

Fliss wriggled her way in between us, tossing her henna-coloured hair over her shoulders.

'I'm very well t'ank you, Fliss. How are you?' Connie replied, using his English voice.

'I wondered what was keeping Daphne. You're DJ-ing at the party, right?'

'Yeah,' said Connie.

'Wicked,' gushed Fliss. 'You've got to play a tune for us, some James Brown?'

Connie was shaking his head.

'Aw go on, There was that track you put on a mix-tape for Daphne from back in the day, Marlena Shaw singing with James Brown's band ...'

'Lyn Collins not Marlena Shaw ...' I mumbled.

'I don't do requests,' said Connie.

'But that's a tuuunne,' Fliss continued. 'Daphne, help me persuade him.'

The girl in the red halterneck brushed past Connie on her way to the loo, touching his arm. 'Don't forget – no ice in my pineapple juice, yeah babe? I like it sweet.' She glanced at Fliss and me, giving us a large fake smile.

'One of your gal dem, I suppose?' said Fliss, giving Connie a nudge. He gestured to the barman. Fliss continued, 'We should all head to the party together. A proper John Evelyn sixth form reunion, eh Daph?'

I sipped my drink. 'Yeah. Sure.'

The High Street was busy. People were milling around outside pubs and bars, and there were already queues at the chippies and kebab shops. The girl in the halterneck was walking arm in arm with the girl in the hoodie; they were leaning into each other and whispering. I dropped my pace to allow them to get further ahead and found myself walking in step with Connie at the back of our group.

'So, is she your girlfriend then? That girl in the red top?'

'Ashanti? We had a t'ing but now we mainly just friends.'

'Mainly?' My voice sounded more judgemental than I'd intended.

Connie raised an eyebrow. He switched his records to his other hand and we continued walking with the carry case between us.

'This party tonight should be a novelty for yuh,' said Connie. 'Make a change from all that indie music I hear yuh get in dem clubs up ah Manchester.'

'There was I, hoping you'd play some baggy tunes just for me. Or perhaps some trance?'

Connie exhaled his big mellow laugh and my footsteps felt light. It had been ages since we'd had this sort of banter.

Some of the drivers from Cheetah Minicabs were out on the pavement liming. Four white blokes stopped to ask them for a light, and the scent of weed mingled with the cigarette smoke. A car rolled by with the windows down, 'All of My Love', by The Gap Band booming from its speakers. A group of women in high heels were singing in Spanish as they headed in the direction of the Mambo Club. It felt so good to be back on my home turf, savouring the South London nightlife. I didn't see the police van that must have been parked in a side street until it pulled up at the curb next to us. Goose bumps spotted my skin as four officers emerged, their radios hissing, the numbers on their epaulets glistening under the streetlights. A square-faced, middle-aged copper reached us first, his index finger pointing at the guys in our group.

'You lot, against that wall.'

Connie paused for a moment, then left my side and moved over to the shuttered storefront of WH Smith.

'Officer, can I ask why you're detaining us?' he asked, his voice slow and distinct, more South London than Jamaican.

'Shut up and spread your arms,' the square-faced copper snapped.

Connie was compliant. I recalled the last time we were together when this happened, but I was older now and I knew my rights.

'You can't just stop and search without a reason.' The

officers ignored me and carried on frisking the fellas. 'Didn't you hear me?'

I'd raised my voice; onlookers were now stopping at the scene, rather than just hurrying by. Good, everyone should bear witness to this harassment. Square-face turned to me, raising himself up to his full height.

'We've had reports of a group of IC3 males dealing in the area. We could smell marijuana and have reason to believe these men may be in possession of controlled substances.'

'We can smell cannabis too; we just passed a group of *white* lads smoking a massive spliff, funny you never saw them,' I said, sarcastically.

The officer leaned forward, bringing his face closer to mine. 'I don't like what you're implying, Miss. But perhaps you and these friends of yours should accompany us to the station and make a formal complaint? There are plenty of women police officers back at the nick; they'd be happy to take you to one side, have a little chat. Would you like to do that?'

Suddenly, I remembered my share of the eighth that I'd stashed in my bra. Images of a strip search, an arrest, a cold police cell flashed through my mind. All my bravado wilted. I looked down at the pavement.

'No, officer,' I mumbled.

After finding nothing on the fellas the police officers finally allowed us to go. There was no apology.

'Keep on Movin'' by Soul II Soul leaked from the basement of a shabby Victorian semi, the rhythm vibrating the blacked-out glass in the bay window.

'Sounds like Emmanuel is on the decks,' I said. Connie didn't answer.

While all of us had made a show of brushing off the police stop, he'd been silent for the entire journey.

I sighed. 'You still pissed off?'

'What d'you think?' Connie snapped. 'And you shooting yuh mouth off didn't help. Acting out the civil liberties text-book like we're in the student union debate club.'

'So every time the police stop us we should just say nothing?'

'What d'you mean *us*? That's the second time mi get stopped this week. The fourth time this month. How many times yuh been stopped recently? Is it in Manchester yuh study-ing or cloud cuckoo land? If they'd searched you and found your stash, they would have found a way to pin it on all of us.'

I could feel my cheeks flush, remembering how easily I'd got scared and how quickly I had backed down. I didn't entirely agree with Connie, but I didn't want us to fall out.

'Fine. I see your point,' I said, trying not to sound too grudging. 'It's really shit. The police are fucking racist arse-holes, but don't let it spoil the night.'

Connie cut his eye past me. 'They always spoil it. Yuh just been spending too much time with yuh posh white friends to notice.'

'What? Like Black women have it so easy?'

'Easier than it is for a Black man.'

That was it. I kissed my teeth and walked on ahead, fuming about what he had said to me. Nevertheless, I was regretting that we were not walking side by side.

*

Multicoloured fairy lights were draped from the hall ceiling. Fluorescent stars were tacked to the walls around posters of Bob Marley and Miles Davis, *La Dolce Vita* and *À Bout De Souffle*. The people in the front room were chatting, skinning up and smoking, unconsciously nodding along to the beats leaching through the floorboards from the basement. Connie pushed through bodies lining the hallway, then stomped down a narrow wooden staircase. I waited nearly a full five minutes before wandering downstairs after him. The basement was dark except for a couple of amber lights that had been swiped from some roadworks, and an Anglepoise lamp over the decks in the bay window. I weaved my way across the makeshift dance floor. Emmanuel was wearing his *'I'M A DJ – NOT A JUKEBOX'* T-shirt. A spliff idled in the corner of his mouth, which he offered to Connie, as a bloke swigging from a can of Stella came up to them.

'Hey mate, you gonna play "Sex Machine"?' he hollered.

'We don't do requests,' Connie barked back.

The guy tutted and sashayed back to the dance floor. Connie took a draw then offered the spliff to me.

'Them damn police chip away at yuh dignity. Dem know it works,' he shouted over the music. 'But I'm sorry I bit yuh head off. It's good that yuh challenge dem.'

'Just best not when you're carrying weed!' I said.

He grinned, then hunched over his record case, putting his discs in order.

I leaned in so I could be heard over the music. 'Got any Stone Roses?' Connie looked up. 'Inspiral Carpets?' I teased. 'C'mon, if you wanna make up then play me a tune.'

Connie kissed his teeth. 'What tune?

I smiled. 'I dunno. Surprise me.'

He gave me a cool upward nod, then bowed so his head was closer to mine. 'I don't do requests. I prefer to read the room. Now g'lang over there-sah and dance nuh! Let mi do mi t'ing.'

Emmanuel was playing 'All Night Long' by Mary Jane Girls and after months of indie nights at the student bars in Manchester, it was a delight to hear that soulful, upbeat classic. But I was also savouring the musicality I'd heard in Connie's voice, how its rich notes had caressed my ear. He so rarely relaxed into his accent these days, but he had just then – with me. It had seemed so natural and so intimate. Ashanti and her friend came to dance right in front of the DJs, their moves lithe and sultry. I ignored them and let the motion of the crowd tug me towards the centre of the room. Emmanuel played three more tracks I loved and it was easy to carry on dancing, my limbs loosening and my senses tuned into the rhythm, the bass line, the bodies around me. I noticed Connie had settled at the decks. As Emmanuel's last track faded, a straight-talking Lyn Collins summoned everyone's attention, especially the no-good fellas. A cheer went up on the dance floor and more people hurried down the stairs. Those of us already assembled were poised, waiting for the beat to drop. Then it did. Lyn Collins was telling all of us that we'd 'better think'; I raised my arms and my hips began to sway, infused by the rhythm of the James Brown Orchestra and the dance floor bursting into life. I looked over at Connie. He couldn't see me, but I know I saw him smile.

Connie played for almost an hour. Dennis Edwards, Curtis Mayfield, Marlena Shaw and George Clinton melted into

Mantronix, Joyce Sims, Queen Latifah and De La Soul. The room heaved with bodies and I was drenched in sweat. When Ann Peebles came on I knew Connie's set had ended. 'Come to Mama' was one of Omar's signature tracks. I saw Ashanti drape an arm over Connie's neck, whisper something, then plant a kiss on his cheek. I looked away and sipped my drink, but I could feel my grip tightening around the bottle in my hand. My attention kept straying back to them. They held each other and kept time to the track's seductive beat, but after the chorus, Connie excused himself and weaved his way across the dance floor and out of the room. I told Fliss that I was hot and needed some water. I wandered out into the corridor, but couldn't see Connie. Neither was he in the crowded front room or kitchen. Now I really was hot, so I stepped out into the back garden. The cool night air hit my face, evaporating the sweat on my forehead, but the chill was refreshing after the sweltering heat inside.

'I see yuh nuh forget how to dance,' said a voice coming to me through the darkness. I saw an orange glow in the space by the basement window; then Connie came out of the shadows and offered me the end of his spliff.

'I thought you didn't do requests.'

'It wasn't really a request. I was watching yuh dance. I was reading the room.'

I suddenly felt shy.

'I'm honoured,' I said, pulling on the spliff. It burnt my lips and I let it fall to the ground. Omar was now playing 'Come into My Life'. 'Didn't you used to play this track? I remember you played it three times at the sixth form Christmas party. Everyone loved it – especially Fliss.'

'That's another reason why I don't do requests – people usually just want to hear the same song over and over again. Especially Fliss.' Connie laughed again. He was fiddling with his box of matches, turning it over in his fingers. I wanted to lay my hand on his. I wanted to touch him.

He cleared his throat. 'Yuh heading back inside to yuh friends?'

'No. Do you have to go back inside to Ashanti?'

Connie paused. 'No. I don't.'

'I've got another request.'

'What?'

'Dance with me.'

I reached up and put my hands on his shoulders. He looked down at me and I felt his hands settle on my hips, tentative rather than assured. We began to sway, moving slowly, our bodies following a beat that seemed to come from within, one we already knew. I felt Connie's hands shift, sliding from my hips to the small of my back, drawing me closer. My hands glided past his shoulders; I was wrapping my arms around his neck, pressing against his chest. We were dancing close-up, like the adults I'd watched in my youth. I was enveloped in his arms, feeling the intimacy and tenderness I'd craved for years. But it wasn't enough. I wanted more. Did Connie feel it too? As the track faded, I shifted my head so my lips were close to his ear.

'This is nice.'

I felt rather than saw Connie's gaze. 'I've missed yuh.'

'I've missed you too. I've been missing you for ages.'

I took one of his hands from my waist and held it before pressing it to my lips. He drew me closer and I kissed his

neck; his warm skin smelled of musk and sugar. I could feel
the rhythm in his chest. I wondered if he could feel mine,
enlivened by anticipation and hope.

'We should go somewhere and maybe talk, or something . . . ' he said.

'I think we've done enough talking.' I took his other hand.
'Don't you?'

Mum was staying overnight with Colin. Even though the
flat was deserted, we tiptoed upstairs like kids coming home
after curfew, excited and nervous. We were standing beside
my bed; Connie moved towards me, then seemed to catch
himself.

'Are you okay?'

'Yeah. You?'

'I'm good. Are you going to kiss me then?'

Connie's shoulders relaxed and he began to laugh. The
dimple in his right cheek appeared. I reached out and
touched it.

'I've always wanted to do that.'

'I like it. Feels nice.'

I caressed his face and neck, my hand sliding down his
chest to his waist, shifting beneath his T-shirt, enjoying the
warmth of his skin.

'Can I . . . ?' He nodded. I brushed the vertical line of hair
that ran from his belly down towards the buckle of his belt.
Tentative yet curious, I undid the belt, unbuttoned his jeans.
'And this?' He nodded, looking serious now. My hand slid
inside his boxers, touching him for the first time; the nerves
in my clit quickening as I felt him becoming hard. Connie

pressed his hand against the base of my spine; he leaned in again, and we kissed.

Our clothes and the bedcovers lay in a tangled heap on the floor. He gripped my hips as I eased myself down. I hadn't realised that I was holding my breath until I felt him moving inside me. I exhaled, pressing down harder. Delighted at the sight of Connie on his back, lying between my thighs.

Later he lay facing me, eyes closed. His arm was resting over my hip, the tips of his fingers meeting the curve in my back. I liked that we were still touching. I liked the weight of his arm. I ran my fingers along the shape of his bicep and up to his chest, tracing where the smooth dark of his naked body ended and mine began. I reached over and switched off the bedside lamp. Connie stirred, but remained asleep. I kissed his forehead. Somewhere in the distance, a siren wailed, the clock on my bedside was ticking and Connie began snoring gently. I closed my eyes, but sleep wouldn't come. I was happy and wired. Wondering what was next.

23

Connie pulled another LP from the crate and studied the sleeve notes. After a minute or so, he sensed the warmth in my stare and looked deep into my eyes. He mouthed, 'What?' I mouthed, 'Nothing.' He smiled at me; it felt like a caress.

It was Sunday morning and Greenwich Market was busy with shoppers scouring the rails of vintage clothes, or hunting for antiques among the bric-a-brac. While Connie was leafing through pre-loved vinyl, I was perusing the spines of the second-hand paperbacks. I couldn't see anything I fancied that I could afford. I'd lined up a job on the estate's summer playscheme and was due to start the next day; until then, money was tight. I left the bookstall and wandered over to Connie; he was flicking through the records in a crate marked '70s SOUL/R&B. He'd already chosen four albums, a copy of 'What's Going On' lay on the top of his pile. I stood behind him and slipped my arms around his waist.

'You've struck gold.'

'Yeah mon! Some good stuff here this week. All dem people ah buy compact discs and ditching dem vinyl.'

'We'd better be making a move if we're going to help Grandma with the cooking. Although you do know she just wants to quiz you before the rest of the family turns up and finds out if your intentions are respectable.'

'I thought I already been t'rough all of that with yuh muddah,' said Connie.

I chuckled and gave him a squeeze. Four weeks had gone by since we had first slept together. We managed to keep it between ourselves until the fourth time Connie stayed over; when Mum, arriving home early from her shift, discovered him in his boxers preparing breakfast. Once we were both dressed, I stammered through explanations. First, earnestly stressing the sincerity of our feelings, then huffily reminding Mum that we were both responsible, consenting adults. She stood leaning against the worktop, arms folded, her attention fixed on both of us. 'Yuh being careful?' We both nodded. Mum said 'Good,' then busied herself with the dishes. Nothing more was said to me, but naturally Mum had told Miss Gladys.

'You know Grandma has to have her say. Don't worry, she's always liked you.'

'Well then, I should probably swing by mi yard, put a shirt on so I look respectable,' said Connie.

'I can come with you.'

I felt his spine tense. 'D'yuh want to? I mean . . . you haven't been back there since . . . '

'That was years ago. It's okay.' My arms tightened around his waist. 'Besides, isn't it about time we told Althea?'

The smell of bacon greeted us as we entered the flat. We paused in the tiny hallway to take off our shoes. Althea called out from the kitchen, her voice sounding clipped and anxious.

'Tobias? Yuh back already?'

Connie hesitated before answering. 'No. It's me.'

I followed Connie inside. The living room was just as I remembered it, although the sofa covers were more faded. Kallai
was lying on his belly watching cartoons, his elbows sinking into
the fluffy beige rug. He was only ten, but his slim body took
up all the space between the couch and the television stand.

'Nuh sit so close, you get square eye,' said Connie, crouch-
ing down.

Kallai shifted his face to one hand, and with the other
bumped fists with his big brother.

'Yuh been all right?' asked Connie. The question sounded
more like an apology.

The boy nodded although he looked uncertain.

Althea called out, 'Kallai! Come get yuh food.'

Connie and Kallai wandered off to the kitchen and I trailed
after them. Connie and I had never talked about what had
happened that afternoon. He'd never brought it up, so neither did I, assuming that he'd rather forget about it and that
I shouldn't rock the boat. An involuntary shiver crept across
my skin as I entered the room, spotting the knives hanging
on the magnetic strip beside the cooker.

'Daphne, yuh here too. Ah the first mi see yuh since time.
And mi see yuh change up yuh hairstyle, it look nice!'

Since deciding to locs-up, Althea had kept her hair under
various wraps. Today, her head was uncovered and the locs
were braided into cornrows rising to a ball at the crown of her
head. She had on jeans and an African print blouse.

'Thanks, your dreadlocks look amazing. I love your top
too,' I said, managing to present a smile.

'T'ank yuh. It's handmade by a gyal mi know, she use

high-quality wax print. If mi ever open mi own salon, mi ah go get her to design some tabards in this sort of fabric and have mi staff wear it as dem uniforms.' Althea looked self-conscious. 'Maybe one day. Anyway, sit down nuh, yuh want a drink?'

'I'm good thanks,' I said, taking the seat nearest the door. Connie leaned against the worktop.

'Mi never realise Connie was meeting yuh this morning. But then mi barely see him these days. Being a student seems to mean yuh carry on like yuh nuh live nowhere.' Connie rolled his eyes; Althea grinned at him. 'Still, it's all right, yuh young. Although me'd prefer if yuh can tan here tonight. Wi nuh back from Wolver'ampton till tomorrow and Tobias nuh like the look of the family who move in two doors down.' She turned to me. 'Tobias's Auntie Sissy t'rowing a big party fi 'er seventieth. Tobias is at Busta's now picking up booze.' She switched back to Connie.

'Yuh nuh mind, do yuh?'

'Fine,' Connie sighed.

Althea sat down and took a sip from her mug. 'So where yuh deh last night? Errol? Omar? Or with some gyal?'

Connie looked at me. I rolled my lips inwards to stop myself from smiling.

'Althea ... The t'ing is ... ' Connie shifted from one foot to the other, like he did when he was a kid.

A grin crept across my face. 'Actually Althea, Connie was at my house. With me. We're together now.'

Althea's dark red lips became an 'O', her smokey kohled eyes were open wide.

'But see 'ere! Yuh 'ear dis Kallai?'

Kallai looked up from his plate and gave a comic shudder. 'Yuck!'

'Yuh face favour yuck, mi t'ink it's lovely,' said Althea. 'Mi always say yuh a lovely gyal, innit Connie? Pretty, intelligent too. Mi glad unnu finally get together.'

'Calm down, Althea,' said Connie. 'We nuh planning marriage or anyt'ing . . .'

Althea winked at me. 'Not yet. Unnu need to finish yuh studies, get good jobs.' Althea cast an eye over at Kallai. 'Tek that into the living room to eat if yuh like.'

'I'm all right here,' he said, his right cheek pudgy with fried dumpling.

Althea sat up straight. 'Mi say galang ah the living room!'

Kallai rolled his eyes before taking his plate next door.

Althea lowered her voice. 'What contraception unnu using?'

'Jesus, Althea . . .' Connie raised his eyes to the ceiling.

'What? Mi just ah look out fi unnu,' said Althea, raising her palms, amused. 'Yuh have condoms, Daphne? Cos plenty women carry dem in dem bag these days yuh know – and nuh just the slack gyaldem neither. The Well Woman Centre on the High Street ah give dem away free.'

'We're good thanks,' I said.

'Okay. Lord mi please fi unnu—'

The front door slammed and Althea leapt to her feet, putting the kettle on, her wooden bangles jangling as she unscrewed the Nescafé jar. Connie took his hands out of the front pockets of his jeans and folded his arms across his chest. He was still leaning against the worktop, looking relaxed, but there was a new tightness around his jaw.

'Hello, sugar,' said Althea. 'Mi just put making a flask for the journey.'

Tobias came and stood in the kitchen doorway, unsmiling. 'Yuh muddah tell yuh to tan here tonight?' he said to Connie. 'Cos me nuh like the look of the people across the landing. Dem make too much noise.'

'Is it dem quarrelling that bother yuh?' asked Connie, deadpan.

Tobias gave Connie an icy look, but he didn't rise to the bait. I felt his eye glide over me and resettle on Althea.

'Yuh wearing that to the party?'

'No darlin', dis is just the outfit mi ah go travel up in.'

'Good. I don't want mi wife in no homemade ethnic smock, when she have nice designer garms to wear. Make us look cheap.'

Althea opened her mouth, and then closed it again. She turned her back and stared at the kettle, chugging its way to a boil.

'Yuh pack the overnight t'ings?' asked Tobias.

'They're in the bedroom. Yuh just need to add yuh toiletries,' she said quietly, watching the steam begin to rise from the spout.

'Mi want to get on the road as soon as possible,' said Tobias, finally leaving the room.

There was a gentle click as the kettle switched itself off, breaking the silence.

'Why yuh let him say that to yuh?' hissed Connie.

'Why yuh have fi provoke him?' Althea shot back.

She poured some boiling water in the flask to warm it, intent on the task at hand, not looking at either of us. Connie shook his head. He wasn't looking at me either. Kallai walked in. I hoped he hadn't heard what had gone on.

'Mum, I don't wanna go to Wolver'ampton,' he said, handing Althea his empty plate. 'I won't know anyone there. And what if I get carsick? Dad will get mad at me.'

'Mi nuh want to hear any of yuh foolishness!' said Althea.

Kallai looked down at his hands. Connie gently punched his arm.

'You'll be okay. I tell you what; I'll let you borrow mi Walkman so you can listen to some music on the journey, help take you mind off t'ings. All right?'

Kallai shrugged. 'Can't you just come with us—'

'No, him can't,' barked Tobias. He'd been walking towards the front door, an overnight case in each hand; now he had our attention again. 'This is a Beckford family affair. Him nuh invited because him nuh family to me.'

'After mi nuh want to be part of yuh family,' snapped Connie.

'So why yuh still live 'ere? Big ol' Mummy's boy is what him is.'

Connie stood up straight, facing Tobias. 'Why yuh always such a bastard?'

'Yuh the only bastard mi see here.' Tobias laughed as he turned and exited the flat.

Althea screwed the lid onto the flask. 'Yuh asked for that. Why yuh come in here looking for a fight? If yuh nuh know how fi bat, yuh shouldn't bowl.'

'Yuh mean mi should be like yuh?'

Althea sighed, exasperated, then ushered Kallai from the kitchen. I could hear Althea in the hallway, gathering her things and trying to shush Kallai's muffled complaints. A few minutes later, the front door closed.

'Connie, are you—'

'I'm fine, Daphne. Just let mi go change my shirt.'

I'd always suspected that Tobias hadn't changed. But now Connie was even less prepared to hold his tongue and maintain the fragile harmony of the house. His normally even temper had spilled over within minutes of Tobias entering the room. I went to look for him.

The bedroom door was wide open. Connie was standing at the wardrobe; he'd put on a fresh vest, and the room had the clean smell of his deodorant.

He picked a shirt off a hanger. 'I'll be ready in a minute.'

'No rush,' I said, leaning against the doorframe.

The two single beds were pressed up against the wall on either side of the room. The bed to the left had various action figures strewn all around it. The other side of the room was neat and ordered. Connie's records were lined up at the foot of his neatly made bed, the collection stretching almost to the door. Textbooks on computing lay on their sides in a pile, keeping the vinyl in place. From what I could see, these thick tomes all looked pristine, their spines unbroken. I remembered how surprised I was when I heard he'd applied to study computer science rather than maths. When Fliss casually remarked that choosing a degree course should be about 'totally immersing yourself in something you loved', Connie was blunt, telling her that for him, the whole point of three more years of study was purely to get a good job at the end of it. I'd also been striving to get to university my whole life because I wanted a good job, but I wanted to do something that I was passionate about as well. Would Connie have shut me down the way he'd dismissed Fliss?

Connie sat down on the bed to put on his trainers.

'Listen, we don't have to go over to Lime Grove, not if you don't feel like it. We can just hang out together, do our own thing.'

At last Connie looked at me. 'It's fine. I'm all right. Let's go.'

'So, young man, what's this mi hear about yuh having sex with mi granddawta?'

Although Miss Gladys was pouting, there was a glint in her eye. I glanced at Connie expecting to see him looking coy, even amused. Instead, his jaw was rigid.

'Blimey! You gonna give us the third degree on the doorstep?' I said, trying to be playful. 'Can we at least come inside before the interrogation?'

Miss Gladys stood back, shooing us through the door. 'Well as mi say to Alma, it's a big change fi unnu so mi nuh entitled fi ask question?'

'Why are you and Mum even talking about things like sex?'

'Eh-eh! Yuh t'ink unnu invent it?' Miss Gladys turned to Connie. 'Look how Daphne embarrass! But mi sure yuh understand.'

Connie forced a smile. Grandma raised an eyebrow. 'Yuh all right? Yuh know mi jus' ah mek joke?'

'Yeah, of course,' said Connie.

Miss Gladys's eyes narrowed. 'Come – dinner nuh go cook itself.'

Now that Miss Gladys had moved upstairs to Marcia and Margery's old room, 59 Lime Grove had a dining room once more. Devon had helped Uncle Earl bring the long table up from the cellar, reuniting it with the sideboard and the good crockery.

All the cousins had now left home, but they usually came by on Sundays. I felt happy to have my family around me with Connie there too, and by degrees he began to relax. When I reached for his knee beneath the table, he placed his hand on top of mine.

It was after 9 p.m. when we left Lime Grove. Mum and Colin walked arm in arm ahead of us while Connie and I hung back, letting the old folks have their privacy. Colin wasn't exactly my idea of Prince Charming, but Mum was happy. A week ago she had asked if I minded if Colin moved in. I said I didn't, and I actually meant it. She was in love and I was pleased for her; she'd spent such a long time alone. I glanced at Connie, wondering when we might move in together and what it would be like. Would there be much more to find out about him? It felt as though I already knew him so well. In my mind's eye I saw a Sunday spent with just the two of us: lazing in pyjamas all day, reading the papers, eating when we felt like it, shagging to our hearts' content.

Mum and Althea suddenly gatecrashed my pipe dream. Didn't they feel happy like this when they started out with Ezee and Tobias? I pushed that thought from my mind. Connie and I were different.

We were walking with our fingers laced together. I squeezed his hand and he squeezed back. Manchester was so far away; how would we cope being apart for ten weeks at a time? Letters and phone calls would never be enough. I'd have to savour every minute with him now.

'Can I come back with you tonight?'

'Aren't you starting at the playscheme in the morning?'

'The community centre isn't much of a commute,' I said.

Connie smiled but I could tell it was fake. 'You don't want me to come back, do you?'

He blew air out through his mouth. 'No.'

'Okay. D'you wanna expand on that?'

'Lord, Daphne, yuh nuh get it? I hate that flat. It's shameful. I'm ashamed of what goes on there. Why would yuh go back there if yuh nuh have to?'

'I want to go back there because I want to be with you.'

'Mi nuh want yuh to see that part of mi life anymore.'

'We've been in each other's lives for nearly ten years. We can be ourselves with each other. Always. Don't hide yourself from me. We're together.'

We'd reached the walkway where the paths diverged; Mum was still strolling ahead, locked to Colin's side. She looked back over her shoulder and I waved her on; she nodded and continued towards our building.

'Come on. Tobias and Althea aren't there.' I gently pulled at Connie's arm. 'Tonight that flat is ours.'

Connie glanced at the tower block, his eyes not quite reaching the eighteenth floor before looking away again. I tugged his arm again, and this time, we slowly began moving towards Hibbert Court.

I sensed that I was alone in the bed shortly before I opened my eyes. The digital display on the alarm clock showed 00:06. Perhaps Connie was in the bathroom or fetching a glass of water. I listened. The flat was still. I put on the vest Connie had discarded by the bedside and padded to the door.

The venetian blinds in the living room were pulled up, and the night sky flooded in through the long, rectangular window. Connie was naked, leaning with his elbows on the windowsill, looking out. The moonlight illuminated his long spine and his thighs toned from all the time spent playing football. Although he must have felt my presence and heard my footsteps on the carpet, he didn't turn around. I wrapped my arms around his waist, kissing his muscled back. His skin felt cool. I wondered how long he'd been standing there.

I'd never seen the view from these windows; usually the blinds were drawn. From this height, the eight-storey housing block I lived in looked squat and boxy, while Lime Grove and its neighbouring streets looked like rows of dollhouses. Slowly, Connie straightened up and put his arm around me.

'Where would you go if you could live somewhere else?'

I looked out, beyond the estate and its surroundings. In the distance I could see the pale yellow security lights in the tall office buildings in the city. Further east along the Thames, cranes dominated the skyline, the huge mechanical structures frozen in action.

'I suppose I wouldn't mind one of them fancy flats they're building over in Docklands.'

'What about North London?'

I pulled a face. 'Nah, never!' Connie smiled and I relaxed. 'Anyway, I'm in Manchester for another year. You better visit me.'

Connie's smile faded. 'Daphne, I'm dropping out of college. I'm going to get a job.'

'Are you mad? There's still million and a half unemployed.'

Connie sighed. 'If I stay in college, I have to stay here. And I don't want to be here anymore.'

'But Connie you don't have to be here. You can move into

halls or get a place with Omar and Emmanuel. You don't have to quit college and get a job. Just move out.'

'If I get a job then maybe I can persuade Althea to move out as well. We'd have two wage packets coming in and she won't have to rely on Tobias.'

'Connie, you know I'd never want to dis Althea or nothing, but she's a grown woman. Tobias is what she wants. Even though God knows she can do better. But dropping out isn't what you want, is it? It can't be.'

'I'm not like yuh. Yuh been ready for university for as long as mi know yuh.' Connie added, trying to smile, 'I don't mind dropping out. I hate mi course anyway.'

'Then why don't you come with me? You could transfer to a course up in Manchester doing something you actually like: maths or physics. You would be away from here and we'd be together.'

'It's too far.'

'From Althea?'

'And Kallai. He's older now; he understands more. He shouldn't have to see what goes on here, let alone call it home.'

'Look, don't make any decisions now,' I said. 'Think about it some more. Come on, it's cold. Let's get some sleep.'

Back in bed, I drew my legs around Connie when he entered me. My arms were already encircling his neck, but I needed him closer. After he'd come, Connie shifted onto his front. He fell asleep with his arm across my belly, but I didn't move. I thought about how he wanted to be anywhere but here. I was determined to help him.

24

The playscheme finished at 5.30 p.m. and once the equipment had been put away and the community centre's hall tidied, I was handed my week's pay and free to go. I would be swinging by One Love to meet Connie, and from there we'd head to the West End. *Do the Right Thing* was still playing in Leicester Square. I brought along the prospectuses I'd ordered from the University of Manchester and the Poly; I was still waiting for the one from Salford. I hoped to get Connie to look at them later. His A-level grades had been good; I was sure he could get onto another course, though getting a grant might be difficult. But then, getting him to leave London was a long shot. But I had to try. I was thinking about what was right for Connie and how he could live his own life for a change. It was late August; I had a little over a month to persuade him.

The bus drew up at the Amersham Arms stop opposite 439 New Cross Road. Although the flats in the building had been let for some time, it still felt odd to see curtains at the windows. The families and survivors of the New Cross Fire had been determined to keep the tragedy in the headlines until the killer was brought to justice. Yet now the national papers and local press barely ever mentioned it. Back in 1982, over a thousand mourners had packed into St Paul's on Deptford High Street for a public memorial service, but over the years, attendance at the annual service had dwindled. In January 1988, the families had decided that year's service would be the last. 'People have forgotten what happened,' one of the relatives had said at the time, 'memories fade quickly.' I remembered how I used to think such a major crime was bound to be solved. Now, I understood this crime would have been handled differently and likely had a different outcome, if the young people who died had been white.

The shutters were already pulled down when I arrived at One Love, so I made my way around to the back alley. The big bin and a barrel tin of cooking oil had been placed on the street at the top of the entry, ready for collection by the dustmen. The back door was ajar and in the empty kitchen the surfaces had been cleaned; the wide stainless steel cooker stood idle.

'Hello?'

There was no answer, although I thought I heard a muffled moan. I parted the beaded curtain that separated the kitchen from the service area. All the tables had been cleared, the mop and bucket were propped against the counter. Connie was standing in the room with his arms around Althea; her head was buried in his chest. He gazed at me over her slumped frame. He looked stunned.

'What's happened?' I paused, thinking the worst. 'Is it Kallai?'

Connie shook his head. 'Papa take sick a few weeks ago. They t'ought he was getting better but him take bad turn. He's dead.'

*

The next week passed in a blur. The playscheme ended and although I'd planned to temp until term started in October, I hadn't applied to a single agency. Connie was never far from my mind.

On Friday afternoon, Mum came home from work to find me sitting on my bedroom floor surrounded by the textbooks for next semester's classes.

She surveyed the clutter. 'Yuh get much college work done today?'

I shrugged. Ever since I'd got off the phone to Connie earlier, I'd lacked the energy and motivation to do anything at all. He'd flown out a couple of days after I'd found him at One Love. Since then I'd called him every day. Mum would have a fit when she saw the bill but I'd deal with that later. Earlier, when we spoke, I could hear the murmur of voices in the background and what sounded like the clanking of dishes. Connie told me that there were always people at the house. 'I help prepare more food for nine night than mi do in a week working ah One Love. I can't keep Gramma out of the kitchen; she say she need to stay busy.' He told me that his gramma looked so tired yet he hadn't seen her cry. 'The funeral's tomorrow so maybe she'll let it out then. All Althea do since we reach here is bawl. Say how she gone for over ten years and the first time she go back home it's to bury her father. Mi know exactly how she feels. Nearly three years wi naturalised, why we never return before now?'

Mum tried to draw me out. 'Colin's coming over later with more of his stuff so I thought we'd get a takeaway. Maybe Indian? Would you like that?'

'Yeah. Maybe.'

She placed a menu at the foot of my bed and left me alone. I sat thinking about how Connie was being strong for everyone and there was nobody supporting him. He'd only been able to make the trip at all because Valerie had paid his plane fare. Bloody Tobias said he would only spare the cash on tickets for Althea and Kallai. The fucking prick. I should be with Connie. I looked at my latest bank statement, which was folded on a corner of the dressing table. My summer job had barely dented my overdraft and my grant wasn't due until October; there had to be a way to raise the money to go to Jamaica and be with Connie. I'd been toying with an idea for a couple of days, but kept pushing it to the back of my mind. Now it resurfaced and I could see no other alternative. I got up off the floor and went downstairs. Mum was in the kitchen.

'I'm going to ask Ezee for the plane fare.'

Mum's eyes widened.

'I want to go out to Jamaica because I need to help Connie. I'll do whatever I can to be there for him.'

'And that includes going cap in hand to yuh father? To big him up and make him feel important? Yuh t'ink he'd be driving BMW and all dem other fancy car if he was quick to hand money to him pickney when dem need it, rather than when him want to show off? Cha!'

'I'm not bigging him up – I'm not a silly little girl; he can't dazzle me anymore cos I know what he's like. And what I *do* know is that he can't resist showing off; he'd love to be able to demonstrate how he can come to my rescue.'

'It's been three years. I thought you decide yuh nuh want Ezee in yuh life. Why give him the satisfaction of even asking?' Mum sighed. 'Yuh can always call Connie and let him know yuh thinking of him. I'm sure he understands why yuh can't be there.'

'I know he does. I know he'd never expect me to come out. But I love him.' Mum was shaking her head. 'I really do love him. If I needed him he'd be there for me, so don't you think I should at least try everything I can to help him?'

'Lord! What mek yuh ears so hard? I'm telling yuh Daphne, nuh go to Ezee.'

'Mum, I'm not a child anymore. Please let me try.'

Mum raised her hands in exasperation but I couldn't wait for more argument when it was clear to me what had to be done. I grabbed my bag and left the flat.

The door opened and a skinny girl in cut-off jeans and a baggy T-shirt stood before me. She looked at me, her brown eyes hooded, like Ezee's. Like mine.

'Oh. Hi there. Is Ezee . . . Is your dad in?'

'No. I'm sorry, he's not home right now,' she said, speaking in the formal style Jamaicans use when they speak to English people. Before I could make my excuses and bolt from the doorstep, the girl had leaned back, and was shouting. 'Mamma Audrey, there's a lady here fi Daddy.'

Audrey emerged from the kitchen; I saw her start, but then compose herself.

'Daphne, hello. How yuh keeping?'

'I'm good thanks. You?'

'Yeah, we good. Yuh just passing by?'

'Sort of. Actually no. I'm sorry to just turn up, but I really need to see Ezee.'

Audrey nodded. 'Well then yuh better come in.'

The photographs that dominated the wall above the fire-place had gone. Now an oval-shaped mirror hung in the space that was once a gallery. Long tapered candles in glass holders stood at either side of the wooden mantelpiece. At its centre were two pictures in busy gilt frames. One was a school photo of Tilda in a burgundy-coloured uniform, the other was a wonky close-up of the little girl and Audrey, with their faces pressed cheek to cheek, staring down the lens. I picked it up to get a closer look. The camera must have been held at arm's length, yet somehow, they had got this lucky snapshot, showing most of their two faces. Audrey's normally pinched face had a smile so wide it narrowed the corners of her eyes.

Audrey had taken the cordless phone from the hall to the kitchen, but I could hear her talking to Ezee, telling him I'd come over 'out of the blue' urging him to 'just come see her nuh'. Tilda pushed the door open with her foot; she was carrying a tray with a glass jug, a tumbler and a plate of biscuits. I put the picture back on the mantel.

'I hope you like the soursop. I make it earlier. Mamma Audrey show mi how.'

She sat on the edge of the armchair, watching as I helped myself to some juice. Nerves made me overpour and I spilled a little on the tray.

'Oops,' I said, licking the side of the tumbler.

Tilda smiled at me. 'What you name again?'

'Daphne. You're Tilda, aren't you?'

'Yeah. How do you know my daddy?'

I wasn't sure what I ought to say. I took a long sip of the sweet drink before answering. 'Well, he's actually my daddy too.'

'Oh! Mi never know that,' she said, the stiff, polite tone relaxing a little. 'I have two sisters back in Jamaica, but mi never know mi have one here as well. I like yuh hair,' she said, pointing at my latest Afro experiment.

'Thanks. I like yours too.'

'Mi have loads of ideas for hairstyles, mi have some beads upstairs and I practise t'reading them. How old are you?'

'Twenty.'

'You have a job?'

'I'm at university.'

'I plan to go to university when mi grow up. Either Oxford or Cambridge or the University of the West Indies. I ask a lot of questions. I'm a curious sorta person. Mamma Audrey say me'd mek a good lawyer.'

She made me smile. 'It's good to be curious. I like asking questions too, but I think I'd like to be a journalist.'

I heard the front door open. I put the glass down on the table. Ezee walked into the room and Tilda stood up and wrapped her arms around him, pressing the side of her head flat against him. I felt a lump in my throat, remembering when my head only reached his chest. I wondered if he still used the same cologne. Ezee gently prised the girl away.

'Tell Audrey that me nuh staying for dinner; mi have business to attend to,' he said. Tilda's face dropped but she nodded.

'I'd really love to see those beads,' I said. 'You could maybe thread some in my hair if you like.'

The girl's face brightened; she giggled and left the room. Ezee placed his lighter and a packet of Bensons on the coffee table; I noticed he didn't remove his jacket. He perched on the arm of the sofa.

'It nice yuh come visit, true say it's been a while, but mi have plans this evening. Yuh should have call first.'

'I know it's been a while. A long while. I came to see you now because I need your help.' Ezee raised an eyebrow while I paused, wiping my hands on the legs of my jeans. 'A week ago, my friend Connie had to go back to Jamaica.'

'What? Deported?'

'No, all that got sorted. His grandad died. He's gone back to bury him.'

'Oh. Mi sorry to hear that.'

'Connie's in bits, but because his grandma and his mum need him, he's having to be strong for them all. I want to go out to Jamaica and support him, but the thing is I don't have the money for a flight, so I was wondering if you would lend it to me.'

Ezee was stroking his neat beard while he listened. 'When is the funeral?'

'Tomorrow.'

'But wait! Yuh want spend t'ree hundred pounds on a plane ticket when yuh'll na'eve make it to the ceremony? Yuh t'ink mi pluck money from tree? Mi nuh see yuh for over t'ree years and yuh come round here a beg money for a holiday?'

I bit down my irritation. 'I know I'll miss the funeral, but it's not just about that. Look, Connie is not just my best, my oldest friend. He and I are together now. I love him and I want to be there for him. I've never asked you for much before, but this would mean a lot to me.'

'Huh! So yuh and the lanky bwoy finally get together,' said Ezee. 'Listen darlin', Connie ah big man, the head of him household. It's him *job* to be strong for everyone else; it's what a man does for him family.' He chuckled to himself. 'Sounds to me like yuh just worried him nuh go come back.'

'He's not like you.'

I glared at Ezee and he stared back at me for a few long
seconds – the self-satisfied smile had vanished.

'Yuh truly yuh muddah dawta. Take offence when yuh nuh
get yuh own way. He picked up the cigarette packet and lit
a fag. 'My money's tied up at the moment. P'raps t'ings will
ease up in a couple of months' time, but probably by then
yuh boyfriend will be back anyway, so nuh need yuh run off
to yard after him.'

I looked away, not quite believing what I was hearing. The
living room door opened and Tilda entered, carrying a wicker
basket containing a hand mirror, a comb and assorted beads.

'Can I do yuh hair now?'

My throat was dry so at first I just nodded, then managed
to say 'sure'. She plonked herself down beside me. Ezee got
up and left the room. I pressed my lips together to stop them
from trembling. Tilda was sorting out her beads, telling me
which colour combinations were her own personal favourites.
I tried to concentrate on her sweet face, her hands, on what
she was saying, but my mind was replaying my exchange with
Ezee, weighing every word. Even though I could see Ezee was
wrong and strong, how was it possible that he had managed
to make me feel so small? A few minutes later, I heard him
shout, 'See yuh likkle more,' and the front door slammed.

I arrived back home just after 7 p.m. Tilda had cornrowed
four braids at the front of my head and threaded red, yellow
and green beads on the ends. I hooked the plaits behind my
ears to stop them dangling in front of my eyes. Mum was
sitting at the kitchen table with *The Voice* spread open at the
recruitment pages. She'd put a circle around a couple of ads

for Ward Sister positions. She looked up as I slumped into the chair opposite her.

'Yuh see him then?

I nodded, uncertain that my voice would remain steady.

'Him give yuh money for the plane fare?'

I shook my head; then I looked away.

I heard Mum sigh. 'Here. Take this.'

She slid a slim book with a blue plastic cover across the table. The words POST OFFICE SAVINGS BANK were written across the front in faded gold lettering.

'I was planning to give yuh this after yuh graduate. So yuh could ... mi nuh know. Put it towards something practical. Sensible. I wanted to give yuh the sort of financial start in life I never had. But ... yuh must make yuh own decisions and mi need to learn to respect that. Spend it how yuh feel and if yuh need to spend it now, then spend it now.'

I hesitantly leafed through the pages. The entries showed the £2, £5, sometimes £10 or £20 deposits Mum had made dating back to 1973. With interest, the balance had grown to the sum of £557.80. I looked at her, speechless. Mum gave a breezy shrug, but she held her head with an air of quiet pride.

'Just so yuh know, Mamma's friend Rita Daniels always ah go pan holiday. She know a travel agent who can likely get a cheap ticket. Mamma also ask Wishbone to call his nephew Travis. He owns a car service and can collect you from the airport.'

I got up, put my arms around my mother and held her tight. I realised that I'd got everything I was ever going to get from Ezee, that even when I was foolish and headstrong I could always come back to Mum. She, Miss Gladys and Connie were more my family than Ezee would ever be.

25

The tarmac on the dual carriageway glistened with damp, evidence of the short, sharp downpours Miss Gladys warned were frequent for the time of year. I sat up front in the minivan, passing bus stops and strip malls busy with shoppers. Scenes that would be ordinary were it not for the palm trees tilting their heads over the roadside and the fact that for the first time in my life, everywhere I looked there were people whose skin came in shades of brown. The view from the aeroplane had been astonishing. As we broke through the clouds, I saw the Jamaica I'd seen on postcards and TV travel shows: the sandy beaches crowded with the hotel complexes jostling for access to the sea. But these sights from the minibus filled me with a different delight.

I thought about how Mum and Miss Gladys still referred to Jamaica as *home*, even though they hadn't been back in decades. This is where their skin colour and the way they spoke didn't automatically mark them as outsiders – foreigners. And for once in my life, I was in a place where I wouldn't be the only Black person in the room, the café, the lecture theatre or the nightclub – I was the norm. I let myself sink into the grey vinyl seat, feeling my heart lift. Connie would have been twelve years old when he left here – now that he was back, did these scenes feel strange to him too? Probably he hadn't thought of it at all, he was grieving. I had to remember that I was here to support him, which I'd be able to do better now we were under the same sky. And my goodness, what a sky!

'Yuh want to stop off and get a likkle refreshment?' asked Travis.

'I'm peckish but I think I can wait. How long will it take to get there?'

Travis screwed his mouth to the side in thought. 'T'ree, maybe t'ree and a 'alf 'ours.'

'What? Is it really that far?'

He chuckled. 'Dis the first time yuh come ah yard?' I nodded. 'Ah nuh small island dis yuh know. Dis is Jamaica.' He kissed his teeth in amusement. 'Mi know a nice place along the way where wi can stop.'

Travis continued talking as he steered his minivan away from the coast; we were heading inland. Through the windscreen I saw rugged hills in the distance, broad and densely covered with trees. I smiled and whispered to myself, 'behold, a green and pleasant land'.

We were two hours into the journey when the sun began to set. Unlike the gradual fade into night I'd known in London without really noticing all my life, here darkness dropped like a stone. Outside of the big towns the highways were mostly unlit; Travis's headlights illuminated only what was immediately in front of us, yet I was thrilled rather than afraid. He drove with the confidence of experience, only slowing down to negotiate the giant potholes in the road, and after a three-and-a-half-hour drive, we were crawling along a dimly lit street. The houses sat far apart from each other, all slightly different in design and surrounded by gardens. Travis was peering at the names on the letterboxes pitched at each property's boundary. Finally, we pulled up outside a white iron gate with a path leading to a single storey house. Connie emerged from the shadows of the veranda; I wondered how long he'd been sitting there, waiting for me.

'I can't believe yuh here,' he said, the bass in his voice vibrating into my body. I held him closer. 'Everyone is sitting out back, but yuh nuh need to stay up if yuh tired.'

'After a ten-hour flight and a three-hour drive, I'm probably beyond tired. But a kiss would revive me.'

Connie stroked my cheek and tilted my face so his lips could brush against mine.

We held hands as he guided me through the house. In the garden, a group were sitting around a low wooden table, their faces lit by oil lanterns.

'But look who it is! Everyone, dis is Connie's lovely girl-friend, Daphne. She come all the way from London,' said Althea, setting her glass down and embracing me. 'Lemme introduce yuh. This is Cousin Wally and him wife, Bea.'

The couple, a broad man with silver-grey hair and a thin woman in a curly wig, smiled and mumbled hellos.

'. . . and over deh is Cousin Maurice,' said Althea, nodding towards a man of about her age. 'Mi remember when 'im was a likkle barefaced yout', now 'im run 'im daddy construction business.'

Grinning, Maurice rose and took my hand. "Owdedoo, isn't that how unnu make acquaintance ah England?' he said, making his accent mild.

I shook his hand. 'Yes. Or you can just say, "wah gwaan?"'

'Woah! She speak Jamaican,' said Maurice, his grin widening into a heartfelt smile. 'Wahm Daphne! Yuh good?'

'Fine, thanks. Nice to meet you.' I was pleased to have broken the ice with Connie's relatives.

'Where's Gramma?' asked Connie.

Althea's tone softened. 'It's the first evening the house nuh full up with people. She gone ah bed, say she'll see yuh in the morning. Daphne, come sit by mi 'ere.'

As I settled onto the bench draped with a patchwork blanket, the pungent scent of kerosene wafted across. I felt a wave of pleasant tiredness, but raised a hand to hide my yawn.

'Is this the first time yuh come ah Jamaica?' asked Bea.

'Yes, although my mum and grandma are from a little place in Manchester. I would have come for the funeral, but I couldn't get a flight.'

Connie's hand was resting on his knee; I placed mine on top of it, interlacing my fingers with his.

'Never mind,' said Althea. 'Yuh 'ere now. Yuh come all this way to support us. That's true love and loyalty, innit Connie?'

'Yes,' Connie whispered, gently squeezing my hand.

'Wi can talk plain in front of she?' said Wally to Althea, lowering his voice a notch.

'Yes mon! Mi love 'er like a dawta.'

'All right. Well as mi was saying plenty people ah open up dem place as a guesthouse, seen as more tourists ah come down this way now. Yuh see dem with dem backpacks. Call demselves independent travellers. The couple over there-sah return from foreign, someplace name Notting Hill. Dem building a second storey, the woman say when 'er children nuh visiting dem ah go do bed and breakfast. It's that what give Florence and Christopher the idea to do the same 'ere, especially seen as dem likkle drop o' pension nuh stretch too far these days. It would be a good enterprise cos this is a nice place and Florence is an excellent cook . . . '

'True, but mi nuh t'ink she can go ahead with that plan now. It'd be a lot to take on by 'erself,' said Althea.

'But she nuh need to take it on by 'erself if yuh could see yuh way to staying on a likkle longer. Just for a couple of months to get t'ings up and running . . . '

While Cousin Wally talked, my mind drifted. Yesterday, I was in London; now, I was sitting out in the balmy Caribbean night, watching the moths dance and hearing the other insects call to each other, somewhere in the deep darkness beyond the patio.

Althea's foot nudged mine as she leaned forward to pick up her glass, bringing my attention back to the table. She was shaking her head but Cousin Wally pressed on, his voice becoming stern.

'Yuh land ah England now, yuh nuh tek out dual citizenship. Yuh must can tan a likkle while and help yuh muddah. It's over ten years yuh gone and yuh na'eve come back for vacation in all that time – even though yuh know yuh daddy was frail.'

I felt Connie's hand tense; his eyes darted towards Althea. Bea touched her husband's arm; it seemed to calm him, although he still looked vexed. Althea was silent for a moment. When she spoke her voice was sombre.

'Mi wish me'd ah come back sooner. It was a mistake to stay away so long and mi ah go regret for the rest ah mi life.'

Wally took a sip of rum. Nobody spoke. I shifted in my seat, feeling out of place. Connie was still looking at Althea, but she was focusing on her glass, running a finger around its rim. Wally leaned forward and patted her knee.

'What's done is done. Christopher always said yuh had to find yuh own path. But if yuh cyaah stay then mi suppose Florence nuh have much choice. The alternative is she sell up. Move to a smaller place. Maurice and me can fix up the house fi 'er. So she can get a decent price for it.'

'Yuh ah guilt trip mi now!'

'Is it working?'

Althea sighed. 'Mi need to t'ink about it. And talk to Tobias.'

'Yuh 'usband, 'im English?' asked Bea.

'Nah, 'im born 'ere. 'Im parents tek him ah England when 'im was young. He's a very supportive husband and father.'

Althea sipped her drink. Connie's fingers were squeezing mine so tightly they hurt.

'Mi sure he'll understand,' said Bea. 'But it's right fi yuh to discuss it with him.'

Wally frowned. 'Yuh understan' mi just ah look out fi yuh muddah?'

'Of course,' said Althea, refusing to meet her cousin's eye.

Connie reached for the bottle in order to top up Wally's glass but he waved it away.

'Wi best mek tracks.'

'Yuh cyaah stay for another?' said Connie.

'It's late. Dem need fi go,' said Althea.

An alarm clock was ticking on the bedside table. I pressed my hand against a fold in the mosquito net, thinning the mesh so that I could read the time. It was ten past nine. I wondered where Connie had gone, but rather than getting up I lay still, listening. I couldn't remember ever waking up to a quiet of this quality. Sunlight leaked through the cracks in the shutters, glinting on the whitewashed wall. I got up and opened them.

I'd sensed that it was a fairly well-kept garden last night, but now I could see it was the sort of Eden that Miss Gladys had always sought to create in the meagre backyard at Lime Grove. Although she'd managed to dig a space she called her ground and grew callaloo, scallion and herbs, she'd had to make do with the sort of flowers that grew in a London climate. I didn't know the particular names of the blooms in this garden, but I saw how their size and colours were similar to Miss Gladys's taste. I could see for myself how Grandma's preference for bold pinks, oranges, purples and reds was because it reminded her of home.

I pulled on my dressing gown and walked stealthily along the corridors, conscious not to disturb the stillness. The front sitting room door was ajar and I was struck by how much it resembled the room Auntie Sybil still set aside for best. The lacy net curtains, crochet doilies, smocked cushion covers and embroidered chair backs; everything was 'just so'. Charmed by the similarities, I wandered inside and was drawn to the dark wood sideboard; above it hung a picture of the last supper, alongside that was a photo of a handsome, ebony-skinned man, half-smiling although his gaze was steady. A black ribbon had been draped over the picture's wooden frame. There were other framed photos delicately placed on each end of the sideboard. I recognised the old-school photograph of Connie propped against a ceramic shepherdess, and one of Kallai's baby pictures. Then my eye was drawn to a silver frame with a family group shot, Connie and Kallai with Althea and Tobias, taken outside the registry office in 1985. I picked up the picture to examine it more closely.

'Yuh Daphne, I presume.'

I turned around and was met with the frown of a tall, pale woman; the lenses in her dark-rimmed spectacles made her eyes large. She stood in the doorway in a faded corduroy shirt, her left arm crooked around a tatty willow trug loaded with fat mangoes.

'Hi. I mean, good morning. I woke up and wasn't sure where everybody was ...' The woman walked towards me. 'Mrs Small,' I said, extending my right hand. 'I'm very pleased to meet you. Although I'm sorry it's under such sad circumstances. Connie always spoke so fondly of his papa. Please accept my deepest condolences.'

The woman peeled off a pair of dusty gardening gloves. 'Yuh may call me Miss Florence,' she said, taking my hand while eyeing the picture frame in my other hand.

Still feeling as if I'd been caught in the wrong, I burbled on, 'I was just looking. Remembering ... It was a nice wedding. Althea looked stunning.' I plonked the picture down.

Miss Florence drew herself up. 'Wi would have liked to be there. Wi wait years for Althea to set a date fi her wedding. Then quick time dem go marry ah registry office – na'eve give us time to save plane fare for one, let alone the two of us.'

She stood beside me, looking at the wedding photo. 'Wah yuh t'ink of him?'

'Tobias?'

The directness of her question caught me off guard. I let my eyes drop to the sideboard again, focusing on the intricate design of the crochet runner. I could feel Miss Florence looking at me, waiting for a response. There was a muffled cough from somewhere down the corridor, then silence.

'It's the latest mi dawta sleep since she come here,' said Miss Florence. 'Mi pleased she finally rest. Now it's mi grandson ah rise early. Mi meet him sneaking down the hallway, ah head back to him room.' Miss Florence's tone was as dry as tinder. My cheeks grew warm. 'Him need fi get up earlier to outsmart mi.' She reached over and adjusted the position of the picture frame, moving it a couple of inches left of where I'd put it down. 'Him out with him breddah. Yuh want breakfast?'

'Yes. Please. Thanks. It's nice of you to let me stay here. Especially at such a difficult time. If there's anything I can do then please just say. I'd like to help.'

'Mi going to go to the market to pick up a few t'ings. Perhaps yuh can carry mi groceries. Although yuh mawgasah. There's ackee and saltfish in the dutchie. Or if yuh just want fruit mi have these, dem only common mango but dem fresh.'

My mouth was watering at the prospect of fresh ackee and ripe mangoes plucked straight from the tree. 'I can't decide. Might it be possible to have both?'

For the first time, Miss Florence grinned at me.

'Eh-eh, yuh nyami nyami! So long as yuh eat up quick time, or there'll be nuttin' left to buy.'

The vast covered market was noisy with traders competing to flog their produce. Everywhere I looked, there were the

Caribbean staples I'd grown up with: from yam, breadfruit, green banana and plantain, to chocho, Scotch bonnet and dasheen. I listened to the Jamaican voices all around me, tuning into snatches of conversation and feeling a buzz of pride when my English ears understood what was being said. Miss Florence took her time and was meticulous. She inspected the soursop for signs of bruising, pinched the tips of the okra to assess its freshness and haggled over the price of everything. She reminded me of Miss Gladys. I wandered over to a souvenir stall, selling island-shaped coasters and 'Jamaica No Problem' T-shirts, but Miss Florence steered me towards the fish stall instead.

'Is pleasant experiences yuh want to remember yuh stay here. Mi already can tell that yuh like yuh food, so tonight I'm gonna cook snapper with mango and green pepper sauce. Call it a welcome meal.'

'Thank you,' I said, touched by the warmth she was extending to me.

There was just one bag of shopping to take back to the house but Miss Florence had filled it to capacity. I kept having to shift it from one hand to the other in order to ease the load. Miss Florence's pace was slow but purposeful. As we walked down the street she greeted neighbours, but didn't stop to talk. In the daylight, I was able to properly see the neighbourhood. Most of the houses were well-kept, some were painted in pastel shades and surrounded by orderly gardens. We passed a peach-coloured dwelling with large gates and ornate burglar bars; a scaffold had been erected at the side of the house. This must be the returnees' place Wally mentioned last night I thought.

'Have you lived here long?' I asked.

'Over t'irty years. We move here after Christopher get a promotion at the bauxite plant. Back then plenty people with pickney live round here. Bit by bit dem all grow up and move away, only we ol' folk left.'

Although she didn't break her stride, Miss Florence's voice was halting. It was a change from the matter-of-fact way she had spoken to me all morning.

'Connie has really missed you. He's so sorry he never had the chance to see his granddaddy before he passed.'

Miss Florence's shoulders dipped and for a moment she seemed to shrink. She paused to regain her composure.

'Connie change a lot. Mi nuh just mean how him grow. He was always a happy t'ing when he was little. Positive. Him nuh seem like that anymore. And mi know it nuh just grief because mi see how him is whenever Althea mention dem life ah London.'

I looked away, swapping the bag over again, considering what to say. I remembered the last time I meddled with Connie's affairs. Would he want me to say something now? I thought about the fights I'd seen between Connie and Tobias over the years. I thought of the physical, emotional and financial control Tobias had had over that family for the last ten years – of course Connie had changed. His gramma had a right to know why.

'You asked me about Tobias earlier. The truth is he makes Connie unhappy. He's a bully – to everyone, especially Althea.'

'I t'ought so. Her letters were always too upbeat. She never badmouth him at all—and nuh mek joke about him neither.

That nuh normal in a marriage. More than once mi say to Christopher that it all sound false. Mi beg her to come home, but she hell-bent on making a life ah England, becoming a successful businesswoman.' Miss Florence shook her head. 'She meking up for dropping out of school when she pregnant – like as if wi ever disappointed with her.'

'We all thought ... hoped she would leave Tobias, especially after she got her British citizenship. But she's still there. Connie thinks he can persuade her to walk out. But she loves him. Or maybe feels dependent on him. I don't know really. Either way he has a hold over her.'

'Mi love mi dawta,' muttered Miss Florence, 'but she always choose watless men and make life a devil fi herself. At least here she nuh under his control. P'raps time away from him will mek her see sense.'

I wasn't sure it was as simple as making Althea see sense, but I didn't think I could say that to Miss Florence, so I said nothing.

Althea was up and about in the sitting room when we returned from the market. Her voice could be heard through an open window, which looked out over the veranda.

'Of course mi nuh forget mi have responsibilities ah England. Ah nuh holiday mi here having yuh know, mi just bury mi father ... '

Hearing the screen door creak open Althea immediately lowered her voice. As I passed the room, I saw her cup her hand around the mouthpiece and mutter a few more terse words. By the time I reached the kitchen, I heard the chime of the receiver being replaced in its cradle. Althea walked into the kitchen, her flip-flops slapping against the floor. She poured herself some water from a jug in the fridge, averting her eyes from us.

'The bwoys nuh wid yuh?'

'No. The likkle one wake early. Mi ask Connie to tek him out,' Miss Florence replied.

'That was Tobias on the phone,' said Althea. 'Him hope wi all bearing up okay. Him sen' him love.'

Althea had the nervous air of a schoolgirl who had been chastised. Miss Florence filled the coffee pot, making no comment.

'Cousin Wally tell mi more about the plan yuh did have to turn this place into a guesthouse. And that yuh'll need help now Papa is ... now Papa pass. Mi want fi help yuh. It's what Papa would have want. Only Tobias say clients ah ask when mi coming back. Naturally dem understand the situation. And cos mi come here on an open ticket mi can stay a couple more months, p'raps longer. But Tobias t'ink mi shouldn't leave mi customers for too long. And he nuh want Kallai educated here. Says he'll fall behind. And of course, him missing us.' Althea's hand slid down the glass; she began drumming her fingers on the kitchen table.

Miss Florence lit the stove beneath the coffee pot, then sat down across from her daughter. Althea would not meet her eyes. I was unpacking the groceries and wasn't sure if I ought to excuse myself, but then Miss Florence spoke up.

'And what is it yuh want fi do? Ah the first mi see unnu since time, and the first mi ever meet mi youngest grandson. Yuh nuh just say that yuh clients understand? Yuh must can stay a likkle longer. Unless of course yuh husband ah insist?'

'Him nuh insist!' said Althea, sitting up straight. She forced a laugh. 'Tobias just finish a long shift. Him tired. It wasn't a good time fi talk. Mi call him back tomorrow and discuss it properly.'

The back door opened and Kallai bounced inside, followed by Connie who winked at me. I was relieved to have more people in the room.

'Where yuh deh till now?' asked Miss Florence.

'Some yout' ah the sports ground kick dem ball and it fly pass wi.' There was more of a lilt in Connie's voice than I'd heard in years. It suited him. 'So Kallai kick it back and likkle after dis him join in dem game. Mi cyaah get him off the pitch.'

'They were thirteen; they couldn't believe I was only ten. Can I go back and play tomorrow too?' asked Kallai.

'We'll see,' said Althea, leaning forward to plant a kiss on his forehead. 'That's from yuh daddy. Mi call him earlier. Him say him missing yuh.'

Kallai's smile faded.

Althea peered at him. 'Yuh all right?

The boy nodded. 'I'm going to play out in the front garden.'

'Okay babylove.' Kallai trudged off. 'Wi make lunch soon eh?' Althea called after him.

Kallai continued down the hallway without answering. Althea rose and began fussing about the kitchen, forcing small talk about my trip to the market, asking Miss Florence if she was ready to begin sorting through Papa's things. I realised that even from this distance, she was still within Tobias's grasp; his presence had caused a shift in the atmosphere. I intercepted a look between Connie and his grandmother and saw that they felt it too.

26

'Why yuh nuh tek yuh Daphne on a trip this afternoon? Show 'er round,' said Althea.

It was the following day and we'd just had lunch. I held my breath but kept my head bowed as I took the dirty crockery to the sink. I wanted to see more of the island, but I didn't want Connie to feel like he had to play tour guide while he was mourning his granddaddy.

We'd all risen early that morning, and while Althea and Miss Florence began the sombre task of going through Papa's papers, Connie and I were tasked with keeping Kallai amused. We decided to take him back to the recreation field where he had joined in with the football the day before. Our walk to the sports ground took us through the neighbour-hood, past houses that were similar in size and style to Miss Florence's. It seemed a shame to me that such pretty houses should have ugly security bars around the windows and doors. Even though I knew from reading *The Gleaner* and *The Voice* that crime was a problem in Jamaica, I wanted to believe that it was overblown or mainly affected particular areas of the island. Uncle Earl still talked about buying land in St Thomas, the parish he hailed from, but these days whenever he mentioned it Auntie Sybil merely smiled. I'd once asked Ezee if he planned to retire in Jamaica; he'd told me that if he ever left London for good it would be to go and live in Florida, but for now he was 'happy just going back and forth'. Of course, now I knew why he was 'going back and forth'. To think, I had relatives in this parish! I wondered if they lived in a neighbourhood like this. I wondered if Ezee's babymothers did too? I pushed the thoughts away. They may well be relatives, but it didn't necessarily make them family.

At the sports ground earlier, Connie and Kallai kicked the ball about while I sat in the shade of a tree with lanky branches and tried to read *Daniel Deronda*, one of my set texts for the coming semester. But after a few pages, I had set the book aside and took a stroll around the perimeter of the field. I was only going to be in Jamaica for another eight days. I felt restless. I wanted to go and explore. But then I reminded myself that I was here for Connie and I was being selfish.

But now Althea had brought up the possibility of sightseeing. I was eager for Connie to agree.

'It's the first yuh come to Jamaica, innit Daphne?' Althea continued. 'Yuh nuh want to come all this way and spend every day lock up inside.'

'Well . . . I don't mind, really,' I lied. 'I'm happy doing whatever you and Connie want to do . . .'

'Mamma and mi ah go start sort t'rough Papa's clothes and t'ings,' said Althea.

'Yuh nuh need me for that?' asked Connie.

'It's more a muddah-dawta t'ing.'

'Are you sure? Yuh nuh go get upset?'

'I'll get upset, but it's a part of mourning. And yuh have fi mourn in yuh own way too. Besides, it's years since yuh deh here, yuh nuh curious to see the place? Tek Daphne to the Bay. Yuh did love it deh when yuh likkle. Mamma say it build up a bit more now. A couple of cafés and bars for the tourist dem.'

'Why yuh nuh come too?'

'I will another time. But it's good for Mamma to have mi here. And to be honest, it's good for mi to be with Mamma . . . '

Kallai jumped in, 'Can I go too?'

'Eh-eh! Yuh want play gooseberry?' said Althea, smiling now. 'Let yuh breddah and him girlfriend spend some time together.'

Connie wouldn't tell me anything about the Bay; he didn't want to spoil the surprise. I packed a bag with a towel, swimsuit, camera and a purse; then, ten minutes later, we were at the top of the street with Connie flagging down an already packed minivan. I ended up sitting on his lap with my arms around his neck, saying 'sorry' to the woman in the seat beside us every time the van swerved around a pothole or cyclist. A voice from behind called out, 'One stop drivah'. The van continued for another fifty or so metres, then pulled up in front of a church. A few of us stepped out to allow a man and a woman to get off, then one by one, we all got back in. I got a seat of my own, beside Connie and next to a window.

I was surprised how quickly the landscape shifted from suburban to rural. I'd spent my entire life in large urban settings, first inner London and now Manchester. The countryside was somewhere it was a hassle to get to without a car or the money for rail fare; I could count on one hand how much time I'd spent there. Here, in Jamaica, it seemed like it was never far away. For a while, we travelled along semi-deserted roads, passing lone buildings or half-built structures. While some of the houses dotted along the route were similar in size to Miss Florence's, others were more modest and even more were considerably smaller. I was unprepared for the sight of the meagre dwellings just off the roadside; houses with zinc roofs that looked as though they would topple over in a gust of wind. Outside one, I spied a young woman who was about my age washing her clothes in a plastic basin, while nearby, a barefoot child was playing with his toys in the dust. Further along the roadside we passed a shack where men were already sipping white rum from quarter-sized bottles. Then, a couple of miles on, the van stopped in a town and the scene changed; here were men and women in smart shirts and trousers, shoppers carrying their groceries to shiny cars and children suited and booted in stiff school uniforms walking down the street in pairs. The van ride was giving me glimpses of a real-life island – not a fantasy one. I was excited to be in Jamaica, but it was different from what I'd expected. I wondered how much of all this Connie remembered. What was it like for him to be back home after being away so long? I was curious, but I felt wary of asking, as if it would be too much of an intrusion, as though it might spoil the mood.

We'd been driving for around thirty minutes when we turned onto a narrow road where tall vegetation on both sides cut off any other view.

'We're nearly there,' said Connie. He was smiling, more to himself than at me. 'Keep yuh eyes looking out to the left. Wait now ... wait ... there ...'

The dense trees and hedgerows fell away revealing a curved

stretch of pure yellow sand reaching towards the deep blue sea. But here there were no hotels and no sun loungers; all I could see were beach shacks, a few modest-looking houses behind them and several small boats moored together.

'Look at that. It's nice innit?' Connie said, his voice steeped in pride and the dimple in his cheek unable to conceal his delight.

I peeled off my swimming hat and the Caribbean Sea water dribbled down the nape of my neck. Reggae beats thrummed from a beach bar where some tourists were speaking English with a Dutch accent. Connie was sitting with his elbows on his knees; he was still wearing trunks but had thrown on his shirt. He held a squat brown beer bottle in his hand. I sat down beside him, but he kept his eyes fixed on the horizon.

'It's here Papa teach me how to swim. I was nine. I ran out of the water and Althea hug me up and say how brave mi was. That mi must always be her brave bwoy. Likkle after that she was gone and I never see her for t'ree years.'

Connie's thumb was sliding up and down the beer label.

'It must have been a huge decision for her,' I said, stroking his arm, trying to draw him back to me.

'After she get pregnant and have fi drop out of school, she feel she have something to prove. Mi sure she never t'ought she'd be gone so long. Nor get mixed up with a man like Tobias. He's trampled on her dreams. I'm sad to be here mourning Papa, but if I'm honest, I'm glad to be far away from that man.'

Connie's tone was flat. I lifted his arm so that I could nestle beneath it.

'I wish I could stay longer.'

He finally looked at me, a hint of a genuine smile breaking through.

'I'm pleased yuh like it here. It's one of mi favourite places. If anyt'ing, a couple of bars has made it better. Although what it really needs is a restaurant.'

'I'm sure if you mentioned it to Valerie she'd be here in a shot, scoping out the business possibilities,' I said.

'Yeah mon, One Love Brasserie and Grill. Let's see . . . '

Connie stood, picked up a piece of driftwood and began drawing lines in the sand.

'This would be the bar area; customers would sit here drinking cocktails and look out at the view. I'd stand over here in one of dem open-style kitchens, where they can see me cook up the food before it serve. Lobster, prawns, snapper – all freshly caught then grilled or boiled or fried.'

'I can just see you running t'ings!'

'Then maybe one night a week I'd DJ and we'd have dancing as well as food. We'd keep the prices reasonable so the people who live here and the tourists can mix.'

'Sounds great. But what would I do?'

Connie exaggerated a thoughtful look. 'Front of house, the Yanks would just love yuh English accent. With my cooking and your charm, we'd make quite a team.'

'Now I know you're joking!' I said, packing away my beach things.

'I dunno, I'd like to think that it was an option,' said Connie softly.

'Leaving college with good degrees will give us more options. Working at One Love is all right part-time, but you wouldn't want to make a career of it. Besides, I got fired from a waitressing job after one shift – apparently I've got no patience and I'm not that charming!' I nodded towards the beach bar. 'Now, this way, sir, if you please.'

Connie stopped smiling and dropped the driftwood. 'Okay,' he sighed.

It was after 5 p.m. when we got back from the beach. Althea was sitting in one of the easy chairs on the veranda. She looked up from her magazine.

'Yuh have a nice time?'

'Wonderful. It's such a beautiful beach. It was like paradise!' I saw Connie and Althea exchange glances and I felt embarrassed for being so effusive. 'I sound like a proper tourist.'

'It's nice yuh like it,' said Althea. She turned to Connie, 'It was one of Papa's favourite places.'

'It made mi t'ink of him, but in a good way. And now wi have another convert; Daphne spend so long in the water mi did think she float back to England.'

'The sea was so warm. I'll have to wash my hair though – it got soaked; that swimming hat is useless.'

Althea smiled. 'Come out here after and mi will oil yuh scalp and plait yuh hair, give yuh a likkle more protection from the sand and salt water next time.'

I quickly showered and once dressed, I made my way back through the house. Cooking smells were already fanning into the hallway; Connie and Miss Florence had gone to work preparing dinner. I pushed open the screen door and went out onto the veranda. Kallai was in the garden doing keep-ups with the football. As I came out, he missed a beat and the ball dropped to the ground.

'Damn!'

'Uh-uh! Wi nuh use that kinda language here,' said Althea.

'But that was twenty-four I did just now, Mammy. Did you see?'

'Sorry babylove, mi never notice, but try again. Come Daphne,' she said, gesturing towards a cushion on the floor. I sat down between Althea's legs. The scent of honey wafted from an open jar of hair oil on the little side table. Kallai abandoned the football and was attempting to climb the mango tree. From inside the house came the faint sound of Connie's and Miss Florence's laughter. I thought about Miss Gladys and wondered what she was doing now. Most likely she was asleep, Mum too unless she was on a night shift. Perhaps one day we'd all come to Jamaica together. On the bus back from the Bay, I'd seen a road sign with directions to Manchester. 1½ Spring View was in a tiny settlement in the northern side of the parish. I was curious to see the place where Mum had been raised. I wondered if somehow I could convince Connie to take me there.

'I feel so lucky to finally be here. I only wish it could have been a holiday rather than ... well, you know,' I said.

Althea dipped her finger in the jar and smeared hair oil onto the back of her hand. 'It's been tough losing Papa. He understood me better than anyone.'

She gently tilted my head to the side and made a narrow parting just above my ear, applied the oil and then silently began plaiting the shaft of hair.

'So, you fall in love with Jamaica? Yuh nuh tempted to stay 'ere, become an island gyal?'

'I'm already an island girl – although the sea around

Britain is nowhere near as warm!' Althea tittered softly. 'I'll definitely be back and next time I'll stay longer. But term starts soon, and getting a degree is also something I've always wanted to do.'

'It's good yuh have ambition and nuh just stand still.' Althea's tone had become wistful. 'It's important not to just let time pass. It was Papa who first tell me "wi run t'ings, t'ings nuh run wi". But sometimes yuh forget and yuh get yuself stuck.'

Althea trailed off into silence again, running the comb over the crown of my head and dabbing more oil on my scalp.

'You grew up here, didn't you? In this house, I mean.'

'Yes. It was a big deal to Mamma to show her family that the man she marry was a good provider – even though him skin black like pitch. Not that any of 'er family ever see the house. None of dem visit in the thirty-odd years she deh 'ere. But Papa never care what dem did t'ink of him. He mek a home for us. He was a kind man. Him never raise his hand to Mamma. Or me. Or Connie. A proper gentleman.'

Althea fell silent once more. I wasn't sure if I should force polite conversation on her or whether I should ask what was on her mind. I figured that she had been through so much the past few days that I ought to take the lead from her; it was largely what I'd been doing with Connie. We continued in this way until the phone began to ring. We heard Connie go into the front sitting room and answer the call; his 'hello' was bright and friendly, then his tone became brusque. He came out onto the veranda to tell us that Tobias was on the line. Althea sighed and stepped over me. She patted Connie's shoulder and then went to the sitting room, closing the door behind her.

Connie came out onto the veranda and leaned against the banister.

'It must be gone midnight in London. Why is he ringing at this hour?' I asked.

'He still want her at his beck and call innit,' said Connie.

We were quiet, straining to hear the conversation through the closed window. Althea's voice was low, so her exact words were indistinct. But after a faltering staccato start, she appeared to be doing more talking than listening. The call seemed to go on for ages but in reality it only lasted around fifteen minutes. When we heard the chime of the receiver being returned to its cradle, Connie and I hurried inside, and met Miss Florence at the sitting room door.

'Well. What him want?' asked Connie.

'What yuh t'ink him want?' There was a slight edge in Althea's voice. 'Tobias wants us to come home.'

Miss Florence crossed the room and sat heavily down on the sofa beside her daughter.

'So when yuh planning to return?'

Althea took her mother's hand. 'I tell him that I'll come home after mi finish mi business here. He wasn't happy at all at first. But I tell him that mi muddah needs mi, and that I need her too. He quiet down after that and just listened. He actually listened to mi. I tell him that over ten years mi been away from here, and although t'ree months can't make up for the time that gone already, it is a start.' Miss Florence let out a sob. Connie went over and put his arm around her as Althea continued.

'I explain that mi can enroll Kallai at the local school for a term. Plenty people in England sending dem pickney back ah yard to school these days. For the good teaching standards and to keep dem from inner-city crime. The Seventh Day Adventist School near here is good – it strict too so Kallai nuh gonna fall behind. We can start to get this place set up for bed and breakfast like yuh plan. Then Tobias can come out in December and wi spend Christmas here. Connie and Daphne too if dem want. I say we need to keep this place for Papa and for the future. It's more than just a house.'

'What did Tobias say?' I asked.

'Him say Christmas is a long way away.' Althea put on a smile. 'But then mi tell him absence mek the heart grow fonder. That mek him laugh! He say that he understands why mi feel mi must stay.'

Miss Florence dabbed her eyes with a paper hanky from the ornate box on the coffee table. She squeezed Althea's hand. 'Yuh come home at last.'

'Yes, Mamma. Mi home.'

Althea seemed to have reached Tobias's heart. They were all hugging and might have stayed like that for a while had the screen door not banged open. Kallai entered, asking how soon it was until dinner because he was starving!

Connie had been experimenting in the kitchen and presented us with a small dish of curried ackee that had even impressed his gramma. When she quizzed him on which spices he had ground to make the seasoning, Connie grinned and re-mained tight-lipped. The main meal of the evening was Miss Florence's Brown Stew Chicken; the meat was seasoned and caramelised to perfection, and the rich gravy of carrots and red pepper had just the right amount of onion and thyme.

After finishing my second helping, I laid my knife and fork on the plate and slumped against the high-backed chair.

'I can't eat another thing. Honestly that was just delicious.'

'I'm not full. I'd like some more,' said Kallai.

'Good bwoy. There's a likkle more left in the pot on the stove,' said Miss Florence, pushing back her chair.

'No Gramma, yuh stay there. I'll go,' said Connie.

'Mamma, yuh nuh remember that time Connie ruin yuh escovitch?' said Althea.

'Like as if mi can forget! Mi turn mi back for a minute to go to the larder and him decide to t'row more vinegar in the pan.'

Connie returned with Kallai's plate. 'Bwoy it vex yuh!'

Miss Florence turned to me. 'Mi should have beat him, but Christopher say, "what will that teach the bwoy?" So wi start it again and this time mi stand over him so him learn to do it properly. Him only seven at the time but even then yuh papa say that p'raps yuh mek a good chef.' She winked at me. 'Or some woman a good husband.'

I shifted in my seat, although it made me glad that Miss Florence was so at ease that she felt able to tease me. It felt good to be accepted as one of the family.

Later, when we were getting ready for bed, I told Connie how glad I was to see him and Althea the way they were at dinner. I also told him about the conversation I'd had with Miss Florence the morning after I'd arrived. I hadn't mentioned it before, as I wasn't sure how he would react, but I wanted to have everything out in the open. He was quiet when I'd finished speaking, and I nibbled at some loose skin around my thumbnail, waiting for his reaction.

'I'm glad yuh tell her. Mi sick of the secrecy. It's right that

Gramma know. It's good Althea is here, away from him, and helping Gramma is a good excuse for her to stay. I just hope that by the time Christmas come around she grow stronger still in her mind. The longer she stay away from that man the better. D'yuh see how much happier Kallai is too? The best thing would be if she could move back here permanently.'

'But wouldn't you miss them? They'd miss you, especially Kallai.'

Connie grinned; he had a glint in his eye. 'Yes, but we'd have somewhere nice to come for Christmas and the summer vacation.'

He pulled me onto his lap. I sat with my legs astride, gazing into his eyes.

'It would take the pressure off you. It means that you could stay on at Poly.'

Connie caressed my face with the back of his fingers before he kissed me. It was a long deep kiss. One hand moved down to my thigh while the other was stroking the skin between my shoulder blades. I pressed down into his lap, kissing his neck, ignited as he unhooked my bra.

'Or if you really can't stand another year of computer studies then come to Manchester; we could get a place together.'

I giggled as he swivelled to one side and lay me down on the quilt, but Connie suddenly looked serious.

'There's so much I wanna do. And so many different possibilities now,' he said. 'I love you, Daphne.'

I felt the pulse at the base of my throat quicken, and the words came easily.

'I love you, too.'

27

Connie gave the market trader his half-sceptical, half-amused look.

'Why yuh charging mi that price?'

'Cos it's the price.'

Connie made like he was turning away to leave, but his movement was cool and unhurried.

'All right, hol' on. What say yuh gimme an extra two hundred for the yam?' said the stallholder.

Connie countered. 'What say yuh include a quarter kilo of the okra yuh have deh and some of dem Irish, and *then* mi give you the extra two hundred for the yam?'

'Him trin' ah bleed mi?' said the man, raising his eyebrows at me. I shrugged, trying my best to look nonchalant, even though I was impressed with the way Connie haggled – I would have just handed over whatever amount was asked.

The trader turned back to Connie. 'Two-fifty. That's mi best price.'

'Done.'

We left the shade and hubbub of the market and walked in the sunshine along the main street. For the past week, we'd fallen into a pattern of mornings spent doing chores, then heading off alone somewhere in the afternoon. Connie had one more week left of his stay, whereas I'd be returning to London tomorrow. I threaded my arm through Connie's, drawing him near.

The builders working on the returnees' house were taking a break; they sat on the first storey with their legs dangling over the side, swigging from water bottles and smoking. They'd made progress on the extension. The grey breeze-blocks looked solid but drab against the rest of the building's peach exterior. Miss Florence's plans for a guesthouse were on a far smaller scale, but over the course of the week, they had begun to take shape, mainly because Althea was more at ease. A couple of days ago, Wally had stopped by on his way back from Guinep Grove, a small resort up by the Bay. Since getting a mention in a couple of tourist guides, their reservations had increased and the owner, Abisai, asked Wally for a quote to build a couple more beach cottages. He also mentioned that several of his white guests often asked how they could start to locs-up their hair or get it drilled in cornrows. Wally told him about his cousin, 'a hotshot stylist, just back from London'. Althea had gone off that morning to meet Abisai for a chat; she was barely able to contain her delight. I could tell that Connie was relieved. He smiled more. He was the most relaxed I'd seen him in ages.

He held my hand as we walked down the street towards the house.

'So d'yuh want to head to the Bay now? Make the most of yuh last day at the beach? Maurice has lent mi his scooter so wi nuh have to take the bus.'

'If it's all right with you, could we take a trip into

Manchester? I really want to see if I can find the house where my mum grew up. Perhaps take a photo of it for her and Grandma.'

Connie took my hand. 'Of course. We can look at the road map when we get in.'

By mid-morning, we were ready to set off. Miss Florence came to the gate reminding us to always wear the helmets, stick close to the edge of the roads, watch out for potholes and go heavy on the horn. 'Some of dem taxi drivers t'ink dem own the road!' The grey-blue Vespa possessed more noise than speed, tootling along the inland highways and farting its way up the more hilly terrain of Cornwall County. I wrapped my arms tight around Connie, but I felt safe. Despite the bumps and the swerves, I knew the tingling in my tummy was excitement rather than travel sickness.

Eventually, we crossed the border from St Elizabeth to Manchester. Miss Gladys had often told me that her home parish was mountainous, over six hundred meters above sea level; it was wetter and cooler than other parts of the island, making it even more lush and tropical. She called it 'the bread basket of the island', famed for its coffee and Irish potatoes, as well as the occasional fog.

We'd been on the road for over an hour when we arrived at the biggest town we'd passed through so far. Telegraph lines criss-crossed the High Street that bustled with shoppers going in and out of stores, banks and supermarkets or milling about the market stalls perched on the pavements. The traffic kept slowing for pedestrians who crossed the street as they pleased. I could hear 'Fast Car' by Tracy Chapman being played through a transister radio, but the tinny music was soon replaced by the sound of drilling from a nearby construction site. It was just an ordinary day. I fancied that Connie and I were the only tourists here – and he was far less of an outsider than me. I wondered if they could tell that I wasn't really Jamaican – at least, that this wasn't my home. I joked that now I could compare this Manchester with my Manchester.

'But this is your Manchester,' Connie shouted over his shoulder. 'It's where yuh people are from.'

I looked around at this Manchester with its vast blue sky. The clouds were white dots, high above us, rather than the grey ones that crouched above the university campus and my digs in Chorlton almost every day of the year. The two Manchesters couldn't be more different. I felt an unexpected pang of affection for the place where I'd been living the last couple of years. I'd chosen to be there, and although I was excited about being here, the other Manchester felt more real to me.

Mum and Miss Gladys left Jamaica years ago; there would be new people living in the house now. Why on earth should some stranger – some foreigner – feel entitled to turn up on their doorstep? Was it too late to turn back now? After fifteen minutes we had left the town behind. Once again the buildings were spaced further apart and the road was taking us to even higher ground. Ahead of us were hillsides densely covered in various shades of green with the odd single dwelling peeking out from amid the foliage.

'I think wi nearly there,' Connie shouted over his shoulder. 'That's great,' I shouted back. Hoping to convince myself.

*

We stood at the gate, looking down a pathway that split the front garden. I had seen this path before, in the black-and-white photograph Miss Gladys kept on her mantel. The house and garden, however, looked very different – it was so much smaller than I thought it would be. In the photograph it was painted a lighter colour and there were no thick bars enclosing the veranda. I stood at the gate just staring, trying to sense some sort of connection but feeling nothing at all. So much for my roots.

'Can ah help yuh?'

The voice carried down the path to the gate; an old man had appeared behind the screen door.

'We were just passing through . . . I mean . . . I have family who come from around here. Actually, they come from right here . . . this house.' I was jabbering, idiotic. What must this old man be thinking? Some strange British woman just turning up out of the blue and loitering outside his house. 'I'm sorry we're disturbing you. We'll go.'

'What name?' asked the man, his tone unruffled, direct.

I was speechless for a moment. Connie stepped in.

'Johnson. Gladys Johnson.'

'Ahh . . . mi nuh hear dat name in a long while . . .' He pushed open the screen door and stepped out onto the veranda. A wiry man with a craggy face, tallish but now stooped.

'Unnu would like some carrot juice?'

The drink was cool and refreshing, the nutmeg leaving a satisfying warmth on my tongue. We were sitting on Mr Dodds's veranda and the old gent was soon waxing lyrical about my grandparents. He knew them from when they first settled in the district, having blown in from the town.

'D'yuh know Johnson chat Gladys up when she was in the back of him taxicab?' The old gent chortled, shaking his head.

I nodded politely.

'Yes mon. Mi never get another decent suit since James Johnson pass. Mi never seen such hard workers in all mi born days; mi t'ink being orphans was what drive dem both. Gladys make mi sister Hyacinth's wedding dress and dem chat like women do. I remember she tell Hyacinth how she t'irteen when she was taken out of school, packed off to Mandeville to keep house for a cousin with a devilish husband, a controlling man unable to keep him hands to himself – yuh know the type. Is when she turn eighteen that finally she ran away from that deh house; she get downtown but catch 'fraid. Say she sat alone on the street corner ah weep.'

I was sitting up now. This story wasn't the version I knew. Miss Gladys had always been vague about the family who raised her; I knew she wasn't close to them, but not because they had been so unkind. Not because they never loved her. The man paused to sip more of his drink.

'Then Johnson pull up in him taxi, him ask if she was all right and if she had a place to stay. It turned out there was a room going spare in the place where he lodged. On the way there, he remark on the quality of the smock stitches on her blouse; him tell her that he was a tailor by trade and said dem should go into business together.' The man chuckled. 'Yes mon, one of the best chat-up lines me ever hear – and the most sincere! Dem both spend their childhood being moved from pillar to post. Gladys tell Hyacinth how this place was the first proper home she ever have.'

My mind was buzzing, trying to process this new version of

my family's history. Miss Gladys had been a constant presence in my life – to me, she was indefatigable, straight-talking, even sassy. Hearing that she had been so vulnerable, alone and frightened, made my heart heavy. Mr Dodds continued with his reminiscing.

'... And she raise her dawtas well. Both of dem get high school diploma and gaan ah foreign. Which one of dem yuh muddah?'

'Alma. The younger daughter,' I croaked.

'The boasy one,' said the man, nodding sagely.

An unexpected smile relaxed my face. So Mum was considered boasy as well!

'After yuh grandad pass, mi did propose to yuh grandmuddah – twice! And twice she turn me down. Say she cyaah marry again, not after Johnson. Still, wi had a likkle t'ing going until she leave in '70. She keeping well?'

'Yeah. Very well, as it goes.'

Mr Dodds smiled. 'Yuh grandfather bury up a yonder in the cemetery deh. He was a fine man. Taken too soon. Remember mi to yuh grandmuddah. Tell her howdy from Wallis Dodds.'

The black engraving had faded. In places it was barely visible. My fingers traced the words etched into the small rectangular stone.

IN LOVING MEMORY OF

JAMES JOHNSON

HUSBAND AND FATHER

1918–1958

I lay down the posy of agapanthus picked from Mr Dodds's garden.

'You okay?' asked Connie.

I nodded.

Connie came over and put an arm around me.

'Grandma says he was the finest man she'd ever known.' I gulped back the emotion that was rising up my throat. 'I knew that Grandma left school early, it's why she pushed us so hard with our learning, but I never knew all that stuff about running away from home – from some predatory old bastard. God, her life was hard! And unfair. I've been so lucky. I've had love and stability my whole life. In part because Grandma gave up so much.'

'What d'yuh mean?'

We sat at the graveside while I told Connie about Mum, Ezee and the real reason why Miss Gladys came to England.

'1½ Spring View was the first proper home she ever had, and she gave it up to come to London when I was born. She hasn't been able to visit her husband's grave in all this time. It makes me so sad. I'm not sure why I came here now.'

Connie shifted so he was closer to me.

'The way mi see it, is that Miss Gladys move to England because her dawta and her granddawta needed her. She stayed because that's where you and yuh muddah were – Sybil dem too. Her family.' Connie put his arm around me. 'She love unnu with all her heart. A house is just bricks and mortar. A home is where yuh heart is. I was glad that I was able to be at Papa's funeral. I've seen where he's buried. But I don't need to visit the grave to remember him. I'll carry him in my heart. I bet if yuh ask Miss Gladys she'll likely tell yuh the same. Yuh can tell yuh grandma that you come to visit yuh grandfather's grave, I think she'd appreciate it. I think it's good for yuh too.'

Connie hugged me. It was good to feel his warm skin. We held hands as we made our way out of the cemetery.

'It's funny how in England we both live on the estate, but here . . . d'you think we would have even met?'

'Wi were destined to meet.'

I laughed. At last, I felt my melancholy lift a little. 'You and your bloody astrology! Come, let's take our time heading back. I want to stop off and do touristy things. Create more memories with you.'

The sky had darkened when we returned home; the clouds now looked bruised and heavy with rain. From the top of the road I could see a tan-coloured car parked outside Miss Florence's house; its boot was open. 'But see here . . . ' I heard Connie exclaim as Althea appeared. She was carrying a suitcase and tugging Kallai's arm; he was fighting against her. Miss Florence came out after them. She was shouting, but over the distance and the noisy scooter, I couldn't make out what she was saying. My mind was racing. They must have had a row, but over what? Everything seemed fine earlier. Althea slung the case into the boot. Kallai jerked again, this time breaking free and scrambling back towards Miss Florence. It was then that the driver's door swung open, and out stepped the tall, distinct figure of Tobias Beckford. My gut twisted.

I heard Connie say, 'What the fuck?' as Tobias swooped on the boy, grabbing him by the scruff of his neck. Kallai swung his little fist at his father and missed; Tobias raised his hand and the boy shrank in fear. Connie revved the scooter engine to make it go faster. He'd driven with care and diligence all day, but the sight of this uproar made Connie reckless, swerving around the potholes at speed rather than slowing down to avoid them. Heart pounding, I clung to his tense body, fearing what would happen if the front wheel dipped into a miniature crater, fearing what would happen once we reached the commotion. Althea began running toward us, her arms waving, trying to flag us down. Connie lurched to the left to avoid hitting her. I could see Tobias jostling Kallai into the back seat. Connie did too. He sped past Althea and kept going until he pulled up in front of the hire car. I clamboured off the scooter; my legs were shaking.

Connie took off the helmet and flung it on the ground.

'Wah the hell yuh doing here? he shouted.

'Come out of mi way,' said Tobias.

He took a step towards us, his body squared, ready for conflict. I'd seen this before. Nervously I inched closer to Connie so I was ready to grasp his arm, or fling myself in front of him if need be – anything to prevent another fight. But then Althea ran up, panting and tearful; she blocked Connie with her body. He rounded on her.

'What the fuck is going on?'

'Him turn up nuh long after unnu left this morning,' she said. 'Wi had a talk. I'm going back with him. Please nuh try and stop me.'

'Of course mi ah go stop yuh,' Connie shouted, leaping off the scooter. The vehicle clattered to the ground. 'This is foolishness. Kallai, come out of the car.'

Tobias took another step towards us. 'She make her decision. We're going home.'

'This is her home! Please nuh do this!' Miss Florence wailed.

Connie lunged. Althea pressed her hands against his chest and I quickly grabbed his arm.

'Yuh come all this way to drag her back. Yuh can't bear not to have her under yuh control. Why can't yuh just leave her alone?' Connie shouted.

Tobias smirked. 'Yuh t'ink it's mi she come for? She can tan 'ere if she want, but my son is coming back to England with me.'

Connie looked at Althea. She was shaking her head.

'Him have rights. I cyaah let him tek Kallai from mi. So mi have fi go with him. Please nuh make this any harder fi mi.'

'Then don't go!'

Althea shook her head, tears leaking from her eyes. Tenderly, she tapped Connie's cheek. He stood motionless as Althea walked away, getting into the back seat beside Kallai.

'And nuh bother t'ink yuh ah go come back to my yard neither,' said Tobias, stabbing the air with his index finger. 'I only want my family living there and yuh nuh family to me.'

Hearing Tobias's voice snapped Connie out of his trance in an instant.

'D'yuh t'ink mi care? I'm done with living in that place. Fuck you.'

Tobias scoffed and got back in the car, slamming the door.

We stood watching the car until it had disappeared from view. Kallai's face grew smaller in the rear window; then he was gone.

Tears filled Miss Florence's eyes. 'First mi lose mi husband, now mi lose mi dawta. Mi cyaah tek anymore.'

Connie's body was stiff with rage, but now his arms grew slack. He went over and hugged Miss Florence; she buried her face in his shoulder. He led her inside and I trailed after, just as it began to rain.

I'd slept badly and by the time I awoke, Connie had already risen. I remembered how on my first morning here I had revelled in the quiet; no LBC news headlines burbling through the wall next door, no front doors slamming along the landing, no traffic noise, no sirens. But this morning, the house felt eerily still. I wondered where Althea and Kallai were now. They'd probably already landed in London and were being frog-marched back to Hibbert Court by that bastard Tobias.

My half-filled suitcase lay open where I'd left it on the bedroom floor. Last night, the thought of packing made me feel heavy inside. I gazed at the ceiling, my mind busy devising plans. Travis was due to collect me after lunch, but I wondered what time the airline's office opened so I could call and see about changing my flight. Maybe stay another week or so and then Connie and I could fly back together. It would be okay to miss the start of term, although Mum would be pretty pissed off with me. And what about the cost? Would I have to fork out for a new ticket? So stupid of me not to have bought an open flight. But then, I didn't have the money. In fact, I couldn't really afford to stay. No . . . it was unrealistic. I couldn't miss my flight home. I heaved myself up, put my dressing gown on and went to look for Connie.

In the kitchen everything had been tidied and left just as Miss Florence liked it. She had been too distraught to do anything last night, we all had been. Connie must have straightened the room this morning. I wondered where he was now. I made some tea in Miss Florence's favourite cup and took it to her room. There was no sound when I knocked on her bedroom door. I sighed and padded back to the kitchen where I sat down at the table and waited.

I was sipping my second cup of tea when I heard the screen door slam. Connie entered the room carrying a bag of groceries. I could sense the agitation beneath the businesslike show he was putting on.

'Morning,' I said gently.

Connie nodded and proceeded to unpack the shopping.

'I made your gramma some tea but didn't want to wake her yet.'

'I got her to take a pill last night. Probably why she's still asleep.'

'I see you've been to the market already.'

'I woke early and couldn't get back to sleep.'

Connie scrunched up the empty shopping bag and then slumped onto one of the kitchen chairs. He placed his elbows on the table and began massaging his temples.

'Would you like a drink?'

'No. Thank you.'

'They'll be all right.' I tried to soothe. 'You will be too. I'll try to go and see them as soon as I get home. We'll have to find out when Tobias is at work so we can get your things out of that flat. Hopefully, he won't do anything vindictive like chuck your stuff out before you get back.'

'I'm not going back.'

'But we should try and get your stuff.'

'Daphne, I'm not going back to England. I have to stay here

with Gramma. I'm going to look after her and help set up this bed and breakfast.'

I was stunned. 'But ... Miss Florence wouldn't want you to do that.'

'I've told her it's all right. That mi nuh mind. Yuh know mi hate mi course anyway.'

'When did you tell her this?'

'Last night. When I put her to bed.'

'You make a massive decision just like that?' I said, snapping my fingers. 'And you tell your gramma before you bother to discuss it with me?'

'I'm sorry. I didn't think before I said it. She was so upset and it just come out. But mi know this is the right t'ing to do.'

'Right for who? You? Your gramma? What about me? For fuck's sake, what about us?'

'It was Papa and Gramma who brought mi up. We're close, just like how yuh close to Miss Gladys. Gramma needs mi right now. This is the place where mi been happiest. It's my home.'

'But aren't you happy with me?'

'Yes. Of course I am. But yuh could stay too. Yuh like it here, don't yuh? Stay here with me, Daphne.'

Connie's eyes were red. For several long seconds I was silent, trying to avoid the truth, though the words were right in front of me. I spoke slowly, through deep swallows, as though each word were a dirty confession. 'This isn't my home.'

Tears filled my eyes. I turned away to hide from the disappointment on Connie's face; he pulled me back, trying to wrap me in a hug. I shrugged him off.

'What was all that bollocks yesterday about home being where the heart is – not bricks and mortar. You said you loved me, but you put everyone and everything ahead of us, you always do. You once told me that nobody has looked out for you, that nobody understands you like I do, but what about me? When will you start to understand and look out for me?'

'Daphne, this is where I belong right now—'

'What about Cousin Wally? Cousin Maurice? Can't they help her?'

'Daphne, I want to stay! It might just be a couple of months . . .'

I had been so naïve and so trusting. All the time I thought we were making plans for *our* future, he saw a very different future altogether – one based on what he wanted. I was merely being tacked on to his scheme. He seriously expected me to give up my dreams and aspirations overnight. I was angry with him and angry with myself.

'No! I'm not waiting for you any longer. This is what you want. You don't want me. If you don't come back next week, then we're finished.'

Connie was shaking his head. Now he looked impatient, irritated. 'Daphne, yuh being unreasonable. It isn't that simple.'

I took a breath and forced myself to look straight at him. 'Yes, it is.'

1993

28

From my desk I could see into Ted Bennett's office. The nicotine-stained louvres were partially open and the door ajar. Whenever the news editor was reading copy he sat reclined in his chair, a biro tucked behind his right ear and a cigarette between his index and middle fingers. Geoff Glover, the *South London Star*'s chief crime reporter, stood in front of him, waiting for feedback on his latest piece. CID officers had arrested three men and charged them with the murder of Stephen Lawrence, the Black teenager stabbed to death in Eltham. Ted sat upright, placed his fag on the ashtray and reached for his pen. Geoff raised his hands in exasperation as Ted began scoring the page with red ink.

'Look, according to my sources the police received an anonymous tip-off the day after the killing took place. There was a handwritten note left on a police windscreen *naming* the suspects, yet it's taken them over two weeks to make these arrests,' said Geoff. 'All I'm saying is, there's a whiff about it.'

'Unless you can prove it, we can't print it,' said Ted in his usual monotone. 'Also, there is no "a" in definite.'

I carefully scanned my copy once more, checking for typos and misplaced commas. Five minutes later, I stood chewing my bottom lip, feeling like a schoolkid called to the head-master's office. It was the longest piece I'd ever filed for the paper. Normally, I'd have been hanging around the local Magistrates' Courts, reporting on fines and sentencing for *News in Brief*. But at the start of the week, I'd been given permission to follow up on anti-racist groups' demands for the British National Party's headquarters in Welling to be shut down. The brief was to go to the area and get 'strong opinions' and 'varied points of view' about the premises on Upper Wickham Lane.

Ted tilted his chair back as far as it would go, rocking it back and forth. Still somehow managing not to drop ash from the end of his fag.

'You were all right, were you? Going down there . . . '

'It was fine,' I said, forcing a smile. Ted's eyes returned to the page and I let my smile drop.

Welling was far beyond the South East London that I knew. As the train pulled into the station, I'd taken the attack alarm Miss Gladys gave me out of my bag and slipped it into my coat pocket.

One local parent told me that she was frightened for her son after a gang of white youths had attacked a Black boy outside the school gates. So far the police had done nothing about it. Another mother, a white woman with two mixed-race kids, was desperate to be rehoused. An elderly Asian man told me that he knew two families whose homes had been targeted by racist groups. Still, several white people I had interviewed felt their area was being unfairly maligned; the murder had taken place in Eltham, not Welling, and there was no proof that the crime was necessarily racist. Besides, hadn't the council visited the place and found that it was just a bookshop?

'Have you got a photograph?' asked Ted, interrupting my thoughts.

I nodded. There, on a fairly humdrum High Street with regular shops interspersing the neat post-war houses, was an unassuming pebbledash building at the end of a terraced row.

'It was shuttered. But I took pictures of the outside. Apparently it's been closed all week,' I said.

Ted's chair made a snapping sound as he sprang forward to lean over his desk. He stubbed out the fag and removed the biro from behind his ear.

'Start here,' he said, putting a line through the whole first paragraph, then other sentences I'd spent hours crafting. 'Lose the references to Nazis,' he added.

'But – with respect – the European Parliament's Committee on Racism and Xenophobia describe the BNP as an openly Nazi Party.'

'Well, *with respect*, as far as our readers are concerned, the Nazis were defeated in 1945; they're not camped out in Welling.' Ted handed me back the copy with a dispassionate flourish. 'You can cut lynching an' all. You know the page four deadline is twelve thirty?'

'Yes, I'll have it done by then.'

'You'll have it done before then; I want it back in thirty minutes. Oh, and Daphne ... ' Ted paused to light a fresh cigarette, lifting his chin to exhale. 'Good work.'

A silent sigh of relief escaped from my chest.

'Thanks.'

The yellow Post-it had been stuck to my desk lamp while I

was in with Ted; Miss Gladys had called to remind me about Greville Dunne's nine night. Mum had to work so I was to represent her. The message said come at 7 p.m. and wear something respectful. I had on denim capri pants and Adidas Stan Smiths; I'd have to go home and change. I folded the note and began revising my copy.

It had gone 6.30 p.m. when I finally left the office. I looked at my watch; I had no hope of catching the 18:44 to South Bermondsey and it would be half an hour until the next train – if it wasn't cancelled. I'd have to try and get a bus. I saw a number 1 and a 133 pull up at the bus stop. The crossing lights were still red but I launched myself onto the street.

'Oi, watch it!'

I sprang back onto the pavement as a cycle courier swerved to avoid me. 'Wah mek yuh gwaan sah? Yuh want fi dead?' he tossed over his shoulder as he disappeared down Borough High Street.

Across the road I saw both buses pulling away from the stop. There wouldn't be another for bloody ages now. I looked at my watch again. There was nothing for it, so I held out my arm to hail a taxi. It was a bit of an extravagance for a Thursday night, but I had enough cash. I knew my biggest challenge would be getting a black cab to stop in the first place. I spied two Hackneys coming down the road, their amber lights gleaming. Sure enough, as the first one drew near to where I was standing, he glanced over, then continued along the road. The second cabbie blanked me as he passed by yet stopped thirty yards on to pick up two white guys in suits.

'Fucking arseholes,' I muttered to myself.

I kept my arm outstretched as I continued along the pavement edge. At this rate it would be quicker to walk back to Rotherhithe. Another Hackney lumbered past, but pulled up at the kerb a few feet ahead. It stayed there, with its engine making a juddering, growling sound. Surprised and relieved, I scooted towards it.

'Thank God,' I exhaled, as the driver wound down his nearside window.

He smiled and I stepped back in astonishment.

'Daphne Johnson, as I live and breathe. How are you?'

I was lost for words so just stood there, aghast.

Mark Barrett grinned. 'D'you wanna cab or was you just holding that arm out for fun?'

'Of course I want a cab!' I spluttered. 'But the cabs don't seem to want me – or my money.'

'Did they have their lights on?' he said, nodding after the other two taxis.

'Yeah, the pricks.'

'I know the type,' said Mark. 'So, where we heading then?'

The taxi trundled down Great Dover Street; I sat back in the seat marvelling at the chances. During the time I spent living in Manchester, I'd often reflect on how big and anonymous London was. Yet here I was in the back seat of a taxi being driven by my first ex-boyfriend. It was like a scene from a modern-day Thomas Hardy novel. There was a Millwall FC sticker above the 'No Smoking' sign, and a sandalwood-infused Magic Tree dangling from the rear-view mirror. Mark glanced back at me, his grey-blue eyes just as arresting as I remembered.

'How long have you been driving a cab?'

'Been out since last September. I passed in twenty-six months – it takes most people years and years to learn The Knowledge. Turns out I'm good at something.'

'Mark, you were always good at something.'

He winked at me. 'Nice of you to remember!'

I rolled my eyes as I chuckled. He always did know how to make girls laugh.

'What are you doing with yourself then? You'll have to speak up. This is my first lease and it's a bit of a tank. I can hardly ever hear what the punters are saying.'

We'd slowed down for the roundabout at the Bricklayers Arms. I switched to the jump seat so I was sitting behind him and could speak closer to his ear.

'I'm a journalist; I work at the *South London Star.*'

'Of course you do! You always had your head in a newspaper if it weren't in a book. So what's tomorrow's headline?'

'Stephen Lawrence. They've made arrests.'

Mark didn't respond. He kept his eyes fixed ahead. The cab rattled on past the old Peabody Trust Tenement and the pub that had been converted into a mosque. Eventually Mark broke the silence.

'So you left Marsh Town?'

'Yeah. I'm subletting my cousin Devon's place. I'm sharing with a mate from uni.'

Mark glanced at me through his rear-view mirror. 'Not Connie then?'

'No. He was in Jamaica last time I heard,' I replied, deadpan.

We lapsed into silence again as the cab continued down the road and we hit the next set of traffic lights.

'Nana passed away. I got her flat, but I've put in for a transfer.'

'I'm sorry about your nana. You fleeing to the suburbs?'

'Nah. I'm hoping to move down Vauxhall way if the council flats ain't all been sold off to yuppies. Be nearer Maisie.'

'Girlfriend?' I asked in a knowing tone.

I watched Mark's profile as he smiled, remembering how those creases always softened his face. Without taking his eyes off the road, he reached down and produced a wallet that he flicked open and handed to me through the gap in the glass partition.

'That's my Maisie.'

The child in the photo had pale brown skin; her dark hair was held in bunches by yellow baubles. She had her father's smile.

'She's lovely, Mark.'

'Yeah. Coming up to a year old. I see her every other Saturday. We go to Battersea Park Zoo. She loves the meerkats.'

'What does Phil think?' I asked carefully.

'Dunno, I never see him. But thinking was never his strong point.' He laughed and I found myself joining in. It was so nice to see him after all this time.

'You're not with her mum?'

'Nah, never worked out. It ain't easy with a family like mine. They still hate Blacks and ain't too keen on having a half-caste in the family neither.' Mark spotted me shaking my head. 'What have I said?'

'Nothing . . . well actually it's not nothing. I just think that your daughter might prefer the term mixed-race rather than half-caste.'

'Oh, so that's racist now too, is it?'

'Actually it was always pretty offensive.'

Mark tutted. 'You ain't changed much. Well, the PC brigade don't tend to include me on their circulars. Probably why my ex refers to me as "the unfinished article".'

I'd been out with several different guys over the last seven years – white as well as Black, and only occasionally ever thought about Mark. But when I did, he was frozen in 1985. I never pictured him as grown up, that he'd be a father already – and to a Black child! Was he just hell-bent on pissing off Phil and his dad? No, it was more than that. He had made some definite choices. The main one being that he wasn't going to be a version of his grandfather, his dad and Phil. If I had met Mark now might I have considered getting off with him? Perhaps. I still liked fellas who could make me laugh. Might *I* have had his child? Probably not. We'd arrived in front of my building. The whole journey had taken around fifteen minutes and I was sorry it was over so soon. I stepped out of the cab and leaned into the front window to pay.

'Did you ever get that note I sent you . . . telling you that I was sorry?'

'Yeah, I did.' He sighed, drumming his fingers on the steering wheel. 'I didn't reply because, well . . . I had a lot going on. I appreciated you sending it – not at first mind. But later on.'

I felt a lump in my throat. 'So, am I forgiven now?'

'We were just kids, Daphne. Besides, young hearts heal easily.'

Mark looked serious. I mostly remembered him with a

lively look in his eye, now he seemed distant and reflective. I
didn't want us to part on any bad terms again.

'I'm sorry. What I said about mixed-race, I must have
sounded like a right know-it-all. I didn't mean to judge. You
love your daughter and that's what counts.'

'Yeah, I really do love her. The thought of someone setting
on her because of the colour of her skin . . . ' Mark turned to
me. 'I just can't imagine what it must be like to have to bury
your child. What they did in Eltham, to that young Black lad.
It's fucking awful. I hope the family gets justice.'

I reached inside the cab and lay my hand on his. 'You know
what, Mark? I never had a dad, not really. Maisie's lucky to
have you. And I don't think you're the unfinished article. I
think . . . you are a work in progress.'

Mark fetched up something close to his familiar grin. He
handed me his business card.

'In case you ever need a ride out to the airport. It's good to
see you, Daphne. Mind how you go.'

'I'm sorry for your loss,' I said, my voice muffled by the fur
collar on Valerie's cardigan.

Valerie sniffed and brought a hanky to her nose. 'Thank
you, dear. Mi really appreciate all what yuh muddah and her
nurses did to mek Greville comfortable. She run her ward
with real compassion.'

'She's sorry not to be here, but she is coming to the funeral
tomorrow.'

The doorbell rang and Valerie excused herself. I squeezed
between the guests that lined the hallway. Three little girls
with fussy blouses tucked into their matching plaid skirts

dodged past me and ran into the sitting room. Beneath the hum of conversations was the gentle beat of an old ska tune and the clink of dominoes being shuffled.

'So yuh reach at last,' said Miss Gladys, calling me inside and raising her cheek for me to kiss. 'This is one of mi grand-dawtas,' she said to the three women sitting closest to her.

'Is this the one that lecture at the university?' said a woman in a grey blazer.

'No, that's Marcia. This is Daphne. She's a newspaper journalist.'

'Oh,' chorused the elderly women, their tone a mixture of awe and approval.

Bawdy cackles suddenly erupted around the dominoes table. Wishbone laughed the loudest.

'Well yuh know Greville would always say yuh as old as the woman yuh feel! Mi cyaah believe him gone at just seventy-t'ree. Nah-sah! An untimely death.'

'There's no such t'ing as *untimely death*,' said Dennis, who owned the butchers on the High Street. 'When it's yuh time, it's yuh time.'

'Ah true!' Another lady dressed in mauve was nodding sagely. 'The Lord God Almighty already mark out every day yuh deh pon this earth.'

'Amen!' said the woman in grey.

Miss Gladys kissed her teeth. 'Then what about murder? What about the murder of a young person, yuh mean to say that nuh untimely? Unnu remember Rolan Adams, that fifteen-year-old dem kill up ah Thamesmead two years ago? And what about the bwoy kill in Eltham last year?'

'Rohit Duggal,' I muttered quietly.

Miss Gladys continued, 'And now Stephen Lawrence. All of these youngsters that have dem whole future ahead of dem killed by racists for nuttin'. Nobody is gonna convince me that dem murder nuh *untimely*. Cha! It's a tragedy.'

There were murmurs of agreement and a more melancholy air descended. I excused myself and went to get a drink.

A group of teenagers had commandeered the stairs; they were listening to music on their personal stereos and taking turns at playing mini *Pac-Man*. The aroma of spice wafted along the busy hallway; they'd made curry goat. In the big kitchen there were guests clustered around a buffet table while others were pouring themselves drinks. There was a step down into the room but I stopped in the doorway. Frozen by the sound of his laughter, my breath caught in my chest. Connie was wearing a Chelsea FC top; a blue-and-white striped apron was tied around his waist. He put the lid back on a large cooking pot and turned to a girl in designer jeans who was exclaiming how she hadn't eaten such amazing food since that last time she went back home. His eyes were fastened on her, listening attentively. Greville and Valerie were like family to him. Why hadn't it occurred to me that he would be here?

The little girls in matching plaid dashed past again, this time squealing and brandishing cartons of juice. Connie's dark eyes followed them as they charged out of the kitchen, then found me hovering at the entrance to the room.

He hesitated, before producing an enormous smile. 'Hello, stranger. It's been a long time. Yuh good?'

'I'm fine, thanks. Really ... good.' I winced at the bland accent I'd acquired since university. 'You?'

'Yeah, I'm well. T'anks.' I could hear his diction tilting

towards Standard English. Stiffening. He excused himself from the girl in jeans and came over to me. I stepped into the room but remained by the doorway.

'It's so sad about Greville. I had to come and pay my respects.'

Connie nodded. 'Yeah. He and Miss Valerie always looked out for me. You'll be at the funeral tomorrow?'

'Yeah. Mum too.'

'Good. I saw you grandma when she arrived earlier. She nuh look a day older than when I last see her, and that's over four years ago, at least.'

Had it really been that long? 'Yes . . . four years. It's good you were able to come back for the funeral.'

'Nah, actually . . . I'm living here now.'

My eyes widened before I could mask my hurt.

Connie looked down at the lino. 'I've been back . . . gosh, eighteen months.'

'I see.'

Eighteen months ago I was still in Manchester, exiting a stale relationship. But even so, I couldn't believe that he'd been back for over a year and hadn't been in touch. That I'd stumbled into him at a wake.

'Gramma get the B&B up and running. Cousin Maurice's daughter Shanna helps her out now. She always asks after you. Now I can tell her that I've seen you.'

'Yes. You can,' I said, hearing the resentment in my voice and hating the sound of it. I groped for something to say. 'How's Althea?'

'She seem okay. She's managing a salon up Sydenham way. Said it's like having her own place. Mi seen her a couple o' times since mi return, but mainly we talk on the phone.

It's easier. Besides, she's still on the estate and I live over in Hackney.'

Guests were coming from the kitchen, balancing paper plates laden with curry goat and rice. They paused to compliment Connie on the cuisine and say what a great help he'd been to Valerie these past weeks. He nodded and mumbled his thanks.

'Let's go out there,' he said to me, unbolting the back door.

The evening was meandering toward night-time; but light from the kitchen window illuminated the side return. I perched on the ledge.

'The food does look nice,' I said.

'I'm working as a chef now at a place in town. It's kinda modern European–British food, although the head chef is from Uruguay. It's okay. Long hours but I'm learning a lot.'

'You always loved cooking. You were good at it.'

He looked shy again. 'How's your muddah?'

'She's good. Married Colin two years ago and they went to Jamaica on their honeymoon. One of the resort's security guards practically barred the gate when they wanted to take a stroll. He told Mum that Jamaica was too dangerous for English people. It was the first time she'd ever been called English in her life!'

Connie chuckled. I'd made him laugh. I let my mind wander back to the time we danced together in the garden at Emmanuel's party, then stopped myself.

The back door made a scraping sound as it opened and a familiar voice said, 'Whaap'm, babylove. Yuh have a hug fi mi?'

There stood Althea with her plum-coloured smile; her

plaited dreadlocks hung loose past her shoulders, which were more hunched than I remembered.

Connie stepped forward and Althea leaned into him, resting her chin on his shoulder. Finally she drew back from him and brushed his cheek with the back of her fingers. 'Yuh look good.'

'T'anks. Yuh too,' Connie replied.

'But wait! Daphne here as well. Long time mi nuh see yuh!'

'Hello, Althea,' I said, leaning in for a hug.

'Look at yuh, all grown and with locs too. Mi always knew yuh was a conscious woman. Mi see yuh granny at the butcher's sometimes. She say yuh working as a journalist!'

'Yeah. Grandma tells everyone.'

'Yuh always so clever and modest. Now, look who mi bring here with mi. Come out here darlin'.'

She beamed at a slender youth loitering at the back door. He wore his hair in neat skinny braids and had on a baggy NWA hoodie. With everyone's attention now switched to him, Kallai looked at the ground, shifting from one foot to the other; it reminded me of Connie at that age, but his sharp jawline was unmistakably Tobias's.

'Hey Kallai . . . Wah gwaan? You good?' asked Connie.

'I'm okay.'

'Come give yuh breddah a hug. T'ank him for the money him send yuh at Christmas,' said Althea.

Kallai stared at Connie. His lips pouting. Vexed.

'It's all right. I was never one for hugging people up when I was his age,' Connie said to Althea, although he was looking at Kallai.

'Him save the money and buy one Walkman. Now him can play him rap and it nuh trouble him father.'

Althea's laughter was hollow and nervous. Nobody else joined in.

'Jerome and that lot are sitting on the stairs. I'm just gonna go chat to them,' Kallai mumbled.

'Yuh nuh see yuh breddah since time. Yuh can chat to Jerome and dem later.'

'No I can't cos you told Dad we'd only be here an hour.'

'It's okay, Althea. Let him go and be with the young people,' said Connie.

Kallai grunted then sloped away.

'Teenagers! Sorry about that,' said Althea.

Connie shrugged. 'Mi wasn't sure yuh'd make it tonight. Will yuh still come to the funeral tomorrow?'

'I'll be there. Mi nuh t'ink Tobias will come. Him have fi work. Probably just as well.' Althea smiled at Connie. 'The food smell nice. Yuh use Gramma recipe for the seasoning?'

'With a likkle twist of mi own. Let mi get yuh somet'ing to eat.' He traipsed off into the kitchen, walking from his shoulders, just like I remembered. His movement was still graceful.

Althea came and sat by me on the window ledge. 'It's a nice surprise to see unnu standing out here together.'

'It was a surprise to hear that he'd moved back here – over a year ago.' I laughed, Unable to hide my bitterness.

Althea's ebony eyes fixed me. Her makeup was expertly applied as usual, but she looked tired. 'I was sorry when I hear that yuh and Connie split up. Mi did t'ink that unnu would have found a way to stay together.'

I felt an uncomfortable sadness pressing against my chest. 'It's just one of those things. We were too young.'

She regarded me. 'What about now?'

'I'm glad to hear he's doing well and he's settled.'

'Him not as settled as yuh t'ink. He's not content.'

I looked inside. Connie had been waylaid by another of the guests who was no doubt complimenting him on the food. Connie was nodding with a broad smile on his face.

'He seems okay to me,' I said.

Althea gently scoffed. 'Yes, but yuh of all people should know how good wi are at hiding t'ings in our family.'

29

Valerie anticipated around sixty people would attend the funeral. In the end, the number was closer to ninety. It had been a bright but cool morning, and although the air was still, train announcements from Hither Green station carried on the breeze across the cemetery. I'd joined in with the singing around the graveside, mumbling through the hymns I couldn't remember, trying to keep my mind off the chill creeping through the soles of my shoes. While the women sang and held each other, the men took turns with the digging, muddying their smart black shoes and the hems of their trousers, their faces streaked with tears. The local authority gravediggers stood at a discreet distance waiting to get their shovels back. By the time we got to the Dew Drop Tavern, Miss Gladys was complaining of cold. Concerned that she might have a chill, Mum had taken her straight home. I got myself a brandy and sat watching the people at the bar. Wishbone cracked a joke, making the other old gents groan and then laugh; they raised their glasses and muttered 'to Greville' before downing their drinks. Althea appeared at my table carrying a plate loaded with food.

'Hello, Daphne. Is it all right wi sit 'ere?'

'Yes, of course,' I said.

Kallai was wearing a voluminous puffa jacket. He slumped onto the stool opposite and began shovelling up the rice and peas with the sort of commitment that reminded me of his brother at that age.

'Hey, Connie, mi find a seat 'ere with Daphne, come!'

Connie gave Althea a look, then nodded me a greeting. He was clutching a pint and two straight glasses. He set a Coke down in front of Kallai, the teenager hunched over his food.

'Yuh know probably the only good t'ing that'll come out of this sadness is if we realise we should make the most of the time we have,' said Althea. 'It's good that it bring us here together. Old friends like unnu.'

Connie and I sipped our drinks while Althea beamed at us. 'As well as mi two handsome sons.' She reached over and pinched Kallai's cheek.

'Mum!'

'Wah? Yuh can act like a big man but yuh'll always be mi likkle bwoy.'

'I can't believe how much you've grown,' I said to Kallai. 'You look way older than fourteen.'

'Thanks,' Kallai said, with quiet pride.

'Mi suppose that's why police stop him the other day,' said Althea.

Connie was about to take a sip of his drink but brought the glass back down on the table. 'What dem stop yuh for?'

'Nothing,' said Kallai, keeping his eyes on his plate.

Connie leaned forward. 'Yuh know dem can't just stop you on the street for no reason. If the police approach yuh, ask if you are being detained.'

Kallai sighed impatiently but Connie continued, 'Did they search yuh?'

'I was with my friends. They searched all of us.'

'Dem can only search yuh if dem have reasonable grounds. Unnu have anyt'ing illegal?'

'We were coming back from school innit!' said Kallai, sulky and irritated.

Connie kissed his teeth. 'Typical. Next time dem stop yuh, make the officer tell yuh dem name, the station dem work and what they're looking for. You'll have to put up with it for the rest of yuh life so it's best if yuh know yuh rights—'

'Have you finished?' snapped Kallai.

'Yuh should listen to yuh breddah,' said Althea, slicing the meat from the chicken leg. 'Seen as yuh never listen to me. Cos if yuh'd come straight home from school like mi tell yuh, instead ah stand up pan street corner with yuh frienddem, maybe police wouldn't stop yuh in the first place.'

Kallai let his fork fall out of his hand; it clanked against the rim of the plate. 'Can't you both just shut up about it now?'

'Calm nuh! Althea is concerned for you and mi just ah school yuh. Why you acting so facety?' said Connie.

'Cos I don't need *you* to school me. I've got me mates. Me bredren.'

'And we nuh bredren?'

'Can't you see I ain't a little kid anymore, or are you fucking blind?'

'Watch yuh language,' said Althea, straining to keep her voice low.

Kallai groaned before getting up and striding off.

'Come back 'ere and tek yuh plate.'

Kallai ignored her, barging past the other mourners.

Althea was incensed. 'Kallai!'

'Leave him be. I'll take it back.' Connie picked up the plate and marched off to the function room, striving to conceal his own irritation.

I felt the urge to go after him, but then I'd done that so many times before, why should I do it again? We'd already created enough of a scene. It was painful to see Connie and his brother not getting on. They were so close once, but then, so were we. Althea pushed her plate away, the food uneaten.

'Yuh nuh need to rush off after yuh had yuh drink, do you?' Althea's tone was even but her eyes were imploring. 'Please stay.'

I touched her hand. 'Of course, I will.

Valerie slipped away at 7.45 p.m., but the funeral crowd showed no signs of going home. Connie, Althea and I sat among the other mourners, listening to them reminisce about Greville. Althea hadn't seen many of these people in a while; they were her friends rather than Tobias's, and as a couple they seldom strayed beyond his social circle. But Tobias was not there now, and the familiarity and the ease that came from the company of old friends made Althea vibrant and funny. Connie seemed more relaxed too; at least, he was smiling a bit more now. I was on my way back from the loo when I noticed Kallai sitting alone in the tiny beer garden, huddled in his enormous coat. I waved at him and to my surprise, he waved back. He sat up a little and hooked one of his headphones behind his ear, so I went outside.

'What you listening to?'

'Hip-hop, some old-school stuff. A friend taped it for me. Eric B. and Rakim.'

'"Paid in Full"?'

'You've heard of it!'

'Are you kidding me? Connie had a recording of that same album! He played it so much the tape stretched. Your dad used to go on about rap not being proper music; he said it would never last.'

'He still says that now.'

I laughed, and Kallai did too. His face grew rounder, the sharp features softening. For a moment, he looked more like Althea.

The pub door rasped open and Connie looked out. Kallai stopped laughing.

'I see the two of you stand up out here. Unnu nuh feel the cold?'

Kallai said nothing.

'Pah! You don't know what cold is until you've lived up north,' I said.

Connie came over to join us. 'Is that yuh new Walkman? The one Althea say yuh save up for?'

Kallai cut his eye past him.

'What's going on with yuh?'

Kallai scoffed. 'You think that chucking a bit of money at me and sending a few stinking birthday cards will make everything jiggy? Jesus! I don't *know* you!'

'Wah yuh mean you nuh know me? I'm yuh brother.'

'Some brother! I've been here all this time with her. And with him. Even when you got back here you never bothered to come see me.'

'All the time mi was in Jamaica mi didn't just send money. Mi write yuh letters too, but yuh never once write back to me.' Connie kept his voice low, but I could hear the resentment underneath. 'And now whenever mi call, yuh nuh come to the phone or yuh never at home.'

'Are you surprised? Oftentimes I have to go and cotch at friends' houses to get away from that bloody flat.' Kallai leaned forward, his body tense with fury.

The two of them were silent, looking daggers at each other. I stood rooted to the spot, wondering what I could say to help. But then Connie spoke up.

'When I come back to London, I figured it was best not to come to that flat. There's nothing about me your daddy likes. So if I come there he gets angry, and when he gets angry he takes it out on our muddah. You nuh remember what it was like back then—'

'I do remember. I remember you putting your hands over my ears to block out the sound of them fighting. I remember you telling me that everything would be all right. Well it was all right for you, but when we got back here, I was all on my own. I'm still on my own.'

Connie's shoulders dropped. He sat down across from his little brother, squeezing his big, tall self between the bench and the tabletop. I'd expected Kallai to storm off, but instead he folded his arms and sat glowering at Connie, spoiling for a fight.

'Daphne, can yuh leave us a moment please?'

I went back inside and perched on the end of the sofa beside Althea. Dennis was holding court now, laughing about a time back in the '50s when he and Greville got lost in the London smog. I kept sneaking a glance at the doors that led to the beer garden. The brothers were still outside. I hoped that was a good sign.

'Greetings everybody.'

I immediately tensed. It was a difficult voice to forget – the deep patwah with a trace of South London. Tobias was making his way over to our table, holding a short glass tumbler in his big hand. His hair was cropped close to his scalp, the way men did to hide a receding hairline. He'd hardly lost any of his bulk or his sharp features with age. Althea fell quiet; she looked down at the table, while everyone else murmured 'hello'. Dennis continued with his story, while Tobias lingered like a cloud. He took a cigarette from a packet of Bensons. No doubt he didn't like being ignored, so he turned to me.

'So, Daphne, it's been a long time. Althea tell me yuh is a journalist now. A career woman. Good for yuh.'

'Thanks. How come you're here now when you weren't at the funeral?'

'Couldn't get the time off, so mi come down after work to pay mi respects.'

My eyes shifted over Tobias's shoulder. Connie and Kallai had come back inside together. Tobias followed my gaze; he looked them both up and down. Kallai seemed to shrink under his father's stare.

'There yuh are Kallai, darlin. Yuh been outside all this time. Come sit down with us now, warm yuself,' said Althea.

'I wanna go home now,' said Kallai. 'Is it all right if I head off?'

'Yes of course babylove—'

'No. How can yuh rush off when mi just reach here?' said Tobias in his genial, light-hearted tone.

'I've been here all day, Dad . . . I'm tired.'

'Tired! It was a funeral, how can yuh be tired? Try working a twelve-hour shift, then yuh'd know what tired is.' Tobias was grinning, addressing his words to the people sitting all around, attempting to cajole them into agreement. 'This yout' just want to go back and run up mi phone bill, calling his friends. No! Stay here, show yuh respects and we'll all go back together.'

'Just let him go, can't yuh?' said Connie.

Tobias lit his cigarette and coolly angled his head, blowing smoke from the side of his mouth. When he finally spoke, all the jocularity in his tone had drained away.

'Excuse me, but what's it got to do with yuh? Yuh back five minutes and telling mi how to deal with mi pickney. It's none of yuh business. Yuh t'ink cooking in a fancy uptown restaurant make yuh some kinda big shot? Cha! Yuh wouldn't last five minutes in a proper man's job.'

'So yuh is a proper man? Why don't yuh show me how yuh is a proper man?' said Connie. 'Come nuh!'

Silence rippled across the pub.

'Eh-eh!' said Tobias, feeling everyone's eyes on him. 'Why mi go waste mi time on a good fi nuttin' like yuh?'

Connie sprang, landing a punch on Tobias's jaw. He staggered back but Connie stepped forward, ready to punch him again. Some men placed their bulk against Connie's chest, holding him back. Althea hurried over to Tobias. He shook her off. Connie was straining against the men who'd formed a human shield.

'I always thought the reason yuh treated me so bad was because I wasn't yuh pickney, but it wasn't that, was it? Seen as you nuh treat yuh own son good neither. You are a bully and one day yuh'll get what's coming to yuh.'

'What yuh come threatening mi now?' Tobias snarled, holding his face.

'Ah nuh threat mi giving yuh, what mi giving is a promise.'

'Fuck you!'

The landlord's booming voice cut straight through the clamour. 'Mi nuh want no trouble, come out of me pub!'

Kallai was staring, open-mouthed.

'Remember what I told yuh,' Connie said to him, before snatching up his coat and walking out into the night.

Connie walked faster than I remembered. By the time I'd grabbed my things, his long, angry strides had taken him to the end of the street and onto the main road. I ran to catch up with him.

'Where are you going?'

He stopped. 'Mi nuh know. Mi nuh know a damn t'ing.'

'Come. Let's just walk. You can calm down.'

The pavements were busy with young people, students mainly, judging by their vintage garms and zany coloured DMs. They meandered along in groups towards the pubs dotted along the main road, or clustered at bus stops waiting for rides into town. The smell of hot oil and savoury spice wafted from the fried chicken shop where a rough sleeper was hanging around the door, begging for change, chips or fags. I remembered walking along this road with Connie before. I wondered what we looked like, walking along together now.

I slipped my arm through his. He accepted my gesture and drew me nearer. I slid my hand into his coat pocket, finding his hand and grasping it. It felt so easy.

'I ruined the funeral.'

'Valerie wasn't there, and even if she was, she'd have understood.'

'I never should have let him take them back to England. He's poisoning their lives.'

'It was Althea's choice. There was nothing else you could have done back then. But it's different now. Althea is older and so is Kallai. They don't need Tobias; they need you.'

He stopped and turned to me. 'What about you?'

'What do you mean?'

'You know what I mean. Kallai wasn't the only one who never answered mi letters.' My shoulders tensed. 'I love Kallai and I care about Althea. But I came back to England to be with you.'

'Come off it! You've been back eighteen months. If you really came back for me, then how come you never got in touch?'

'Errol said he hear that yuh got trainee reporter position straight out of college. You had yuh degree and get a proper newpaper job, the t'ings you've always wanted. Yuh wanted that more than to stay in Jamaica with me—'

'Oh here we go.'

'Mi nuh criticising yuh! I know how much it meant. I was gonna call and congratulate yuh. But then I began picturing yuh living yuh life. Dating guys with degrees. I put off calling. A month passed, then two, then six, till eighteen months were gone. I don't know what else I can say. I fucked up four years ago. I thought I belonged in Jamaica because it was the right thing to do. But where I actually belong is with you.'

Connie stood, waiting for a response. I touched his face, his cheek warm despite the cold air. A familiar drop of pleasure radiated through me, spreading beneath my skin, making my stomach tremble. It was surprising – no, disconcerting. My mind was telling me to *stop being so fucking weak*. Connie tenderly placed his hand on mine. Pinched by fear and pride, I stepped back and put my hand in my coat pocket.

'I don't know. I need to think. I have to go.'

30

I spent the next two weeks burying myself in work. According to the Association of London Authorities, racist attacks were up by 16 per cent, with a 36 per cent rise in South East London alone. In 1992, 811 racist crimes had been reported, but for all my phone calls and trawling through data, I couldn't find out how many of those crimes had been solved. I was trying to write a bigger piece about race hate crimes and whether the police were taking them seriously.

I was also trying not to think about Connie, but he was never far from my thoughts. He'd paged me a couple of times. Just bland messages, hoping I was okay. Then on Wednesday he'd shown up at my office, dropping off homemade soup because he'd heard from Miss Gladys that I'd been working long hours. 'I figured yuh'd need some proper nourishment to keep you going. I mean, look how yuh mawga-sah!' I'd been moved by the sound of his accent poking through. Although I'd fixed my face to appear unimpressed, Connie seemed undeterred, his tone cheery. 'No hurry to return the thermos. Mi 'ave another. Although I'm off this Sunday. We could meet up. If yuh want.'

Now it was Sunday and I'd been standing at the St Mary's

Gate entrance to Greenwich Park for ten minutes. There was no sign of Connie. I'd tied my locs in a favourite kente wrap. It matched the tote bag I had bought to hold Connie's flask. But apart from that I was dressed down in jeans, a simple black top and tinted gloss rather than lipstick. I was pleased that there was some real warmth in the late-May sunshine. Connie had surprised me when he suggested meeting here as it was a schlep for him. I wondered if it was for my convenience – maybe he was conscious that I might want the option of a quick escape. I looked at my watch again, promising myself I'd only give him another five minutes, but then I caught sight of him steering his bike through the tourists along King William Walk.

'Sorry I'm late. As it turns out yuh not allowed to cycle t'rough the foot tunnel. T'anks for waiting.'

He seemed tense; maybe it was nerves. He was talking to me the way he had at nine at night, in that precise English voice.

I gave an insouciant shrug. 'Me should 'ave realised it was BMT not GMT, you mean.'

Connie made no remark on my terrible Jamaican accent, instead his face relaxed into a grin. 'It's turned out nice. I brought a picnic. You hungry?'

'Why are you always bringing me food?'

'Dem say good food is the best way to a man's heart, then why that cyaah work for woman too?'

'Oh, so you're wooing me?' I teased, thrilled to hear the rhythm of his accent again.

'P'rhaps. How mi doing?'

I ran my thumbnail along the edge of my bag strap. 'D'you wanna have a look around the market?'

'Nah, I hear it's not as good as it used to be. Lemme chain mi bike and wi take a stroll around the park.'

Our conversation went in fits and starts: we discussed the weather, he asked about my week at work and I asked about his. Grasping at straws, we commented on the kids in the play park and the couples on the boating lake, before we fell into silence. I wondered what I was doing. I'd mentioned to Mum and Miss Gladys that Connie had dropped by my work, bringing me food. Miss Gladys smiled. 'He was always a t'oughtful bwoy.' Mum was slicing cucumber, the knife tapping loudly against the chopping board. 'How yuh can call him thoughtful when him broke yuh granddawta's heart.' The two of them had continued back and forth, while I picked fluff from the knee of my tights. I remembered those light blue airmail envelopes arriving, that initial jolt of joy I felt knowing that Connie was thinking of me, but the delight would always dissolve into bitter resentment. He had chosen to live in Jamaica rather than be with me. I never replied because I couldn't bring myself to read them. I wanted him to feel as bad as I felt.

Miss Gladys had turned to me. 'All mi saying is that mi know from experience that ol' fire stick easy fi catch.'

Mum scooped up the cucumber slices and dashed them into a bowl. 'Then how come mi never feel that way about her father?' she said dryly.

'Enoch Edwards is a hard man fi love. Anyway, mi ah talk from mi own experience, and what mi know is sparks fly when former lovers meet, cos if it's meant, it's meant.'

I looked into Miss Gladys's warm eyes. 'And what if it's not meant?'

'Then yuh move on,' said Mum curtly.

Connie and I had reached the statue of James Wolfe and were looking north towards the city, where for years mechanical cranes lumbered about on the old docklands. Now shiny skyscrapers soared. So much time had passed since we first met, many things in our lives had changed. And yet we shared so many experiences. There was still so much about him that felt natural and familiar.

Connie sighed. 'This isn't going too well, is it?'

'It's not unpleasant being with you. Just strange.'

'Would you have called me if I hadn't come to yuh workplace?'

I shrugged.

'Was it out of order me coming to your workplace like that?'

'A bit. The soup was nice though.' He looked at me and I grinned. 'What have you brought me this time?'

'Let's find a good spot to eat and I'll show yuh,' he said. 'Plus, if we're eating, we don't have to talk if we don't want to.'

An hour later, we were still sitting on the blue-and-white checked cloth Connie had spread on the grass close to The Queen's House. All that was left of the picnic he'd brought was half a baguette, a few olives and a couple of carrot sticks. He offered me the last falafel; I split it in two, dipping my half in the homemade hummus.

'I read yuh article in the paper. The one about the BNP. It was good.'

'I never knew you could get the *Star* round your way.'

'I picked one up at the newsagent, when I was here meeting Kallai.'

'You've met up with Kallai?'

'He phone mi the day after the funeral. Tobias was working so wi were able to talk. Wi arranged to meet here cos it's not too far for him to come, and this is the closest mi ever want to be to that flat.'

Connie twisted the lid off the bottle of fizzy water and handed it to me. I took a swig and handed it back, waiting for him to continue.

'The quarrelling is bad. Dem barely civil to one another. He tell me that he's begged Althea to leave but she nuh listen to him, so him nuh have any respect for her anymore. Of course him nuh mean it, he loves Althea like I do, him just talking out of frustration. I hate that man. I hate that he made me feel helpless for such a long time. Him doing the same t'ing to Kallai. But I told Kallai that I'm here for him now as much as I can be. And that when him sixteen he can come live with me.'

'It's really important that you stay close with him.'

'He t'inks he's so grown up but he's still a kid. Some of the t'ings he comes out with crack me up. Yuh know he still knows all the lyrics to "Rapper's Delight"!'

Connie laughed, the warmth in that sound was always so seductive. 'Everyt'ing isn't all better between Kallai and me yet, but it feels like we're making a start.'

'Good. I'm glad.'

'So am I. Now that just leaves you.' Connie looked at me, serious yet uncertain. 'I can't undo all that is already done—'

I became aware of a knot in my chest, a mixture of fear and

delight. I remember Miss Gladys's and Mum's words, 'If it's meant, it's meant. If it's not meant then yuh move on'.

'I've . . . missed you,' I said.

'I've missed you too. Can we be friends?'

'Yes. I'd like that.'

Connie shuffled across to me, lifted my chin and kissed me. 'Can we be more than that?'

A delicious shiver rolled through my body, leaving me giddy. I exhaled. 'Let's see.'

31

Connie was lying on his front; his face was turned towards me, partially concealed by the pillow. I could see an eyebrow and a row of lashes, a thick, black semi-circle against his dark brown skin. I listened to the sound of his breathing, watching the gentle rise and fall of his back. A week, then a month, now six weeks had gone by since that afternoon in Greenwich. The clock radio switched itself on.

Connie stirred, opening his eyes. 'Morning.'

'Hey,' I said, slowly running my hand over his arse. 'D'you want some coffee?'

'In a bit.'

Connie rolled onto his side, lying with his elbow denting the pillow and his hand supporting his head. He looked sleepy but interested. Still with my hand beneath the sheet, I felt my way along the side of his body; when I reached the top of his thigh I moved my hand to his front, brushing the line of hairs that ran from his belly down to his cock.

'Let me see yuh.'

He pulled back the sheets, my skin pimpled in the cool air. He ran a hand along my thigh, sliding over my backside, caressing my spine.

'I like it when you do that,' I murmured, shuffling closer.

Then we were kissing; brief, soft kisses, the stubble beneath his chin grazing my lips and neck. Connie eased me onto my back, gently parted my legs and began touching me. After I'd come, I got on top of him. We carried on like this for a while but the orgasm had sapped my energy. We swapped places. I lay on my back, lethargic, horny, enjoying his weight and the smell of the shea butter on his chest. I wrapped my legs around him, whispering fantasies until he finished.

We must have dozed for a bit because when I awoke, it was just after 10 a.m. Connie got up and rummaged about in the drawer I'd cleared for him, finding a fresh pair of boxers. 'I should swing by my yard later after work.'

'I didn't realise you were working today.'

'Juan has more immigration problems. He asked if mi could cover part of his shift. I should be done by four.'

'So you'll miss the demo.'

'Afraid so.'

'I don't know why you don't just leave more of your stuff here,' I said, putting on a T-shirt. 'In fact ... ' I paused, uncertain whether or not to continue. Connie looked at me, expectant. 'Well ... you know, Milly's moving in with Jo at the end of the month. You could move in here. If you liked,' I said, hoping that I sounded breezy.

Connie smiled. 'Yuh nuh t'ink it's too soon? How would me moving in here with yuh go down with yuh muddah?'

'Colin's been working on her and you know Grandma is on our side. It doesn't matter that it's only been a few months, we've known each other for such a long time. If it's meant, it's meant. Think about it, you'd have more privacy than in that house share you're in now. The rent's not bad. You'd be closer to Kallai too.'

Connie looked thoughtful. 'True. Actually he'll be here soon for the money I promise him.' I gave him a questioning look. 'An end-of-term seaside trip, all his friends are going but Tobias won't hand over the money. Let me go jump in the shower then get on with breakfast. What yuh have in the fridge?'

'Dunno. Whatever you left there the last time you came over.'

Connie rolled his eyes at me.

Half an hour later, I was skimming through the newspapers, sipping coffee and reading articles aloud while Connie cooked. He looked at home in my little kitchen; I couldn't resist imagining what it would be like to have him here with me all the time. There was a knock at the front door. I recognised Kallai's silhouette through the frosted glass.

'Hey, your brother's cooking up a storm in the kitchen. Come on in,' I said, standing back, inviting him inside. He hesitated. I noticed how frowsy his clothes were, like he'd been sleeping in them. 'Kallai, is everything all right?'

He looked up at me from beneath the brim of his Malcolm X baseball cap. The bruise was faint but his eye was bloodshot. He looked embarrassed. I stepped out onto the landing and guided him inside.

A shadow of anger crossed Connie's face when his eyes fell on Kallai. I could see Connie biting down on his rage, trying hard not to be like Tobias. But the more questions Connie asked, the more Kallai masked his fear and shame with truculence and monosyllables; he was just like Connie at that age, when he was enduring the same treatment.

'Does Althea know what happened?' I asked softly.

Kallai shook his head.

'Did you stay out last night?'

'I slept on Marcus's floor. His mum was on a night shift. But I had to leave early before she got back. I ain't had no breakfast.'

I dished up the scrambled eggs, toast and bacon and we all squeezed around the table. Kallai ate up everything we put in front of him, while Connie and I picked at our food. When he'd finished eating, Kallai remained hunched over his plate, not looking at either of us.

Connie reached into his jacket, which was hanging on the back of the chair, and placed a brown envelope on the table.

'Here, I got the cash for yuh trip. Keep it in yuh room and hand it in on Monday morning. Don't let Tobias know you have it. Althea neither.'

As Kallai reached over to take the envelope, Connie laid his palm over his brother's hand. 'D'yuh know I'm here for yuh. Yuh can talk to me.'

Kallai nodded, eyes down. 'Can I use your loo please?' His voice shook. I sensed that he was trying not to cry.

Connie waited until he heard the click of the bathroom lock before he spoke. 'That bastard. I should go round there now and beat the crap out of him!'

'You getting done for assault isn't going to help Kallai.'

'There is no way him can tan in dat flat with dem for another day, let alone until he's sixteen. Mi need to do somet'ing now to get him from dat place. He needs to come and live with me. Mi ah go move him in with me tonight and call social services first t'ing on Monday. Mi nuh care if it put

Althea in trouble too; dis t'ing cyaah go on. Mi nah go put up with it any longer.'

'I agree he can't stay there. But you need to think about this. You live in a room in a shared house. I know you're all friends but where would Kallai sleep? And what about school? Social services would be more likely to take him into care than let him live with you in those circumstances.'

'Yuh have a better idea?'

My thoughts were swirling; I was desperate for a solution.

'Look, you have to get Althea on your side somehow; you have to get her to agree to let Kallai come and stay with you – at least in the short term. Then maybe you can make enquiries with social services, but you can't go in all guns blazing. It will just blow things up and that will be worse for Kallai. He acts all tough, but he's just a child.'

Connie still looked irritated. I softened my tone. 'How about what I mentioned earlier? If you moved in here when Milly moves out, there would be an extra room. Kallai could come and stay here whenever he wanted. He could still go to the same school and be close to his friends. Maybe, eventually, we could sort it so he could just live with us. What d'you think?'

'You'd do that? You'd take on Kallai?'

'Of course! I love you and I love Kallai as well. I'll check with Milly, but I'm pretty sure she'll be at Jo's all weekend. Kallai can sleep on the sofa tonight and tomorrow at least; then we can figure something out. It'll be all right. Go to work, then go and talk to Althea later.'

'I love you,' Connie said, caressing my cheek. I stood on my tiptoes to kiss him.

The pink beaded curtain that hung over the kitchen door jingled before it parted and Kallai peered inside.

'Connie's staying at mine for a few days. D'you wanna come and stay here too?'

Kallai shrugged. 'I don't think they'll let me.'

'What if I was to come over after work, say around five? I can talk to Althea, sort it out with her. I'll tell her it's just till t'ings cool down. What yuh t'ink?'

Kallai nodded, giving us a tight little smile.

'Okay. Thanks bruv.'

There was a large crowd gathered at the entrance to the town hall when I arrived just after midday. My flatmate, Milly, was chatting to my cousin Marcia, who had propped her pregnant belly on the 'NO MORE RACIST KILLINGS' placard she held in front of her. Kwame, her boyfriend, stood by looking anxious. Their baby was due any day now, but my cousin refused to sit this demonstration out. I'd been briefed to write 150 words for the paper, but I was there in solidarity too. A few weeks ago there had been a march through Norbury, passing the place where twenty-four-year-old Ruhulla Aramash was beaten to death by six white youths last July. Following that march there'd been a rally where Bishop Desmond Tutu and Neville and Doreen Lawrence gave speeches. Although this demonstration was smaller, we made a lot of noise: we had to keep on raising awareness. I composed most of the copy in my mind on the train back home. As I walked through the estate, I noticed the number of St George flags draped across windows and balconies. It was true, there were more Black people living in this particular side of the borough now than when I was younger, but the flags made me ill at ease – I still associated them with BNP marches. Even though I was born and raised right here in South East London, I never felt that flag belonged to me. I never felt English enough.

I let those thoughts slide away and focused on Connie instead; I found myself smiling once more. I'd told Milly about Kallai turning up at the flat with a bruised eye and she understood straight away that he ought to stay at ours. She was defending a fifteen-year-old joyrider on a TDA charge at Highbury Corner Magistrates' on Monday morning so it was easier to stay in Chalk Farm with Jo. It was after 6 p.m. when I reached my block of flats. Rather than waiting for the lift I took the stairs, thinking about the prospect of Connie coming home to me that evening. In a few weeks, we would quite possibly be living together, with Kallai too. Our own unique family.

As I drew near the front door, I could hear the phone ringing, but by the time I got to the living room it had stopped. The red light was flashing on the answering machine; I had six missed calls. The phone began to ring again and a feeling of dread shot through me. For a split second, I considered waiting for the answering machine to kick in. I shrugged the feeling away.

'Hello, Daphne Johnson.'

'Daphne? It's Valerie.'

'Oh, Valerie, hello. Were you after Connie? Cos I'm afraid he's not with me at the moment. I expect to see him later though.'

'Daphne, listen to me . . . no wait . . . me nuh know how to say it.' She began to cry, big, deep sobs. I pictured her body shaking.

'Valerie ... what is it? What's wrong?' The fear was back, creeping up inside me cold and slippery. 'Valerie, calm down. Breathe slowly ... that's it. Now, tell me what has happened ... please.'

'There was a stabbing. It's Tobias ... him dead.'

Cruel apprehension now flooded my mind. I couldn't move or speak.

'Daphne, yuh still there? Yuh listening? The police arrest Connie. Dem charge him with murder.'

32

Leigh, Fitzsimmons & Partners were based in a modern building on Lower Road. That morning neither Leigh nor Fitzsimmons were available. Instead, Althea and I sat in the office of Miss Eleanor Walsh, who was going over what she kept calling 'the particulars of the case', in a brisk, dispassionate tone.

This was the longest Althea and I had spent together since The Magistrates' hearing seven weeks ago, when Connie had been remanded in custody. She sat in the chair nearest the window with her hands clasped, silent except for the occasional sigh. Either she didn't want to be there, or she didn't want to be there with me. Perhaps it was both those things. I wanted to shake her. Now that we had a trial date, something had to be done. We needed a united front.

'So, Mr Small confessed to the crime when the police arrived at the flat, which is why they arrested him. My colleague advised him to stick to "no comment" in the interview which Mr Small disregarded.'

'He was in shock,' I said. 'He's not a violent person. It must have been self-defence ... or something.' I turned to Althea. 'Don't you think?'

Althea looked at her hands.

'Then we need to prove that the force Mr Small used was reasonable. I have to be frank with you, the CPS are going for a murder conviction. Mr Small is a fit young man in his twenties, while his victim was a forty-seven-year-old with hypertension. If he's found guilty, he's looking at a life sentence.'

I felt a wave of sickness. I breathed deeply, hoping it would pass.

'Now, there was an altercation at a wake in May, where Mr Small—'

'Connie,' I said. I couldn't stop myself. 'Call him Connie, not Mr Small.'

Miss Walsh opened her mouth; then nodded before continuing. 'Where *Connie* threatened Mr Beckford in front of witnesses. Also, a friend of Mr Beckford's, a Dalton Bustamante, alleges Mr Beckford confided that Connie threatened him with a knife in January 1986. If the Prosecution can show that he'd always harboured a hatred of his stepfather then it shows motivation. Now, you say Mr Beckford was violent?'

'Mi nuh know what to say.' Althea's voice was little more than a whisper. 'Tobias was unkind. I will say that.'

I couldn't listen anymore. 'Althea that man abused you and your sons – especially Connie – for years and years! *Unkind?* He was monstrous!'

Althea fiddled with the buckle of her handbag, refusing to meet my glare.

Miss Walsh cleared her throat. 'It's a very stressful time. I understand that emotions are running high.'

I felt nausea swelling again, this time deep breathing

didn't help. I mumbled 'Excuse me . . . ' before dashing from the room.

After vomiting, the sickness ebbed away. I cupped my hand under the cold tap and swilled my mouth with water. There were tears in my eyes. I was worn down with the pressure of the situation, with being brave and practical. I'd been playing that role ever since the first time I visited Connie in custody. I'd sat in the visitors' room across from him feeling anxious and out of place but trying not to let it show. He was wearing a grey sweatshirt with frayed cuffs, a baby blue T-shirt poked out beneath its sagging neckline. His jogging bottoms skimmed his ankles and on his feet were the carefully shined black shoes he'd worn to work that afternoon. They looked ludicrous against the rest of his hand-me-down apparel. I'd left a care package at the visitors' reception when I arrived at the prison; it contained clothes and Nivea cream. Now I saw that his hair looked dull and matted; next time I'd bring hair oil and an Afro comb too. I wondered how many more of these visits they would allow.

The tasteless instant coffee was too hot for the thin plastic, so Connie held the cup by its rim. It looked dinky and fragile in his right hand. I pictured a knife in that hand, then quickly shoved the thought away.

'Has the solicitor been to see you?'

'Yeah.'

'What did you tell them?'

'That I never went there to kill him. That we got into a row. It turned into a fight. It was an accident.' He spoke like he was reciting lines.

'And . . . what did they say?'

'The woman say next time I go to court, mi have to make a plea. She can't tell mi how to plead. Mi must decide for meself.'

'You'll plead not guilty, right?' Connie grunted and I continued, 'Mum and Grandma and me were talking about it. With Tobias's history and Althea's and Kallai's testimony, there's a good chance. You could say you were provoked, or he came at you with the knife and you somehow turned it back on him so it was an accident.' He continued looking down at his coffee cup.

'Connie . . . what actually happened?'

'I can't remember. It was all so fast.'

'Okay. I hope your defence are talking to Althea and Kallai, so they can build a better picture. They're staying at Valerie's. I could swing by; it'd be better than a phone call—'

'Leave dem be.'

'But they're witnesses. You'll need them to testify on your behalf.'

'They weren't there.'

I scoffed in disbelief. 'The reason you went over there was to see Althea and talk about Kallai.'

'They weren't there, then I got into a fight with Tobias. Look, the two of dem have a lot to contend with right now. Mi nuh want yuh to bother dem.'

'Bother them? Connie, you're in jail! I'm entitled to think Althea might want to help you. You're her son!'

'Yes! And she have another son whose father is dead. The two of dem have a lot to deal with. If Althea wants to she'll contact you, but until then, leave her alone.'

Now, as I dabbed the corners of my mouth with a paper

towel, I remembered the sight of Connie following the other inmates back to the wing, his head down, looking at the sludge brown tiles. Already defeated. I gazed at my ashen reflection in the mirror. Why was I the only one still trying? I wiped my eyes with the back of my hand. Instead of composing a neutral expression, I watched my jawline harden. A terse, straightforward voice inside my head was saying *this cannot go on*.

Miss Walsh glanced up from her papers as I re-entered the room. 'Better now?'

I nodded. I could feel Althea's eyes on me but I blanked her.

'Good. I was just saying to Mrs Beckford that it would be helpful if we could find Connie good character witnesses—'

'How far along are you?' Althea's voice was gentle. I thought I detected a tone of hopefulness.

How dare she ask me that question, as if we were sitting in a park, rather than a solicitor's office discussing her son's murder trial.

'Althea, I'm sorry, but this is neither the time nor the place—'

'But it's Connie's, isn't it? Have you told him?'

I kissed my teeth. 'I figured he has enough on his plate right now and frankly what is the point of telling him when . . . ' I trailed off into a sigh and looked away.

'When yuh nuh intend to keep it.'

Miss Walsh rose. 'I think I ought to give you two a moment alone.'

The solicitor closed the door behind her.

Althea looked crestfallen, like I'd dangled a treat, then fiendishly withdrawn it. I hated her.

'D'you know what? I'm not sorry. This is none of your business – or his either for that matter. He's going to jail for life. He seems resigned to the fact. And you're just content to stand by and let it happen. I feel like I don't know you and Connie anymore. You've all given up – maybe I should too.'

'But he loves yuh!'

'And you loved Tobias, that didn't have a happy ever after. Even now you cannot bring yourself to tell the solicitor the truth about that evil man. What is wrong with you? Why won't you help your son?'

'I am helping my son!'

'How are you helping him?' I yelled, exasperated.

'I *am* helping my son. I'm helping Kallai!' She exhaled a moan. 'And so is Connie.'

Although I heard the words, it was only after Althea started crying that I realised what she had really said. I drew back from her.

Althea took a pause to wipe her eyes. I waited for her to continue.

'Connie t'ought it was the best t'ing to do and I went along with it. I should have told yuh before. I'm sorry I didn't. But mi know he loves yuh. Whether yuh decide to keep the baby or not, mi nuh want there to be any secrets between unnu.

'Mi buck up on Connie outside the flats. He'd been ringing the entryphone but Kallai nuh answer. Mi joke that most likely he was listening to music and nuh hear the buzzer.' She sniffed. 'Instead, when wi arrive wi find him standing over Tobias in the kitchen doorway. Him screaming at him "Daddy". Crying. A bloody knife in him hand. I tek the knife from him and Connie grab a tea towel and press down on

Tobias's belly, trying to stem the blood. Trying to save him. Such a small wound, but so much blood. It seep t'rough the cloth like it was tissue.' My mind's eye conjured up the scene, sensing the blood and the panic.

'Connie tell me to call an ambulance and get a blanket or somet'ing for Kallai. I pick up the phone, then Connie say, "Wait. If yuh call an ambulance and say him been stabbed, then the police will come too." Mi said, "Wi cyaah worry about that now." But he just repeat, "the police will come too". Mi look at Kallai. The bwoy just stand there shaking, weeping. That's when Connie tell the two of us to go. He say when dem ask wi fi tell dem that wi wasn't there when it happened.'

I covered my mouth, trying to slow my breathing. Connie was innocent. He wasn't a killer. Although this had been what I'd wanted to hear all along, I felt myself rocking slightly, trying to quiet the roar in my head. Yes, I felt relieved, vindicated even; but I was also furious. Connie told me not to bother Althea and Kallai. He had kept this from me. Would he ever have said anything? He was prepared to sacrifice his own freedom for his brother. I knew it was noble, maybe even the right thing to do, but four months ago he'd told me I meant more to him than anyone. Now he couldn't even tell me the truth. 'What do you expect to happen now?' I lashed out. 'Am I supposed to play the dutiful babymother and wait for him to do his time?'

Althea shrugged. 'I just want you to know what really happened that night. Yuh could do it though. Yuh a brave, clever woman Daphne – mi seen it. If I'd been braver, then my boys would have had a different sort of life. Mi did tell yuh that we're good at keeping secrets in our family. This is a secret I don't want to keep – at least not from yuh nor mi grandpickney, that is, if yuh decide to keep it. Yuh nuh remember how mi used to say "wi run t'ings, t'ings nuh run wi". Neither one of my sons should be in this situation. So mi ah go do all mi can to help unnu.'

She leaned over and took my hand. My first instinct was to pull it away, but I didn't. Her touch made my shoulders drop. Her voice was soothing and I let myself sink into calm.

'Mi cyaah face Connie till all of this is over. But when yuh see him next, please ask him to forgive mi. I should never have let t'ings go this far. And Daphne . . . will yuh forgive mi too?'

She was looking at me. Her appearance had changed; the distracted, fragile woman now had an air of quiet determination. I couldn't hate Althea; I'd known her for so long. There was still fear in her eyes. But I knew true courage meant being able to act in spite of fear. I felt my chest tighten; I nodded so I wouldn't have to speak.

Althea smiled. 'Call the solicitor lady back inside. I know what I want fi tell her now.'

Two little boys in matching combat trousers push wooden beads around the multicoloured wire maze. I've seen these brothers before. This is my daughter's first time here. Although Mum and Miss Gladys thought that a prison visiting room is no place for a child, Connie and I feel differently. Despite being one of the last in, we were shown to a table at the end of a row. These offered slightly more privacy, even though over the past year I'd got into the habit of talking low and sitting forward with my shoulders rounded, elbows resting on my thighs. When she begins to cry, Connie jiggles her in his arms. He is anxious to soothe her but his movements are too jerky. She can tell that he isn't relaxed. He places her on his shoulder and rubs her back. When that doesn't work either, he hands her back to me. She nuzzles against my breast and settles.

'She's beginning to look more like yuh now. My two English roses,' he says.

'I'm sorry I couldn't persuade Kallai to come.'

'You did yuh best. It's gonna take time. And we have a long while yet.'

His tone is flat. He is always more nervous than he lets on. I hold out my hand and he takes it, squeezing my fingers a little too tightly.

'It won't always be like this. We're gonna appeal. Tobias's ex-wife has come forward. Her testimony will help. We mustn't give up hope.'

'Okay,' he says ruefully.

The prison officers from the B wing appear and the inmates begin filing in. Althea's smile doesn't reach her eyes but she waves. Connie and I stand up, ready to greet her.

Author's Note

While this novel is a work of fiction, the history included is real. Initially, I hadn't set out to chronicle the events that took place south London during the 1980s and early '90s; I was only scanning contemporary newspapers in order to get a feel for the period. Reading the letters pages, in particular, revealed what people were concerned about, what they were really thinking and the prevailing attitude towards race. As I delved deeper, this research brought back my own memories of growing up here at that time and it was impossible to ignore the impact this mood and these significant moments would have on Daphne and Connie. These events are an important part of Black history. They are an important part of British history.

I mention Cherry Groce, Cynthia Jarrett, Rolan Adams, Rohit Duggal, Ruhullah Aramesh and Stephen Lawrence. These people died or were murdered as a result of racist attitudes and the racial politics of the time. Sadly, they were far from the only victims. I also reference the New Cross Fire and I would like to acknowledge all those who lost their lives as a result of that arson and its impact: Patrick Cummings, Andrew Gooding, Peter Campbell, Gerry Paul Francis,

Steve Collins, Patricia Johnson, Rosaline Henry, Lloyd Hall, Humphrey Geoffrey Brown, Owen Thompson, Yvonne Ruddock, Glenton Powell, Paul Ruddock and Anthony Berbeck.

In many ways things have improved and there has been some positive change in this country. However, we now live at a time when that positive change feels as fragile as I can remember.

Acknowledgements

It has taken many years to get this novel out of my head and onto the page. There have been many people who have helped along the way. My deepest thanks to my agent Nicola Chang. Thank you for checking in with me over the years, for the encouragement you gave me when I was finally able to hand you a draft and for the tough love I needed to whip it into shape. As we say in Jamaica, 'time longa dan rope'. I'm so grateful to have you in my corner all these years. To my editors Sharmaine Lovegrove and Maris Dyer. You both pushed me to dig deep, to really think about all the characters in this book, the themes I wanted to explore and ultimately, the story I wanted to tell. This novel is so much stronger because of your important questions, keen insights and for making me feel that I was in safe hands. Thank you for believing in this book and continuing to push for the best.

To David Evans and Sophia Rahim and everyone at David Higham Associates, thank you for your support and expertise. To Stephanie Delman and the team at Trellis, thank you for your enthusiasm for this novel, your patience and wise counsel.

Many thanks to the fantastic team at Dialogue Books and Knopf Doubleday who have been so enthusiastic about this novel, and have worked so hard to bring it into the world.

Big thanks to my literary sistren: Natasha Bell, Heather Binney, Emily Selencky and Maria Thomas. There aren't adequate words to describe how honoured I am to have your friendship. Thank you for your generous feedback, your wisdom and encouragement. You are talented writers, excellent human beings and tremendous fun to be around.

To my early readers: Rita Daniels, Kate Smith, Lauren Shukru, Jaimie D'Cruz. I inflicted some pretty ropey drafts on you guys; thank you for responding with warm praise and incisive comments.

The London Library Emerging Writers Programme provided fabulous mentoring and gave me structure during the dark days of the first pandemic lockdown. Particular thanks goes out to Claire Berliner, Head of Programmes, and my peer group Sarah Marsh, Yosola Olorunshola and Chez Cotton. Chez, thanks for also taking the time to provide legal insights and opinions, apologies for the artistic liberties I've taken.

To my tutors at Goldsmiths, Ardashir Vakil and Tom Lee, thank you for being such attentive readers and for the thoughtful guidance. I'd also like to thank my MA Creative Writing cohort: Claire Bullen, Angela Chan, Lauren Hughes, Oli Hudson, Eleanor Lee, Shauna McAllister, Kajal Odedra, Leanne Wimhurst and Sioban Whitney Low.

Thank you Clare Dowdy for telling me about print journalism in the '90s; any inaccuracies are down to my artistic licence rather than gaps in your knowledge.

To Matt Bourn and Aaron Clarke, you were the first to

suggest that Daphne's and Connie's lives might need to be longer than a short story. Thank you for the nudge.

Access to good research was key in the writing of this novel and I found that there is only so much information that can be gleaned from a Google search. I'd like to thank the staff at the Black Cultural Archives, the British Library Newsroom, the Southwark Archives at John Harvard Library and The London Library.

To my mum, Hyacinth Smith, thank you for teaching me the value of reading and imagination. To all of those who lived at 90 Evelyn Street and my dear siblings, Sharon, Lorna, Mark and Sheila, thank you for the support – and for providing the inspiration! And speaking of inspiration, thanks to my grandma, Miss Beryl. 'She likkle but she tallawah', gone but not forgotten.

Finally, to Jon and Ella, thank you both for putting up with me, for loving me, for everything. Thank you, thank you, thank you.

Sources

- *South London Press*, 20 Jan 1981
- *South London Press*, 30 Jan 1981
- *South London Press*, 10 Feb 1981
- *South London Press*, 17 March 1981
- *South London Press*, 1 Oct 1985
- *South London Press*, 11 Oct 1985
- *South London Press*, 25 March 1986
- *South London Press*, 15 Jan 1988
- *South London Press*, 29 June 1993

Bringing a book from manuscript to what you are reading is a team effort.

Dialogue Books would like to thank everyone who helped to publish *Jamaica Road* in the UK.

Editorial
Sharmaine Lovegrove
Adriano Noble
Eleanor Gaffney

Contracts
Anniina Vuori
Imogen Plouviez
Amy Patrick
Jemima Coley

Sales
Caitriona Row
Dominic Smith
Frances Doyle
Ginny Mašinović
Rachael Jones
Georgina Cutler
Toluwalope Ayo-Ajala

Design
Nico Taylor

Production
Narges Nojoumi
Kelly Llewellyn

Publicity
Corinna Zifko

Marketing
Emily Moran

Operations
Kellie Barnfield
Millie Gibson
Sameera Patel
Sanjeev Braich

Finance
Andrew Smith
Ellie Barry

Copy-Editor
Josephine Lane

Proofreader
Karyn Burnham